Seventh Street Alchemy

Seventh Street Alchemy

A selection of works
from the Caine Prize for
African Writing

First published in 2005 by Jacana Media (Pty) Ltd
5 St Peter Road
Bellevue, 2198
Johannesburg
South Africa

ISBN 1-77009-145-9

Cover design by Disturbance

Printed by Pinetown Printers

See a complete list of Jacana titles at www.jacana.co.za

Table of Contents

Introduction

This is the fifth anthology of Caine Prize shortlisted stories, and the third to include the proceedings of a Caine Prize African Writers' Workshop. Out of the twelve countries represented on the five shortlists to date, three have been North African, three East African, three West African and three from southern Africa. So the Prize has a truly pan-African reach. It is widely referred to now as 'the African Booker' and 'Africa's leading literary award' – in Africa, in the UK and increasingly in the US.

The impact on the writers' lives has been dramatic. The first two winners, Leila Aboulela and Helon Habila, have both had outstanding success with their work since. Habila won a Commonwealth Prize for his first novel in 2002 and his second novel is with the publishers. Leila Aboulela's second novel, *Minaret*, has just been published by Bloomsbury. Chimamanda Ngozi Adichie (Caine Prize shortlist 2002) was on the Orange Prize shortlist for her first novel, *Purple Hibiscus*, published by Harper, and it won the Commonwealth First Book Prize in 2005. Hassounah Mosbahi's story, *The Tortoise*, which was shortlisted in 2001, appears in an excellent collection of stories from North Africa, *Sardines and Oranges*, published this year by Banipal. And Doreen Baingana, shortlisted in 2004, was given a Writers' Programme Award for her collection, *Tropical Fish – Stories from Entebbe,* published this year by Massachusetts University Press.

The 2004 Caine Prize winner was the Zimbabwean writer, Brian Chikwava. Also on the shortlist, with Doreen Baingana, were Monica Arac de Nyeko, also from Uganda, Parselelo Kantai from Kenya and Chika Unigwe from Nigeria. Their stories appear in this volume. Except for Kantai, who was busy on a Reuters' Fellowship at Oxford University, they participated in this year's Caine Prize African Writers' Workshop, as did Charles Mungoshi (Zimbabwe) and Jackee Butesda Batanda (Uganda), who were both highly commended by the 2004 Prize judges.

Other participants in the Workshop, which was held inside the rim of an extinct volcano – at Crater Lake, near Naivasha, Kenya – were from Kenya and from South Africa. The animateurs were Veronique Tadjo, from the Ivory Coast, and Binyavanga Wainaina, Kenyan Caine Prize Winner in 2002 and editor of *Kwani?* The stories produced at the Workshop all appear in this volume, along with Charles Mungoshi's *Letter from a Friend*, which he read at the Workshop and which, although it was written beforehand, has not previously been published.

Once again we thank Jacana for their patience and perseverance in producing our anthology. And we thank our principal sponsors, the Ernest Oppenheimer Memorial Trust and the Gatsby Charitable Foundation, for keeping the Prize going through three more years. Without them, we would simply not exist.

Nick Elam
Administrator

Caine Prize Stories 2004
Winner and Finalists

Seventh Street Alchemy (Winner)

Brian Chikwava

By 5AM HARARE'S STRUGGLING inhabitants are out of their hovels. They are on their varied ways to innumerable places to waylay the dollars they so desperately need to stave hunger off their doorsteps. Trains and commuter omnibuses burst with exploitable human material. Its excess finds its way onto bicycles, or simply self-propels, tilling earth with bare, frost-bitten feet all the way to the city centre or industrial areas.

The modes of transport are diverse, poverty the trendsetter. Like a colony of hungry ants, it crawls over the multitudes scattered along the city roads, ravaging all etches of dignity that only a few years back stood resilient. Threadbare resignation is concealed underneath threadbare shirts, together with socks and underpants that resemble a ruthless termite job. In spite of poverty's glorious march into every household, the will to be dignified by underpants and socks remains intact.

Activities in the city centre tend towards the paranormal. A voodoo economy flourishes as daylight dwindles: fruit and vegetable vendors slash their prices by half and still fail to sell. The following morning the same material is carted back onto the streets, selling at higher than the previous day's peak rates. In some undertakings the enthusiasm to participate is expressed in wads of notes; in some, simple primitive violence – or the threat of its use – is common currency. As the idea of ensuring that your demands are backed up by violence is fast gaining hold among the city's prowlers, business carried out in pin-striped suits is fleeing the city centre, ill-equipped to deal with the proliferation of scavenger tactics. Pigeons too have joined the new street entrepreneurs: they relieve themselves on pedestrians when least expected and never alight on the same street corner for more than two days in a row. Even the supposedly civilised, well-to-do section of the population, a pitiful lot typified by their indefatigable amiability, now finds itself anchored down by a State whose methods of governance involve incessant roguery. Instead, facing up to their circumstances with a modicum of honour, they weekly hurl themselves into churches to petition a disinterested God to subvert the laws of the universe in their favour.

At the corner of Samora Machel Avenue and Seventh Street, in a flat whose bedroom is adorned with two newspaper cuttings of the president, lives a fifty-two-year-old quasi-prostitute with thirty-seven teeth and a pair of six-inch-heeled perspex platform shoes. It has been decades since she realised that, armed with a vagina and a will to survive, destitution could never lay claim to her. With these weapons of destruction she has continued to fortify her liberty against poverty and society. Fiso is her name and like a lot of the city's inhabitants she has concluded that death is mere spin, nobody ever really dies. On the night a street kid got knocked down by a car it was a tranquil hour. A discerning ear would have been able to hear two flies fornicating several metres away. But to Anna Shava, a civil servant, soaked to the bone with matrimonial distress, the flies would have had to be inside her nose to get her attention. Her tearful departure from home after another scuffle with her husband set in motion a violent symphony of events. Security guards who scurried off the streets for safety could not have imagined that an exasperated spouse in a car vibrating to the frenzied rhythms of her anguished footwork could beget such upheaval. Right in the middle of the lane, at the corner of Samora Machel Avenue and Seventh Street, a street kid staggers from left to right, struggling to tear himself out of a stupor acquired by sniffing glue all day. The car devours the tarmac, and in a screech of tyres the corner is gobbled up together with the small figure endeavouring to grasp reality. Sheet metal grudgingly gives in to a dent, bones snap, glass shatters. The kid never had a chance. His soul's departure is punctuated by one final baritone fart relinquishing life. Protruding out of the kid's back pocket is a tube of Z68 glue.

A couple of blocks from the scene, blue lights flashed from a police car while two officers shared the delicate task of trying to convince a grouchy young musician to part with some of his dollars for having gone though red traffic lights.

"You've been having a good time. That's no problem. But you must understand we also need something to keep us happy while doing our rounds," one of the officers said with a well-drilled, venal smile before continuing. "Since you are a musician we know you can't afford much, Stix, but if you could just make us happy with a couple of Nando's takeaways..."

Anna, realising that they were not going to pay her any attention without some effort on her part, marched over to the officers. "Will you please come to my help, haven't you seen what happened?" she said, donning that look of nefarious servitude that she often inspired on the faces of applicants at the immigration office. She knew better than anybody that being nice to people in authority could render purchasable otherwise priceless rights, and simplify one's life.

"We are off duty now, Madam, call Central Police Station," one of the officers yodelled over. Returning to her car and periodically glancing over her shoulder in disbelief, she saw the offending driver stick out of his window a clenched handful of notes to pacify the vultures that had taken positions around his throttled freedom. His liberties resuscitated, he sped off in his scarlet ramshackle car.

Two days before, Anna, no less fed up with her errant husband, had followed him to the city's most popular rhumba club. She had found him leaning against the bar, with men she did not recognise. They talked at the top of their voices in the dim, smudged lighting. Her husband, who had been tapping his foot to the sound of loud Congolese music, recoiled at the sight of her. Befuddled, he grappled with the embarrassment of having been tracked down to a nightclub crawling with prostitutes. And then there was the thought of his mates saying that his balls had long been liberated from him and safely deposited in his wife's bra. His impulse was to thump her thoroughly, but lacking essential practice, he could not lift a finger.

"What do you want?" he asked, icily.

"Buy me a drink too," she brushed the question aside.

He stared at Anna as she grinned. Outrage lay not far beneath such grins, experience had schooled him. Reluctantly he turned to the bar to order her a Coke, struggling to affect an air of ascendancy in the eyes of his peers. He tossed a five-hundred-dollar note at the bartender, as if oblivious to his wife's presence.

Half an hour later when Anna visited the ladies toilet, transgression would catch up with her husband. There a lady with greying hair, standing with what looked like a couple of prostitutes, cut short her conversation to remark innocently, "Be careful with that man. He's a problem when it comes to paying up. Ask these girls. Make sure he pays you before you do anything or he will make excuses like, 'I didn't think you were that kind of girl.'"

Anna was transfixed, hoping – pretending – that the words were directed at someone else.

"You could always grab his cellphone, you know," the woman added kindly.

That woman was Fiso who, at the time Anna ran into a street kid, was engrossed in the common ritual of massaging her dementia, having spent a whole day struggling to sell vegetables – a relatively new engagement imposed on her by the autumn of her street life.

She was exhausted and was not bothered by the screeching tyres down the road. It did not occur to her that what had registered in her ears was an incident precipitated by her well-meaning advice. Beside her, sharing her bed, lay her daughter Sue, a twenty-six-year-old flea-market vendor. In the midst of her mother's furious campaign against a pair of rogue mosquitoes, which relentlessly circled their heads before attacking, Sue came to the tired realisation that in spite of all the years on the streets, her mother still had undepleted stocks of a compulsive disorder from her youthful days. In the sooty darkness her mother blindly clapped, hoping to deal one or both of them a fatal blow. Precision however remained in inverse proportion to determination. The mosquitoes circled, mother waited, her desire to snuff out a life inflated. They would dive, she would clap. Sound and futility reigned supreme. At last, jumping off the bed, Fiso switched on the light. A minute later one of the mosquitoes, squashed by a sandal, was a smudge of blood on the president's face, but Fiso could not be bothered to make good the insignia of her patriotism. A few months before, she would have wiped the blood away. But the novelty of affecting patriotic sentiment in the hope of dreaming herself out of prostitution to the level of First Lady had long worn off.

The following morning Sue switched on her miniature radio, to be confronted by the continuously recycled maxims of State propaganda, which ranged from the importance of being a sovereign nation to defending the gains of independence in the face of a 'neo-colonialist onslaught'. Leaning against the sink, she failed to grasp the value of the messages to her life. She gulped her tea and went to the Union Avenue flea market. There, among other vendors slugging it out for survival, she could at least learn where to get the next bag of sugar or cooking oil.

On the same Saturday afternoon that marked the climax to Anna's marital woes, Stix, a struggling, young jazz pianist, had a call from his friend, Shamiso, inviting him to an impromptu dinner at Mvura Restaurant. Her friends and elements of her 'tribe', as she liked to refer to her cousins, were to be part of the company. With only the prospect of being part of a nondescript crowd at a glum, low-key music festival in the Harare Gardens, Stix committed himself to Shamiso's plans. At 7.30pm he made his way to the restaurant. By midnight he had made a pathetic retreat to his flat, having shared part of his meagre income with two police officers fortunate enough to witness him driving through red lights. From his flat he had called Shamiso, and threatened to cremate her for inviting him to a restaurant where they would be saddled with a bill of over $15 000 each. That it was a restaurant with 'melted Mars Bar' on its dessert menu wickedly swelled his appetite for arson.

"So don't say you have not been warned about Mvura Restaurant," Stix said to Fiso the day after the incident. "If, however, out of curiosity you decide to go there, your experience will approximate to something like this: you get there, the car park is full of cars with diplomatic registration plates and there is not even space to open the car doors. At this point a security guard..." Stix pauses to light his cigarette, "... will run like a demon to find you a parking space – but since you don't own a car, Fiso, you won't experience that bit."

"So you're not going to take me there?' Fiso asks, but Stix ignores her and continues.

"You may be at a table where you sit back to back with the Japanese ambassador, and you will be confronted by a waiter wielding a menu without prices. By the end of the evening you will be sorry. Never assume that such restaurants price their food reasonably!"

Fiso listened, thinking what a curious person Stix was, and well aware that save for living in the same dilapidated block of flats, they did not have much in common. The nice restaurants, elitist concerts and well-dressed friends existed only in the stories that Stix told her on their doorsteps on sluggish afternoons. They were just another spectral reality that Stix was fond of invoking. And after an hour or two of reciprocal balderdash, one of them would just stand up and walk into his or her flat, leaving the other to wean him or herself from that hallucinogenic indulgence.

Defining one's relationship with the world demands daily renegotiating of one's existence. So far-reaching are the consequences of neglecting exigencies imposed by this, that those unwilling or unable to participate eventually find themselves trapped in a parallel universe, the existence of which is not officially recognised. These are the people who never die, Sue and her mother being a quintessential sample. Sue has no birth certificate because her mother does not have one. Officially they were never born and so will never die. For how do authorities issue a death certificate when there is no birth certificate? Several other official declarations only perfect the parallel existence of most of Harare's residents. Officially basic food commodities are affordable because prices are State-controlled. Officially no one starves because there is plenty of food on supermarket shelves. And if it is not there, it is officially somewhere, being hoarded by Enemies of the State. With all its innumerable benefits who would not want to exist in this other world spawned by the authorities – where your situation does not daily remind you what a liability your mouth and stomach are. It was therefore towards this official existence that Sue and her mother strove. Fed up with galloping food prices in their parallel universe, they took a chance and tried to take the leap into official existence.

It was an ordinary Monday morning when mother and daughter walked to the Central Registry offices hoping to get birth certificates, metal IDs and, eventually, passports. Sue had been told she could make a good income buying things from South Africa and selling them at the flea markets. But because the benefit of her deathless existence did not also confer upon her freedom of movement across national boundaries, she needed a passport. Fiso had decided to assist her daughter and get herself a passport too. Little did they know that they would find the door out of their parallel existence shut, and bolted.

By mid-afternoon Fiso was on her doorstep relating the events of the morning to Stix. Back in her humble flat she felt better, having spent half a day surrounded by the smell of dust, apathy and defeat.

Such were the Central Registry offices: an assemblage of Portakabins, which had outlived their lifespans a dozen times over. With people enduring never-ending queues, just to have their dignity thrown out of rickety windows by sadistic officials, inevitably a refugee camp ambience prevailed.

"If your mother and father are dead and you do not have their birth certificates, then there is nothing that I can do," the man in office number 28 had said, his fat fist thumping the desk. He wore a blue and yellow striped tie that dug painfully into his fat neck, accentuating the degradation of his torn collar.

"But what am I supposed to do?" Fiso asked, exasperated.

'Woman, just do as I say. I need one of your parents' birth or death certificates to process your application. You are wasting my time. You never listen. What's wrong with you people?"

"Aaaah you are useless! Every morning you tell your wife that you are going to work when all you do is frustrate people!" Fiso stormed out of the office. Having learnt the false nature of authority and law from the streets, she was certain that he was her only obstacle. Men, she knew, could have the most perverse idiosyncrasies and at least one vice. In her experience, doctors, lawyers and the most genteel of politicians could gleefully discard their masks to become the most brutal perverts. It was a male trait, an official trait, and it accounted for her failure to acquire the papers she and her daughter needed.

Fiso's parents had died long back in deep, rural Zhombe where peasant life had confined them to a radius of less than a hundred kilometres, and where an innate suspicion of anything involving paperwork was nurtured. Back in the forties, stories of people having their names changed by authorities horrified semi-literate peasants such as Fiso's parents, who swore they would never have anything to do with the wicked authorities of that era.

"We were told to go to office number 28, but there was no one there. After about forty minutes, we went back to the office that had referred us, but there was no one there either. Returning to office number 28, and seeking help from an official who was strolling past we were told, 'Look? Can't you see that jacket? It means he is not far away. Wait for him.' So we waited – for three hours – only to be told to bring one of my parents' death or birth certificates."

"Civil servants are like that, Fiso. They all have two jobs you know," Stix said, mildly. Fiso was being too naive for a seasoned sex purveyor, he thought.

"Look: a Japanese firm is making big money generating electricity out of sewage waste. All you have to do to bring your electricity bill down is shit a lot!" Stix, his eyes on the newspaper, was trying to steer the conversation in another direction.

That afternoon, it was Fiso who disappeared into her flat first, inexplicably regretting that she had let Stix have sex with her a couple of months before. They had been drunk, and she had found herself naked and collapsing onto Stix's bed, his fiendish shaft plumbing her hard-wearing orifice. "Ey, you! That's not a good starting point!" was her only protest, and she cursed the alcohol that still swirled inside her head.

15

"If you'd been a virgin, Fiso, I would have washed my penis with milk, just for you," Stix said after contenting himself. Fiso ignored the remark. More incensed with herself than with Stix, she simply decided to sleep over the anger in the hope that it would go.

In Harare, vegetable vendors can yield useful connections. After Fiso and Sue had failed to get their papers, a woman at the Central Registry was brought to the attention of Fiso by a fellow vendor. This woman, a relative, could assist her to get any form of ID for a fee. Because the vendor and her relative went to the same church, she suggested that this would be the ideal place to introduce Fiso.

Less than a hundred metres from the church building, a man of Fiso's age stood by a corner selling single cigarettes and bananas. Fiso, sensing her increasingly disagreeable nerves, sought to calm them down with a cigarette.

"*Sekuru*," she addressed the man, "how much are your cigarettes?"

"I'm not your *sekuru*. Harare does not have any *sekurus*. They are all in the rural areas. If you desire a *sekuru* then make one for yourself out of cardboard."

"How much are your cigarettes?" she asked again, avoiding the contentious term.

"Fifteen dollars."

She quietly retrieved three brand new five-dollar coins from her purse, handed them over and picked a Madison Red from among the many on display. Contentedly lighting the cigarette and avoiding eye contact, she heard the man ask, "What time is it?"

"If you need a watch why don't you make yourself one out of cardboard?" she retorted, and walked away, victorious.

With what panache does fate deliver the person of a harlot into a church building? Cockroaches appear through the cracks in the walls and wave their antennae in response to an almost primaeval call. The priest, beneath his holy regalia, shudders, aware of the relative paleness of his cloistered virtues in the face of a salvation cobbled together on street corners. Against the tide of attrition of the human condition, what man of cloth can offer a soul a better salvation than the sheer dogged will to live? In the priest's mind, however, such sentiments only manifested themselves in vague notions of jealousy and contempt. As Fiso strolled in carefree, the holy man recoiled, the congregation's heads turned, and the Devil chuckled. A Dynamos' Football Club t-shirt, fluorescent green mini-skirt and six-inch-high perspex platform shoes upstaged the holy word.

Destructive distillation is a process by which a substance is subjected to a high temperature with the absence of oxygen so that it simply degenerates into its several constituent substances without burning. After her silent confessions and having received the body and blood of Christ, Mrs Shava found herself subjected to destructive distillation by an ogling congregation. Like anyone being introduced to a person of dubious appearance on sanctified premises, she degenerated into her constituent attributes of self-righteousness and caution.

"The church services are short here – or was I late?" Fiso remarked after being introduced to Mrs Shava by her vending friend.

"No, we're not like those Pentecostal churches, we're less fanatical." Mrs Shava said, unable to look Fiso straight in the eyes and bewildered, her mind whirling with an elliptical sense of déja vu as she wondered where they had met before. She could also feel the stares of the congregation pecking at her back from several metres away. She resented them but neither did she like talking to Fiso. However, having listened to her plight, she agreed to help her out. Everyone had to live, after all.

"Eeeek, ahh, it's complicated." Mrs Shava moaned, a technique that she had perfected after helping several people. "It's no easy task," she continued, wanting to justify her fee.

"I understand, but I must have a birth certificate. And my daughter cannot get one if I don't have one – and she needs a passport."

"I can try, but it is a risk, I could lose my job." Mrs Shava assumed a pious expression. Fiso knew that it was time to tie up her end of the deal. She understood what Mrs Shava meant when she said that success depended on a number of factors; Fiso knew it meant one thing only.

"I understand it's a big risk, but I intend to reward you for your efforts." Fiso glanced at her friend for clues but the vendor's face was as blank as a hospital wall. "I don't know what you would like, but I'll leave you to decide, my sister."

Mrs Shava's lips parted dispassionately to reveal her white teeth, "Okay, call me on Wednesday and I will see if it's all right for you to come to my office. People at my workplace will be on strike but I can't risk my job. If it's okay, I'll give you the forms, you fill them in and I'll take them back. And don't forget my fee: $15 000!" She smiled for the first time and turned to walk away.

"Uhh, huh, your phone number at work?" Fiso stammered.

"Nyasha will give it to you; I have to see someone else," came the reply.

Fiso turned to Nyasha, and they smiled at each other.

Contentedly walking off, Mrs Shava could not have guessed that in less than a minute she would be caressed by more poltergeistic echoes of a recent past. She was walking out of the church premises when Stix stopped by to pick up Fiso in his scarlet car. A shiver descended Mrs Anna Shava's spine as she recalled the night she killed the street kid. Fiso's face, though, defiantly refused to fit into the jigsaw puzzle, and Mrs Shava could only watch in bewilderment, as the old harlot jumped into the car, which rattled away, accelerating sideways like a crab.

In a mortuary at the central hospital, clad in a blue suit, white shirt, and seemingly asphyxiated by the tie around its neck, lies a slightly overweight corpse. A cellphone is still stuck in one of the pockets and when it rings for the third time, it is answered by a being who, after years as a mortuary cleaner, picking his wages from its floor, has become indifferent to death.

"Hullo, Central Hospital," he answers.

"Hullo, I'm looking for my husband. Is that his phone you are using? Who are you? Is he there?"

"Aah, I don't know, but unless this is the body of a thief who stole the phone from your husband, your husband is dead. The police shot him in the head. They said he was rioting in the city centre."

The previous night Anna's husband had not returned from work. That he would have come to such a rough end, no one could have guessed. But, being in the insurance industry, he would have appreciated it if he'd been told that the value of his life was equivalent to twenty condoms, and in all likelihood would not have contested such a settlement being awarded to Anna. His death, though, had consequences that reverberated through to Fiso, because on the day she was supposed to call Mrs Shava, grief and its attendant ceremonies had already claimed her. Then, on Monday, having spent all night at Piri-Piri, the city's sleaziest nightclub, Fiso decided to take the Central Registry juggernaut head-on. Suffering from a hangover, and caring not about consequences, she went straight to the Registrar General's office.

"I've been trying to get a birth certificate and can't, because your staff members only care about getting bribes!" The Registrar General's secretary remained calm, picked up the phone and dialled but, before she had uttered a word, the RG had emerged from his office. Being a constant target of ridicule by the press as the man heading one of the most inefficient and corrupt government departments, he was very sensitive to criticism.

"How can I help you, lady?" he demanded impatiently.

"I only need a birth certificate, but your staff is only interested in frustrating people into paying bribes!"

"Those are serious allegations." The RG's interest lay only in smothering public objections.

"All I want is a birth certificate, Sir. My womanhood is an old rag. I've paid the price of living. Please do not waste my time, I'm too old for that."

The Registrar nearly had convulsions. "Sandra, call security!" he ordered.

The secretary fumbled, dropped her pen and spilt her coffee.

"Your staff members all want bribes. I come to you and all you do is get rid of me! I suppose you want a bribe too? What else can you do apart from sitting on your empty scrotum all day?"

In a little less than half an hour Fiso was behind police bars facing a charge of public disorder. The police, however, soon found their case stalling. There was no way of establishing her identity because she did not have an ID. After she told the investigating officer that she was trying to get just such an ID when she was arrested, the officer called the Registrar General, who offered to quickly process an ID if it was in the interest of facilitating the course of justice. That afternoon Fiso was bundled into the back of a Landrover Defender in handcuffs and taken to the Central Registry to make an application for an ID. Predictably she refused to co-operate, so she was later thrown back into the vehicle and taken to the police cells.

Two days went by, each bringing a new face into the cell she shared with six other women. On the third day two cellmates went for trial and never returned – either freed or sent to Chikurubi Maximum. Then a new inmate arrived. From her appearance one would have surmised that she was a teenager picked up from the vicinity of a village while herding goats. It was her carefree disposition that won her the attention of her cellmates.

"What are those for?" she asked, looking up at the left corner of the cell. The officer who had brought her had hardly locked up. No immediate answer came until the officer had disappeared.

"Those are CCTV cameras," someone finally answered her.

"What is CCTV?" the girl asked again.

"Closed Circuit Television. It enables them to watch us from their offices all the time on one of their televisions."

Later in the evening, when another new face was brought in, the goatherd girl asked the officer: "Is it true that you have a TV and that you are watching us?"

The officer just continued with his duty of locking up the gate as if nothing had been said. Goat-girl was, however, unfazed.

"I think you people are going to be in trouble when the president finds out that you are wasting TVs on criminals. I'm sure he would like to be watched on TVs too. Or watch himself so that he's safe from assassins and perverts."

After five days in the cell Fiso was cautioned and released without charge – not even that of failing to produce an ID. The investigating officer, seeing that the case was going nowhere, had managed to convince his superior to release her with just one statement: "It's only an ageing whore."

Brian Chikwava is a Zimbabwean writer and musician who is based in London.

Strange Fruit

Monica Arac de Nyeko

Southern trees bear strange fruit,
Blood on the leaves and blood at the root,
Black bodies swinging in the southern breeze,
Strange fruit hanging from the poplar trees.
Billie Holiday, 1939

★★★

IT'S EVENING IN MY dream. The Kitgum sun has disappeared behind the hills. Dry leaves crash under my bare feet as I race among the *yaa* trees at the foot of Kidi Guu hills, looking for Mwaka. Burnt tree stumps and thorn bushes let me through their sheltered trunks with a few scratches and cuts. The looming night falls upon the lush and short shrubs inch by inch. I am alone and frightened. I need to find my husband. I need to sniff that familiar fruity scent in his breath. I need to touch his unblemished face.

Mwaka emerges from behind the anthill, standing amidst a thicket of overgrown spear grass. The enormous acacia trees on the breasts of the hills sway and crack like the hinges of a breaking door. Darkness shields his face. In his heavy footsteps is the same man who went with the liberation war two years ago and drifted like the August tide of Aringa River. His feet carry him with the poise of a mountain spirit. I stretch out my hands. I beckon him to come to me. Every step releases him like a blooming hibiscus. I have waited so long for this moment. Nothing can spoil it. My heart gains the momentum of an *orak* drumbeat. Just like that

21

day he held me in his arms under the full moon and released himself inside me.

Mwaka pulls closer. My head feels like a roaring flame of eucalyptus tree logs. I bury my face in my palms and close my eyes tight. His footsteps hasten away, over the dry leaves. I open my eyes and scan the darkness. There is no sign of him.

"Mwaka!" I call out.

His brisk strides fade faster than a sigh. He melts into the night. My cry spatters into the air.

"*Maaadooooo*! Mwaka!"

Mwaka's motion is steady like a straight-line. He descends into the wilderness. I am left with no husband. No petal of mirth to call my own. No wind to carry my weight. My risen hope evaporates. My frail arms hash forward. I crash to the ground. I start to sink. At the end of this tunnel, the glimmer of light becomes a pencil point, and blinks to black. It leaves me with nothing, except Piloya's hand at my feet and her scared voice, "M-a, wa-ke up! Wake up! Maaa, Maaaaaaaa…"

Piloya's voice plunges me into her world. I stretch my hands and legs. Piloya kneels at the foot of my bed. She has left hers at the other corner of the room. Her little hands pass rapidly over my feet and make their way upwards searching for my hands. I release my fingers into her open palms. She squeezes gently. I read the words buried in her motion. I bend over and bring her off her knees into my bed. We say nothing. I swallow hard and pass my fingers over my arms. The roughness of the goose pimples settling upon my skin teases my fingertips. Piloya curls her body. She searches for my hand again. She finds it and leans her head upon my elbow. Her soft breathing comes through the darkness, tender and pure like rainwater.

I lie on my back and take heavy sighs to conjure calmness from the tip of every vein that runs through my body. The desperation I felt when Mwaka disappeared has leapt into my consciousness. I feel a certain heaviness sit on my chest. I pull Piloya closer. I hold her tight. It's a language she picks up quickly, and draws even closer to me. She places her hand upon my stomach to make sure I am by her side. It's a habit she picked up when Mwaka was gone.

Safe like a secret, Piloya lets sleep immerse her and take her to another universe. For me it's blink after blink with no sleep. My eyes travel to the corrugated-iron sheets and to the little hole in the roof. The moon shines bright. I can see the headstrong woman in the moon staring at the earth below. She brings to life the Acoli folktale of her journey there. Her story has been told for generations. She was cast into her sky prison for going to the forest to pick firewood when her husband had refused to let her go. She makes me think of Mwaka before he was the man whose face hides behind the darkness in my dreams.

Mwaka was the young man whose voice soared with the tempo of the *orak* dance that night I first met him. He stamped his feet to the ground, raising fumes of brown dust up the other dancers' noses in the dance arena. They shoved him with their dancing gourds. The girls crushed him between their bosoms. He struggled to make his way through. When he got to me, his feet sprung him up and down like a rapid eye blink. This was the *orak* dance of the New Year. Young men and women came with keen eyes to search for potential partners.

I had escaped from home to come and stare at village dating and courtship with city disdain. I was the nineteen-year-old city girl from Kampala, come with Ma and Pa to spend Christmas with the family. Mwaka was the village boy who enchanted all metropolitan care and class out of me. He had enormous strength in his limbs and danced with the lightness of a feather. I stared at him, and then focused my eyes on the woman in the moon. As a child, Ma had told me the moon woman's story. I gave her a name from the Acoli word for moon – *dwe*. Her name was Nyadwe: daughter of the moon.

Nyadwe never aged. Puberty pimples spread upon my face like black beans. I kissed goodbye to my childhood. She was still as young. Nyadwe was as enchanting as she had been when I first saw her. Through the years, I stared up into the skies. I imagined she could hear me. I felt sorry for her as much as I did for myself. We developed an intimacy of deprived souls, in our nightly symposiums of morbid revelations. I whispered to her the contempt I felt for my parents whose concept of discipline was synonymous with whip lashing. Nyadwe knew those things about me I had never told to anyone. When the moon did not adorn the sky during some nights, I missed her dreadfully. I stared aimlessly at the heavens waiting for her to pop out of the clouds.

As Mwaka's eyes settled upon my waist beads, I looked up to her for an answer. Nyadwe was smiling right above my head. She was brighter than I had ever seen her before. I joined the dance and surrendered to the dance rhythm. I cast my hands in the air and laughed delightfully. Mwaka came so close to me. I could feel his breath upon my neck. It was a sweet and fruity scent, like ripe mango. He placed his palms upon my hips. I swayed and gyrated to the tempo of the drums. Our voices rose robustly with the rest of the dancers in this heated celebration of youth. The obscene lyrics slid out of our vocal cords with a carelessness that belonged to puberty only:

> *eyo eyo eyo*
> *open your wrapper*
> *let the big mortar in!*
> *eyo eyo eyo*
> *shake it shake it*

The tune poured into the night. It was not just melody; it was ecstatic passion that sprung Mwaka and me to the long grass under the trees. The moon shone generously upon our naked bodies. We yielded ourselves to the night. We let it take us beyond the music and the darkness.

I had met Kiden my loud-mouthed cousin at the dance. I did not find her when Mwaka and I got back. I came back home in the morning with a pot pretending that I had been at the river to collect water. The dance arena dust still clung to my feet. My hair was full of grass twigs. I had forgotten to pick them out in my haste to get home before anyone woke up.

Ma stood by the door to the main house. She had her hands at her waist. The morning splendour dissolved in an instant. My heart, which had danced with the morning dew on my way home, now thumped inside my chest like *orak* drums turned sour. Every muscle in Ma's face busted with anger. Her hands shook. She grabbed me by my collar and took me inside the house. Ma pushed me to sit on the floor. She summoned Pa in the house, like she always did when she learned something bad I had done before he did.

"You are from Kampala. Kampala for God's sake," she shouted.

That was Ma. Always going on and on about the city and how different people from the city should be when they come to the village. Pa looked at me fidgeting with my fingers and staring at the floor.

"Don't do it again," he said in his faint voice.

Pa's voice had always been faint. He looked at me. My eyes trickled with humiliation. The floor felt hot. My teeth chattered the way they do when it is too cold.

"Don't do it again," Pa repeated sternly.

I nodded.

"She won't do it again," he said to Ma.

Pa got up slowly and went outside. I was shocked. So was Ma.

24

She slapped the mahogany table, moving her head with so much force. Those dangling wooden earrings she never took off swung like ripe fruits in the gusts of June. She swallowed hard. Ma stormed out of the house, banging the door behind her. She snapped at everyone the whole day, including Pa.

I thought she had even forgotten all about it. In the night she came to me. I was already asleep. She shook hard at my feet. I woke up, sat up and rubbed my eyes. Ma spoke in a tone barely audible to herself.

"Lakidi," she started.

She rarely called me Lakidi. I dreaded it when she did. Ma had given me the name herself. Lakidi meant stone. Ma believed I could shoot up into the sky one day and twinkle like a star. I hated that my name was a constant reminder of Ma's hopes in me. Ma's eyes burnt like a flame when she spoke of me sometimes. Her words sounded almost magical at such moments. She said there was much more in me than I gave. That buried deep within me was subtle warmth that could blossom in the driest season and survive a long drought like a cassava stem. But, when I did something wrong, Ma's magical voice grew harsh and sharp. It fell upon my body like thorns.

"If your father thinks men pulling at your breasts in those stupid dances is okay, I don't," Ma said. "Do it again and I will tie your feet to iron bars and lock you inside the house until it's time to go back to the city."

"Maaaaa," I said.

"What?"

"Nothing."

"What was that tone?"

"Nothing."

"Do you think I am stupid? You think I did not hear that tone, huh? Yesterday God knows what you did in that stupid dance. Today you don't respect your parents. What will you do next, huh?"

I shut my mouth. I held the blanket to my chest and pressed it closer. At such moments I regretted that when the temptation arose I had not poured hot water on her vegetable seedlings in her nursery beds in Kampala.

"Answer me, huh?"

Ma's voice rose sharper. She sounded like she was about to burst into tears. That is how Ma was. After raising her voice, she always cried. Ma cried if anything got her very mad. I hated listening to her outbursts. She slapped her hands upon her thighs and rocked her body to and fro crying, "Aii aii." Listening to her at such times was worse than any whiplash.

"Talk to me," Ma repeated.

I got out of the bed and tried to make my way outside amidst the darkness.

"Where are you going, huh?"

"I am just going outside to the toilet."

"Oh… toilet? I see. If I hadn't woken you up, would you be thinking of a toilet, huh? Is that all you can think of when I am talking to you?"

I walked past her, brushing her shoulder. Pa's voice was right at the door.

"What is going on in there?"

Ma pulled me back by the shoulder. I staggered and almost fell.

"Slut, slut!" she cried.

"What is going on in here?" Pa asked again.

I heard several other voices outside.

"Look at your daughter. *Aiii aii aiii. Lutwaaa!*" Ma wailed in Acoli.

"What is this, all about?" Pa asked.

Ma continued to wail loudly.

"*Aaii aiii aii.*"

"What is wrong in there?"

"She does not even respect me anymore. Slut, you think I did not hear what happened with that stupid boy Mwaka. I sat the whole day today trying to tell myself you are smarter than that. Do you know how I felt the whole day, huh? Do you?"

I stomped out of the house. Pa tried to hold me back. I busted through the door and almost knocked him down.

"Why did you start all this now?" Pa said to Ma.

My cousins were all outside, even Kiden. They all stared at me like I was covered in shit. I ran in my petticoat. I did not know where my destination was. My feet just brushed the grasses along the way. I went with the flow of the night. Nyadwe was not there in the skies. She would have led me to a safe haven. She would have calmed me.

Then it hit me – Mwaka!

It took me a while to find his place. When I did, I banged on his door. He took one look at me and held me in his arms for a while. He did not ask any questions. Gradually, he released me. He took my hand and led me to his bed. He got into the bed and put his hands around me, like a fragile object that should not get tarnished. His sweet mango breath was upon my neck, so fresh, so warm. It calmed the tears, the shame and the anger.

Pa came early the next morning. He stood by the door like a chicken beaten by hailstorms. He said nothing except, "Lakidi, everyone expects you home."

I insisted Mwaka take me home with Pa. Mwaka did not argue. I was so afraid that Pa would lose his calm and beat me up along the way. Ma refused to come out when we got home. She refused to talk to me for days. Everyone said very little. But it was Pa's silence that worried me. I would have preferred that he snapped at me and his eyes burnt with anger. He did not. I felt guilty. It did not feel right. He caught me looking at him often trying to seek the words behind his silence. He smiled lightly and passed his hand upon his beard and looked at something else.

The following days, Pa let Mwaka come home. He had learned that I met him at the church gardens. Mwaka loved bougainvillea with a passion I could not understand. The church gardens were full of well-pruned bougainvillea plants in different shapes and sizes. They stood and held up their green leaves and pink petals to the heavens. In some parts of the gardens, red and white roses bloomed. The thorns never let me pick a single rose bud, without a prick. Mwaka liked it. He took my bleeding finger into his mouth and licked. It was strange. But he said it was a pact. That it meant we would always be together. The thought of Mwaka and me forever lighted my eyes. When he spoke like that, I felt like I was lying on a carpet of morning glory petals and floating over Lake Victoria.

Mwaka's passion for the flowers was replaced with the love of card games with Pa when he started to invite him over. Pa laughed softly. He did not say much. Sometimes he joked with Mwaka and they seemed at ease with each other. I did not see Ma anywhere in the compound when Mwaka was around. One day as I passed by their room, later in the night, I heard Pa and Ma talking.

"She is not young. She's got her teacher certificate you know," Pa said.

Ma grunted and jeered.

"Anyone but not him."

★★★

The marriage did not come as a surprise to anybody. Not even Ma. But she did say it would not last.

"Not even this planting season." She said and laughed the way she does when she wants to get people angry.

She came to see me often after the marriage. She coaxed me to reveal any problems I was having.

"That's what mothers are for, dear," she said sweetly and smiled.

Year after year, it was the same words from Ma. I hated the way Mwaka bought every useless thing that caught his whim, and our accounts suffered. I loathed his snoring in the night. We fought about so many things that seemed stupid. Sometimes I refused to talk to him when he got me so mad. One time I packed my things and threatened to leave with Piloya when he sold a cow after I told him it was not necessary. He came home that evening with a dress. I had seen it once before, in a shop window. I commented on how nice it looked. Mwaka had bought it. He handed it to me. I tried to look even angrier. I broke down and laughed. I took the dress from his hand and went to try it on.

"It won't work next time!" I shouted from the bedroom.

"There won't be a next time," he said and laughed.

When Ma came, she always seemed disappointed that we joked and laughed. She was astonished that Mwaka held my hand and stroked my face when she was around. Mwaka came home as soon as he had rounded off the accounts as the chief cashier at the Acoli Farmers' Association.

"Look at him," Ma, said with contempt, "at home all the time, trying to impress me, isn't he?"

"Ma, that's him, he comes home every day like that."

"Well I don't buy any of it. He does not deserve you. Lakidi, you could have…"

"Maaaa."

"Oh I see, I am not even allowed to say anything about him, am I?" she said and called Piloya. Ma started to tell her a tale of a time long ago, when elephant refused to listen to his mother and lost his long, beautiful tail.

In the night Mwaka whispered in my ear the funny names she had called him. Her favourite one was *obibi*. Ma called him that even when I was there. She stopped when Piloya asked her, "Is that Pa's name? Ogre?"

★★★

One day however, Ma came to see me without sending word.

It was one of those days when the sun fell upon the skin like red-hot charcoal. March had ripened the millet in the fields. Every inch of our compound was spread with sunflowers, groundnuts and sorghum, all ready

28

to be stored away in the granary. Mwaka's favourite mango tree stood in the front of the house, carrying drying leaves that poured to the ground with the slightest breeze. Piloya's lips cracked. They even dripped blood sometimes. Her dark skin grew too pale and she was tired all the time. Ma emerged hunched and sweating from the car that had brought her to our compound. Without sitting down, Ma walked towards me and clumped her hands on my shoulders.

"You have to come to the city, everyone says so, even your Pa."

"Ma, not that again," I frowned lightly and hugged her.

"No no, this is serious."

"Maaaa, come on, we have talked about that before."

"Yes, but…"

Ma had come because of the rumours. Everyone was talking about the rebels. Strange stories had penetrated the market places and the churchyard on Sundays. After village meetings, people gathered in small circles. They whispered stories they had heard from other people. At the river, women stayed longer and spoke of men who came and abducted men and young boys to force them to fight. The same kind of stories had infiltrated the radio stations and newspapers like a plague.

"Everyone is talking about it; this is serious," Ma said.

Mwaka spoke to her himself. Ma listened and did not grunt or pass foul comments.

"Everyone is okay, like they have always been; radios are full of lies, and everyone knows that. The rebels are not fighting us. It's the government they want, " Mwaka said.

"They say it's different this time, it's different, they changed tactics…"

"Nothing will happen, give it time, you will see, we have heard rumours like this for years and nothing has happened."

Later in the day, Ma smiled and said, "He is not so bad, you know."

Mwaka always spoke about the rebels with a lot of contempt. Sometimes he lost his temper and lamented about how stupid they must be to follow a guerrilla leader who had no formal education at all but wanted to form a new government. When he spoke to Ma, his voice was calm. He paused in between his sentences beautifully. I was so proud of him.

★★★

A month later, I was in the family cemetery weeding my uncle's grave. I heard voices chanting, "*Harambe, Harambe!*"

They drew closer and filled the air. The chants echoed with a kind of intensity that made me very unsettled. It was one of the slogans the Mau Mau fighters in neighbouring Kenya had used, when fighting the British before independence. It was a pledge of togetherness, but something about this chant was different. The voices rose with the thumps of heavy gumboots. Then the bullets started. The wind held still as the air filled with skittering bullets that made my head pound and ears ring. When Mwaka heard the guns, he followed me to the cemetery. He found me darting through the massive undergrowth in the gardens making towards the house. He grabbed my hand. We all rushed inside. A few minutes later, men and young boys busted into the compound like hailstorms flung by lightning. The heaviness of their footsteps echoed their number. They were many.

"*Toka nje, la sivyo tutaichoma nyumba yako.*" Come out or we burn the house.

Silence.

"*Tunajua kwamba uko ndani.*" We know you are there.

We remained silent, engulfed in a fear that could drill holes through the ground. Mwaka held my hand. Piloya, only eleven then, lay under our wooden bed without any movement. The voices outside rose sharper than Waragi Extra Strong Spirit as they started to chant: "Death to the traitors! Death to the traitors!"

People had spoken about such things. They said the rebels considered every male a traitor if he refused to join the liberation war. He was an enemy of the Acoli people, and the great rebellion to oust the government. Mwaka held my hand and squeezed it till it hurt. He raised his feet where we lay and covered ourselves with blankets and other things. Mwaka never said anything more. He went to the door and opened it. Daylight rushed in. Hands raised, he walked towards them and I knew it was real. These locusts who had desecrated distant villages, swarmed several homes and seemed so alien to me had come to take my husband. I held Piloya's hand. It stuck in mine like glue. I tried to block the voices out of my ears, but they glided through too eagerly.

"*Je, kuna wanaume wengine ndani ya nyumba?*" they asked.

"Only my daughter and wife," Mwaka said.

"*Watowe nje.*"

Mwaka did not come. A young boy who stunk like a he-goat came, stood before me, pointed his barrel at my head and stammered, "Ge ge ge ge geee-t out!"

Piloya and I scampered out of the house. We stood near the door. Most of the young boys had new green army uniforms that were tacked into their gumboots at the ankles. The endless sight before me was of guns slung on shoulders, a knife on the waist, a few pistols here and there, and new gumboots whose black plastic was caked in dust that seemed to have risen to their hair and turned it brown.

I remember standing there and getting ready to find myself in the next life. If my daughter and I should die, I prayed that it should be quick and painless. A young man held his AK-47 to our heads. Piloya soaked herself in urine. She held onto to my hand while her eyes flapped around like a duck about to be slaughtered. She had never seen so many men like that. The endless number of men overwhelmed her. She cast her eyes upon the earth. The number of young boys was greater than the adults. Some boys even seemed weighed down by the size of their guns. Their blood-shot eyes scared me. The air was heavy and stuffy. Everything smelt rotten.

Some of the boys hit at dry mango leaves with their guns. Mwaka always said the tree had saved his grandfather from the Karamojong cattle rustlers. He climbed up on it and the leaves hid him. The Karomojong could not figure out where he was. Mwaka carried his grandfather's name. He had a very strong attachment to the old man. He said, when the man died, he came to him in a dream and said the tree was special and he would be its guiding spirit. The rebels broke off branches and they dropped to the ground. Mwaka glared at them and tried to look away. That tree was as good as his grandfather.

The others walked around laughing in loud voices with several rounds of ammunition rolled around their waists. Except for the fear threatening to pound my heart out of my chest, everything remained calmer than I expected. I did not speak. Just in case I said the wrong thing, and they sliced my guts and I woke up in a pool of blood covered with flies and maggots.

Whether there was someone in command, I did not put much effort in trying to notice. A boy, who looked not more than eleven, searched our house. He came out, smiling at me and revealed teeth, which I imagined smelled worse than our pit latrine. He said to me, "*Harambe!*" and offered his hand for me to shake. I shook it and quickly clasped my hands together.

An older man announced that they should be on their way. A good number had started to drift away, taking the route of the cattle kraal, towards sunset. Mwaka's animals had filled the kraal enclosure before the notorious Karamojong rustlers who believed all cows in the world belonged to them raided it empty. The rebels did not bother with Piloya and I. One punch on his back and Mwaka started to walk slowly away.

I stayed with the feeling that Mwaka had gone to work and the evening sunset would bring him home to me. As he disappeared among the figures, Mwaka stole a glance at Piloya and me. Then he looked straight ahead, walking on, never wavering until there was no single figure I could pick out from the distance. I stood there and refused to acknowledge that although Mwaka was a strong man he was not a fighter at all. He would not survive the forests. Mwaka was wearing his sapphire blue and red striped Acoli Farmers' Cooperation uniform. That image of him stuck in my mind like a portrait. When I see him often in my dreams, the merge of blue and red seems calm and tranquil, but I cannot embrace its beauty and let it envelop me. It is always too remote for me to reach.

We stood there and watched him march out of our lives. The men and boys chanted with vehemence. The earth moaned softly beneath. Only the luckiest of men escaped. The rebels descended back to the wilderness, which had released them, chanting, *"Harambe! Harambe! Harambe!"*

Morning came without Mwaka. Piloya cried for her father. She hated that the schools had closed. She had to stay home every day. Words got lost in my mouth, like a child's burble, uttered and gone. My heart started to soak in a maze of unspeakable gloom. I sought a smile behind the shadows of my grey clouds. I found one in the vague memory of a meaningless childhood song:

thunder thunder
the king has sent me to fetch his son thunder
oh you bigheaded one, give him back thunder
or else this shall surely end in jail

Day after day, the song became remote like distant *raa* smoke. Weeks later the dreams started. Sometimes I was looking for Mwaka's whisper in the bougainvillea petals in the church gardens. Other times I was a ripple in the ocean growing bigger and bigger. Most times, I was at the foot of Kidi Guu hills, looking for him among the acacia. In the mornings, I woke up and stretched out my hands, searching for him. Any sign of him, his sweet mango breath, his laughter, anything.

Sondra and I used to teach together at Lacep Primary School, before it was closed down. Her husband was taken the day Mwaka was taken too. She came to me often. We sang folksongs under the mango tree until we fell asleep. After her husband was taken her face no longer had any scars.

He used to beat her up thoroughly. When anyone on the staff asked about the scars on her face, she always said she had fallen down.

In the days after Mwaka and her husband were taken, we went down to the river to wash clothes like many other women and girls often did. Like the rest, we sat by the bank waiting for our clothes to dry. Sometimes even when they had dried, we remained seated a little longer. We said very little. Most women came to the river too often. Some came even when they had almost no clothes to wash. Sometimes laughter came through, but it was dry and lifeless.

The Aringa River was a seasonal tributary of the Nile. It passed through distant lands, filled with man-eating crocodiles and grouchy hippos that sliced people in two. Sometimes, the water brought with it blood-sucking leeches that stuck to the skin. They did not fall off until they had siphoned enough blood. Very often, when people swam, the leeches found their way into their noses. They lived there unnoticed for weeks sucking blood painlessly out of their unsuspecting host. Once found, people conquered their thirst for blood by sticking sharp thorns into their slippery black bodies. Then they sent them back to the water as dead beings to be cast away by the tide.

On one of those days when we went to the river to wash some clothes, Sondra started to hum a funeral song. Then she buried her face in her hands. She had never done that before. I moved over to her and held her in my arms. She lifted her head up. Her eyes were red. Tears flowed down her cheeks.

"I don't want to, but I miss him," she said and sprung up.

Sondra went over to the *mvule* tree a distance from the river. I thought she wanted to be alone for a while. But, she started to hit at the trunk instead. Her braids swung upon her head. She shook like something was driving her to harm herself. I ran up to her and grabbed her by the blouse. Her hands were badly bruised and there was blood.

"Sondra, Sondra," I shouted.

Her eyes stared at me blankly. Piloya was scared. I held Sondra and shook her.

"Sondra, Sondra."

She stared at me, even blanker. I slapped her hard across the face more than once. She dropped on the ground. I sat down beside her and lifted her head to my lap and stroked her head.

When I lay on my bed that night, I thought of my own tears and I buried them even deeper. They begged to be let out. If I cried, it meant I had surrendered. That time had not yet come. Not yet. I looked at Mwaka's metal case. If I could just get my hands to open it, I could sniff his presence. Maybe then the gathering tears would go away. But I could not bring myself to open his case. Everyone said luck lay there. Opening his case would scatter his luck away and expose it to the wind or bad spirits. They could snatch it away. If there was anything Mwaka needed so badly, it was his luck! The case would stay that way.

Grandma had long moved to the city. Ma promised to come to see me from Kampala. She said she was coming to take me home. She said the village was killing me. Mwaka was dead. I should get that straight, cry over him and move to the city where I belonged from the start. I agreed. The following day, I was going to lay four large stones in the cemetery to evoke Mwaka's spirit back home to rest with his ancestors under the big *kituba* tree and leave for Kampala with Ma. Ma had not seen me for a while. When she finally came, she took one look at me and shrieked in Acoli, which rolled off her tongue like the edge of a sharp butchers' knife.

"If you had not married that village boy, you would be in the city where none of this stupid nonsense exists. Nothing would be driving you to the verge of a nervous breakdown! Look at you! *Woi woi woi ma weee…* Allah! Allah!"

She clapped her hands upon her mouth. Ma started to cry, heaping curses upon the war, the village and anything else she could think of. She called the night I had met Mwaka, the impotent night, which should be flung into the river with shit, shit and shit! She sat on the ground and slapped at it with both her hands raising them to the heavens and shouting my name like I was dead. Piloya burst into tears and ran inside the house.

That night, as Ma slept, there was a knock on the door. I knew the rebels did not knock. They barged in. But I opened it ready to expect anything. A young man stood in the darkness. He refused to come in or look at me. He stammered. There was a memory of such a stammer somewhere inside my head.

"Me me me me sa-ge."

He held out his hand. I picked out the little paper that sat in it. I held it up to the kerosene lamp inside the house. It was Mwaka's handwriting. *Meet me by the river, tonight, urgently.*

It was one year and two months since he had been taken from me. I put my hands upon my chest and swathed myself in the hope of seeing him again. After I had buried him, there was a promise of his resurrection by the river. I was glory triumphing to glory. Each hope that had faded, sprouted up like dying sunflower stems blessed with life after the long awaited rains finally come. I held out my hands to Nyadwe and spoke with her. The universe still granted wishes, smiles and fresh-water springs after all. I saw Nyadwe that night in a new light. She was not the headstrong woman of Acoli folklore. Nyadwe was earthquake. Nyadwe was lightning. Nyadwe was time. Nyadwe was power. She had watched over my husband each night like I beseeched her. She had brought him back to me. Nyadwe had sat in the night sky defying wind and darkness to torch up memories such as mine. When I looked at her, Nyadwe promised me a future, she promised me new memoirs not stained with blood.

Sitting by the river I waited for my husband. My hands were curved tightly around my folded legs as I rested my chin upon my knees. I tapped my toes lightly upon the sand under my bare feet. The Aringa River reflected a glassy smoothness from the skies. Each ray of moonlight fell upon the water surface, sharp and fresh in a fuse of red, gold and white beams. When I listened carefully, I could hear the still and quiet water flow slowly by. It reminded me of a time before the war, when I came to the river and Piloya had barely started to crawl. I sat her by the water and let her hit at it with infant excitement. Bare-chested women dived into the river and emerged with small streams of water sliding down their naked bodies like gods performing a purification ritual. Children's voices floated about. Aringa flowed, heading towards horizons whose end only the sky knew. A few women tried to catch fish in the full waters with their hand-woven baskets. They laughed with each catch and their voices could reach the sacred caves at Kilak. During those days before the war, the legend of the Aringa River Bridge as it is told now, did not house so many troubled spirits under it. The river was not filled with too many leeches like it is now. Lost souls did not cry in the night begging for rescue. Our dreams rolled us into tomorrow with promises of rainbows, seas, corals and mollusks.

I did not hear Mwaka come until I felt a tap on my shoulder. I turned to look. There was my husband before me; resurrected from the dead debris where I had buried him. His woolly hair stood like a crown of untamed fur. He had grown much thinner and looked ragged holding his rifle under his arm. He never kept his beard when I had known him. Now it was plaited into one lock of hair. It hung like a small rope. There was a huge burn scar across his forehead. It sparkled like it had been massaged with *simsim* oil.

35

"*Min ot*," he said in Acoli the way he always referred to me: Mother of the house.

Mwaka threw his rifle on the sand when I could not stop staring.

"Are you okay?" I managed to say when he sat near me.

"Are you okay?" he asked back.

I nodded. I was at a loss of words. My heart raced like the first time I met him. He breathed softly. He had come along with other men who slouched around us like fallen angels. In hypnotic craze, I tried very hard to see only him and me under the clear night sky by the river in this reunion of two lost lovers.

"Piloya," he said.

"She is a woman now," I said.

I studied him stealthily. In his soldier uniform, Mwaka looked like an image I had seen before but could not recognise anymore. The youthfulness that had glowed upon his face was gone. There was no sweet honey in his reckless bandit-like poise. I thought he smelt of gunpowder and decay. He touched me lightly. His fingers did not burst with life. My hands clung to each other, unsure of what to do. He was so distant, like he had been in my recurrent dream, impossible to reach among the acacia trees at the foot of Kidi Guu hills.

"What have they done to you?" I asked, my palms tracing his cheeks. I brought them back quickly and tucked them safely in my cardigan. He articulated every word. He sounded distinctly Mwaka, but I could not find him underneath his whisper. The valour of his voice had grown mould. He cleared his voice.

"I came to let you know I am okay."

I looked at him and said nothing.

"You don't talk much these days," he said.

Mwaka had risen in the ranks and was now a commander. I was ashamed that I had thought a single day in the forests would crush him into pebbles that get washed away by a slight drizzle. He was far from that. Mwaka was rock. He saw his tomorrow bursting alive like an amplified electric guitar. He saw himself as part of the ascension leading the country to a Promised Land. Canaan was so near.

"I smell it!' he said and spread his fingers before me.

"Our harvest is coming soon, very soon," his breath came close, and I smelt something sour, something I couldn't quite place, like the smell of rotting vegetation in forests perhaps. I'd smelt it before, on another soldier. The question formulated itself slowly through the dark and silence.

"Have you taken the oath of allegiance?"

"Yes."

So that was the smell on his breath. He'd tasted human blood, licked at it, and smeared it upon his body.

"They made you?" I gasped.

"No. I chose it. It will bring us a big harvest after the long struggles of the war."

I looked away, stretching my hand across my stomach.

"Come back home with me, Mwaka, you do not belong there. What have they done to you?"

My voice was low and unsure like a baby's first steps on cement. None of us said anything for a long while. Mwaka stood up, kicked at the sand and avoided looking my way. Our silence carried no single grain of seed to the panicles of my famished wishes.

"You have to wait for me. You have to wait for me. I will come to you when it's over."

For a moment I thought he was going to break into tears. His voice bore a crack of emotion I had not felt until then. Without saying anything more to me, he turned away.

"*Harambe*," he shouted.

His few companions echoed it back and they started to move. Mwaka walked away from the river, onto the upward stretch that leads to the main road busting out of Kitgum town. They disappeared just above the bridge. I watched him and the men till I started to see faint ghostly figures coming and going over and over again. I made my way home almost invisible to myself. I had no tears in my eyes. They had just been buried under silt, and shadows had cast a spell upon them. I told Ma about the meeting when I got back. Her surprise gave way to a loss of words, then to anger.

"*Obibi!*" she shouted. "Are you going to stay?"

"He is my husband," I said, nodding my head up and down and carefully avoiding her eyes.

"If I ever set my eyes on him, I will toss him in the river with shit, shit and shit. That's where he belongs!" she said and soaked herself in tears the whole night.

Ma left the following morning. I thought I saw something in her eyes. A certain fear that she had lost me and would never find me. She did not see my point, but staying in my marital home was a battle I had chosen to fight even with no promise of a victory.

★★★

Days, weeks, months passed by.

Then tonight I put off the cooking fire in the kitchen and got ready to go to the main house, where Piloya was already asleep. A voice suggested itself from the darkness under the mango tree as I passed. A voice which swished with the leaves in the night breeze. A voice such as his.

"Don't cry," he said as I rushed at him, the bulge of his white eyes finally betraying where he stood in the shadow of the tree. My hands went up to his face, feeling for the scar. Was this the old Mwaka returned? But he smelled of gunfire, decay and something else I could not figure out. That smell of blood on his breath again. I lowered my hands from his face and neck.

"Just hide me in the old house with a jar full of water; don't come there, I will be okay," he said.

He refused to look my way like he always did. He kept insisting I should hide him away and go to sleep immediately. I stood there, an eerie presence hanging suspended in the air. My knees were weak. My ears rung and my head spun like someone was pulling at the nerves in my neck and forehead.

He had run from a battle at Kilak. He said they had a mole in his commanding camp. Someone had been feeding government troops with intelligence information. Someone in his battalion. Soldiers had penetrated their camp at the foot of the Kilak hills and caves. Many of his fighters were dead. As the commander, he did not trust anyone. He had to hide. The army was after him. He said he would hide with me for a few days. No one would think of looking for him here.

"You have to bathe first, and you need clean clothes," I said.

"No no no," a heated protest from him.

"This is my house. You do as I say," I said in a tone of a woman weighed down by heaps and heaps of broken hopes and wishes. This woman had surrendered and submerged herself in shallow pools of water that could not sink her.

I did not wait for Mwaka to say anything more. I held my wrapper and tied it around my stomach tight till I felt my guts knot like a girl scout's rope. I went into the kitchen. He remained outside. I promised myself to try, just to try and see what I could do. He was my husband, to have and to hold, till...

What if they had followed him here? I sought in my heart and I found that the fear did not weaken my spirit. Not yet.

I sat on my small curved wooden stool by the fire, boiling water, poking at the wood, confused. The kerosene lamp lacked paraffin. Its glow was weak and died. The darkness of my kitchen offered nothing but a mustiness of a kind that lingers in a place such as an Acoli woman's kitchen only. Sharp flames with scarlet billows bit into my skin. I carried the hot aluminium saucepan with my bare hands. I felt the blood in my fingers heat up and I thought my nails would fall off. I poured the water into a big metal *galaya*. I poured some more cold water in. I dipped a finger to gauge the temperature. It was okay. As I carried it out, I noticed that shadows from the trees surrounding our home fell clockwise to the centre of the compound to congregate there as the silent and brief visitors to the earth in the night. Something about them reminded me of my dead uncle. Unknown people had stabbed him to death on his way home one day. His coffin was placed at the centre of grandma's compound. Everyone congregated around it, humming sad melodies, shocked, angry.

I carried the water to the bath-shade Mwaka had built himself a little distance from the house. My slippers slapped at the earth below and made soft sounds. I called him. He came closer. I sniffed out the smell I could not make out before. It was stale sweat that smelled like decaying mango. Mwaka was limping, but he did not look terribly in pain. He refused to let me look at his leg. I put him on the big stone that I sit on when taking a bath. He held out his hands. He let me take off his filthy uniform. I tossed it over the bath-shade. It fell outside. He had no gun. I did not bother asking why. I took his trousers off and tossed them outside as well. I got the sponge I had cut out of an old Vitafoam mattress, and started to scrub his body. He relaxed, raised his head. I lifted my head up as I worked. It felt like someone had stuck something powerful up my nostrils and my nose, eyes and mouth were inhaling the pressure without resistance. My eyeballs heated up. The way they do when I am about to cry. It was not the tears. It was the invisible chains that tied a noose around my neck and tried to choke me. Heat rose to my head. A throbbing headache started. It felt like a stone had been planted right in the middle of my skull. I handed Mwaka a towel to dry himself and a dress to wear. He held it before him, shook it, then gave it back to me.

"I can't wear this."

"Then you will have to be naked."

"Why can't you bring me some of my old clothes?"

I poured the remaining water out of the *galaya*. Anger consumed me like lightning. A force drove itself inside my hands. I struggled very hard to hold myself from falling upon him and pounding at him till my hands bled and blood trickled upon the bath-shade stones under our feet.

"Why can't you bring me some of my old clothes?"

"Mwaka, you came here after two years, you do not know how we have been living."

"Why can't you bring me some of my old clothes?"

"Look Mwaka, your metal case, um… I have never opened it, since they took you away."

"Well, now I am back."

"You wear that dress or you walk naked!"

"Let me go get it myself, or I want my uniform back."

"You wear that dress or you walk naked!"

I started to collect the *galaya* and sponge. He fitted the dress on without any more protest. I walked him to the old house where we kept things we did not use. It was an old house that could collapse at any moment. Everyone expected it not to last into the next year. It lived on, weak, daring everyone, bravely. Mwaka fitted himself amidst the piles of old boxes and old furniture with difficulty. The dust choked me. The boxes were many. Inside was dark. It had been untenured for a long while. Mwaka covered himself with a blanket and fell onto the mattress I brought him.

"I will be okay, lock the door and go away. Don't come here. It will look suspicious."

I went to the house, brought a flask of hot water with a jar of cold water, some cassava and potatoes and peanut butter. Then I closed the door behind the dark room and fastened the padlock. I went back to the bathroom. I collected his clothes, stuffed more wood into the fireplace and threw them upon the flames. The fire devoured the green uniform reluctantly. I shivered a little. I tried to remember a tune to sing. I wanted to lure my spirit to calm. No tune or calm came. I waited patiently for the foul-smelling cloth to burn up, then left the kitchen. I came to the main house and into the bedroom. Piloya was asleep. I stayed with no single lure of sleep in my eyes for a long time. When sleep finally came; it whisked me off to a dream and sent me to search for Mwaka's sweet breath among the acacia. I had to find his unblemished face. In my dream, I had spoken to the large bougainvillea tree that stood like the queen of the night in the darkness next to my house. I asked her for that first petal she had bloomed with the start of the new season. When she gave it to me, I placed it in my pocket and went off to find my husband. I wanted to place in his palm that single and freshest pink petal from the flower tree. He had planted it the day Piloya was born, to celebrate her birth. One day he had told her jokingly when she asked him about the flower: "It's a powerful plant with special powers. If you can find that petal which blooms first when a new season comes, if you place it in my palms, I will hear you wherever I am and come to you whenever you call my name."

★★★

Blink after blink. I have no sleep again. My memory has chosen to take me back to the day they took Mwaka. He wanted to go drinking with his friends in the trading centre. I sulked till my long face weakened his feet. The simmering midday sun brought the rebels. They found Mwaka at home like a good husband and wheeled him to the end of a mirage. My hands beat into my lap resonating the wail of an Acoli woman who widowed herself.

"*Atim ango?*" What shall I do?

My hands still beat into my thighs. I yearn them to reach out and feel his affectionate recognition in the curves of my memory. When I release myself and reach for his reflection, I find none. Everything is marred with the squeal of defeat. Mwaka is a memory of shackles that have hoarded layer upon layer of guilt in my heart.

"*Atim ango?*"

Piloya sleeps on, unaware that the father she longed to see so badly, now lies in the old house.

"*Atim ango?*"

My knees quiver. My feet carry me off the bed. I let them do as they will. They lead me to the corner of the room. I grope and find Mwaka's metal suitcase. Two years it has lain cold and alone, holding his luck securely. I pass my palms over the metal. The power in my arms goes lukewarm, but my hands proceed to press it open. It cracks and falls into the silence of the room, like a whisper. The crickets outside jumble the night calm with chitchat whose meaning is buried in the mysteries of a diviner's cowries. My hands fumble and grope for the contents in the metal case. I land on the polyester on top. Chills spread through my body faster than a rumour. The colors of the fabric play in my mind as clear as the day Mwaka fitted it on for the first time. It is the yellow suit I bought him, to celebrate our

Aluminium Anniversary. Our ten years of union as man and wife was going to be a special occasion. The time had come to watch my mother swallow her words and get smacked right in her face for predicting that my marriage would not last longer than a planting season. I chose yellow. Yellow was a happy color. It was a bright and uplifting celebration of our coming sunny days. Mwaka did not get to wear his suit beyond a single fit. That scent of the one fit lingers faintly in the yellow. Maybe it's all in my head, like the voice that springs out of nowhere and sounds exactly like mine.

"*Oui. Oui. Maadoooo*, Mwaka!"

It is faint, but it never goes away. It echoes an abyss of loss and losing, on and on, till it gets me dizzy and zonked. With Mwaka's suit now in my hand, it gains momentum. I try to ignore it. All I want is to feel Mwaka. The way I knew him. I bring the fabric to my nose. A fire starts to burn through me. I crack louder than old wood and cry like the day he asked me to marry him. I shriek as every laughter, touch and sunshine comes to surface. The room gathers my wail into an embrace. Piloya's voice comes through the darkness.

"Ma, Ma..."

The tears can't stop. They flow ceaselessly, adorned with the kind of innocence only present in the reverberation of a baby's first laugh. What am I going to do with him? What am I going to do with myself? Thoughts chill me, like syncopations of slave jazz. They do not scare off the chanting voice in my head. It goes on throughout the night. Sure, undeterred and resilient, like Father Lagoro reciting mass...

Oui. Oui. Maadoooo, Mwaka!
Oui. Oui. Maadoooo, Mwaka!
Oui. Oui. Maadoooo, Mwaka!

★★★

The cock sounds its rapturous morning crow. I am a plant groping for sunlight. Mist floats over the hills. Day has come. I turn the radio on. The airwaves bring a haunting song by Oryema Geoffrey, the Acoli musician based in Paris. His melody floats for a while in the air before it settles on the ground like a fluff of feather. The News's main points start soon after. They carry messages that wear my ears with their bulk.

"The rebels have crossed the Aswa River into Kitgum district after a battle at Kilak. Twenty rebels and seven government soldiers are dead. A landmine hit a double cabin and killed four people along Kitgum road..."

Sounds of morning bring the long squawk of dawn bird-song. It is beautiful and blissful to the last dot. Daylight breathes life into the yellow, ripened June mangoes. Tens and tens of half-eaten fruit are spread under the trees. That always got Mwaka very angry. He got out of the main house; looked at the *alima* mangoes spread under the tree, and lamented about the bats that wasted his best fruit in the late hours of the night. In the afternoons he sat and gazed up into the tree completely engrossed. Piloya was sure her father counted the mangoes up the tree.

Time limps and drags itself along like a wounded antelope. My eyes keep going to the old house with the lock on the door. My nerves are tense. I sweep the leaves from under the trees. My hands are reluctant. My limbs carry me sluggishly.

"I will be okay," I repeat what Mwaka said last night, until it starts to sound true.

A few hours into the morning finds me under the mango tree. Sitting here, I can see Kidi Guu just before me, lying very peaceful and calm. Under this mango tree, the pale layers of rolling grasslands, which remain almost cheerless and scanty regardless of the season, inspire a hidden beauty whose colour dazes but does not pour any excitement into my heart. The ragged tree barks, dry acacia, moist thickets, shrubs and bamboo are all blooming with the freshness and change of season that comes with June. The leaves and trees also cheer each other brightly.

Piloya joins me in casting an eye at nature from this distance. A big basin full of water and ripe yellow mangoes sits between us. I keep thinking that Mwaka could do with a few mangoes. I remind myself, I can't take them to him.

My legs are too long for the papyrus mat on which we sit, so I rest my ankles on my red slippers. Piloya's eyes are like the newest leaf on a plant. She flaps them beautifully, reminding me of Mwaka's two pigeons. He sold and resold them to different people. They always came back. Her eyes are so bright today, like a shaft of light hatched a new beauty in them suddenly. When she laughs, they look like beads. Piloya's laugh gets me envious sometimes. It carries an attitude that makes everything stop to listen to her. She sits and faces me, picks a mango from the basin and cuts into it. She casts me quick glances. My fingers work nervously at my hair. Sometimes we love to talk. Sometimes we just sit and sleep under the mango tree.

Today we do not talk much. In the distance Father Lagoro beats his drum reminding us of the Sunday mass tomorrow. After Piloya's mock pounces that send the chickens scattering away, she gets on the tree and shakes at the mango tree. The door to the main house is slightly open, letting in daylight. It falls upon my scattered books at the foot of my bed. I bite my lower lips between my teeth and pass my palms over my face and sigh. I catch myself holding my two fingers in front of my face, moving them fro and back, and talking to myself. Embarrassed I fold them back in my hands. They drop upon my lap making a very light *pwah* sound. Mwaka always made me hold my fingers like that and move them back and forth touching his nose and mine in turns saying *somwa*. He coined that word using my first name and his Acoli name: Sophi and Mwaka.

Without fighting the confusion going on in my head, I pick a mango and start to cut at it, putting each succulent piece in my mouth. Piloya shouts from the mango tree.

"Do you want some more mangoes, Ma?"

"Get off that tree before you fall down and break your hips," I say.

"I will not fall down."

On other days I would have yelled at her till she got down. Now I just stare, as if seeking a truth buried in mud. I catch myself raising my two fingers to my face saying *somwa* again. I laugh. Ma spoke to herself a lot. She scattered her hands in the air and quarrelled with the wind. Sometimes she stared at one spot for minutes. Her mind took her somewhere unknown. Her strange engrossments always made me laugh. I laugh now, not because it is so funny. I laugh to send the tears away.

I am thinking of evening, when the dreams come. I could maybe check on Mwaka as well. Piloya climbs down the mango tree. She kicks the dust under her feet as she gathers the mangoes that have fallen on the ground and are spread around. She carries them in her t-shirt. They look like they could tear through and fall out any moment. She bends over the plastic basin before her and lets the mangoes fall in. The water splashes upon me. She laughs at her own clumsiness, fixing her eyes upon me. Then she sits next to me.

"Is something wrong, Ma?"

I am thinking. Mwaka could do with a few mangoes. How is he doing? What if the search for him brings his pursuers to my doorstep? What would I do? It can't happen, I tell myself. Then I think of Sondra, my friend, who comes in the afternoons sometimes to sit, laugh and cry. I pray she does not pass by today.

Piloya's elbows rest upon my lap. She stares at my long dark hair, which I normally plait in two neat rows. Toilet flies are trying to get to the little

44

bits of mango sap stuck accidentally in her hair. She starts to yawn. Suddenly she springs up. The fat toilet flies buzz shamelessly. She grabs a tree branch lying from the earth and waves it frantically. Thoughts pound at my head. I feel them blind me. I open my eyes wide and pretend I can see something flying just before me. When I am wrapped in darkness, I always imagine I can see a butterfly gathering wind under her wings and passing the redeeming feeling to me. Today my mind refuses to see any butterflies.

"Lets go inside," I say to Piloya.

I pick up the mats. She gathers the mango peels spread all around. She throws them in a nearby bush. As she is coming back, she stops midway.

"Ma, look," she says.

I cast my eyes her way. She holds her hands on her waist then points them about in the air, and says, "One two three, *kamata!*"

She places a leg front and one back, shakes her waist and sways here and there. Her lilac skirt sways with her, slapping its hem against her tiny legs. The lilac is so steady, so pure against her dark skin. Hands in the air with soft dance movements, very gentle, very graceful, my little girl charms me. She barely raises her feet off the ground. Piloya smiles, making her beady eyes glow like a polished conch. Her hands go up and down, sometimes almost up to her face. Then she sways slowly like a river wave. Her shoulders rock her body and swing her to a Lingala dance. I feel the desire to throw the mat down on the ground, join her and together swing to soft Lingala. But I just stand and watch Piloya sing and dance:

excellent Sofia,
I lovuyou ela mama,
excellent Sofia,
I lovuyou ela mama…

Her voice settles a calm aura around me. It's a song addressed to a Sofia. That is my first name. Piloya insists it was for me, because it says mama somewhere and I am her Ma. Piloya dances with infant innocence. She laughs and tries to cheer me. A fire threatens to burn my throat. It dries my chest. I feel the heat rise up to my eyeballs. My daughter continues to dance for the mango leaves and the bougainvillea plant that celebrated her birth. The petals stand out ecstatically pink just near the verandah of the main house. The grasses shake lightly as Piloya sings. She dances on, completely absorbed, like no one is watching.

I move and sit on the verandah, resting my back against the mud walls. Piloya moves over and sits beside me. We stare at nothing and everything.

The skies are so blue. The clouds glide about carrying a certain kind of order and logic beneath their elegance. There is silence for a long while. It is broken when Piloya starts to hum another song. I close my eyes, gradually picking up the tune. Together we hum the melody of the folksong that tells of a world a long, long time ago, when Atunya the lion could talk, when there was no drought and famine in the world.

The music stops. I open my eyes. Piloya's eyes are still closed. Her head is raised up towards the skies. Tears have escaped through. They flow down her cheeks.

What could possibly drive my thirteen-year-old goddess to tears? I grab her into my arms; place her head upon my shoulder and rock her back and forth, back and forth. She clasps me tight to her chest and presses against my shoulder. When she lifts her head, she holds her hands before her. She speaks amidst a threatening sob.

"Pa, will be okay, won't he?"

I draw away from her, a sudden fear.

"I saw you last night."

I am at a loss for words. I sniff softly and clean the tears off my eyes with my cotton skirt. We hold together again and rock to and fro. Our cries crush us into one hope. But the feeling that madness is down the hill waiting for me does not go away. After a while, we release ourselves and look at each other. Piloya is still crying. I tap her twice on the shoulder, put my hands on my knees and slowly pull myself up. I am thirsty. I have to go to the house to drink some water.

The sun, what heat! It is too bright. My shadow is lost in the sand. I turn to make my way to the house with slow steps. Crash! I turn sharply around. Like gunfire on steel, a Land Rover crushes into the village. The lone vehicle tears through the overgrown grasses. They fall flat to the earth and lie still under the alloyed wheels of this metallic monster. Piloya and I look at each other. We never see four wheels here. Our eyes rush to the path that comes out of Grandma's deserted home near the family graveyard, and leads to my house.

The army Land Rover makes its way to my compound and brakes hard in the middle, where the night tree shadows love to congregate. It spins its wheels and spits gravel at Piloya and me. Its shape and colour fade behind a huge cloud of dust that spreads across the compound. Then the engine is silenced.

I try to keep calm. It is nothing, I say to myself. Piloya stands close beside me pulling nervously at her hair and her dress alternately. Eyes on the vehicle, she blinks rapidly and looks up at me occasionally. When she stands next to me, Piloya reaches my shoulder.

The sun falls upon the vehicle windscreen. It deepens the brown tint. I can't see a thing inside. We used to call these kinds of vehicles IFA. We thought they were Imported for Accidents. They caused so many.

The vehicle faces me. The headlights look straight at me like a buffalo getting ready to charge. The docile headlights of this rough terrain giant drive me to tremble. Heart pounding, my head goes dizzy. A dull shade seems to appear for a second or two. Then it's suddenly bright again. The door opens. A loud crack and a black army leather boot slips onto the earth, glinting. A body follows through, pulling itself slowly until a man, probably six foot, stands much taller than the vehicle itself. The man has a neat moustache, chocolate skin, and a slight smile that slits across his face like a small razor cut in heavy fabric. It is not enough to reassure and calm the tension bubbling inside me. He starts to walk towards me. His is the walk of an over-confident man.

Men, probably five or six seated at the back, get off the Land Rover. They are all clad in army uniforms. They seem all clean apart from the dust. The road here can be dusty. Sometimes dust sticks and dyes the eyebrows brown. The man comes before me. I am a mess. I look like a depreciating widow who has not stopped mourning her loss for years. The man offers his hand.

"Lieutenant Kanyehamba," he says.

I shake his hand quickly and hold my hands to my chest. My conscience accuses me as if I have just stolen a little child's wish. The man whose name I have already forgotten reverses two large steps backwards with the same overwhelming confidence. He holds his hand behind his back. I don't like it. It is the way the soldiers who trained us during *muchaka-muchaka* stood and ordered us to fall on our stomachs, rise up immediately and run a hundred metres forward to assemble a weapon. I did not complete the course. That compulsory basic military training for everyone could go hang itself.

The man has a pistol at his waist, sitting slanted towards his right arm in a leather pouch. It's a beautiful thing with silver lining and looks like a trophy. He has tied his army trousers and his brown leather belt right above his big stomach, holding the trousers up and straight. He wears a red cap, but I can tell that his whole head is shaven like most high-ranked government soldiers.

The driver gets out of the vehicle and leans against it, looking my way first, then elsewhere. He is a young man, with shyness in his eyes. He looks around at the scanty green that surrounds my house. His eyes settle on the orchard a little distance from the house. The others, probably lower-ranked soldiers, hold huge AK-47 guns under their arms. They stand behind their boss. They never look away. Their unrivalled attention on me gets me more uncomfortable. I tell myself, keep calm. It's not what you think. They can't possibly...

The lieutenant takes a red Sportsman's cigarette packet from his pocket. He tears the silver lining off, takes out one cigarette, parts his mouth lightly and fixes a cigarette in. He turns his head around as if to study the place and starts the lighter with his thumb. A fire springs up from his lighter, burns briefly and coils shyly back inside. The man smokes his cigarette, raises his head up and puffs the smoke up into the air. When he speaks, his Swahili is almost as good as the kind spoken in Tanzania.

"We come in good faith," he says and smokes his cigarette again.

His voice is deep and sounds trained, sort of like those lads who go to Catholic boarding schools. His words fall one after the other. I can imagine him standing in the army barracks, pulling hairs off new recruits in the barracks, still sounding terribly cultured.

"We mean no trouble."

I nod once. My body tingles, but it's one tingle I can't scratch even if I tried to. I hold my hands together and squeeze them, reminding myself it is nothing.

"You know, some funny characters have been causing quite a bit of trouble, don't you think?"

I nod twice and fix my eyes on his boots. They scare me with their bright shine. I look at my own hands. My heart promises to pop out of my chest. It pumps so loudly that I cover one hand upon my heart and try to control it. My hand trembles over my blouse. It begs to be brought down. I bring it down quickly and hold a fist to keep calm.

"Where is your husband?" He blinks rapidly. The cultured tone is gone.

"Huh?"

"Where is your husband?"

My initial surprise wears off a little. I hurry to respond before he even finishes his sentence again.

"I don't know," I say.

"Oh, oh, not like that, not that tone, we mean *no* harm," he says like a conman.

He almost fools me into a reassuring moment that is as slim as a sesame pod. He nods his head up, down and signals his men something. I don't know what it means. He laughs as the men dash into my house. He starts to whistle a tune. His lips pull forward. He nods his head to the beat of his whistle. I turn to look where the men have gone. Things are being flung outside. Saucepans drop. A few cloths drop lightly. Something falls even louder. It's my radio. It cracks revealing an interior of ugly red and green wires. The men in the house are busy. Things heap up one upon the other outside my doorstep. The lieutenant comes to me.

"You see, cooperation, cooperation," he says.

I nod.

"Now, where is your husband?"

My voice threatens to break into a sob. I look helplessly at Piloya whose face fills with utter terror.

"Where is your husband?" he spits again. His eyes protrude like a frog's. I coil and draw back as he comes forward. I almost fall to the ground in my hasty retreat. Father Lagoro's drum beats again reminding us of mass tomorrow. A dog barks from a distance. The sun burns upon my skin like a flame. Sweat forms around my mouth. I clean it off and gesture to Piloya that she is to sit on the verandah. She resists. I push her too hard. She falls down and bruises her knees. My anger shocks me.

"Hey, what has the little girl done?"

Mwaka's clothes are flung out of the suitcase and scattered around. My eyes pick out the yellow suit that I buried my face into as I wept last night. One man gets into the kitchen. I avoid looking at the old house where Mwaka is hidden. It's falling down, it will not catch their attention surely. Don't you think?

A man comes back. He shouts something. I look. He holds on the tip of a short stick, a blackened remnant of Mwaka's uniform from my fireplace. The lieutenant motions with his head, a tight smile presses on his face. One of the men grabs Piloya. They take her to the lieutenant. Piloya struggles to break loose. She starts to cry softly.

"Ma, Ma..."

"Now," the lieutenant says, "where is your husband?"

I stand and look on. It's all I can do.

"Where is your husband?"

"Umm... they took him, two years ago..." I struggle to say. I stop. I start again and stammer. The words are lost.

"What is it?"

He draws closer and grabs my chin up. He fixes his hand just under it. The old house attracts the other men. They approach it and kick at the door. The weak hinges give way. The wooden door falls flat on the ground. They crash inside. Piloya rushes to me and clings to my hand. I look to the old house. Sounds of a struggle come through.

"*Atim ango?*" I shout out.

Mwaka is hunted from the boxes and dragged towards the centre of the compound. He looks ridiculous in the dress. The army boss says something about hiding himself pretending to be a woman. Two men hold Mwaka's hands. They pull the rest of his body on the soil. He winces his face in pain. I feel dizzy. I cover my eyes with my palms till I can't conjure any flickers of light. The kicks start. Kicks, kicks and kicks. The smell of fresh blood rises to my nose. The kicking does not stop. Mwaka says nothing. Just moans softly, sometimes loudly.

I try to gather strength. I want to run and do something. My feet refuse to move. I fall to the ground. I chant to the Virgin Mary. My chant is not loud. It spits inside my head, trying to rise beyond the sounds of kicks.

"Hail Mary, full of grace, the Lord is with you, blessed are you among women and blessed is the fruit of your womb Jesus…"

They ask Mwaka questions. Where are the rest of them? Where is the stock of ammunition? Where is the next planned attack?

"Go FUCK whoever sent you!" Mwaka shouts.

They kick him more. Mwaka's cries get higher and sharper. My daughter clings harder to my hands. Father Lagoro's worship drum beats its melancholic refrain reminding us again we should not miss mass tomorrow. Piloya springs from my grips. She rushes forward.

"Pa, Pa, where are you taking Pa? Leave my Pa alone!"

One kick. She falls down. Piloya moans softly. The earth welcomes her silenced cries and lets her lie still. Her large lilac skirt spreads upon the earth around her, so pure, so calm.

The kicks stop after a while. I hear a faint sound from Mwaka, then everything goes dead. Terrible chills sit upon me.

I start to crawl towards Piloya. I take a quick glance towards the mango tree. I notice something. Two hands knotted behind a back and a frozen stare, curled over a rock plate of bulged eyes. The figure is almost too peaceful to touch. It hangs on the mango tree. It is the new branch grafted to the tree with a sisal rope around its neck like an offering to the sun, to scorch, to ripen and to rot. Mwaka does not swing with the powerful afternoon wind draft. Thirty-three. That is his age. All he is. A number scribbled on a page, a vocal parting of lips, as light as a hair strand. I watch him. My defeated warrior hangs like strange fruit, waiting to be plucked.

50

I resume my crawl towards Piloya. Two hands pull me back by my legs. I bruise my knees badly, but I struggle still to crawl on towards my daughter.

I am grabbed again. I dig my nails into the soil. I scratch at the earth till blood soaks underneath my broken fingernails. The veins in my head strain. It feels like I could explode at any moment. My breath heats up into a pant. I fight to let some air in my lungs. The lieutenant leans upon the Land Rover smoking his cigarette with a disinterested stare like a lioness leaving a carcass for her cubs after a kill. About six men surround me. They shout things I can't hear. I have to get to my daughter. Where she is lies the melody whose tune I can hum.

One man holds me down. His hands look weak, but he puts my hands together and holds my two wrists in one grip. His other hand separates my thighs. I kick about trying to fight. My hands turn me into a tiger. I scratch. I don't get anywhere. I am scratching air.

His zip goes down. His pants let go of his body. The power in me starts to fade. His grip is as strong as a waterfall. My back is planted to the ground. Gashes of current shifts rush through my head. The world spins. I spin with it, like a whirlwind. My cotton fabric is ripped off. My nakedness is revealed. The man lies on top of me. I close my eyes. The action starts and gradually heightens. It eats away at me bit by bit like snake venom. I take my lower lip between my teeth. I bite till I taste blood and feel it flood my mouth. In the background there are cheers, "Go go go…"

The world is empty. The sounds of the birds and the barking of the dogs seem muffled. Anguish. My cry is too weak to travel beyond any brick wall. It is too frail to hustle its way through the mud houses in the distance, whose pale corrugated-iron sheets reflect the fading sun with mild interest. My muted voice hangs loose like a funeral tune. It holds in a fragile moment. The action is untouched. Like a bush fire, it burns without hesitation. My eyes open and look up the mango tree where Mwaka hangs. I can't bear the sight of him. I shift my eyes to the leaves. The green overwhelms me with its enormous stretch. I start to drift away like a canoe. I am powerless against the waves sailing me.

" *Aii aiii aiii.*"

I am an end giving birth to another end. I don't realise it when the weight above me is lifted. It does not matter. I am already too heavy to fight the stormy seas. I am sinking. There is a kick to my thigh and a command, "Let's get lost."

I hear laughter. It mounts the great Kilimanjaro and withers its grandeur. Movement around me becomes faint. Sounds of gumboots thudding upon the earth draw away. Sounds of feet jumping and stepping onto the back of the Land Rover come through. There is a long ring of laughter again as the vehicle starts. It spits gravel and raises dust, which floods the compound. It is quiet for a while. Then the cry of a lone *openo* bird pierces through.

"*Cu cu cu.*"

Piloya's voice also comes through.

"Ma, Ma..."

The lingering filth in my depth is stronger than death. I struggle to keep my eyes open. I seal layer upon layer of restraint over my emotions, till they are tighter than a hymen. I am sprawled over this very earth Piloya took her first footsteps upon. The red earth has blended with my naked thighs. My breasts point up to the heavens like two small anthills. The sun sheds a gloomy light. It is dull and shifts the hours slowly. I hang to the hem of sanity like an antelope in a snare. I remind myself; my name is Lakidi Sofia. I am stone. I am warmth. I am sky.

Born in 1979, **Monica Arac de Nyeko** comes from Kitgum district in Northern Uganda. She is a member of the Uganda Women Writers' Association (FEMRITE) and the chief editor of *TAP Voices*. She taught literature and English at St Mary's College in Kisubi before pursuing a Masters degree in Humanitarian Assistance at the University of Groningen. Her personal essay *In the Stars* won first prize in the *Women's World* Women in War Zones essay writing competition. She has been published in *Memories of Sun*, *The Nation*, *IS Magazine*, *Poetry International* and several other publications. Her novella *The Last Dance* is forthcoming with Fountain Publishers.

Hunger

Doreen Baingana

My PRIVATE Diary
Patti Mugisha
Gayaza High School
Kampala, Uganda, Africa, the Universe

Sunday, April 10, 2pm
BOARDING SCHOOL IS LIKE purgatory, or prison – being sent away to wait
– that's mainly what I do: wait for time to pass.

There are five more hours to supper, and I'm hungry already. I'm up
here in an empty classroom, writing in my diary when I'm supposed to
be studying 'cause it's one week till finals. Three more long weeks, then
home, home at last. Please, God, help me concentrate on this stupid
history book. I don't want to study at the dorm with the others. I prefer
to be alone with the leftover scribbles on the blackboard and the
disorderly desks and chairs abandoned by the last class of girls on Friday.
The scratched and beaten-up furniture looks like wreckage after a riot, it's
so old.

We had sweet potatoes and peas for lunch: not as bad as the usual
mash, but not enough. It's never enough. There is no privacy in the dining
room, nowhere to hide – that's what I hate about school. No moment to
myself. Even my thoughts feel exposed. We are squashed fifteen girls to a
table, girls from all grades, so that we can learn from our 'elders'. Thank
goodness for the wide windows along both sides of the room with their
wooden shutters flung open for air and light. At least I can take in the
flourishing trees outside.

There's a mural at one end of the room, which I have stared at for three long years now, to avoid looking too hungrily at the food being served. I need to disguise my greed. Nobody remembers which art class painted the mural or when. It's one of those paintings that show every activity under the sun: a church with musical notes sailing out the window to heaven; a school (ours) with classes full of round, dark heads; an aeroplane flying over cows in a field; a red-orange (but fading) fire in an office building, with fire engines and ambulances and running figures around it; a street with small children crossing, holding hands; angels flying in place, stuck in the sky; and the yellow sun above it all. Only the sun isn't shining yellow anymore. All the colors have faded to a greyish-creamish-brown that matches the dining-room smell of burnt beans, rotting cabbage, oily plastic plates, and about two hundred sweaty girls. I study the busy picture's comic details while wishing and praying for enough food to satisfy my stomach. Today at lunch it was Joyce's turn to serve my table. As usual, she gave each of us so little I could have cried. After we quickly clean our plates, there's a long wait while the seniors gab on forever about nothing, when they know very well that the rest of us are waiting for seconds. But the dishes are placed at the head of the table, where the older girls sit. So even though they are fat enough already, they get second helpings first and finish all the food, leaving us younger ones staring at our empty dirty-grey dishes that look like shapeless, open mouths. Even now, after lunch, my stomach is growling. Oh, God, I pray for something good today instead of all this suffering. You promised to fill our cups to overflowing, told us to 'bring your vessels, not a few'. Amen!

Worst of all is watching Linette not eat because back at the dorm she can slowly munch a whole packet of biscuits or a loaf of bread. Her father is minister of agriculture; she can afford to play with her dining-room food, mashing it into a creamy mess that she stirs round and round her plate. I can't stop staring. Linette brings hot sauce, margarine, or mashed avocado to the dining room – anything to make the weevil-filled beans and *posho* taste like food. Even then, she doesn't eat much of it and makes disgusted faces as we gobble down ours. Oh, I wish I could eat her leftovers. I'd lick the avocado right off her plate. No, no. My Father in heaven fills me. He satisfies my spiritual hunger. Yes, Lord, I do believe. I think I'll stay here, there's no point in going back down to the dorm for tea at four. That sugarless, milkless, so-called tea is just bitter black water.

5.30pm

It's so hard to believe in God sometimes, when I think about what He puts me through. And He says He loves me. I went back to the dorm at teatime anyway, because I was so hungry. I trusted God for a miracle. Why not? I am His child, His chosen one. Maybe I could ask Linette to lend me some money, I thought. Just five shillings to buy a few oily *kabs*. I was going to get my tea when Linette asked me to fetch her some tea too, because she was busy getting her hair done. She was sitting between Mary's legs on a sisal mat on the floor, surrounded by the bright black metal frames of our bunk beds. Every week Mary plaits Linette's hair in complicated *biswahilis*.

Linette took my cup from me roughly, spilling some of the tea and exclaiming, "Eh! Now look what you have done!"

"Sorry, Linette."

"Don't 'sorry' me. Here's your sugar."

She poured *four* spoons into my cup, not bothering to stop the precious silvery grains from trailing down to the floor. *That* was pure malice. She knew I could have put some of it away for tomorrow, at least. I climbed onto my top bunk and buried my face in my history book. I still feel it. The shame. The frustration. I have no energy for anger. My tea now was lukewarm and so ghastly sweet it hurt my throat, but I forced it down. I wasn't reading, but thinking, Oh, God, how unfair You are! How can You give someone this evil all the food and things she has? Why did I torture myself by going back to the dorm for tea? I should have stayed in the empty classroom till supper, chewing on my tongue, swallowing saliva. I wanted to cry. I couldn't ignore those two, who were eating, talking and laughing as if nothing had happened. Linette usually did all the talking while Mary listened and applauded, acting amazed and impressed by everything Linette said. Being a *koty* isn't easy. Or does it come naturally to her, the – No, please, God. No bad words. But Mary was the one gobbling down handfuls of groundnuts, not me. Dear God, what sort of lesson am I supposed to learn from this? I walked back to the classroom, past the dining room and the other dorms, where clusters of girls sat on the verandahs, eating all sorts of nice things – *kabs*, roasted maize, biscuits – as they talked and laughed. The cement path up the slope to class was bordered by severely chopped, stifled grass that moved me to pity. It was too neat to be natural, like a newly pressed army uniform.

God says we suffer for a reason. What reason? Maybe, just maybe, God will answer my prayers and Mama will come see me this evening. Or what if Jesus comes back? I mean, *what if?* Oh, the promised Rapture! I would be lifted up with the holy ones, leaving Linette and Mary behind to burn in hell as they screamed and pleaded for mercy. No, that's silly. And evil. Forgive me, Father. Give me a heart to love them no matter what, because right now I don't; I don't love them. All I can think about is my stomach. I'd better get back to history, which to me sounds like lies: the past reheated as moral tales of good versus bad, strong versus weak. 'Shaka Zulu was a man of humble origin', and so on and so forth. It's all about how he fought and killed everybody and became king. All I have to do is quickly cram it in for exams, and then I can just as quickly forget it. But I can't concentrate; I'm so hungry, so empty. What do I want? I wish a prefect would come running in right now and announce that Mama's here. A miracle! Please, God, please. The bell also means the end of visiting hours for the week. That's it. At least another five days of hunger without hope. My Jesus, You alone know what's best for me, but it's getting harder to wait for Your will. It really is.

8pm

We had *cas-kat* for supper: starchy white cassava cooked with fat brown beans. The cassava was hard to chew, but there was a lot of it, thank you, Jesus! I ate it hungrily. Everyone stared, but what did I care? Shame disappears when hunger arrives. The bell rang before I finished eating, but I wasn't going to leave my food behind. I pretended to ignore the gaggle of girls as they scraped back their benches and streamed out into the cool evening air, carefree and confident, comfortable in the company of their friends. They had nothing to worry about, except maybe a few pimples cropping up. Only two other girls remained in the huge, darkened dining room. We bent over our plates, and our private hungers, silently. It's only the most *malo* girls who stay behind: the villagers, the greediest ones, the ones who desperately and completely clean their plates of the so-called food. Everyone else stares and snickers at us as they walk out. Us versus them. *Malo* versus posh. How can we not care what they think of us, as we expose our poverty and greed? We are ashamed of having no shame. The worst of it is, I think I'm better than the villagers. I'm not really *malo*, not from the village. I grew up in Entebbe. My father used to be the deputy director of public health services. Tata went to England and Europe many times for work and brought us back dresses and shoes you couldn't find in Uganda. I mean, we used to have a Benz! But when his drinking became a day-and-night obsession, he lost his job. It was announced on TV that he'd been retired 'in the public interest'. I don't want to describe that shame. Now Mama has to dig in the evenings after work and on weekends. She plants beans, maize, *doh-doh* – anything to save money. Poor Mama. She doesn't have a car or the time to come and visit, or the money. Sure, everybody's worse off after Idi Amin's regime, but *we* shouldn't have been. Anyway, why am I writing about this? I'm tired of thinking about these things, chasing what might have been round and round in my head, looking for someone to blame. Why can't I be happy and chatty and simple, like the other girls? Life would be so much easier. Maybe it's because I am a child of God. He says we are different. We are not of this world. We should not want to be part of it. But I can't help it; I do.

Doreen Baingana was shortlisted for the Caine Prize in 2004, has won the Washington Independent Writers' Fiction Prize and received an Artist Grant from the District of Columbia Commission on the Arts and Humanities. Her *Tropical Fish – Stories out of Entebbe* was published by the University of Massachusetts Press in 2005.

Comrade Lemma and the Black Jerusalem Boys' Band

Parselelo Kantai

I

LAST NIGHT I HAD the dream of fish again, in which my departed mother Petrobia is a young woman throwing a party in the afternoon. All the people of God are coming to our house in Jerusalem estate, and she is a whirlwind of movement, shouting, *get-ready get-ready, how can the visitors find you so dirty as if there is no woman in this house and you are orphans,* washing and ironing, and scrubbing the courtyard with soap and water, brandishing the broom of my childhood, the long, thin sticks tied together with strips of tyre from the abandoned lorry that leaned drunkenly against the outside of the courtyard wall, its axles resting on crumbling construction bricks. The smell of frying fish on the fire in the stone-slab stove in the corner tickles my nostrils. Then the guests begin to arrive, the men of the church and their wives in their stiff Salvation Army suits with their black Bibles, propping their bicycles against the courtyard wall in the hot afternoon sunlight. The only place the sun does not intrude is our small living room, crowded with new wooden chairs, their backs draped with crocheted *vitambaa*, Jesus on the wall, his hands extended in blessing. And there is singing and clapping, the fried fish sizzling in the centre of this circle of the people of God and all of them, all these people who died so long ago, are calling me by my childhood name, smiling and saying, eat, Sylvanius, eat, and Petrobia my mother picks up the fish and holds it out towards me and I am ravenous and radiant like her in my spanking new clothes and I reach for it. And then, suddenly, I am an old man again, my face sagging and creased, my guitar-playing fingers gnarled and bent, and there are blue-bottle flies buzzing over the fish, and Martha is sitting next to me. The people of God are still smiling kindly and saying eat, Sylvanius, eat. Then their faces melt, become skeletal. Even in the dream, it is at this point that I know I am going to die soon.

I was woken up this morning, the eve of our nation's 40th independence anniversary, with the gift of an old jacket and a song of freedom. A delegation from the community arrived at my front door, surprising me with a long-forgotten song I had composed in my youth as the leader, lead vocalist and lead guitarist of our neighbourhood group, Comrade Lemma and the Black Jerusalem Boys' Band. They were singing *Joka*, a song I stitched together from sleepless nights spent with my ear against my departed mother Petrobia's shortwave radio, when the shrrr-shrrr of static would part like clouds after the rain and allow some music through, the little transistor shivering at the forbidden sounds coming from a thousand miles away with the shaky, faraway voice from a sad, sweet, heavenly place singing: "*Ayeee Afrika-e/Ayee Afrika-e…*" Then you couldn't hear the rest because of the shrrr-shrrr of radio quarrels and the announcer's Queen's English interrupting them in an in-out whisper, like a man calling out from a well that is being opened and shut.

Among those forbidden faraway songs called up by my mother Petrobia's transistor radio, there was one in particular that had me in fits and sweats of how can this be? Who is this God of Music whom I have never heard of? Every night at the same time, the transistor clouds would part for long enough to allow a voice from the pits of hell to cry out in the accents of the damned:

There is a train from Beira!
There is a train from Namibia!
There is a train from Zimbabwe!

And then the voice would make the choo-choo sounds of a train and the clouds would close again, the train's shrieking whistle fading into "shrrr-shrrr-shrrr-you-are-listening-to-shrrr-shrrr". As the train sounds faded, I would close my eyes tight and travel to lands I had only heard of in my geography class in Primary 6, from which I dropped out because Mr Clarke, the headmaster, wanted to separate me from my departed mother Petrobia and send me away to a boarding school, and then who would take care of my sickly mother who had already lost so many children to small-pox and influenza? I would soar over the clouds and find myself riding in a train of doom from Beira, the wailing voice chasing behind, like so many demons escaped from hell.

It was a time when words were heavy as stones and could get you into trouble. Certain words especially, certain names, were only whispered. Dedan Kimathi Waciuri, General Mathenge. But most of all it was Comrade Lemma, the founder of the liberation struggle, who strode into our boyhood games of war, carrying away the children, the cowards, the irritating little girls who wanted to play boy games on the street on which our dusty, pink mud-brick flats were located in Nairobi's African quarter. Our mothers used his name as weapons against us, as in if you don't come in now Comrade Lemma will come and take you to the forest and eat you up. At night he would invade my dreams wearing his long, brown leather jacket, his shaggy knotted hair obscuring his face.

The delegation from the community was chanting in rapid verse, their younger members cutting the air like those exponents of martial arts in the makeshift cinema halls in my neighbourhood, cutting the air and chanting "*Nairobi Kambi ya Utumwa*", and in doing so, taking me back to a long time ago.

We heard of other places that people went to; and they would return dispossessed of the gift of speech during the day so that only during their nightmares could they tell stories of the quicksand torture of the prison camps, of how the earth had swallowed them, them and the stranger next to you, Prisoner Number 1234 – No *Afande* Sir I am not belonging to the proscribed group otherwise known as Mau Mau, *Afande* – and all you saw was an acre of heads and eyes, heads and eyes, and all the time the earth sucking and swallowing, like shitting in reverse. One night my father failed to come home and my mother started to grow old.

So I became a musician, leader, lead vocalist and lead guitarist of Comrade Lemma and the Black Jerusalem Boys' Band, and composer of *Joka*, the song that the nation has long forgotten after so many years of its being banned. And now I wake up to hear my neighbours singing it as if to mock me first thing in the morning after my premonition of my own death. Franco and Stish, the grandsons of Martha, my next-door neighbour and friend indeed over these gruesome years, are a pair of teenage poets whose rapid verses of our life here beneath the bridge, beside the river, regularly bring tears to my eyes when I remember my own youth of saying heavy things from the side of my mouth. I usually treat the sounds of their rapid verse with the contempt they deserve because it is a parody of music and to encourage it is to repudiate all those years of my youth.

And so I am especially wounded by their mannerless mistreatment of *Joka*:

KutokaKwalehadiKampala
MwendowaJokasiyohalaka
KutokaKisumuhadiKisauni
Jokalinanyonyanyinyiwahuni
Linatambaa, hiligarilamoshi
LinasafishaReserve, linakaushaardhi
Linawabwagawahunijijini
Huku Nairobi kampi ya utumwa

I remember how I became a musician as clearly as the evening of our nation's independence day, when my departed mother Petrobia was excommunicated from the Army of God for forgetting herself and simulating the tribal dancing of her people from the west of the country, thus forcing us to leave our one-roomed Jerusalem flat in disgrace and begin our journey to the banks of the river where I buried her. But that was much later, when my musical career was already flourishing. My career began on the same day that we saw Comrade Lemma for the first time. A photograph on the front page of the *East African Standard*, showed a man of about 40, his head resting peacefully beside his bullet-riddled torso in the Ngong Hills, the victim, said the report, of a group dispute over dinner.

As usual on that night of my adolescence, I had my mother Petrobia's radio glued to my ear, my borrowed Salvation Army guitar cradled in my arms, a tentative Ten Cent cigarette drooping from my mouth and pen and paper at the ready just in case the clouds parted long enough for me to decipher the music beyond. The God of Music began speaking in my ear in that terrible voice – there is a train from Zimbabwe. But he was not taking me to the mines of Johannesburg. Instead, he chased me through the clouds, his voice ripping through the heavenly peace, and I watched down below my fellow Africans from Kisumu to Kwale and Kampala to Kisauni climbing into train carriages. Regard them, said the voice, with their life's possessions wrapped in bedsheets, arriving in the city for a better life. But that was not yet a song. But my heart damn near burst out of my chest.

Then I was back in my room writing to the music coming from the transistor, the strident church voices of Southern Africa accompanied by the penny-whistle tunes that evoked so much sadness. I also wrote to the hypnotic guitar rhythms of Dr Nico and Le Grand Kalle, those Congolese gentlemen who were especially favoured on the transistor. I wrote a chanting chorus from the drumbeats of my childhood spent under the umbrella of the Salvation Army, which promised hell on earth and victory in heaven. My words burned with blasphemy. I woke up in the morning full of the joy of a religious conversion and the realisation that my voice had been transformed overnight from the lilt of puberty into the deep tones of my lost father's Salvation Army choir's voice.

It was Humphrey, one of those bullies from my childhood, who together with Tairero and Solomon now constituted the popular neighbourhood band known as the Black Jerusalem Boys' Band, who saw the possibilities of my song *Joka*. In fact, he intervened when Tairero threatened to beat me up when I suggested that I join the band. Humphrey was the vocalist, both Solomon and Tairero played guitar in the frenzied high-pitched tunes of those days.

"Hold on," he said lazily, leaning against the old lorry next to our courtyard wall. Humphrey and I were neighbours. Our mothers detested each other. They waged a never-ending war over which religion was superior and you Salvation Army people are so primitive, marching about like a herd of sheep and you Catholics pray in unwashed clothes, we are God's true army, we wear uniforms.

"Let him sing his song at the end of our show tonight," Humphrey said. "The crowd will laugh him out of Jerusalem. That will teach him."

Mr Ben's bar in the shopping centre had the dubious reputation of staying open long after the beginning of curfew. Mr Ben was partners with a police sergeant who made sure that his men went deaf to the noisy bands that played in the bar after 6pm, the onset of curfew. Mr Ben was a respected member of the community, being the only African licensed to sell beer.

I was quite nervous. The small bar was packed. There were customers squeezed on the narrow, wooden benches, standing and smoking at the dimly-lit counter, leaning against the dirty windows, blocking the corridor that led to the toilet at the back. I gagged on account of the pungent scents of Ten Cent cigarettes and Roosters, and the odours that blended with the scents of beer and urine. The fat barmaids sweated as they delivered orders, and would scream dramatically when the drunken men reached for their breasts. Behind the counter, Mr Ben was yelling orders to his skinny assistant, his balding head glistening.

People were calling out Francisca, another round here, and don't forget my change this time, Anna. Nobody saw how uncertainly I held Humphrey's guitar. I closed my eyes and went to Beira.

It was the sound of a man weeping that made me realise that something strange was happening on that night in Mr Ben's bar. My fingers were racing over the guitar strings like a reckless soldier on the run. Then I was in Nairobi; there were people weeping and clapping, weeping and clapping and I was singing *Joka* again. After that night, *Joka* was always the last song we played because, as Mr Ben, whose paunch grew steadily bigger, once said, it keeps the customers drinking.

Humphrey disappeared after that night. We heard he had got a job as a music librarian at the *Voice of Kenya*.

I took the name Comrade Lemma, not so much to honour that man with the burning eyes in the newspaper photograph, but to prevent my mother Petrobia from hearing that her son was a bar-room singer on Saturday nights. Every Saturday, people came to Mr Ben's to weep, people from all over the African quarter, from Pangani and Kaloleni and Ziwani and Bahati. Mr Ben continued to insist that it was a mortal sin, boys, a mortal sin, to pay musicians any more than they could reasonably drink on a single night.

Rumours about me grew. I was a Mau Mau leader disguised as a musician. No, no, no, he is actually a South African who sailed to Mombasa where he learned Kiswahili from the ghosts in the Old Town and come to Nairobi to steal the souls of respectable city residents, like us. And on and on. I wore my black cap lower, fearing my mother's wrath.

When we began to smell freedom, *Joka* was being seriously discussed as a contender for the new national anthem. By this time, however, I had been cut loose from the song.

Within the first year of the new independent government's life, the song was banned. It was said that the song's disturbing lyrics had annoyed the new leader.

Mr Ben became uncomfortable with us, and paid us off with enough money to launch Tairero's career as a drunk, and finance Solomon's trip back home to Uganda, and transform me into a vegetable dealer who, during those slow times in between customers, would read anything he could get his hands on and especially the classics of Charles Dickens. Then my mother Petrobia danced in church. We moved to the empty land by the river.

II

I was therefore in a furious mood this morning by the time I had put on my usual trousers, my brilliant white *kanzu* from those days of Rehema

– an old flame of my active years who had come to comfort me as I mourned my poor departed mother Petrobia's death from tuberculosis and shame, and who had left a few months ago convinced that my mourning period was over – and my sandals which I designed myself from strips of abandoned lorry tyres to accommodate the crisis of my twisted feet. I have a distaste for mimics as I have suffered greatly because of them, and I therefore intended to reprimand these young men. I was instead met by cheers of "Comrade Lemma! Comrade Lemma!" and Martha herself staining the newspaper page in her hand with her tears.

"Look at you!" she exclaims accusingly, her voice quivering with an emotion I have never witnessed in all these years of our friendship. She brings the page close to my eyes as only she and a very select few know of the special problems of my eyes. There is a grainy picture of three young men, dressed in the band outfits of my youth. Next to it, incredibly, is a passport-sized photo of myself with my Comrade Lemma locks and all the stains and distortions of my advancing years. The headline reads: 'Comrade Lemma found!' And then there is a sentence below that takes me a moment to decipher because of the special problems with my eyes and the fact that my spectacles have been missing ever since the mysterious early morning departure of Rehema some years back. I am just able to make out the sentence below: 'Independence musician and national hero lives in Nairobi slum squalor'.

Around me are the shining faces of my neighbours, regarding me as if I were a stranger, even after all these years of our collective struggle for a better life. I was once told, in private, that when reading, an amused expression comes to my face, as if I were laughing at a private joke. I can feel Martha's gaze boring into me, confusing, like she always does, my squint for a smile, because why else would you be smiling if you were not staring at that picture and recalling the heroic years of your youth.

There is a long pause. They peer at me. I squint my way across the tear-stained page, recognising in one paragraph the lyrics of *Joka* that I wrote those many years ago, and how my poor departed mother Petrobia, on discovering that I was Comrade Lemma on the day of our country's independence, had begun her retreat into shame and silence.

"*Ni yeye!*" It's him, declares Martha, her voice quivering, fading eyes alight with something I shall have to investigate later. There is a roar of approval. Franco and Stish, her poetic grandsons, are already chanting, in their youthful rapid verse, "*Joka! Joka!*" and it is soon answered by the feminine response of "*Mwendo wa Com-ra-dé siyo halaka*" and an impromptu festival of cheering and rapid verse takes over the normal morning noises of my narrow street. Another young man has taken up a tin and a stick and is beating out a rhythm, and I find myself hoisted up in the air, on the shoulders of my neighbours, my *kanzu* flapping ridiculously about me like a flag that is looking for an anthem.

They put me down long enough for Martha to hold an old black jacket against me. "It fits you," she says. *Inakushika.* The way she undresses the word provokes a stir in me that I experienced last with Rehema.

"It's from Marehemu George, a present for you." She is dressing me with her deft housewife's hands and undressing me with her look. "He says you must look presentable for today's meeting." Her faded eyes sparkle in the morning light, and take her back to the days when, I now strongly suspect, she was the unintended tormentor of young men. I am hoisted up again.

And so I begin a new journey with my old song.

Marehemu George has pulled out another miracle from his little bag of imported hand-me-downs. A year ago, he arrived on foot in our neighbourhood with a bale of second-hand clothes. They were a donation, he said, from a rich, departed American named George whose organisation he worked for. And so we took to calling this young man Marehemu, the late George, who provided us with dead people's clothes at a discount price. But a resurrection has taken place in Marehemu George's personal circumstances in the months since his organisation embarked on a new project to dispense free condoms. He is now an evangelist of new afflictions and beware the next victim could be YOU, you are never too young or too old to die.

It is only from my perch on the shoulders of friends and neighbours that I realise how my neighbourhood has grown in the years since I moved here to bury my departed mother Petrobia near the river so that her soul would be carried away from this city of misfortune. We head deeper into this valley of cardboard walls and tin roofs and the greenish sludge of sewers running like snot-nosed kids on a Saturday morning. It occurs to me that all these years my world – of narrow streets and afternoon chats with Martha about how are your late daughter's boys doing, that is a good colour for a growing boy's cardigan – has been this neighbourhood that is Kwa Lemma, where the city's newest immigrants have always settled.

I was the first one here, so they named it after me. Now I can see at least eight distinct Kwa Lemmas, collapsing against each other like a completed game of dominoes. There is the bridge, belching with the arrogance of city traffic, the old stadium in the smoky distance where all those years ago they played the first football match of an independent nation. We are singing *Joka*, and the women with their clutched babies hanging from them like an extra, cheering hand, are peeping out of their tin-roofed shacks. Spirals of charcoal smoke rise in the early morning air. In my present mood of a conquering neighbourhood hero and without my spectacles, I see a phoenix rising from the ashes. For the first time in many years, I welcome the chemical and plastic stench of the river.

Parked by the smart wooden office at the end of the street, I recognise the immaculate four-wheel-drive vehicle that Marehemu George has taken to driving. Then I see other vehicles, untidily parked. Suddenly, my narrow street has become a cul-de-sac: unmarked saloons and pick-ups, dark-blue Government of Kenya vehicles block off the side that leads to the open field where we have our football matches. A small horde of journalists brandishing biros, notebooks, cameras and complicated electronic equipment. This unexpected sight has the quite embarrassing effect of making me fart, briefly and pungently, on my new porters.

I realise Marehemu George has a hand in this morning's unexpected events. I had mentioned to him on several occasions that while condoms were very much appreciated, we must also bring to the attention of the authorities that many people here also fall victim, often even die, to the hidden diseases of our polluted river water. That it is not enough to dispense rubber for the protection of our people during their nocturnal embraces when the same prophylactics end up clogging our already overworked drains in the morning and floating on our river in a most unacceptable manner, especially as this is the same river we all depend on for our domestic needs. It is a subject that I have, in fact, written extensively about. Being one of the more literate individuals in our community, I took it upon myself some time ago to agitate, through the press, for external assistance to help us resolve this problem. Curiously, and it might have something to do with the deteriorating handwriting of an old man with special problems of the eyes, these lengthy articles were never published.

We were seated in my darkened parlour, Marehemu George and I, sipping his mineral water on the evening of our potable water discussion when his attention was diverted to the collection of framed photographs by my bed honouring my departed mother Petrobia. Among them is a misplaced photo of the band outside Mr Ben's bar and it is the one that has Marehemu George's attention.

"Who are these people, *Mzee*?"

"Oh, nobody really. It's just an old picture."

"Yes, a very old picture. Is one of these young men you?"

I wanted to get back to the subject at hand so I told him impatiently that, yes, I was one of them.

"Which one?" Marehemu can be very persistent.

"Isn't it obvious? The one in the middle, with the guitar and the hat."

"That's you? *Mzee*, I never would have… What was the name of your band?"

"Comrade Lemma and…"

"… The Black Jerusalem Boys' Band! My God, I've found you!"

Marehemu George is a big, imposing figure, a man of quick ideas. He has put on a lot of weight since he joined us. Now he is excited like a little boy. He is gesticulating hugely, so that his fingertips brush the walls, telling me how till the day he died his late father always talked about my band.

"Especially that song of yours, remind me, *Mzee*, what it was called…"

"*Joka*."

"That's it!" He snaps his fingers. "He said *Joka* had changed the way he looked at the world. My family owes you a debt, *Mzee*. Which one were you, if I may ask?"

"I am Comrade Lemma."

He looked at me intently for a few moments, then, I am afraid, he removed his scented white handkerchief and carefully wiped a waiting tear at the base of one of his eyes. Then he said in the voice of a man in a Charles Dickens novel: "And so, this is what it comes to."

He kept on repeating, "So you are the Comrade Lemma?" and standing up and sitting down, trying to catch up with his accelerating thoughts. By the time he was leaving, he had the look of a man who has found his destiny.

Next day, in the afternoon, when the light is especially good by the river at the back of my house, Marehemu George took me to meet a straggly-bearded man with dead eyes, a bush-jacket and a camera. You must look broken, Comrade, Marehemu George had said, with all the years of suffering etched on your face.

Marehemu George appeared at my door the following evening with a copy of the newspaper under his arm and a knowing smile. As we sat down to our drinks of mineral water, Marehemu George spread out the newspaper. On one of the inside pages was a photograph of me the day before, the shimmering river hiding its dirty secrets through a trick of sunlight so that we appeared to be in a better part of town, out in the countryside. Above my name was the question: 'Who is this man?'

"Even as we speak, Comrade, the nation is scratching its head in bafflement. Who is this man, indeed, Comrade, indeed," said Marehemu George, tapping the photograph with his hand of shiny rings. Underneath the photograph, there was the hint of amazing prizes to be won, and you could be the lucky winner of a year's supply of Careful Lover Condoms, a donation from the American organisation Marehemu George represented.

The next day, I was visited by an overweight and sweating young woman clearly experiencing difficulty with her luggage. She spoke with a strange accent, a little like Marehemu George in those first days when he was explaining, "No folks, you just don't get it, I've just come home from America. I've been living there for the last two years!" She described herself with the curious statement that she was "in radio". I invited her into my house where she took out a complicated array of electronic gadgets, attached one to my *kanzu* and asked me to laugh. I finally managed to emit a long, drawn-out croak. She said thank you and left.

A little boy woke me the following evening with the message that Marehemu George wanted to see me. The big desk in his office had been cleared of everything but a big radio, from which a young lady whom I thought sounded like my visitor of the previous morning was shouting as if her house was being robbed, saying you are listening to Clouds-Aif-Aim-Ninety-Eight-Point-Five and reporting on the chaos of evening traffic. Marehemu George told me to sit down, Comrade, our plan is taking shape.

There was a pause in the music. Then a machine voice said, "Whose laugh is this?"

And the woman said: "Okay-so-it's-the-moment-you've-all-been-waiting-for. It's time for 'Whose-laugh-is-this?'" There was the sound of clapping and cheering from the audience. "For two-thousand-five-hundred-shillings, a year's supply of condoms from Careful Lover Condoms, two bottles of Count Pushkin Vodka, a Coke and a smile, can you guess which celebrity is laughing?"

There was a drum roll and then the sound of a frog in distress.

"That's right, folks. Call me on four-four-four-four-double-four and tell me 'Whose-laugh-is-this?'" Again there was the sound of clapping and cheering from the studio audience.

Moments later, there was a telephone call and an uncertain voice said: "Could it be the President?"

A sheep bleated and the audience laughed mockingly. Then the disembodied voice of the machine said: "*Kondoo*! You-are-as-dumb-as-a-sheep."

And the young lady said dismissively: "Wrong! Next caller, please." I had the impression of a long line of people at a telephone booth, waiting patiently for their chance to call in and become sheep.

The next caller suffered the same fate when he suggested the laugh belonged to the Minister of Finance. The prize went up to for five thousand shillings tomorrow, a year's supply of Careful Lover Condoms, four bottles of Count Pushkin Vodka, a Coke and a smile, Whose-laugh-is-this?

Marehemu George's teeth flashed in the evening gloom, like a block of white flats in a run-down neighbourhood.

"Comrade, you outdid yourself!" he said. "Even I wouldn't have recognised that laugh as yours."

"Is that me?"

"But of course, Comrade. You remember laughing for a pretty lady yesterday morning?"

Marehemu George informed me that I was now officially on the nation's celebrity list. For the modest sum of ten thousand shillings, which he had personally pledged, my laugh of a frog in labour would be identified in a few days when he, Marehemu George, made a call to the studio and became the surprise winner of 'Whose-laugh-is-this?'

"It is all about knowing people, Comrade. But I digress. At that point, Comrade, the whole nation will be asking, 'Who is Comrade Lemma?' On that very day, my friend the editor assures me that your identity in the photograph competition will also be revealed. Then the action will really begin." Later, as we sat there on his verandah, he wondered aloud what it would take to mobilise the community, "Comrade, you know these people better than anyone else," then reached into his pocket and presented me with some money, saying, "No, please accept it, Comrade, as a small token of my respect for a figure of national importance."

Things started to happen very fast from the time we got back to my street. The newspeople moved quickly towards our party of throbbing, gyrating youths honouring an old man in his hour of glory. For a moment, I forgot my aching back, twisted feet and fading eyesight in the flash of lights, the click and whirr of cameras and rapid-fire orders, of stop there so that we can take a picture, Sir, no right there so that these shacks form a backdrop for your remarkable face, isn't it remarkable, and more calls of exactly like that, Comrade, yes, that's right, that's perfect, Sir. The years of heaviness, and the price paid for saying heavy things, fell away as I recognised that I, Comrade Lemma, was being honoured, finally, for services rendered to the republic. I stood alone, in this broken-down neighbourhood that had been my home for all these years, in my old *kanzu* and my morning gift of a black jacket, and shed tears.

When I opened my eyes, I was alone in the middle of my narrow street, the glorious vision replaced by dust, screaming and chaos and the throb of a helicopter overhead. I could dimly discern that the crowd, as well as the newspeople, had diverted their attention to the helicopter landing in the dusty field next to our neighbourhood.

"Marehemu George said he was expecting a cabinet minister," I was startled by Martha's voice behind me. I turned to face her. She was smiling.

"I wonder which minister. I lost track of them in the late '60s." I must admit, I was putting on a brave face. I had not expected that my moment of glory would be so brief.

"Marehemu said maybe the Minister of Culture. But it doesn't matter. You are the man of the moment. Even the minister is here to honour you." I found her hand in mine for the first time in all the years I had known her. I was astonished to discover how tender her eyes could become, how they could, in moments like this, defy her grief of burying her own daughter; this world can be cruel.

"Don't forget your neighbours now that you are famous. I will cook your favourite meal tonight. Come." And she was gone. In front of me, the surging mass of people were trying to get a glimpse of the minister and meeting instead the solid resistance of the police, who were clearing the way for the minister with threats of whipping and shouts of "*Ondokeni! Ondokeni!*" and arranging the crowd into a wave of placards in front of Marehemu George's office.

After the radio broadcast our verandah had been turned into a museum in my honour. The photograph of me by our shimmering river taken the other day was a huge poster covering the main window of the office and overlooking the table, now draped in a brilliant red cloth. The poster said in big, bold lettering: 'Careful Lover presents Comrade Lemma, a genuine Kenyan hero. Careful Lovers Last Longest'. Then there was a line at the bottom: 'Careful Lover Condoms Supports the Search for a National Hero'.

There were smaller posters on the walls and windows, all with 'Careful Lovers Last Longest' emblazoned beneath my photograph. This irritated me because I have sometimes suspected that Rehema of my active years left out of frustration at my impatience in these matters.

The Minister of Culture is a gentleman of the first order. To the utter astonishment of Marehemu George and others, he refused to take the high chair reserved for him and instead left it for me, saying that this was my day and besides, I was the older man.

I was unsure of how to behave after so many years out of the limelight. I was the hero, the man of the moment, and yet I had the distinct impression of being a servant to this event amid all the clicks and whirrs and "like that, *mzee*, right there", and the attending minister and the welcoming flash of teeth of a grave and resplendent Marehemu George, more spectacularly dressed than ever. My face felt tight and dry with the effort of suppressing my need for the toilet. His ease around all these strangers and their gadgets acted like an anti-laxative and I relaxed beside him. I was, however, struck by the unnecessary thought that his lips were so close to the cluster of microphones that he appeared to be performing unspeakable acts to several men at the same time, without the protection of Careful Lover Condoms.

When he started speaking, the verandah went quiet. Even the crowd on the street strained to hear what he was saying.

"There was once a young man who wanted to change the world through music. At the time, there was a war on and his people were dying in their hundreds and being detained for their opinions and their defence of a struggle for national liberation. Yet this young man ignored the dangers of subversion and sang his heart out…"

The exertion is affecting me. Look at me, the hero of the nation, the old warrior battling to stay awake. My eyes won't remain open and my mouth hangs embarrassingly as Marehemu George weaves his way in and out of my story.

And I can see Humphrey that night so long ago when he surprised me after so many months of being away, in that suit of the new, upcoming African manager, made to measure by the Indian tailors on Biashara Street.

"Comrade Lemma," he announced grandly, "I am going to get you on radio. You will be a national hero. I will make you rich beyond your dreams." As he was leaving, he asked me for the words of *Joka*. "It has become my favourite song. I hum it on my drive to work. Now I want to be able to sing it." I wrote them down for him. And he was gone. And then later, on that first morning as an independent nation, putting on the radio to hear: "And now the song the nation is dancing to, *Joka*, by Humphrey W. Gatonye, the man of the moment…"

My eyes jerk open to find Marehemu George killing off all my old friends and band members.

"…Save for Comrade Lemma, who survived death on numerous occasions, all the other members of the Black Jerusalem Boys' Band died heroically in the service of the nation. For two years he was a detainee in Hola…"

He talks of my long and traumatic experience in several detention camps, where quicksand torture was liberally applied (I was considering suing the British Government for the crimes of torture and illegal confinement), of how Tairero Omondi died at the hands of thugs after a Comrade Lemma concert in the City Stadium; of how Solomon Olimba died trying during a colonial police interrogation after his arrest for subversion; and Humphrey W. Gatonye, in a British Army bombing raid in the Aberdares as Mau Mau soldiers wept with sheer joy at his vocal talents.

"Now on the eve of our 40th anniversary as a free nation, and under the new leader of a truly democratic government, Careful Lover Condoms is proud to return a national hero to his rightful place in society!"

The smell of fish begins to invade my nostrils.

I have difficulty recalling in exact detail what happened when I stood up during the question and answer session on Careful Lover Condoms' role in the search for a national hero, and went looking into the eyes of the seated newspeople, of the Minister for Culture, for the owner of the fish, my muttering growing louder and louder until I was screaming in my hoarse, old man's voice, I am not Comrade Lemma, Comrade Lemma is dead, over and over and there was a roaring in my ears like that of the doomed train from Beira. And I was seizing one of the microphones from Marehemu George and I could see them as if they were written in the air in front of me, those words of the last verse of *Joka*, which had eluded me for all these years and the sound of an old man who is speaking out after so many decades of silence, was fading in and out as if from a well that is being opened and shut. And I was saying *kifo ni rahisi*, death is easy, it is living in silence that is difficult, which one will you choose my brother, in these days of bondage, don't be an old man who can't explain why he didn't die young or why his children walk in chains. And I remember seeing Martha's eyes so clearly in the middle of that surging crowd, please understand why I have to do this, and hearing the commotion of chairs falling over and the smell of gunpowder and asking why were you there, Martha, in the dream of fish.

My own understanding of the riot, Inspector, is as follows: as the event wore on and the people began to tire, Martha's grandson, Franco, decided to check that his money from Marehemu George's early morning payment was still intact, and realised that his pocket had been picked. It is therefore incorrect to assume that the ensuing cry of *Mwizi* – thief – and all the commotion had anything to do with accusations levelled against me on the podium by Marehemu George that why did I want to wreck his event after he had paid me such a large advance. The late Martha, being an elderly woman and ignorant of how to get out of the way during a stampede, was therefore a victim of circumstances.

Yes, Martha is dead, and I, I am still alive. But the stench of rotting fish is everywhere now.

Parselo Ole Kantai is co-editor of *Ecoforum*, a Nairobi-based journal concerned with environmental and developmental issues in East Africa.

The Secret

Chika Unigwe

TODAY, THERE IS SOMETHING on the news about women in France who give birth under X. It means that they choose to abandon their babies. They keep their names anonymous and the children grow up never knowing their roots. You imagine the children floating, rootless, with nowhere for their tentacles to grasp.

You wonder what would push a mother to abandon a child. Why would a mother carry a nine-month pregnancy only to choose not to raise that child?

It must be a western curse you conclude. Where you come from, a child has many mothers. When one mother is tired, another takes over.

Loneliness secretes a stench that clings to you. It is not one that you can easily eradicate like you can the stench of sweat (you swear by Avon all the time) or morning breath (Macleans does the job for you). You never knew it was possible to be this lonely.

"Eby, your friends are here," Mother announced.

They filed in laughing at a joke and flying high on youth.

"There is a party tonight. Loads of good-looking men. Are you interested?" Angel asked.

Angel. What a name to give a roguish child. She looked like a rabbit.

She had protruding front teeth, which, to her friends' amazement many men tended to find alluring.

She was the unrivalled sex-goddess of the gang. De-virgined at twelve by choice, she had bedded more men than one cared to count.

She introduced Eby and the other girls to tampons.

And gave them tips on how to catch a man's attention.

They looked up to her, but that was before she became ill.

Angel.

She no longer lived.

Her parents said it was juju.

They said somebody had hexed her, made an effigy of her in Ijebu Ode and stuck pins all over it.

They said she cried at night that she was being pricked with a thousand needles. The last time Eby saw her, she looked like a drawing on a sidewalk: devoid of flesh.

She had a silk scarf around her head.

The scarf kept slipping off and whenever she lifted her hands to tie it back in place, Eby saw how bony her fingers had become.

Her cheeks looked like she had them sucked between her side teeth. Eby wanted to hug her, but did not know how to. Eby did not hug her. She went home and cried.

In your first month in Belgium, you smile at every black person you see. You feel that your colour brings you together more than nationalities ever can. In the sea of pale yellows and yellows tanned by holidays in the sun and days spent under suntan machines, your eyes frantically seek out blacks for fraternal greetings. The first one you speak to replies in French, "*Pardon, mademoiselle, je ne parle pas d'Anglais.*" Tears gather in your eyes and you turn away in disappointment. The ones that speak English with a very West African accent tell you that they are Portuguese. Sudanese. Somalian. Anything but the truth you see lurking at the corner of their eyes, hiding from you. You stop wondering why they lie, but turn inwards to yourself. You do not smile unless you are smiled at. Do not speak, unless you are spoken to. You think perhaps the smell of your loneliness drives them away.

Angel died of AIDS.

Everyone knew that.

Eby saw how her body went.

Bit by bit like a yam being prepared for supper by a bad cook: too much flesh is taken with the skin.

The left-over yam is half the size it should be.

Then it is chopped into even smaller pieces.

Angel looked like an *izaga* masquerade by the time she died.

Her mother cried and stood her ground that she was hexed.

Being a victim of the evil eye was better than being a victim of AIDS. You do not realise how bad your loneliness is until you start looking forward to the invitation for coffee at Lisa's. And the barrage of questions that accompany it. Lisa, your neighbour and friend. She asks you around for coffee and sometimes you reciprocate the goodwill. But you know nothing about her. She does not open up her life to you. You have never even been upstairs in her house as you always have your coffees in the kitchen or on the porch. Loneliness and curiosity are the major ingredients, which bring you together. And a shared smile on a warm sunny day, which instigates a conversation:

"You are new here?"

"Yes."

"Are you from Surinam?"

"No. I am Nigerian. West African."

"Oh. You like Belgium?"

"Yes."

"You miss home?"

'Yes.'

"Lovely weather today."

"Yes."

"*Precies afrikaanse* weather, no?"

'Yes. The weather is almost tropical.'

"I am Lisa."

"I am Eby."

"Nice name."

"Thanks."

"*Totziens.*"

"See you."

After that, the coffee invitations follow. "You drink your coffee black, no?"

"Yes."

"Sugar?"

"Yes."

"Ah, you like sugar. I do not like sugar in coffee."

Coffee. Black. The colour of a winter night. Biscuits with chocolate cream in between. So sweet they made you sick once. And the questions that always come piling up, every day a new one.

"So, in Africa, did you eat biscuits?"

"Yes."

"But not this type. Which type did you eat?"

"English biscuits."

Eyes widen instantly and then dilate in acceptance of a logic behind English biscuits in the heart of darkness.

"Of course, English colony, Neegeria, no?"

"Was."

"Huh?"

"It was an English colony. Not anymore. Nigeria has been independent since 1960."

1960 Nigeria nwelu independence

Na ime aro ozo anyi achiba onwe anyi oo

Azikiwe

Nnamdi Okpala

Jisie nu ike

Anyi ga enwe mmeli

1960 ooo

1960

The song came unbidden to Eby.

Her mother sang it all the time, but it was one she sang without joy, contrary to the message of the song.

Eby could feel the weight of the sadness her mother carried when she sang the song that celebrated the independence of Nigeria.

Her mother did not talk about the day much but Eby had seen pictures.

Her mother at one side of the green-white-green Nigerian flag.

She was smiling.

It was a smile that lit up the picture.

It was almost tangible, alive.

Whenever her mother spoke of the independence day, she chopped her words like firewood.

They fell in bits, heavy with a thud:

In. De. Pen. Dence.

Mess.

The. Nation. Is. A. Mess.

It was the same when she spoke of the Delta Region.

She was from Biara.

When Shell's construction of pipelines destroyed her uncle's farm along with those of others and her uncle came, looking like a man who had been out in the rain, crying in the quiet way men do and complaining of crops killed, she cursed oil.

She walked around for days saying Doom. Doom. Doom.

When the community demonstrated, she drove down from Enugu to

Biara to wave placards she had written.

Placards which denounced Shell.

And the military dictatorship.

With the bad roads and traffic jam, it had taken her more than four hours to get there.

"Do you come from a large family?"

"Yes."

"Oh. Very African." She smiles across a coffee mug. Black. No sugar. No milk.

"How many brothers do you have?"

•Three."

"Sisters?"

"Four."

"I am an only child."

"Very European," you say in a voice spilling over with sarcasm.

She smiles. You do not think she notices the sarcasm.

"One child is enough for us in this country. We do not have the stamina of African mothers."

White folks are very selfish. One child! Eby thought.

How much more trouble does it take to raise a few more children?

They have everything to ease the job for them.

Washing machine.

Drying machine.

Self-cleaning oven.

Food in tins.

Drinks in cans.

Microwave oven.

Running water.

Electricity.

Her father often said that both heaven and hell were on earth. This was heaven.

Her first days in Belgium, she had played with the light switch like an excited child. Off. On. Off. On.

The sheer magic of light flooding a room at her command was something she had to get used to.

She no longer needed to stock up on candles and kerosene for the nights NEPA was unable to provide electricity.

Gunther.

The first time you hear the name, you make him repeat it. You practise rolling your tongue to its exotic sound. Gunther! Gunther! It is a name that tastes of nothing you have ever eaten.

He is not easy to miss. The only white face at the club you go to on a Friday night. You know immediately he is not Lebanese. You steer clear of them. They are everywhere in Enugu, buying up businesses, getting young girls pregnant and leaving them.

He walks over to you, plants himself between you and the man you are dancing with and asks if he can dance with you.

You like his confidence. Your dancing partner complains that he is rude, but you like his rudeness. Besides, the young man you are dancing with is beginning to bore you. He is a poet, he says and, while dancing, has begun to recite poetry to you:

your eyes
shine like the moon
bright
sending shivers
down my spine

You do not like men who recite poetry.

Gunther is built like a wrestler. He looks like the sort of man you will always feel safe with. Yet, when he speaks, you cannot believe that that is his voice. He has a child's voice. It is a voice that is innocent, untainted by the bitterness that comes along with maturity. It is easy to fall for him. And when he asks you to marry him, you do not need to think. Your "of course" carries the conviction of your feelings, even more so than the kiss that follows, which tastes of mint.

Eby insisted on a traditional wedding. It would make her feel more married, she said.

Gunther got caught up in the preparation: getting measured for a wedding outfit and dropping off invitation cards.

He had a black brocade gown trimmed with gold thread and pants to match. He drove down to Garki and bargained for two goats.

He was very proud of himself that he got the trader to reduce the price by half.

Nobody had the heart to tell him that even with the 'reduction' he had paid too much for the animals.

Although he complained that a cow cost too much, he nevertheless paid for one.

He marvelled at the list of presents he was expected to give out:

Bales of cloth for Eby's mother.

A live goat for Eby's father.

Two cartons of maltina for Eby's paternal aunties.

Three cartons of beer for her paternal uncles.

A carton of maltina and twenty naira in an envelope for her oldest sister. Two crates of soft drinks for the Young Christian Girls' Association.

Two crates of soft drink and the waist of a goat for her committee of friends.

He said it was robbery, but he laughed and presented the gifts with a smile that did not waver.

And stored up an archive of stories to regale his family with back in Belgium.

Your first Christmas with Gunther is white. You spend Christmas morning watching the snowflakes fall, not quite believing you are in Europe. Abroad. You put on the thick brown jacket with white lining, which Gunther's mother has given you, and run out in the snow. You ask a mirthful Gunther to take pictures of you, proof that you have arrived. Gunther laughs, his dimples unbelievably deep, and obliges you. Your foreignness intrigues him. He says that being with you is like having a box of pralines: you know they are all delicious but you delight in their differences.

Now, he wonders if life will not be simpler with a wife who is more like him.

Eby wanted a white Christmas this year.

In some puerile way, she felt that if it snowed on Christmas morning, it would be a sign that her problems would soon be over.

That was the miracle she was hoping for. It was Christmas Eve and the forecast for the following day was cold but dry.

No postcard Christmas for her, with snow on the outside and a fire on the inside (even if it was just central heating).

They do not have an open fire in their cramped apartment above a children's clothes shop.

The table is laid in an array of cutlery. You wonder about the etymology of the word. Like, does it come from clutter? There are the fish knives and the fish forks. Then the soupspoons. Then the dessertspoons. And the multitude to choose from. For just one person. You think of the washing up ahead of you.

You remember your first Christmas dinner. And how a delighted Gunther tells the table that the cutlery both amuses and confuses you. Would the fish taste different if eaten with a spoon, for example? You remember the indulgent laughter, which follows this.

These days, Gunther does not tolerate your questions. He is too impatient and when you ask the order in which you should place the glasses, he grumbles like a man who had to clean up his dog's mess for the umpteenth time in one day.

He is making turkey stuffed with minced meat and mushrooms. You hate mushroom, you cannot stand its rubbery taste like that of a used condom. But that does not matter to Gunther. He has the mushrooms halved and marinated in red wine. Like he was trying to drown them. "Drunken turkey," he says, "I'm making drunken turkey."

There are potatoes to go with the turkey. Boiled and dipped in olive oil. There are three bottles of red wine.

"Apéritif?" you ask Gunther. He grunts a "*Ja, graag.*" You pour him some red port. And pour a glass for yourself. You like the taste of red port. Uncharacteristically of you, you drain your glass in a single gulp.

Soon the guests will begin to arrive.

Tante Miet is the first to arrive. Bowing under the weight of her fur coat, she comes as usual in a cloud of perfume. Today it is Eternity for Women emanating from every pore. Kiss. Kiss. Kiss. Three times. The kisses that do not touch your soul but leave lipstick stains on your cheeks.

"Merry Christmas," she says and hands you a meticulously wrapped package. Even without opening it you know it is a bottle of perfume. Tante Miet is predictable. You wish life were like that: predictable with a sweet smell. Your life has taken a turn you would never have predicted.

Next to arrive are Stijn, your father-in-law and Charlotte, his girlfriend.

Charlotte has hideous taste in make up. Her eyelids are coloured purple, which gives her a battered, worn look. Her lips are orange. You hold the impulse to laugh.

Stijn looks dignified. He looks like he could be a professor. Or a banker. To see him, one would not believe that he was a mason. It was difficult to imagine him, knees on the floor plastering somebody's kitchen.

You kiss them, kisses that sail in the air.

On TV is some scientist — you do not catch his name — talking about mummies that they have unearthed. He is saying proudly, his glasses perched on his nose, that they have solved the mysteries of some of the mummies. Perhaps now, their spirits can rest in peace. You want to scream at him to solve your problems. You are angry that some hefty research grant went into disturbing the rest of people long gone and forgotten about. What about you? You want to ask. What about finding a cure for the cancer that has lodged itself in your breast.

You are only twenty-five and it is not fair.

Eby had known she had cancer for a while now.

Doctor Suikerbuik told her already a week ago.

The knowledge weighed heavy on her chest.

She re-played the moment in her head when Suikerbuik told her, "I am sorry, Mevrouw, but the result shows that the lump is indeed cancerous."

She had cried but decided not to tell anyone yet.

Not even Gunther.

Gunther, Eby sighed. She was wearing thin on Gunther, she knew it.

He had had enough of a wife so different to him.

There were cracks in the marriage and she could see them as clearly as if someone had drawn them on a piece of paper and handed it to her.

He complained when she made *egusi* soup.

He said the smell of *egusi* was too powerful for their apartment.

He complained when she watched TV, could she not reduce the volume? Thank you.

He no longer noticed her lingerie, her hair, her eyes. All the things that had intrigued him.

She wondered how long it would be before Gunther told her what she had suspected for a while now. She was almost sure that he had a mistress.

She would not tell him about her cancer.

She was going to be a martyr and suffer on her own.

He had to stay because he loved her, not out of a sense of duty. She could not bear it if he stayed out of a sense of duty.

Or worse, if he stayed out of pity.

She would not tell her parents, they could not deal with a dying daughter.

She had no friends to tell.

Lisa was the closest person who qualified as a friend in this place, and Eby had never been upstairs in her house!

She wondered about Angel.

Dr Suikerbuik had told her that her lumps had been caught in time.

Caught! As if they were fish swimming away from a fisherman's hook.

He had told her she was most likely not going to die.

Yet Eby was scared.

The dreams were responsible.

She was not superstitious, but the dreams disturbed her nevertheless.

It was the same every night: she saw herself wrapped in white muslin and placed in a coffin.

In the dream, she knew she was dead.

She saw her mother pounding on the coffin, asking her to get up. Dr Suikerbuik could not reassure her.

Eby wondered if she would see Angel when she died.

Would they still be friends?

Would she look like she did before she became ill?

She had a lot to tell Angel.

The only problem was that she did not want to go just yet.

You pour wine for the guests and some more for yourself. You clink glasses with everyone. The wine swirls as glass kisses glass.

"To a wonderful year!" Stijn shouts.

"May all our dreams come true," Tante Miet adds.

Your head spins with the terror that her words might come true. You hurriedly put your glass down and spill some of the wine on the wooden side-table. You run into the bathroom while everyone's eyes follow you questioningly.

Dr Chika Unigwe, a Nigerian living in Turnhout, Belgium is a recipient of BBC and Commonwealth short story awards as well as the author of two EFL books published by Macmillan, London. Her debut novel, *De Feniks* is published by Meulenhoff (of Amsterdam) and Manteau of Antwerp.

African Writers'
Workshop Stories 2004

Grasshopper Redness

Monica Arac de Nyeko

OOLA. HE OWNS A LAW firm in Bugolobi. He is choirmaster of the Bugolobi Anglican Church just around the corner after the charcoal market where the women traders sit under the sun. They sit there till they don't feel its sharpness burn upon their skin like the flames of an angry bushfire. When he meets me today, in between a brisk walk and greying hair still uncombed, Oola is almost startled. He wants to look at me but for a moment he is unsure if he should. Like always, he speaks quickly. Almost breaking into a slight stammer, and constantly pulling at his beard with his teeth biting at his lower lips. He bites his lips now.

– Atek! You are growing up like a weed. Only yesterday, you were a little girl!

He lifts and drops his hands in unison like the *one two two one* beat to the tune of *Amazing Grace How Sweet The Sound*. He has this smile which cracks upon his face and vanishes sooner than expected. He pushes forward his hand and waits for mine. He does not look at me, but at my hands.

– Do you like it at university?

His eyes are still on my hands. He is always searching for the words behind my hands as I slowly take my right hand out of my pocket and extend it to him. I withdraw soon after. I have it rehearsed. I always let my hand brush his and withdraw soon after. I have to. If I let him hold on, then he starts pleading. I can't bear to see his eyes like that. He always has that same look. Not exactly a sad one. Not even a sorry one. Just insistent. As if he is demanding me to open myself up and unravel his wounds. I have tried to say this to him, always through the flapping of my eyelids as I avoid his

85

own. That his past is bound with his own, not mine. I have a future to quest after. I can't help him heal. The wounds he caused me are too deep.

– You don't talk much these days? Well, you have never spoken much really! Is your Ma okay? Does she still have trouble with that piece of land?

I nod my head left and right. Standing on the road like this will get us knocked by these bicycle men who pay no attention to anyone. They are hurrying past Bugolobi church and towards the market, which sits in the valley, below where we stand now. Without making a huge effort, you can hear market vendors calling out to buyers to come finish off their merchandise so they look into another day and earn more shillings. Things do not always work that way. There are always the unsold tomatoes, so red on the stalls and almost daring to stain the wooden stands to a deeper red! The drying pepper is almost as red as the oil paint on the stalls. Everything is so red. Sometimes I want to wrap a bandage around my eyes to avoid this redness that lacks tenderness I can sniff.

– I should be on my way now. I say.

My voice is still. I can barely hear myself. Oola has not heard me. I try to look at him again. I can't hold onto a long gaze! Not with his eyes, as red as meat and beamy with the residue of *waragi*. Maybe from last night, or the night before. Everyone in Bugolobi church knows. They pretend they don't notice, after all the man is a good choirmaster. Today, when the sun shows up its rays, Oola will be at Mama Damali's place, asking for a tot. Now I must be on my way, to see Ma.

★★★

I dreamt of meat last night.

Meat? Meat is bad! Bad! Terrible. Ma always says. Ma wishes my recurrent dream was about water. You see, according to Ma, although water steals from us, water also extends the night into the day with promises of birth or life. Meat? Meat is bad! Bad! When Uncle Giwa joined the army 12 years ago, Ma always dreamt of big chunks of meat in big pots. She was always stirring the meat with the big *ogwec*. The one Uncle Giwa carved out of the guava tree in Grandpa's compound. The same one he crushed upon Ma's back when Ma tried to block him from taking the army recruit bus to become a cadet. He became a cadet. He even came home with his friend Oola the first day we ever saw him in his new uniform. Ma pulled my ears for saying its colour green was very beautiful, like Mother Nature.

86

– Mother Nature? What do you know about Mother Nature, Atek? You think you are so good about colors that we should all listen to you now? Eh! You open that no-good mouth of yours again and I will pull your ears till you fart like Mother Nature itself!

Ma does not speak like that often. When she does, it's because she has been looking into her cowries. Ma likes to cast them on the floor. She searches for hidden tongues, patterns and revelations. She cast her cowries on the floor the day Uncle Giwa and Oola came home. She said she could see a storm forming in the skies. The lines on her face grew deeper. Ma stood behind the house and held her hands across her face searching for some clearing in the clouds. Then she held her hands upon her breast and muttered.

– I don't like this. This is not good.

Grandpa used to say – after some of Ma's revelations, holding his stick and pointing at nothing in particular – taking your Ma's cowries too seriously is as good as throwing oneself in the river, Atek, do you hear me? Do you?

When he spoke like that, his eyes focused on a particular spot, and he seemed transfixed there for a long time. Grandpa liked to hum songs. For some reason, his songs always bore a certain hint of sadness that matched the pace of his greying hair. It did not matter if it was the happiest song I had heard the women or girls in the church choir sing with so much mirth the day before at so-and-so's wedding. When Grandpa picked it up and started to hum, slowly tapping his walking stick on the ground or scribbling unreadable symbols and letters on the ground, it seemed he was struggling to calm some thoughts laying deep within him, throbbing or tossing and rendering him in this constant state of melancholy.

It was hard to imagine Grandpa the way Ma described him. Grandpa with stooped back and knees, which seemed hardly able to carry his weight, was not exactly easy to see as the leader of the rogue village boys who took matters into their own hands and constantly terrorised men who made a habit of beating up their wives. Ma said that, at a time before she was born – and before Grandpa lost his young wife, who one day fell in the middle of the large compound and never got up again – Grandpa had made a name as the de facto head of that gang, which for a long time had most men scared of even lifting a finger to hiss at any woman. Ma knew I laughed when she told me these stories about Grandpa, which I hardly took to heart. How could I, when Grandpa, constantly grumpy, chewing at his tobacco in the middle of a hot afternoon, never hesitated to swing his stick at the chickens in the compound, which, innocently clucking and searching for left-over nuts in the dust, never anticipated the possibility of a stick aiming at their feet. It seemed ours was the only compound with no short supply of limping chickens.

Ma tried to look into her cowries to ask about Grandpa and the chickens despite Grandpa's mantra, which he often uttered in between clenched teeth, saying:

– There is absolutely, no point in asking for answers from the dead when they always obscure the world of the living with stains and worry. When I get my hands on those cowries I will throw them in a blazing flame!!!

I am not sure what Grandpa says now. Especially when Ma sometimes throws cowries on the compound on which he once sat and aimed at the chicken's feet. Ma likes to evoke his name and conjure his presence, seeking answers to the question Grandpa never got to answer. Did Grandpa blame Ma for Grandma's death? Why did Grandpa stop believing in Ma's cowries? What harm had any chicken ever done him?

Everyone knows Grandpa liked everyone to believe he was never into Ma's cowries and 'that kind of thing' – the way he referred to whatever Ma did. Ma says the old man liked to think he was too rational for his daughter's unexplainable complexities. That is why he let Uncle Giwa's friend Oola spend the night with us, although Ma had told him there was something not quite right about the man. He – Grandpa – was tired of listening to Ma and being called names for it. Ma never did tell me this, but the day Grandma died was the day Ma started to see the future in her cowries. That's when everyone started to tell Grandpa that there was something not right about this. People said the cowries had gained power by sucking out life from someone as dear to Grandpa as Grandma. That only Grandpa did not see anything wrong with Ma because he was only too happy to let his wife go so that his daughter could terrorise everyone by seeing things that no normal person ever saw.

Grandpa used to say:

– I can't stand those fingers pointing in my direction when I go to drink some *liralira* in the evening like everyone else. Do you know that no one wants to sit with me?

Grandpa wanted the whispers and accusations to stop. Perhaps that is why he aimed at the chickens so much and had over the years perfected his little sport. It was not just the chickens, as I learnt after watching him closely one evening. Grandpa's stick seemed sharp and on spot when he sought as his target the hens particularly. Even still, it was not just any hens. They were Ma's hens!

I told Ma. She said:

– You talk like that again and I will feed you with cow dung till you go to search for your good-for-nothing father in Kenya! You hear me?

That was when I was little. I learnt to keep my thoughts to myself. If it was not for the cow dung and Ma's threat to send me to search for a father I had never known, I would have pointed out to Ma that it seemed a little strange that Grandpa always encouraged her to go the river at the height of every flood season. Mudfish were known for swimming far off the banks of the river and hiding too deep in the mud. If you were not careful with the business of catching them, your feet could stick in the mud and at such critical moments the river tide always claimed its offering.

– Strange, how these things happen.

That is how Grandpa would have spoken. Grandpa said that when Grandma died everyone except him seemed to know what had happened to her. Yes, it was strange and so were lots of things. A strangeness that Ma had learnt to live with I suppose, because this river, to which grandpa always sent Ma, never claimed her. It took Grandpa instead, I heard Ma say in passing the other day. That it was what Grandpa wished and chose. He wanted to go at the time when the river, confused if it should rise or fall, remained static and took on a falling offering rather reluctantly.

Sometimes I think of Oola like that. Even as he walks, his strides are reluctant to admit he is falling. Yet, the days come and take him with them. No one will sit near him at Mama Damali's place. The sores on his body declare their presence too willingly and proclaim a pattern even Ma's cowries cannot comprehend. He does not need to go for a test. People know these things by just looking. Each day that comes and goes leaves him with a thinness that is almost hard to bear. His lips are so red and raw with sores that it is hard to lay eyes upon them even for a second. And that terrible cough he has! So sharp, like his chest is cracking open.

– If Oola just goes, then he will not haunt everyone else. Maybe the wounds he created will start to heal.

Ma likes to say that. But Ma's wounds are not about to heal. Even if Oola, with his awkward tallness and knock-knees, was taken today by the water demon riding on the river wave to the land beyond the first death and the second death, Ma would still bleed. Ma would carry her spear into the realm of the departed to demand that Oola be denied entry into the kraal of redemption.

Perhaps Ma thinks that way of Grandpa too. He started it after all. Ma saw the dark clouds in Oola's eyes, even when he smiled shyly, wore his hair and moustache neatly and carried a transistor radio that matched the greyness of his khaki shorts. All Grandpa had to do was believe Ma. Perhaps Grandpa believed Ma but chose to ignore her, like he had often done. Grandpa was tired of everything. He wanted a normal life, with a normal daughter and family like everyone else. Uncle Giwa however did not believe Ma one bit. He shouted in her face that she was extending her hatred for this army uniform a bit too far.

 — I have known Oola for three years. You and your cowries should be cast away. How dare you say you see darkness in my friend's eyes? A man who helped me like a brother. A man who sat by me when I was sick in cadet school and wiped my dirtiest parts! A man who knew I had you for a sister and chose to be my friend!

But there was something perhaps Uncle Giwa did not know about Oola. Maybe that's what Ma saw that day. There was a thirst for innocence untouched by lust. A virgin perhaps? During that time the rumours had just started. Those rumours about the blood test which Oola had taken soon after his wife was said to have died under the spell of the unexplainable illness killing so many people. Uncle Giwa did know that Oola's wife had died, but 'it was cancer'. That's what Oola told him. Yet every rumour knew it was far from being cancer. What cancer made one suffer from incurable bouts of green diarrhoea that left one skinned to the bone? As it goes, someone had told Oola that all he needed to cure himself was a virgin. That was after he had taken the tests, which turned out positive positive positive... and the fear of death started to mount upon him and he thought he would lose his mind.

Meanwhile the dark clouds Ma saw in her cowries started when Oola and Uncle Giwa had come to visit Grandpa for a day. The next day, they would go back to cadet school. It was the grasshopper season. The moon was high. Every ray of light enchanted the insects as young kids got ready with their plastic containers to storm into the night, like their fathers and those before them had done. The grasshoppers, each of them flying towards light, without any knowledge they would be on dinner plates the next day. Oola, not knowing he was the subject of any family discussion, and I getting impatient that Uncle Giwa, Ma and Grandpa would not stop their argument, hurried into the night. I with this kind stranger who was also my Uncle Giwa's friend and had offered to walk me to the spot somewhere near the main road where all the kids who were going to trap grasshoppers that night had agreed to meet.

– If only he had listened to me.

Ma says that often. When she talks like that you know she is talking of Grandpa. She blames Grandpa for the red stains on my cream skirt that night. She never says it, but I know when she stares into her cowries sometimes she is asking Grandpa if the stains drove him into the river. Or if perhaps by some strange inclination of thought he had gone to the river to ask the waves why, after all this time, they had never let Ma stick her feet in the mud.

Ma still goes to the river, to search for Grandpa. Her cowries will not give her any answers when it comes to Grandpa. Perhaps the river will. Who knows? Perhaps the river also knows where she can find her brother Giwa, whose face she can't trace in the cowries, and whose decade of absence haunts Ma, because she can't find him anymore. Not in her dreams of meat, or in mine.

★★★

I met Oola today. When I meet him sometimes, it's hard to believe it has been almost ten years, since that grasshopper night and the red stains. I can't tell Ma I just met Oola going towards Mama Damali's place on my way to come see Ma this morning. She cannot stand his name. It breaks her every nerve till she is weak and drained and her wrinkles draw in deeper. Ma will not show me she is crying. But she does. Often. Her eyes stare blankly into my eyes, not sure why after all this time, I will not let my pain bleed like her own. The stains are mine. Not hers. Ma thinks that's even more reason why I should let the pain bleed out of me more. When she searches into my heart, Ma cannot understand why there is no sign of rage. How can I even offer him my hand to shake? Don't his sores bother me? Do I know what they mean? Do I know?

Ma. My Ma!

Every time I see her I think she has aged. She is sitting on a *toktok* stool today. Her head is wrapped in a *kanga* headscarf with bits and pieces of Swahili words fading into the fabric whose colors were bright like her smile. The patterning of the textile, which carried images of several birds in flight, has also disappeared and the birds have lost themselves around the folding of material around her head. Ma is watching her garden with *sukuma wiki* sprouting out of the ground. The vegetables planted in this front garden of hers have become a rich dark green since I last saw them about a month ago.

I like the way they light up her front yard and flap their large leaves about. Ma tends to them every day. She knows it will not be long before they are ready to leave her garden. That means she should not put too much energy into them for they have their own destiny. But Ma attends to each and every plant as if persuading it to stay a bit longer. Sometimes I catch her whisper:

– Please deliver me that promise. Please!

As I approach the short steps leading up to the verandah on which she sits, Ma lifts her eyes and smiles. It's the same smile she had when she started to look into her cowries after the river and Grandpa. I stopped by Bugolobi market to buy her some tomatoes from a man who offered me a good price. I hand them over to her in the *kaveera* and make my way inside. The sun is mild today and the verandah gets a light breeze from the direction of the mango tree standing at the end of the garden. I have come to see Ma this early morning. I have had this dream of meat several times. Why does it bother me so, this time? Sometimes I think Ma can read my thoughts. Can't she?

– Why have you come home when you are about to write exams?

Ma asks me as she rises and follows me into the cowrie house. There is animal skin over the floor, which Ma says belonged to her ma. She sits in the corner of the house where she usually positions herself when she has guests with requests for cowrie services.

– I just wanted to come home, I say to Ma.

What I want is to talk about my meat dream. But I know surely that even if I do not talk about that, the smell of her animal skin will calm me. I will feel Ma's walls enclose me with a reassurance I feel only when I am inside this space, which belongs to my Ma and her ma before her.

– Can I make you some porridge?

– No, Ma. I am not hungry.

My answer is quick. Ma stops just as she is about to rise and settles back into her position. She rests her back upon the wall. She is humming a song. It sounds like one of Grandpa's melancholic tunes. Of ummmmm… um…

Water has taken
Water has taken
My friend
Water has taken
Water has taken
My friend…

Ma stops. She is smiling. That same smile she had when she saw me come through the gate. The smile she has when she tends her *sukuma wiki*.

– You need to let the pain go. You need to bleed, Atek.

This is not the first time Ma says this. There is firmness about her tone today and a kind of certainty that has been absent from her voice since Grandpa and Uncle Giwa. Very often I want to tell Ma to stop fighting my battles. I do not want to see her lose herself fighting both the living and the dead. She needs to learn to look into her cowries again without seeking the lost or those she will lose. She needs to know when to stop. She has lost interest in everything but tending her *sukuma wiki*, which she is terrified of losing. The same vegetables she refuses to harvest. The women in her neighborhood will not let such good food go to waste. They pluck the leaves every time Ma leaves her verandah. This has made Ma want to sit at the verandah all the time. But she cannot be prisoner to watching over the stems every minute. The night is there, and the night always takes away, even if you are watching.

– Ma, the meat dream again.

She pays me attention without seeming to search for signs of pain and the bleeding behind my eyes, when I go silent.

– Was it the same dream?

– Exactly. Except that this time, the meat smelt of grasshoppers and I could not resist it, so I took a bite. And it was strange as well, because the grasshoppers were red, not green. I say.

– You ate them?

– It's what I just said, Ma.

– I see.

– What does this mean?

Ma is quiet. She sends her hands to fetch her bag of cowries. Then she changes her mind and looks at me intently.

– Grasshoppers? Grasshopper redness? That's not good Atek.

– Not good? What does the dream mean?

– I am not sure.

She is avoiding my eyes now in the same way she was the other day when I told her that I was tired of searching in the darkness and always guessing, worrying, if I was… if I could be… or if it was just a matter of time before I was like Oola, with the sores, and that terrible thinness and the cough. That day I told Ma I would take the test. When? I was not sure. But last night, I lay facing the ceiling. The uncertainty, not knowing and guessing seemed even harder to bear. I made up my mind to take the test today.

– I am not sure, Ma repeats.

– How can you not be sure Ma, how?

Ma is quiet. Her quietness terrifies me. She will not even try to look at me. What does the dream mean? Why does it bother me so this time?

Somewhere in the folds of Ma's silence, I start to get a sense that Ma knows what this dream means. That she just refuses to untangle it for me, because it goes back to that grasshopper night and the red stains on my cream skirt. That same grasshopper redness which returns to haunt me in my dreams!

In this silence, I find myself thinking of Grandpa who went at the time when the waters, confused about whether they should rise or fall, remained just static. Yes, without Ma having to tell me what my dream means, I know it is okay if I let myself start to fall. I should. I am sitting on Ma's animal skin, feeling the claws of the leopard to which this skin belonged. The proximity to such strength loosens my muscles and the weight of these tears, fermented over a decade old, start to hear me down. Ma rushes forward. She lets me fall upon her chest. Her breasts firm like the day I suckled them, hold me before I crash. Slowly I pull away from her. Ma lets go of me, humming...

Water has taken
Water has taken
My friend
Water has taken
Water has taken
My friend ...

Pacing to Ma's hum, my feet lead me out of Ma's cowrie house, off the verandah and into the compound, past Ma's vegetables and off the path that leads to Mama Damali's house.

Monica Arac de Nyeko was born and raised in Uganda. Her short story *Strange Fruit* was shortlisted for the Caine Prize in 2004.

One Woman's Body

Doreen Baingana

HERE I AM AT A SMALL bar on a dusty road, in a dusty corner of Gulu. It is my first month away from my husband and my father and my home, Kitgum. My first month of work selling second-hand clothes with my friend, my saviour, Cantina. I am in a bar at night because I am tired but can't sleep without beer. I am alone because Cantina is saved and does not drink. I am here because I rent a room behind this bar which is a shop during the day. My room and the bar are small, cramped and dark, but my room stinks and the bar doesn't. The bar smells of old *posho* flour, and beans and spilt Omo and cooking oil and Ugandan *Waragi*. And beer of course, which smells a little more pleasant when you are drinking it than when you are pissing it. My room is close to the bar's latrine. Drunkards are not known for good aim or a good conscience and so piss all over the latrine floor and along the wall outside the latrine. The elephant-loud hiss as the piss hits the corrugated-iron walls time and time again drowns my dreams. I prefer to sit here and drink as long as I can.

My shield from the stares of the men is a bowed head, anonymity and my bottle. I sit on the edge of one of the three benches, squashed in and protected by the glass and wood cupboard filled with Nice and Lovely Hair Oil and Vaseline, Ambi lightening cream, Delicious shampoo, and earrings and necklaces of fake gold and other fancy colors valiantly struggling to sparkle under the dust. The wall to my side is lined with shelves creaking with Kimbo tins, exercise books, bicycle tires, hair pieces and long brown blocks of Key soap. The more I drink, the less they look like they will topple over and land on my bare head.

The person I owe rent to, the bar and store owner, is perched like a queen in the small island behind the counter and plastic jars of *mandazi* and sisal balls. Mrs Oketch is a healthy giant the color of strong tea, who wears a wide sea of *busuti* that is defiantly black and red, the ruling UPC colors. So is her headscarf, a flag against the increasingly loud rumbles of rebellion from the south. Her wide, lazy smile, a proud display of a hundred small, bright teeth and large pink gum, reassures anyone who steps in her domain that beer is still flowing freely here, at least. Her husband is a colonel, which helps keep her store stocked. He is away in Buganda fighting, but still she smiles. I can do nothing but twitch my lips in a forced smile back, and hope I am not the joke. The room she rents me is very cheap for a place in town, stink and all, and she lets me pay by the week, and hasn't asked for my story. I can only be grateful.

It is time for a second beer. I relish the first cold sip that is as sweet as a kiss. A sharp nip. I must forget all that. It is now nine o'clock and the bar is filling up with its regulars. Men, of course. Most of them sit outside on benches arranged in a large, crooked circle in the dim dust. The dark, warm sky embraces the group and its murmurs that gradually rise to shouts and frustrated slaps on thighs and barks of laughter that drop to sudden silence. They agree to disagree and seal the truce with a bottle-turned-upside-down long gulp of their drink of choice. Now the regulars simply flick their eyes over me then concentrate on their beers. That is a relief. To disappear. To be background while the men brag and lie and tell tall tales, as alcohol makes their tongues liquid. A few bring quiet women along to listen and laugh and say amen.

On my first day here, one pregnant, red-eyed man greeted me politely after ordering his two UG tots and coke. "I'm alright," I murmured and kept my eyes on the floor. He stood by for a moment, as though counting the grey bags of Kakira sugar on the top shelf, then shrugged and went outside to sit with more willing company. I bought myself another beer from placid Mrs Oketch, and studied my dusty toenails and brown sandals. Half an hour later, the man came back into the store, and boldly ordered Mrs Oketch to give me a beer. "No," I said, and stared straight into his red eyes. He shrivelled under my rude blank stare and shuffled out. Mrs Oketch burped a short, satisfied laugh. It was the response of someone who had seen it all, and all it deserved was a burp or a belch.

"That woman is trouble," I heard the red-eyed man complain to the others as he sat down, settling his belly between his thin legs. "She's ugly too."

The others laughed at his weak effort to save face. I swallowed my beer. Another said in support, "Why is she here alone anyway, if she is not a *malaya?*"

"That one? A *malaya*? Honestly, are women in such short supply?"

The words slid off my body like water. I had heard worse. But I wasn't a fascinating enough topic to hold their interest for long. There was the war. There was always the war and the guerrillas in Luwero, including women, with their big butts and long *busuti* hitched up one large leg as they ran through the bush. They were finishing off our men. And what about their leader, Museveni, who appeared and disappeared in a blink of an eye, in a swirl of dust, and changed form at will, from a snake to a pig to a man again. That is how he crossed borders and never got caught. The Devil was on his side. He was sweeping through the country, moving north with an army full of Rwandese, those foreigners. And he said he wanted to liberate Uganda. All he wanted was to take it for his own people. Moreover, those milk drinkers could not fight. They have won a few battles here and there, but they would be defeated big in the end, the men said, bold with booze. You wait and see. We know fighting, we have protected Uganda, the whole of it, since day one, so what do they think? Those ungrateful, banana-eating weaklings! They should stop playing with us.

The false bravado wears me out. The real men are fighting and dying for us, for these drunkards here. I have my own battles to fight. At 6am again tomorrow, Cantina and I have to go to the border with Sudan, three hours of bad road away, to buy more clothes. Ah, but let me have one more beer then leave. I give Mrs Oketch one thousand shillings. She holds out her immense arm and large open palm as though kindly accepting tribute from her serf, and does not move another inch of her terraced rolls of fat. She is too settled and spread out to get up.

I reach into the fridge and take out another cold one to wash away the what-ifs and could-have-beens. I deserve my drink; I have already been at war. I fought the battle of the body. The battle for new life between me and my husband. I lost, and left, and I am now on my own, with no home except this body which has betrayed me. This body that cannot remake itself. And I thought I was a woman. I carry these breasts that are still upright and pointed expectantly outward. For what? The Baganda say, *Kitalo mabere; nomugumba gamera.* What a pity about breasts; even a barren woman bears them. A real woman bears two fruit on her chest to feed children, not just as a snack for men.

Once, it seems so long ago, my body was mine to play with. I was a fast runner, played dodgeball with my friends at school, jumping high and swerving at the last minute and laughing out loud. I was good. Then, when I was fourteen, a teacher showed me what else my body could do. My breasts were swelling and stretched my school blouse tight. But I had no money for a new uniform. I could not ask my father. I could not say the words breast and bra to a stern preacher. Anyway, all his money came from and went back into his Church of the New Believers, which he started when I was ten. That was when he sent my mother away because she did not believe in him and his church. Who could I turn to when my breasts swelled up like a disease and I began to bleed? This body was no longer mine. I could not run and jump like before. I could not control it as it got bigger than me.

One afternoon a button on my blouse burst off in Maths class. A friend gave me her sweater, but the teacher had seen me, and his eyes glinted like a cat that has spied a mouse. Mr Okurut stared, not at my face, but below at my hands holding the sweater closed over my chest. I looked down at the floor ashamed. Some girls and boys giggled. They too had watched my body swelling faster than anyone else's. I wanted to squeeze myself under the desk and disappear.

The teacher glanced my way throughout class. He would catch himself and turn away, but his eyes did not obey him, and slid back to me as he drawled out equations. Mr Okurut had not looked at me like that before. With such longing. For me. At the end of class, with a dry cough that he covered with his hand, he told me to remain behind. The others tittered and looked back curiously as they wandered out. He asked me gently if I wanted money to buy a new blouse. I looked down and whispered, "Yes, Sir."

"You need a bra too." Did he really say that word out loud? He reached for his wallet, worn and thin, and pulled out 5 000 shillings. "Go to the second-hand market tomorrow. I am sure you will find something."

"Yes, Sir," I smiled gratefully.

He said, "Don't feel bad – everyone is growing." As I turned to leave, he stopped me with a touch on the shoulder, where he left his hand. "Come with me to my office."

I followed him. What could I do? He closed the door and pulled me to him. He moved my hands gently away from my blouse. The button fell from my damp fist. He opened the blouse, smiled and touched my breasts. "So soft," he said, "so fresh." I did not know what to do. My stomach curled up painfully tight. I could not look up. He told me to lie down on the floor and knelt beside me. He said, "You are beautiful," but he did not look at my face. His hands roved all over my body as his breathing got heavier. His face was that of someone looking with longing and inspection and desire at a rack of beef hanging up at the outdoor butcher's. Red meat hung on a hook, swaying in the bright light, flies swarming over it as the butcher sharpened his knife. Red fatty flesh desired by crowds of salivating shoppers. My teacher leaned over me, widened my legs and drilled a deep hole, hurting me and hurting me, but I could not cry out.

When he was done, he said, "You better go home now, or you will be in trouble." I gathered myself from the floor, my mind blank. He zipped up and smoothed down his trousers. Then he reached for his wallet, got out 1 000 more shillings and tucked it into my blouse. "That's where grown women keep their money," he said, smiling. He turned to his desk now calm, as I hurried out.

I had never had that much money before. Never. Perhaps I could buy sweets as well as a bra and new blouse. But my body felt old. It ached. It knew too much. As I walked home through the blue dark, I was dully surprised to hear the evening birds coo as usual, as they did every night that fell.

At home, I prayed and cried for God's forgiveness. Somehow it was my fault. And I shouldn't have taken the money. The next time I entered Mr Okurut's class, in my new loose blouse, I also wore, for protection, a necklace and cross I made out of thread and two thin bamboo sticks. Nothing worked. The teacher stared at me greedily and my stomach tightened again. And again, he squashed and squished my breasts and body like it was ripe fruit. I left school that day and told my father I wanted to serve God full time in his church and he accepted. He was happy not to continue paying fees, perhaps for nothing if I were to marry and stay home and cook, which I did.

This beer makes me think too much. Why am I going back to that when I have left it behind? But my husband, Okello, was a good man. Four years ago, he saw me sweeping my father's church, which began in our house, but grew fast over the years, and so the faithful built a new building. It was a long structure with reed walls that did not reach right up to the thatched roof. The wind blew through gently, cooling the congregation and carrying our songs to the town and beyond on Sunday mornings and weekday evenings. The wind also blew in dust that I had to sweep out every evening. Okello came by one sunny afternoon and stood outside by the wall and looked in. I stopped sweeping and turned, feeling someone behind me. He smiled, but did not say anything, so I asked, "Are you looking for someone?"

"No," he said, but did not go away. I wasn't scared for some reason. Maybe because he was so calm, so himself, like a solid wall. He was dressed well too. His trousers were well-ironed, with two sharp lines down each front, his shirt a bright white against his sombre dark face, and his shoes shone black. Perhaps he was a teacher? I said, "My father is back at the house."

"Who is your father?"

How could he not know? "The Church Leader." My father did not use the title 'Reverend' because he had begun his own church.

"Perhaps I will visit him one day." The man smiled and walked away. He did not say bye. How strange he was. Where was he from? Who was he? Something told me not to tell my father, and the next day, Okello was back.

"What is your name?"

"Achieng, Betty."

"How old are you?"

"Sixteen."

"Why aren't you in school?"

That was embarrassing, and I looked down to the mud floor as I answered, "My father needs me here." Okello remained silent after my answer, as if he knew that was not entirely true. But how could I tell him my shame? "No money," I said instead, quietly. It was partly true. I wish I had told him the whole truth then, perhaps it would have changed the future. Who knows? Okello said nothing, but smiled as if that was okay and I would be okay too. That was all that day.

Later, Okello told me he was a member of another church, The Catholic Charismatic Church of Uganda, that also was new and not part of the main Roman Catholic Church. It started in Arua, and its leaders had sent Okello here, since he was born in this area, to see if it was possible to start a branch. I guess he finished his work quickly because every evening he came back to our church when it was empty and I was cleaning it. I started to wait for him. He would not say much. Each time he would ask me a question or two, then smile and watch me work.

I now waited for his face to rise above the reed wall every evening. I was careful which dress I wore. It would be clean and would cover my knees. One evening after two weeks, he asked if I could take a walk with him the next day. I quickly said yes, and then looked down to hide my eagerness. Again, I did not tell my father, but swept the church as quickly as I could and locked away the few bibles we had. We walked down a path away from the houses, and it was soon just us and the long yellow grass and wind and our footsteps. I liked that we did not talk. He took my hand. His was warm, but mine began to sweat. I took it back and he let me. But he soon took it again and said, "It's alright." We came to a huge green Kituba tree and he said, "I don't think I can climb that anymore. I used to."

"Try," I said, giggling.

"I prefer to sit under it with you."

So we sat. Quiet as usual. My fingers fidgeted with the belt of my dress as I waited, and yes, he turned my face around and kissed me. When he stopped, smiled and said, "I shouldn't be doing this," I pulled his face back to me. This had been done to me before; I wondered why he kept his hands off me. I picked up his hands and put them on my chest. It was not big for nothing.

"Achieng!" He pulled his hands away. I laughed and tried to pull him back, but he scrambled to his feet. "You–!" He did not know what else to say. This time it was I who said, "It's alright," as I got up too.

I held Okello's hand as we walked back, reassuring him with a small squeeze now and then. He seemed a little confused as he said bye, and I thought I would not see him the next day. He was not like my teacher. But he came back, and smiled at me, and we both eagerly set off for our walk. In a week, he became an expert of my body, holding my breasts as though choosing mangos at the market, testing them with his palm for firmness, weight and ripeness before taking a bite. He found my breasts and other parts of my body to his liking, as I did his, but he was a good man, a Christian man, and he went to visit my father. My father wished he was not Catholic, but at least he was not Roman Catholic, at least he spoke in tongues and he was a good Acholi man and gave my father three cows. Perhaps my father had heard of our walks and was glad to get rid of me before there was trouble.

In any case, I wanted Okello, and was as hungry as he was and we fed off each other. And it was good. After marriage, of course, the consummation, the shared meal had a purpose beyond pleasure; I was supposed to lovingly shit out a child. Or two or three. One year, two years, three years and four, and I didn't. I still haven't. I won't ever. Okello is a good man, but the empty years ate at us. We stopped talking and laughing together and simply fucked and prayed. Okello led us, pleading, "Our Heavenly Father, make us fruitful. Bless our marriage bed, and kill any demons breeding in Achieng's belly. Oh Lord God, a preacher must have children, and bring them up well as an example to his flock. You who wrought a miracle by making the Virgin Mary pregnant, can work a miracle again, by bringing my wife's belly to life. We beg you, because we believe in you. Amen." I too said amen because I knew it was my fault. God was punishing me because of what I did with the teacher. But after years of this, I realised God did not want to forgive me. He was mean or deaf and I was angry and fed up. I took up spirits instead. I could no longer struggle at sex without sneaking some *waragi* into our holy house and drinking some before bed. Night after night, after Okello's days spent in prayer and preaching, we feverishly went at each other. He pulled hard at my breasts as he came as if that would send a signal down to my belly. Force it to wake up and make life. Shudder after shudder, in vain. The pleasure was spiked with, was spoiled by, resolute effort and the resultant bitterness. Afterwards, when he fell to the side, drooling and snoring to high heaven, worn out by his heroic efforts, I kept my legs up in the air, not wanting a drop of sperm to spill. In vain. Something inside me killed it. All I could do was wash myself in tears and secretly blame Okello for his bad seed. He blamed me for my constipation.

The silent war between us spread to the street. Walking down the dusty trail to the vegetable market was as hard as the trials of the night. The women I met, my former playmates, ignored my murmured greeting and stared at me as though I had two heads. I felt like choking as I moved through their thick silence. As I came closer, the women lowered their voices and then stopped talking altogether to watch me pass by. As if they had never seen a woman walk before. As if my extra head would rear up and snap at them and infect them with barrenness. I kept my eyes on the ground, but could feel the women shift and bunch closer together in the solidarity of the fertile. They were real women. Their bodies justified them by producing more bodies, while I had been fucked for more than four years for nothing. They watched me with pity, fascination, malicious glee. Their worth was high because mine was so low. My wretchedness increased their happiness. They shifted their fat babies from one wide hip to another, covering the innocent round faces not from flies but from this woman who was not a woman. They feared me too, as one fears what one cannot control. They could have been me: a woman with a hole for nothing. A hole that kills and kills and kills. A dead end.

Okello finally gave up. He said God was punishing us because we had sinned before marriage, or rather, I had led him, a preacher, to sin, and so he was taking me back home. I knew my secret sins and so when he said pack up, I did. I was tired of fighting and endless, fruitless sex. I accepted defeat. Little did I know that he had already seduced a shopkeeper's daughter who was now pregnant. Okello knew this when he took me back to my father's house. Perhaps my father knew too. That hard, bright afternoon when we walked into my childhood home, my father would not look me in the eye, but walked right past me and reached his hand out to Okello, and welcomed him, and apologised. I left the room as they went out the front door to collect the cows my father had received for me. Okello got back his three cows, and the calves of those cows, now ten in all.

After one week at my father's house; I knew I could not go back to childhood. I could not stay in this town where everyone knew my husband had finally, successfully fathered a child with another woman. It was confirmed: I was worse than a prostitute, worse than a mad woman, I was simply the worst. I had to leave, and did, and now I am here, in this bar, drinking beer.

I couldn't have done it without Cantina. She started school with me and left it one year before me, pregnant, and moved to Gulu to marry the father of her child. Her marriage too went sour, but from too many beatings. She left, but her husband would not let her take their four children. She has now lived by herself for two years, trading in second-hand clothes. She sees her children secretly at school and slips them new clothes and exercise books and *mandazi* and her love. Piece meal. They do not understand why and she waits for the time when she can explain. When I called her on the phone for rent at the post office in Kitgum, and told her my story, she told me to leave and join her in Gulu. I told her, at least you have children. She said I was better off without them than having them torn from my breast. I can start afresh, she said. Afresh? I have not felt fresh for years; my stale, bitter body sags like a dry, diseased mango. We do not fully feel each other's pain, but still, Cantina told me to come up and I came. I packed what was mine: a few clothes, no bible, and left. My father, even more relieved than I was, gave me transport money.

The trip in a squashed *matatu* took three long hours. A piece of metal cut through the lace of my old bra and with, each jump and joggle of the taxi on the potted road, dug sharply into the flesh between my breasts like a bad conscience. We drove directly into the sun, eating and drinking dust as Congolese music blared false merriment in our ears. The driver kept it loud; why should we sleep if he couldn't? Let us all sweat, suffer and suffocate together.

We arrived at six in the evening. The sun had reduced its relentless wide grin to a thin smile that seemed to mock me for the day gone by, for my life left behind. Cantina met me at the dusty bus stop and took one of my two bags from me. She had called a *boda-boda* motorbike taxi to carry my luggage, but saw that there was no need. We first went to a little kiosk in the taxi park were she ordered a soda from the shifty-eyed man behind the crooked dusty counter. Cantina spoke loudly, authoritatively, as I stood by like her child. The man pointed to a large blue bucket covered with a sheet made of papyrus. I removed the sheet and wanted to jump right into the bucket and swim with the bottles in the ice water. To keep my face underwater forever. I chose a Mirinda and the man wiped it with a rag. I would have licked the outside of the bottle dry. I gulped it down like it was my saviour, not removing the bottle from my mouth until it was empty. Cantina laughed and bought me another one. I could not refuse. She pulled out a roll of bills to remove two thousand shillings, and I wanted to be her.

Cantina lives not too far from the centre of Gulu on an unmarked side street that has a row of similar small houses with two wooden windows and a door in front. We walked to her place with my mouth still wet and tasting sweet from the soda. The cool air seemed to welcome me, and so did the soft evening sun glinting off the corrugated-iron roof of Cantina's house. We bent low to enter the doorway, and it was dark and cool inside. We removed our sandals just inside the front door. The floor was a deliciously cool heaven for my swollen feet. Cantina opened the wooden windows and my eyes got used to the shadows as a tender light flowed in. These were her own two rooms. She had two wooden chairs, a stool, and a plain table along a wall. On the floor in a corner was a hot plate and a small cupboard. On one wall, a Caltex Calendar, on the opposite one, a picture of an unhappy Jesus. A wooden door led to another room. Cantina quickly made me tea, which she served with roasted groundnuts, then led me to her outdoor bathroom. Cold water on my skin is my only remaining physical pleasure. But now I felt that starting again in Gulu was better than drowning. I slept on Cantina's floor on a mat and thin mattress of grass covered with flowered sheets that she hadn't sold. The very next day, we set off for the Sudanese border to buy my first bale of clothes so I could start my own business. The work is hard but better than thinking too much. And right now, at least I can pay for a room and drink of my own.

So I might as well have another. The red-eyed, pregnant man has come into the store again, almost tripping at the doorstep. Mrs Oketch won't stop the flow of drink as long as the money flows too. He lurches over to my corner and sits down heavily next to me. "By the way, by the path, who are you?" he asks.

"Achieng."

"Oh no," he slurs, "that's the name of my mother. I can't fuck my mother, can I?"

I pick up my beer and pour it over his round belly, watching it froth and spread over and down to his stick legs and crotch. I laugh as I shake the bottle empty.

"Whaaaaa–!" He grabs my wrist as he shoots up, or tries too, but lurches forward. "You stupid bitch, *komanyoko!* A curse on the day your mother fucked your father to get you!" and so on he froths and spits out in English, Swahili, Acholi and English again.

I twist my arm out of his grasp and push him back so I can leave the corner I am trapped in. He pushes me too, but loses his balance and holds me in a smelly, beery embrace instead. We struggle this way from side to side, both of us yelling. I don't see how Mrs Oketch rises and leaves her throne, but she is right by us now, a formidable red and black mountain, and hits the pregnant man on the head with a hard plastic jar full of *mandazi.* He falls forward with me underneath and I land hard on the bench, shouting, "*Aaaiieee!* He's killing me!" His grip is surprisingly strong; he has both my arms fastened down. The empty beer bottle falls out of my hand and crashes down, filling the small dim room with an endless glass waterfall clatter and cracking. I try to bite his neck but can't twist my head enough to it. It takes both Mrs Oketch and a man who rushed in from outside to wrest the drunkard off me and drag him outside and throw him down into the dust, where he moans and curls up, holding his head. She snarls at him, "Take your skinny buttocks home to your miserable wife, you fool." Though my arms and back are in pain and my legs are cut from the broken bottle, I can't help but stare in admiration as Mrs Oketch stands there snorting in the dark, sending the rest of the drunkards home. "Enough!" she says, pointing to the road, the other hand on her broad hip, her legs spread wide. She is a cross between a warrior and an elephant, and I want to be her.

I gingerly limp away from the sea of brown glass and step outside. My legs trickle blood. Luckily, Mrs Oketch sells cotton wool and Dettol too. As I clean my wounds, the man who helped Mrs Oketch tear off the pregnant man says, "Why do you fight with men?"

"But I don't! You saw what happened."

"Ahaa, I fear women these days!"

"And so you should."

Mrs Oketch grunts in approval and we laugh together. He is called Paulo, and he is on leave from the army and is a friend of Mrs Oketch's husband. I say I can't sleep now; I have a horrible headache. He offers to stay with me and she gives him the key to lock up, and waddles mightily away into the night. Paulo gives me Panadol and opens a fresh bottle of UG.

"Why can't you sleep?" he asks.

"Ah, my troubles are not that interesting."

"Soldiers don't sleep too."

I nod in agreement and we drink silently, each for a moment lost in private pasts.

"Tell me," he says. His face is dark and long, with strong cheekbones. His bottom lip protrudes a little and is pale pink. I study him, and he does not turn his face away. It's as if he has waited for ages, and will wait some more. Okello was like that once. I am the one who turns away, because suddenly I want to trace my finger along his cheekbone.

"This is a story that must be repeated," I say, and he laughs at our traditional way of beginning the old stories. "There was once a woman who thought she was a woman."

He laughs again, but says, "Just tell me straight, will you?"

I raise my glass for more sparkling fuel, wipe my mouth and start. He listens as I pity myself and cry and get mad and groan, lunge up and point accusingly and fall back down like a wet rag. I can't help it. Still, he listens. Then as I sit there, a residue of myself, still crying, Paulo says, "Where do you stay?"

"Behind here," I sniffle.

"Let me take you home."

"Home?" I laugh drunkenly, "What home?"

He takes my hand and I follow him out the door, and wait for him to lock up as the cold black wind dries my face. We stumble together over a slat of wood placed across an open sewage drain, and lean on each other for more than support. He is strong and tall. He is a soldier. At my door, I say, "I need to pee first." He knows all my shame now after all.

106

"I see," he says, and I giggle. I am too gone to go to the toilet, and all these drunkards pee outside here anyway, and it is dark, so I take a few steps away and tell him not to look. I widen my legs, squat down, pull up my skirt and pull down my panties, one hand leaning on the wall. The loud sound of pee streaming out and the relief of release make me giggle, but suddenly I feel two warm hands cupping each cheek of my buttocks. I can't stop peeing and I am silenced. The weight of him close to my back and his hands holding me steady tell me there is nothing to do but feel.

Soon, we are in my bed and he is inside me and fucking me with a vengeance, as if to drive and thrash and force out all my history, all that I had told him before. I open myself as wide as I can, my legs pounding his muscled and scarred back, because for once, after so long, this is for no good reason. This is yet another feverish battle. Even though I do not know what he is pounding against, what he is exorcising, it is something fierce and necessary. He works silently, with hardly a grunt of exertion, while I mean to wake up the whole street with my unrepentant loud moans. I am, for once, completely out of myself, but he is here to stop me from breaking. But we do, we break and curse and collapse like dead dogs on the roadside. And soon, we don't even exist.

I am pulled out of nothingness by a sharp rap on the door. "*Kodi?*" It is Cantina. She knocks again. "Achieng, are you there?"

I push Paulo away. He groans, but he doesn't wake up. "I'm coming," I call, and pull a *lesu* over my naked, aching body, stumble to the door, fumble with the lock, and then open it a crack. It is already dim blue dawn outside and Cantina smells sharply of soap, which tickles my nose and I sneeze. "Cantina, I am sick, so sick." I rub my face as she furrows her face with concern.

"What is it? What's wrong? Can I come in?" She pushes a little at my creaky door.

I push it back. "No, no, I just have a bad, bad fever, headache, you know? I just need to rest for one day. You go without me." And I'm the daughter of a priest.

She pauses then shrugs a little. "You know you won't be able to buy new supplies until next Saturday?"

"I know, Cantina, but what can I do? You go. You'll be late. I'll see what to do."

"Okay. I'll pray for you." And finally, finally, she leaves.

Paulo turns over in my small bed. "Who was that?"

"My friend, Cantina. I was supposed to go buy more clothes today."

He grunts and goes deeper under the covers and I join him.

Hours later, the sun pierces through the slats of the wooden window and lands on our faces. We wake up and reluctantly come to our senses. I make tea, which Paulo gulps down as he shuffles into his clothes. As he gets up to leave, he pulls out his wallet and counts out ten thousand shillings, which he hands to me. "I stopped you from going to the border," he says.

I look at the money in my hand and up at him. "Thank you." I am embarrassed as I remember my teacher, but push the notes under my pillow. Paulo gives me a mock salute before he closes the door behind him.

I gather my soap and towel and go outside. Fill the basin with water. A cold wash will help. The bathroom has no roof; it is four pieces of corrugated iron leaning on each other. The floor is huge stones arranged so that water can seep down under them. The sun directly on my bare skin feels just right. This morning, the sun is gentle, and my sponge soaked with soap wakes and soothes every muscle and nerve. The sun and soap caress me everywhere that Paul did and I relive the night as its opposite: a fresh new day. I sing, "*Yesu*, light of my life..." and giggle as I squat to wash my not-so-secret and now swollen leaves of skin. I marvel at how tender and yet hardy they are. How resilient.

What should I do today? I muse with pleasure. I won't sit on the ground in the hot, dusty market guarding spread-out old clothes discarded by white strangers far away and now to be haggled over and thrown back in my face by stingy women. No. I will buy red nail polish from Mrs Oketch's store and paint my toes. And that face cream with a funny name: L'Oreal? I will throw out the boiled beans I made yesterday and go to Sonia's Restaurant behind the post office for lunch. I'll buy pork and chicken and that special sim-sim sauce she makes that goes so well with *posho*. After that I can wash it down with beer if I want. And I'll still have money left over. More than I make in a week. I pat myself dry and stretch my long, lean naked body to the abundant sun.

Doreen Baingana is a Ugandan writer currently living in the United States. Her short-story collection, *Tropical Fish: Stories Out of Entebbe*, was published in February 2005 by University of Massachusetts Press after winning the AWP (Association of Writers and Writing Programs) Award for Short Fiction in 2003. Ms Baingana also won the Washington

Independent Writers Fiction Prize in 2004, and was a finalist for the Caine Prize for African Writing in 2004. She has an MFA from the University of Maryland, and is their Writer-in-Residence. She is a member of FEMRITE, the Uganda Women Writers' Association. She swims like a seal.

Life Sucks... Sometimes

Jackee Budesta Batanda

Being Rasta:

THE MONEY MADE ME quit. Other dynamics could have made me
resolve that I wasn't carved for this job. It could have been the intern
trainee editor, Jackie, who, because of the locks flowing down my face,
asked me, "Are you Rasta?" Looking her in the eyes, I had
nonchalantly replied, "Just a fashion statement, sorry to disappoint
you." *Your frigging arse,* I didn't add because on day one at work, you
don't use curse words and in any case you're eager to please everyone
and smile at whatever baloney they utter. And she had pouted and said,
"Oh, now I don't like you. I thought you were Rasta." I had shrugged
my shoulders. We were seated at the new deep-beech-effect tables that
had been delivered that morning and hammered into shape, making
my mind muzzy listening to the hitting. The sun seeping in through
the brown vertical blinds made dark stripes on the tables. It was a large
one-roomed office where everyone saw your comings and goings and
even eavesdropped on your conversation – a staffroom in every sense.
Jackie sat on a grey high-back swivel chair (she had been here three
months); I sat on a green plastic garden chair. My swivel chair had not
yet been ordered.

"Really?" The grin on my face enlarged exposing my poorly set teeth.
My teeth were one of the things I would soonest change – given the
opportunity.

"I'm Rasta, yeah," she said. My eyes leisurely trekked from her talking
lips to her purple braids, and there was surely no sign of Rasta. Ras. Jah-
Bless. One Black Love. Whatever.

"Actually, I reeeaaally want to dread my hair, but I still live with my *Paros*," she continued.

"You don't have to be dread to be Rasta. This is not a dreadlock thing; it's divine conception of the heart," I counselled. Don't be fooled, not my creation. I just rolled off lyrics from some song by Modern Heritage that I heard eternally played on Capital Radio, *Kampala's Friendliest Station*.

She nodded, "Yeah, I guess you're right. Rasta is an inner thing." She paused and added, "Well, I have something Rasta." She showed me a coloured thread necklace draped in yellow, green, red and black, hanging round her neck.

"It's beautiful," I lied. I didn't give a shit about the Rasta necklace.

"You know my boyfriend has divine dreads. He's Rasta. And he speaks fluent Jamaican patois," she ended proudly.

"Great. Is he Jamaican?"

"No, he's Ugandan."

"Wow," I humoured her. "Did he grow up in Kingston or Brixton?" I asked, suddenly interested in this Ugandan guy who spoke patois fluently, according to the gospel by his girlfriend who was afraid to dread her hair until she fluttered from the parental nest called home.

"No," she said and quickly added, to placate my patent loss of interest, "He has lots of Jamaican friends here." And in the bloody twenty-five years I've lived in Kampala, I'm yet to meet a Jamaican. And shit, I didn't even know we had a burgeoning Kingston. The closest we've had to Jamaica, in my opinion, was when Sean Paul and Shaggy fortuitously performed at Speke Resort, Munyonyo, sometime this millennium.

"So what does he do, is he part of the Blood Brothers' Band?"

They were the only local reggae band I knew.

"He's a visual artist. You should meet him. You will like him!"

This Rasta wannabe didn't know that you just didn't invite another girl you only met 30 minutes ago to freely meet your boyfriend and assure her, 'you will like him'. Especially not this girl. In my other life, I had gained a reputation for snatching boyfriends or in more correct language, leaving a trail of haemorrhaging hearts, but that's not the story I'm chronicling today. Then she reached for her wallet and pulled out a coloured business card – yellow, green, red and black. Now why would anyone give you her boyfriend's business card? To show off that he has one? Why not a pic?

"I'd love to meet him someday," I said and we giggled, our laughter floated across the table, over the half partition to the editor.

"Soon as I complete campus, I'm moving out of home. I've already told my *mithe* about it and she's *kaawa*. It's my *fithe's* reaction I'm anxious about."

"You're above eighteen, he'll get over it." Hell, this was 2004.

"Yeah, I hope he does. You know he's very strict," her hands reached for my locks. "I really like them. I can't wait to dread my hair too. Yeah. Will you do it for me? Actually when I have a child, I'll twist his hair while breastfeeding him," she said dreamily. And I smiled and joined in her dream and saw her years later with locks, holding a dreadlocked baby. Even after this sweet vision, I was still reluctant to dread her hair. I did not want people walking around with my look. Especially real Rastas!

"Piece of advice," I interrupted our dream. "Join a dreadlocks discussion group on the net. You'll learn a couple of things."

"Yeah, that's brilliant," she enthused as if I had revealed to her a discovery worthy of winning the Nobel.

By the time she completed her Rasta fantasy and wanting to immigrate to Ethiopia, I was irritated. When she said, "Abyssinia is the cradle land of black people and I want to be buried there", I knew I had indulged her enough. Her ancestry was Kintu and Nambi, the first Baganda who dropped on Buganda from heaven and filled Uganda. You know all that first-man, first-woman bullshit. The Abyssinia thing didn't relate to her in my judgment. I closed my thoughts in my mind and avoided her from then on.

Les fausses raisons:

Another factor that made me quit my job could have been the four blasted weeks I spent being prostituted from computer to computer. So I spent my days in a mild frenzy as I struggled to get my edits in on time. The newspaper was started when senior reporters stormed out of a national paper to start a bi-weekly. It happened at a time when the newspaper industry was struck with panic. Reporters bounded from media house to media house. I followed the story in the confines of my room, savouring every luscious detail and decided to be a part of this exhilarating experience the Ugandan media would witness only once. And that's how my unfortunate arse landed here at a time when my mind was wondering what the hell to do with the dregs of my life. Considering the fact that the statistics in a previous edition of the *New Vision* had proudly screamed, 'Uganda's life expectancy rises to 47', I had already lived over half of my life and needed to do something useful with the remaining half before I became another digit added to the data computed by the World Bank, IMF, UNFPA...

I had zeroed down on this paper, updated my C.V. and decided I wanted to be an editor, to have control over articles from reporter wannabes flooding the editor's inbox, and in my grand high-back swivel chair, build and obliterate writing aspirations in their infancy, depending on my disposition. If all went well, it would have been wicked.

But something wasn't right. It was like I had landed in a balloon about to explode. I came to this deduction from the whispered conversations within the office, when the managing editor (M.E. we called him) was out. It felt like I was in a crammed elevator that would jam before reaching its destination. The wise thing was to depart before it actually got stuck.

Or I could have grown tired of watching M.E. for signs that he belonged to a cult, after a photojournalist had joked that the black and white rosary lying reverently on his desk was the same type used by the Kanungu cult members, who perished in the 2000 inferno. We had nervously laughed, looking behind our shoulders in case M.E. sneaked up on us. And for days, I had furtively watched him from the corner of my eyes and my computer screen for signs, and realising there was no news here, I probably got bored.

Or it could have been the way the reporters summed me up when I walked to my desk and sat at my computer without greeting anyone. You know days when you don't feel like exchanging pleasantries. I had many such days. I stayed aloof from their 'who is doing what' and 'where and when' sessions.

And behind my back they whispered, "Who does she think she is?"

Or it could have been Charlotte Max, the editor from England via Voluntary Services Overseas. She was brought in to put our editing in order. My guess was it was a plausible excuse to sunbathe in Africa at no cost at all. Hell, she did more mountain gorilla tracking, bird watching, bungee-jumping, kayaking, white-water rafting and touring national parks than editing. It was more like she had volunteered to sojourn in YuuGee, made famous on BBC and CNN for (in this order): HIV/AIDS, Malaria and the Schoolgirl-Abducting Rebel Bandits in the North. She could have been okay if she didn't fucking laugh after every three words she spoke. Laughing is tolerable if the voice is soothing, like camomile tea for menstrual cramps. I seriously wouldn't have minded Charlotte and her exasperating laughter, if she hadn't after one shitty lunch episode, pulled me aside and bloody asked one of the bloody photojournalists to take a bloody pic of us, leaning close, arms on each other's shoulders making a zebra stripe, grinning into the camera like we were best buddies, for a pic she would email her niece back home in Swansea, wherever that was.

A fucking sad story with lots of pain:
The money factor outweighed all the reasons. My editor, after an exhausting day, when most of the reporters had left and the office was cemetery quiet, sat me down and told me management had agreed to take me on.

"On six months probation though." That had not sounded bad, though we had previously agreed on two weeks probation. And I remembered my brother asking me whether I had discussed my terms and I had, in jest, declared, "No. I guess I'm the greatest fool that ever lived, huh, working without knowing my pay?"

"Didn't you go to Makerere?" he had queried.

"Actually the closest I got to Makerere was the gate, during my three year degree."

I watched my editor, across his desk in his high-back swivel chair with armrests, his hands stretched across the table like he was preparing to say the rosary, then grappling for a pen to scribble on a blank page, and waited for him to continue.

"Two weeks is a short time to judge someone and it would be unfair on you too."

Unimpressed.

"Yeah?" I chipped in.

"We shall pay you one hundred thousand a month," he ended.

"Shit! 100k?" I idiotically repeated.

Holy shit! I felt my face get hot like I had been slapped – like all the blood in my body had rushed to my face. Damn him! My first reaction was to slap him and walk away. But since I started yoga, I had learnt to control my emotions. However, the laughter escaped before I could push it back down my throat. Fuck, it chortled like an ancient train – you know the ones, still plying Kampala-Soroti carrying maize and beans, a legacy of our unsuccessful Uganda Railways Corp. And then I couldn't stop laughing. It was like the laughter was waiting to be released all this time I had worked here. My life stretched in front of me like a film clip. Forty-seven-years-life-expectancy. At 25, I wasn't getting any younger and six hundred thousand in six months was an insult. In the clip, I saw myself walking to work because I couldn't bloody afford the cheap taxi fare. The monthly salary wouldn't even buy me tampons let alone lingerie. I wasn't about to live a life so that someday some equally miserable playwright would stumble on my fucked-up sad story and write a crappy script on my wretched existence.

"That's what we pay beginners. But you can think about it," I think I heard him explain in response to my mirth.

I recall promising to think about it as I marched out the sliding door with no intention of returning. I remembered Charlotte's irksome laughter, immensely pleased that I wasn't going to suffer it another day and I smiled. I mean as bloody real a smile as I could conjure – the type that starts slowly as a twitch and blossoms like a morning glory. The first big smile in weeks and I felt my spirits rise from the abyss in my belly where they had taken refuge. Hell, she could keep the fucking pic she had promised to give me.

My smile led me along Kimathi Avenue to the Design Café – an al fresco restaurant on IPS building, speckled with Castle Lager *Africa's Finest*, yellow and brown parasols over the scattered white plastic tables... and chairs like the one I used at my now former workplace – where I had a soiree with my mates. I was late. Thirty minutes late because my left sandal had an incident – the insole and heel had separated, and because the Kampala sun had set, the cobblers that habitually sit along the pavements with little green boxes with inscriptions – 'Expert Shoe Shiner/Repairer' – had packed their wares and gone home. I was at a loss till I saw a newspaper vendor seated on the pavement with sweets, magazines, week-old newspapers and Orbit gum. I bought four packets of gum and chewed it, throwing the wrappers on the ground joining other sweet wrappers and papers, before spreading it between the insole and heel like margarine on bread, and comfortably walked off.

I was also late because I had strolled in loops trying to avoid the rendezvous because I was in no mood for chitchat. I just wanted to go back home, lie on my bed and invoke sadness (my idea was to listen to Sade and finish a whole bottle of YuuGee Gin). But my legs had still led me past our dull brown Parliament building to Kimathi Avenue past the towering glassy blue IPS. Sammy saw me and hollered my name. I turned sheepishly and traced my steps to their table, which faced the nearly inglorious Mayor's Gardens. I pulled a chair to join them; the waitress came running before I could say, "I've had a shitty day and no, I don't want to talk about it".

"What's your story?" Sammy asked in way of greeting.

Ignoring him, "Coffee. Your strongest, blackest coffee and a tot of YuuGee gin," I told the beaming waitress. I wanted to slap the smile off her face.

"Okay, the blackest coffee and YuuGee say something," Sammy teased.

"Give me a break," I snapped, "Someone has to promote the fucked up local industry. Make it two tots."

They were drinking imported Guinness.

"Damn! That hurt," Lumu sniggered.

And when my coffee arrived, it was precisely as I had requested. Again I managed another smile, pouring the YuuGee in my coffee; I sipped and savoured the acridity on my tongue.

"An idyllic way to celebrate joblessness…"

"Not again," Lumu interjected. "What the fuck happened this time?"

"Ah, man, chill. Mine is a fucking sad story without pain, you don't want to get bored."

"Come on tell us," Sammy cajoled. And I told them, exaggerating a lot in my response to my editor. I lied that I had banged the table hard, called him a sucker and told him that we would be doing each other a disservice working together and I wouldn't fucking stand for this 'Gaining Experience' bullshit. We were living in new times where exploitation was out of the question.

"I grabbed my bag, told him that their lunch sucked and stormed out."

I was enjoying this empowered version of the story. I felt like a Cosmo Woman.

"Go sister," Sammy shouted. "Burn the assholes down."

"Geez 100k per month?" Lumu sighed. "Now this is a fucking sad story with lots of pain," he added and ordered another round of Guinness and the strongest, blackest coffee and two tots of YuuGee for me and we drank to a fucking sad story with lots of pain.

Fed up with this shit hole:
When my editor called my cell, wondering why I bloody hadn't reported to work, I told him, "I'm trying to gain the impetus to get out of bed to make it." It was four blissful days since I had walked out with that smile on my face, glad that I'd be spared Charlotte's raspy laughter.

"You're acting unprofessional, especially now that you're on probation."

"Fuck the probation, I'm not coming to work anymore."

116

I liked this version best. I mean I don't know anybody who quits their jobs from the cosiness of their beds.

Later in the morning, I headed to a mate's house for 'a day of reflection', as we favoured to call it. It was a girls' thing. The threesome had one thing in common – we had quit our jobs and we were in transition – rethinking our lives. Kemi's living room was a diminutive square with one window filling half of the wall. It was plainly furnished with a large rug covering one side of the wall, an old rectangular shelf, which held seashells and a couple of books. A hi-tech stereo and more shells sat on the black trolley. A brown clock, which did not work, hung above the stereo. An old ceramic coffee table rested in the centre on the yellow carpet. As we sat curled in the brown chairs, we talked of our future plans.

"I've decided to relocate," Ssubi said.

"Cool. Where to?" I quizzed.

"Canada."

"That's the best bloody news I've heard this week."

"You know I met this Indian-Canadian who told me the Canadian Government had this relocation thing for immigrants. There are forms you fill in and all that."

"Isn't it a hoax?" Kemi popped in.

"The only hoax I know is people putting you on six-month probation for a bloody 100k and expecting you to work your arse off. That I say is a hoax. This Canada thing? It is celestial!"

"Seriously," Kemi insisted. "How sure are you that the suckers aren't con men?"

"Con men or not, life's about taking risks. You know that being Ugandan is a risk in itself?" I pointed.

"Guys, anyway, we need to think about it. There's lots of funding for people in the arts. I'm wasting my skills here. I mean look, what steps are in place for photographers in Uganda?" Ssubi asked.

"The only reason I'm with you on that is because I'm fed up with this shit hole called For God and My Country. Sometimes, I'm sure God gets pissed off at how we're treated," I added.

"What about saving the world?" Kemi asked.

"Moment of truth. I'm no longer interested in saving the world bullshit, whatever," Ssubi said. "Can you imagine, I go through moments budgeting what I'm going to eat during the week. Debating whether it's economical to buy a samosa or chapatti. There is no room for the world."

"Anyhow," I added, "the way to maintain our bloody sanity is to leave YuuGee and try our luck in Canada or wherever. YuuGee is a good place to live when you have the money, then you can live like royalty, until then, we need places which will boost our creativity. I'm totally in for this Canada thing."

Not my bloody tale anyway:

We – my brother and I – had dinner at my Uncle Tendo's crib. Ma's elder brother to be exact. I wasn't a sucker for those family get-together things (you met relatives you had last seen three years ago at a similar event and had to teeth and give them a detailed account of your bloody life like you were in the witness stand). They were normally a meeting of old cronies who are above YuuGee's 47-years-life-expectancy. He lived on Naguru hill; in one of those mansions you only see in copies of *House & Garden* lying at the British Council, with ornately maintained gardens, a long driveway from the gate to the house and the property protected by Falcon Security Guards with a white wooden board on the gate, 'THIS PROPERTY IS ELECTRONICALLY PROTECTED. TRESPASS AT YOUR OWN RISK'.

In red writing.

The only reason I agreed to attend the dinner when my brother called was because I had taken to cooking our meals since I quit my job. So it was the thought of free food that made me attend the insufferable dinner. Uncle Tendo always found reason to celebrate and I still can't remember what it was he was celebrating this time. As long as you were there and laughed at the right time, nodded and pretended to enjoy yourself, who the hell cared what the do was about?

We arrived a little late when everyone had settled on the rattan chairs with beige cushions on the terrazzo porch, which meant we had to greet and re-pump handshakes, teething all the way round. That's no problem if you're greeting five people. It becomes convoluted if the fucking number is close to thirty. Soft R&B music was playing in the background. Thank heavens it wasn't Lingala sounds, because one – Uncle Tendo would have interpreted the whole fucking song and two – I hate Lingala sounds. When we finally took our seats at the end of the row, one of my cousins – Uncle Tendo's thirty-something second daughter – looked me up and down like I was a new specimen and when she opened her mouth asked if I was my sister and smiled like she had asked the most intellectual question. *No, I am not my sister, arsehole.* I looked at her like I was seeing

118

her for the first time in years and realised how dumb she was. Whenever we met, which was often, I had to repeat my name to her. And my name is as simple as it gets. I was about to make a sharp retort, when it occurred to me that the bloody woman must be a slow learner. A very slow learner. And I was sorry for her. Empathy washed over me, and I sucked in my breath. Very slowly, for she might take long to understand my straightforward name, I told her my four-letter name and even spelt it slowly to be in sync with her understanding. Damn! I took a swig of my mineral water and reached for the crisps in the bowl.

Uncle Tendo called out to me to have a glass of wine.

"I'm in my bloody periods," I shouted over the music. "Wine increases my flow."

He laughed. An aunt, Ma's age gasped. I smiled.

Later a cousin hollered, "You're glowing. What's up?" and I cheekily replied, "The sky. I only glow after sex with my boyfriend and he's away." Ma gasped. She's from a generation where sex talk is a taboo and its details are only revealed on the night before the wedding by the bride's *Ssenga*. I knew she would go on and on about how I kept embarrassing her, "Imagine in front of all those people. Especially Uncle Tendo." Then she would sigh and roll her eyes in exasperation, wonder at, "The youth of today," and mutter to God, "What did I do wrong?" In her eyes, Uncle Tendo was the mahogany mantelpiece of integrity. He had taken care of us after our dad had travelled to Russia to study. Mum had taken two jobs to help pay for his education and look after three children. Dad repaid this by coming home with a Russian mistress. That's why I never told her that Uncle Tendo had recently secretly married a university girl in a traditional ceremony in the village. In any case, I was clearly a disappointment to her, save for the one time early this year, when I had had one of the frequent break-ups with my boyfriend and on Valentine's Day had taken her to Grand Imperial Hotel as my valentine and we had talked about her favourite subject, 'ALL MEN, EXCEPT UNCLE TENDO, ARE DOGS'.

We explored this theme over a sumptuous five-course meal, with red roses standing on our table, a live band and a whole waiter to ourselves for the whole evening, and we had ended the night dancing away in Ange Mystique. For those few hours her disillusionment with me, even her hypertension (caused by me) were utterly forgotten.

I watched Uncle Tendo's wife, my soon-to-be ex-aunt, running up and down making sure her husband's relatives were comfortable, keeping a steady flow of food and wines like she had done for the past forty years.

When a plate she was carrying fell noisily interrupting all conversation, I looked at her and had this awful feeling she knew. Our eyes met for a fleeting sec and in her's I read, 'I know that you know that I know he's going to leave me.' Dammnit! The bloody new Mrs Tendo girl had been my classmate at university. I dropped my gaze and concentrated on my water. It wasn't my bloody business.

Later Ma managed to get close to me before I could duck, "You didn't have to embarrass me like that. Not in front of Uncle Tendo," she whispered. This was after we had walked away with our plates laden with food from the large brown dining table in the hall where the buffet had been set.

"I didn't do anything Ma," I replied. I was in no mood for arguments. To quiet her, I added, "I quit my job."

"Why?" she asked surprised.

"I got bored," I answered indifferently.

"Now what are you going to do?"

"Nothing." I saw her roll her eyes and knew what was coming next. "Ma, I will figure something out soon."

Now I knew she would run mourning to Uncle Tendo about the youth of today having no respect for a good job.

Midnight Caller:

Since I quit my bloody job, and didn't have to explain to people, 'No I'm not Rasta', I could afford to lie awake late in my bed listening to *Midnight Caller* on Capital Radio. It was some sloppy show where insecure lovers called in and said, "Good evening DJ P. I want to know whether my boyfriend loves me. Please DJ call him up and ask him who sent the message."

The DJ went on, "Are you sure you're ready for the answer?"

"Yes," the miserable caller responded. It all sucked.

"Will you still talk to him, even if the name he mentions is not yours?"

"Just call him DJ P. I'm ready."

Then DJ P called up the boyfriend and said, "I'm DJ P from Capital Radio and I have a message for you." He played some sob love song and added, "Your girlfriend sent it to you. She wants you to mention her name and then talk to you."

And sometimes, the unfortunate bastard goofed and mentioned the wrong name. The only reason I lay awake in the dark and listened to

Midnight Caller was the DJ, not the insecure calls from his callers. You should have heard him give tips on love and lasting relationships like he was a goddamn expert on love. He was pretty fucked up in that area – he is the fucking bastard I had broken up with when I took Ma as my valentine. I listened to him, because I fell in love with his voice. It was the kind of voice that aroused you in moments of loneliness and awakened dead emotions. Sometimes I cursed him and fancied calling into the show like one of those sob callers and blasting him live on air. Dig that. But sometimes, I am a bloody sucker, and so I try not to sob when I feel the damn tears in my eyes when I realise I still miss the bugger so much.

Jackee Budesta Batanda was born in Kampala, Uganda. She was Africa Regional Winner for the Commonwealth Short Story Competition 2003 and was shortlisted for the Macmillan Writers' Prize for Africa 2004. She has also been highly commended for the Caine Prize for African Writing and Commonwealth Short Story Competition 2004. She is currently Writer-in-Residence at Lancaster University and General Secretary of the Uganda Women Writers' Association (FEMRITE).

Chief Jongwe's Funeral

Brian Chikwava

EVERYONE IN THE VILLAGE knew it. It had happened the week before. On a clear, blue Saturday afternoon, a little innocuous cloud came to squat over the Mudyambanje homestead. It shat two bolts of lightning. They struck the granary, destroyed bags of *rapoko*, maize and black-eyed beans, and killed six hens and a cockerel. Sekuru Mudyambanje, in his advanced age, had taken it all in his stride. He had emerged from his hut, and held his crusty hand over his eyes to protect them from the scorching sun. "You of the spirits of darkness. When I hurl my spear into your heart, you shall be exposed, and your badness shall spill into the earth," he had cursed. Then he shuffled to the granary where he studied the ruins with a severe face, tapped the earth with his walking stick and called out to his 15-year-old grandson.

"Tari my grandson. Bring me my spear, axe and knobkerrie. Please!"

Tari, who like everyone else had been hovering at a safe distance, is said to have run into his grandfather's hut and brought the said hardware. After that, what happened depends on who you hear the story from. Some say Sekuru Mudyambanje threw a pinch of his snuff at the remains of the granary, stabbed the earth with his spear, shook his axe and knobkerrie at the cloud and commanded it to take his spear back to its origin. Others say he threw his spear at the little evil cloud and it went back to its owner. Others say he got possessed by his most powerful ancestral spirit and hurled an incantation in an ancient language that no one understood. But what they all agree on is that the little cloud drifted to the Shambira family's homestead, lowered its pants, and squatting over their property let out a salvo of lightning bolts. A dozen cattle died. Sekuru Shambira, with his no less commanding age, is also said to have come out of his hut, gazed up at the sky and let out a deep sigh of resignation. Then he had gone out for a walk in the forest. No one dared follow him.

But now the District Administration's longest-serving chief, Chief Jongwe, had finally died after a long illness and the whole village was congregating at his home. There was a deep sense of unease among the mourners. Two distinct camps had emerged before the ceremony – one, under the big mahogany tree, surrounding Sekuru Mudyambanje, and the other, just outside the kitchen hut, loyal to Sekuru Shambira. Each camp was sipping and passing round the beer calabash, whispering and refining the sense of itself while affording each of its members the opportunity to realise how alike their thoughts were to everyone else's. How close they were to the truth. Those who were not comfortable being strongly identified with either movement smouldered with distress. Both camps were radiating high-intensity distrust towards them. Even dogs and cats smelt it and kept their distance.

"This Moyo family. Be careful with them. They may be eating from the same plate as the Mudyambanjes. Why else would they be bothering to leave us sitting here to greet Mudyambanje and his people?" Sekuru Shambira dispensed his wisdom.

"That's exactly what I was thinking," a disciple concurred.

"Yes," Sekuru Shambira nodded. "They say you can't bait fish with what they don't eat. Mudyambanje must be having something they have a taste for." Then he retrieved his snuff tin from his pocket, emptied a bit onto his hand. With his other hand he pinched a bit and held it up to his nose. The suction strength of his nose liberated the snuff from his fingers. He sneezed twice. Sekuru Mudyambanje must have already been in the thralls of his snuff's pleasure when Sekuru Shambira sneezed, because disciples turned their heads in suspicion. "He has figured out you are having snuff and is worried. He must be guilty. Otherwise why would he be having snuff at the same time as you," one of Sekuru Mudyambanje's faithfuls observed. Everyone else around nodded their heads in agreement. But Sekuru Mudyambanje waved his hand dismissively in a gesture of indifference.

"Snuff is one of the ways by which people protect themselves from bad intentions. Why would Shambira be rushing to protect himself if he's innocent?" someone queried.

Meanwhile Sekuru Mudyambanje had lit his pipe and puffed away contemplatively. He had unambiguously communicated his message to the entire village: you don't mess with me. His disciples were quietly jubilant that finally Shambira had met his match.

"Isn't he the one who struck the Shava family's home with lightning last season?" Sekuru Mudyambanje's camp recycled the rhetorical question.

"Yes, it's him. That's what the spirit medium MaMkhiza said. People also say he keeps a huge owl inside his hut."

"Ah well, this time it's not going to get him anywhere. You don't play around with the Mudyambanjes. These are not the kind of people to mess with. Sekuru Mudyambanje's father is said to have been a fierce man. He's the man the chiefs of his time used to send into the mountains to apprehend mad men who had become a danger to the village. And they say he used to go up there all alone, and would always come back with a subdued wild man." Simeon, a distant cousin of Sekuru Mudyambanje was spreading the word. Sekuru Mudyambanje continued to smoke his pipe, keeping an eye on Shambira's camp and trying not to be sidetracked by the flattery of his disciples. He didn't want to end up like Shambira, who he believed capable of making a drum out of his wife's skin to play his own praises. He was a Mudyambanje; the one who eats marijuana. That's not a clan to be taken lightly or mess with.

Then something extraordinary happened that afternoon: in the full glare of daylight a huge baboon casually strolled towards the mopane tree under which women were brewing beer and cooking for the mourners. It chased them away, and made off with half a pumpkin. For a brief period the deceased chief's closest relatives, who were separately wailing in the centre hut – the family's biggest hut – forgot about the dead chief. Something was clearly ominous. The chief's eldest son, who had temporarily taken a walk to the bushes just outside the homestead while the baboon incident unfolded, was suddenly needed by the bereaved family for an important decision. Angirayi, the late chief's teenage grandson, was ordered to go and fetch him. He didn't have to go far. The groans coming from behind a *muzhanje* thicket were enough for him to identify his uncle. "Babamkuru, you are wanted back in the centre hut," he apologetically dumped the message before racing back.

When Babamkuru went back to the centre house, he was informed of the bad omen that had befallen the family. The baboon was still on a tall tree a stone's throw away. It looked like it was intent on coming back for the second time. The decision that Babamkuru, as the new head of the family, had to make was whether someone should be sent to fetch MaMkhiza, the sangoma. Her arrival for funeral rites and to find out the cause of the chief's death had been planned for the following day. But things were not looking good. So Babamkuru decided MaMkhiza was to be sent for. He had made the decision with fairly decent quantities of both fear and despondency. But later in the afternoon this would descend into panic, because while he was busy making decisions, the hens had finally discovered the generous deposit he had left out in the bushes and were fighting over it. Anyone with a keen eye could have noticed that something was amiss: there was not a single hen to be seen roaming around. So when MaMkhiza arrived and was solemnly ushered to the middle of the centre hut, there was another matter to consult her about: the chief's eldest son had gone out in the bushes to pee and discovered that his shit from a previous excursion had been taken away. The family was concerned that the person who had bewitched and killed the chief must have let his goblins out on a rampage to bewitch the whole family.

MaMkhiza was a straight-talking, gentle and deeply respected old woman. She was a well-known spirit medium, people from all over the country came to consult her. She did not always have answers for everything ready, though, because when she was asked by the chief's family about the disappearance of the eldest son's waste she laughed briefly and clapped her hands with disbelief.

"Ah! Jongwe's children? What has got into you? Is that what you called me here for? To find your excrement?"

"No, we are sorry MaMkhiza. We were just asking. We look to you elders of the village for guidance," Babamkuru had said.

"Guidance on what? On what happened to your excrement?" MaMkhiza queried before continuing, "What if it has been eaten by one of the many dogs I've seen outside?"

There was an embarrassed silence. The matter was quickly dropped from the agenda and the consultation quickly moved to the baboon issue.

"The baboon approached the women at a leisurely pace, chased them away and took away some food," Babamkuru related the story. "We were all reduced to being mere spectators as the women abandoned their pots in a stampede. No one dared chase the baboon away," he said with a sombre face. MaMkhiza said the family had done well by not doing anything to the baboon because the baboon was now host to Chief Jongwe's spirit. He had come to say goodbye to his family and also to reveal himself to the person behind his death. That person was among the villagers mourning outside. She demanded that a ritual be performed to acknowledge the chief's visit and cleanse his home of evil spirits. Still up on the tree, the chief was keeping a watchful eye, unaware of the pandemonium he was causing. Normally Angirayi would have taken it upon himself to challenge the baboon. He would have excitedly shouted to his young brother: "Tom! Bring the catapult. Quick!" But under the circumstances and following MaMkhiza's advice, he knew the catapult was an unthinkable option. That it was unthinkable, he was certain, but did not quite grasp the reasons. He was happy to leave that to greater minds than his. Moved by fear and confusion, he would however later make a confession to his mother.

"I think it's that one-eyed baboon that always comes to steal food. I always shoot at it."

"Shut up!" his mother would censor him. "That is not the baboon you shot! Are you saying you now know better than MaMkhiza?"

Baffled by his mother's reaction he shut his mouth and wandered off for solitude. He was pitifully out of his depth and nothing was making sense. Something that MaMkhiza had said in the centre hut was continuously tumbling in his mind: *they say men with short legs should not try to jump over streams. They can't jump; they wind up as crocodile food.* He had vague notions of what that meant, but was sure that she had said those words soon after mentioning the lightning incidents that had occurred recently at the village. He also figured out there was a stream someone was trying to jump and that they could end up being food for crocodiles. Then he started to stealthily creep around the two groups of mourners checking out the relative lengths of Sekuru Shambira and Sekuru Mudyambanje's legs.

Outside the centre hut the two factions of mourners continued their murmurs of suspicion. They were not privy to MaMkhiza's consultation. But they had witnessed her cleansing ritual as she walked around with a black cow's tail spraying some concoction on each hut's roof. They had also seen her give the chief's eldest son four pegs made from a tree no one knew and instructed him to go and sink them on the ground at each corner of the homestead. These pegs would complete the family's spiritual defence system. After that the late chief's family had again congregated at the centre hut for MaMkhiza's concluding advice. Rumours that were trickling out to the mourners outside said MaMkhiza had promised she would come back the following day to help with the rites before the burial. But, when a rumour that MaMKhiza had pointed out that the person who was behind the chief's death kept an owl in his hut and will be exposed because the spirits of the village's ancestral sangomas were preparing for an assault on evil witchcraft practitioners and their collaborators, Sekuru Shambira's camp began to shrink. As the whirlwind created by the rumours around Sekuru Shambira gathered speed, it gradually chipped at his delegation, flinging its members off to their homes. Eventually Sekuru Shambira left with a handful of his faithfuls. He didn't even say goodbye to the late chief's family. Soon after his departure Sekuru Mudyambanje was invited into the centre hut by the bereaved family who were eager to have additional advice from him. It's only when Sekuru Mudyambanje finally came out of the centre hut to join his followers that the chief was seen saying goodbye to his family and going down the tree he had spent most of the afternoon on. It was interpreted as a good sign. The family's fortunes could be on the verge of a change.

Then as the west skyline turned copper red, a tiny cloud appeared on the horizon. It caused some considerable concern. Even the disciples who throughout the afternoon had been beer-driven to shovel praises on Sekuru Mudyambanje fell silent. There was no more of "...Oh the Mudyambanjes are not to be messed with. They can show you what you've never seen before: the snake's buttocks." This time there was a real sense that Sekuru Shambira may after all be the one who could show the entire village the snake's buttocks. But to everybody's relief the cloud quickly thinned out and dissipated in the atmosphere before going far.

Bats were just beginning to flutter about the darkness when Sekuru Mudyambanje decided to inform the chief's family that he was going to his home but would be back the following morning. A handful of people volunteered to accompany him, while the rest remained seated around the fire they had just lit under the mahogany tree. They were to spend the night around the fire and assisting with any chores the late chief's family required done. Masculine tasks like roasting meat. A few minutes after Sekuru Mudyambanje's departure an owl came to settle at the top of the mahogany tree and started to hoot. The party that had accompanied Sekuru Mudyambanje came back to find the fire under the mahogany tree deserted. They spontaneously scattered, each embarking on his own search for a member of the late chief's family on which they could dump their goodbyes and disappear.

"Angirayi, say goodbye to your father for me, I'm off. Tell him I didn't want to disturb him."

"Angirayi, tell your uncle I will be back tomorrow. Goodbye."

"Please tell your family I have to attend to other matters. I will however be back tomorrow."

When all but a few of the mourners had disappeared and the owl had flown away, Angirayi was left sucking his thumb, not sure which message to deliver to who and from whom? In his absent mindedness he slowly approached the mahogany tree where he stumbled upon quantities of deserted meat from the ox that was slaughtered that morning. He sat down next to the fire and started to enjoy his finding at a leisurely pace.

Brian Chikwava is a Zimbabwean writer and musician who is based in London. He was the winner of the Caine Prize 2004.

Tracking the Scent of My Mother

Muthoni Garland

MY FATHER WOOED MY mother in a 1200 Datsun pick-up that was sold so soon afterwards that it must have felt to her like a false promise. Senior-mother, his first wife, whose tight religious clothes constricted her breathing, had already borne him five daughters – Mercy, Charity, Faith, Hope and Grace.

His five acres grazed the River Sagana in Ihwagi, on the outskirts of Karatina, where the old Mountain-of-God loses its shadow. By day my mother tilled the land, and by night my father tilled her. She birthed me and my brother in quick succession.

While my brother scowled at us, or napped on a *khanga* under the shade of a *mugumo* tree, my mother and I washed the family's clothes by the banks of Sagana, whipping them against the rocks in a frenzy. If I held back, my mother was just as liable to ignore me as launch a slapping attack on me. She was difficult to predict.

She walked with eyes downcast and the sharp wedges of her cheeks on her broad face pointed to squashy lips that she constantly bit to bleeding. Her pleated dresses, passed on by Senior-mother, grazed her ankles. Still she hunched her body as though to further blur the curves. But when roused, my mother unfolded herself and it would come as a shock to realise she was as tall as my father.

After we'd spread the washing on large boulders to dry, we'd waddle into the depths, me naked, she in her billowing petticoat. We'd stretch our bodies in the water and drift with the current. Even during the rainy season when the rush of water hid the boulders that formed our boundaries, we'd dare the current to deliver us past the patchwork of tea, potato, maize and cabbage farms, past the facing ridges of Mukuruweini and Ithanga; beyond the old Mountain-of-God, and further west of the Yatta Plateau where Sagana became the crocodile-infested Tana.

Afterwards, I'd dry in the sun while my mother applied soap to her long damp limbs like a lotion. Tucking a *khanga* around her waist, she'd bare her breasts to feed my brother. After a while, I would take off to explore and determine the owner of the hidden eyes staring at us.

My half-sister, Faith, hid behind fig trees and wild-gooseberry bushes, and spied on us. When I caught her spying, she ran away. I chased her. I knew she wanted to steal my mother.

I remember the roar of water during the rainy season, and the rickety plank-and-rope bridge on which Nairobi City relatives swayed and groaned under the weight of the flour, sugar, Tree Top orange squash and Cadbury Cocoa they brought us that last Easter.

They had to park their car on the other side of the river under a roughly constructed awning of sisal sacking. While the men slaughtered a goat in a distant clearing, the women pounded *mukimo*, gossiped about the latest city fashions – flares and curly-kits – and practised rolling out sentences in the nasal English-English spoken by my cousins.

After the feasting, the men meandered off to baptise a half-drum of *muratina*, or in the words of Uncle Erasmus, "To partake of the fruit of the hog-dog tree, otherwise known as Kigelia Etiopica."

My father had never been to school because, in the old days when leopards and buffaloes roamed, at least one son remained behind to herd the goats and cattle. Uncle Erasmus, a lecturer at a private university in Nairobi, always made the effort to visit and advise us. In his presence, my father chewed his *mswaki* stick to curtail his tongue, but when Uncle Erasmus was gone, my father said, "Life speaks in proverbs; anyone who is intelligent will understand."

Seventeen-year-old Cousin Wangui's stellar KCSE results punctuated her mother's every other sentence. Nobody complained when Wangui slipped a cassette into father's player, tied a *khanga* around her hips, and wriggled to the spiky notes of Congolese Lingala as though attacked by red ants. Of course, I joined her and discovered that, even at six, my limbs were looser than hers.

My mother hovered on the fringes of the group, and her darting eyes kept lighting on me. She laughed that afternoon for all of Karatina, but the hollowness in her tone confused me. I didn't realise then that my mother was only four years older than Wangui. I didn't understand that a woman who gives birth is like a tall and leafy banana tree that breaks under the weight of its own fruit.

I also remember the roar of water during the rainy season, and the rickety plank-and-rope bridge, because it was there a couple of years later that I pushed Faith into Sagana's rushing waters. It was not my fault that she had never learnt to swim.

There must have been a time when earnings from tea and four grade cattle were good because my father's house, a rectangle with three rooms, was built with cemented bricks. The verandah, whose sloping roof darkened the rooms inside, served as his lounge and observation point. Sun glinted off the roof, but when it rained the *rat-at-tat* hammered the corrugated-iron sheets, and later, water would sneak its way in through rusted corners. When we looked up during bible meetings, I wondered if the echoes of our deafening prayers for wealth – we were already rich in spirit – would lift the room and float our house to the sky, or if patched gaps in the ceiling would leak their potency.

Senior-mother insisted that, along with her disciplined five, my brother and I attend these services, while my mother tended to more practical demands like cooking.

The mud and cowpat orphan of a kitchen squatted by itself in the furthest reaches of the compound. Stabbing *mukimo* with a wooden spoon by the fire, my mother hummed funereal hymns, "*Woii, woii gugika tia ati ninia datigwo.*" Oh dear, what will I do now that I'm the one left behind. I'd sit by her feet on the hard-packed earth and root out jiggers from her toes with the sharp nib of my father's penknife while she wept. The tears and wood-smoke reddened her eyes, and the stale smell lingered and stiffened her hair, but her singed shins gleamed.

Twanging the elastic on our catapults, my brother and I went hunting for birds. We liked to collect the long dark feathers of widow bird tails. My brother followed me, and sometimes drove me crazy by claiming he'd downed my bird. No matter how much I hit him, he'd state, "I shot it" as though declaring a fact made it true.

When a bird dropped, we'd watch it crazily flap or rotate on an injured wing. I cut the neck with the penknife stolen from my father, and plucked off the feathers, gutted the stomach, and cooked the bird in a Blue Band tin over a three-stone fire. We'd munch the meagre mouthfuls of meat, and also crunch and swallow the bones.

As the river of practical demands – for meat, school fees, clothes, cotton wool – rushed its course, the veins on my father's forehead throbbed like rustling snake hatchlings. He regularly visited Sagana Co-operative Society and Kenya Co-operative Creameries and The Co-operative Bank of Kenya to beg for his tea and milk dues, and to negotiate for fertiliser, school fees and tide-me-over loans.

When the chairman of the former, in the Nyayo grabbing tradition of his predecessors, emigrated to South Africa with all the proceeds of the 1988 tea auction, my father broke. That night, and every night for six days, while Senior-mother wailed and beseeched God to let her know how they were going to feed and educate Mercy, Charity, Faith, Hope and Grace, my father cut down every tea bush. He said, "Where there is a shortage of figs, don't birds survive on the bitter fruit of the *mugumo*?"

Senior-mother appealed to the Extension Officer when he brought a red tractor to plough the farm because my father wanted even deeper roots uprooted. From his shrug and the eyes he widened at Senior-mother, I sensed the Extension Officer sympathised with her plight. But he cranked the tractor when my father said, "Nobody regrets what he leaves, only what he does not find when he comes back."

When my mother stopped working on what became a maize and potato farm, her new happiness was as fascinating and unfathomable as my father's proverbs.

She'd plonk herself on a stool in the shade of the compound and thrust in my hands a broken wedge of mirror. Peering into it as though she were a stranger to herself, my mother would style her thick hair using a pick with several missing teeth, and scold me in an indulgent voice for dancing from one foot to the other.

The volume of Senior-mother's complaints and prayers increased as Mercy, Charity, Faith, Hope and Grace dropped in and out of school due

132

to lack of fees. My father sold the cows but the money never lasted. Eventually Mercy left school altogether to work as a maid for an Indian family in Thika. Soon after, Charity eloped with the Extension Officer.

Against the background of Senior-mother's prayers and wailing, my father observed my mother's preening from his verandah perch, and concluded, "Two wives are two pots of poison." But he'd then descend and yank my mother by the hand to his room to taste her brand of poison.

I'd stop sweeping the compound and run to our room – the middle one in the line of three that before our time had served as the sitting room. When important visitors came, like the pastor during bible meetings, the stiff and cracking black plastic sofa and its matching chair squashed against the wall, still served their duty.

I'd lie on the Vono mattress, stained with my brother's urine, on the bed we normally shared with my mother. I'd close my eyes, my knuckle rubbing my mound to the squeaking of my father's iron bed behind the wooden door. I'd listen past my father's grunts and the slap of bare skin to hear my mother's gasping.

By twisting my ear, my mother encouraged me to scramble up the overgrown climbers that grew wild on border fences, to fill a *debe* with wrinkled purple passion fruit. We gouged out the phlegmy insides with spoons she bent into shape for the job, and sieved the black seeds from its dense juice. My mother added water and stirred in the tumeric powder that my half-sister Mercy had brought home on her day off, to intensify the yellow colouring.

Four miles into Karatina we walked, with plastic containers balanced on our heads like Luo women. Trailing behind her, neck throbbing too much to turn, my eyes traced the rise and fall of my mother's big buttocks. I was conscious my eyes were not alone in this enterprise.

At the sausage and chips shop, a Mkorino with a white headscarf tied low on her forehead sniffed the juice and accused us of either diluting it or using unripe fruit. She added that while she didn't want to be unreasonable, only God knew that the cost of the sugar needed to sweeten the juice would leave her with nothing.

Using a handkerchief drawn from the depths of her bosom, my mother wiped the sweat from her forehead, and let her towering silence do its work. My father would have said, "One keeps silence with people one does not like."

With the proceeds my mother bought me a Fanta. I sipped it while a hairdresser in Veeginia's Hair Salon cooked my mother's head with chemicals.

At the sight of my mother's shiny curls and their insinuation of foreign ways and squander, words failed my father. He attacked her on the iron bed in his room.

With my collection of widow bird tail feathers, I bribed my brother to take off his clothes and lie on top of me to listen to my mother's gasping.

A different type of gasp alerted me to hidden eyes spying on us. I pushed off my brother and chased Faith all the way to the bridge. She was fourteen to my nine, but her attention was divided between her fear of the swaying bridge and my angry kicking. I jumped up and down vibrating the rope with my hardened palms while Faith cried, "For God's sake, why do you want to kill me?"

When she tumbled over, only a flash of her thin legs flailing under her long polka-dot skirt appeared in my view because the bridge was rocking. Clutching the rope, I glued my eyes on the facing ridges of Mukurweini and Ithanga, and the snows of the old Mountain-of-God until the bridge and the hammering in my head were still again.

I vomited every time my frowning father, or crying Senior-mother, or location chief, or sub-chief, or policeman questioned me about Faith. My mother rocked me on her lap, and wiped my mouth. My brother went to see them investigate the scene, test the planks and ropes of the bridge, study the boulders and rushing waters. But I burrowed into my mother, until the policeman in his blue, shiny-button uniform concluded that Faith, in the careless ways of children, had died playing on the bridge with me, that it was a most unfortunate accident.

The turbaned pastor from the New Deliverance Church led the service for Faith's funeral, but Senior-mother insisted that nobody had ever seen Faith play with me, and refused to let me, my mother or brother attend.

My father bought my brother a uniform and found him a place in the New Deliverance Church Primary School. When I asked, "And what about me?" my father said, "One clears the bush, the other eats from it."

So my mother twisted my brother's ears and instructed him to teach us. We could soon sing, 'ABCD-el-emu upto zee', and 'Inky-pinky-ponky. Father had a donkey...' I also learned to read, 'See Rabbit Run'.

I never again beat up my brother, and when I shot a bird, I let him claim it.

After another Luo-style walk balancing passion juice on our heads, my mother bought herself some bangles from a street hawker, and Hairglo Curl Activator Gel. She rubbed it into her hair to fluff out the curls. Jangling the new bangles, she placed the gel in the paper bag and pushed it towards me along with a shilling, and instructed me to wait for her by the Ihwagi turnoff.

On the main Nyeri-Karatina-Nairobi road that sliced through the centre of town, *matatus* kicked up dust and clamour as they spilled over the verges to avoid potholes. Lurking behind a red phone booth, I watched my mother remove the *khanga* from around her waist to reveal a flowery skirt I thought I'd never seen before. On longer scrutiny, I realised she'd chopped off the ankle-inches and removed the pleats.

Drawn to the Congolese *katika* music twanging from within Three-In-One Bar, Restaurant and Lodgings, she lingered on the threshold. Two schoolgirls, sweaters tightened around their buttocks, emerged from a Peugeot 405, and were escorted in by a man in a large cowboy hat and another man who looked like the location chief. My mother tightened her belt and slipped into the bar behind them.

Three hours later, my mother staggered to the stage, slurring, "Where are you my daughter?" and jerking her finger at onlookers, "Inky-Pinky-Ponky, your father he is a donkey!"

I wanted to hide from the sniggers of sweat-stained farmers, and the pitying glances of market women on their way back home with empty baskets, but my mother fell. Her legs splayed out from her like the vee of a catapult.

As the clicking of tongues and wagging of heads and scandalised comments turned into curses, my mother laughed. This changed into a braying sound that broke off after each long gulp of breath, changed pitch and rose to a scream.

People shuffled back, sniffed the air in exaggerated fashion, staring at her as though she'd turned into a gorilla right in front of them. Ripples of "*Ngai Fafa!*" "What is that smell?" and "*Haiya*, Devil Worshipper..." tainted the dusky air.

When my mother quietened, I held her hand and guided her into the *matatu*.

Drivers never refused to carry her. In fact they'd insist we sat in front, with my mother in the middle. As her pale-yellow thighs came into view, the temperature in the vehicle rose. I'd fidget. When I couldn't stand it anymore, I'd pretend to be jogged by bumps, and place the paper bag of Hairglo on her lap.

My mother would somehow brush it to the floor. And old Gakuru, who could barely see over the wheel, or Muriuki, with his brown teeth and severely receded hairline, and even Nehemiah, who preferred to speak in English because his wife taught at my brother's school, would flash me triumphant looks. A wonder none of the vehicles veered over the banks of the parallel Sagana!

As we neared home, my mother punctuated the country music playing on the cassette stereo with her own sorrows:

"I took the diamond ring you gave me and threw it way out in the sea," Skeeter Davies sang.

"Shu-a-ray, this is too mush," my mother moaned.

"And I had this awful feeling." Skeeter countered.

"Enough is enough," my mother cried.

"That's just where I ought to be."

"Braaday herro."

My father wasn't normally a loud or violent man, but the chest contains a beehive full of pride. His flailing arms greeted us the moment we emerged at the bridge. He shouted that neither my mother, "…drunken prostitute and Devil's messenger…", nor her useless daughter would ever leave the farm again.

My mother shielded me with her body and urged me to run, run away, before unfolding herself to turn the attack on him. They fought all the way to his room, and all night their wrestling rumbled the ground.

The next morning my mother was gone.

My father didn't look for her. He sat on his chair on the verandah, chewing a *mswaki*, staring at the spot where my mother once styled her hair. Sometimes he lit his eyes on me, but he said nothing.

Later, he'd cough a lot. At the clinic, the doctor told him he suffered bronchitis. But I suspected my father was either emptying his chest or choking on the memory of my mother.

Senior-mother said that my mother probably fell into the river, floated away to where the Sagana became the Tana, and where, God help her, she was most likely consumed by crocodiles. My half-sisters Hope and Grace said that I would now come back to earth, as though I'd flown off it in an aeroplane like the one we'd heard delivered Cousin Wangui to America.

To distract my brother who now urinated in bed every night, I read him his '*Hadithi za Abunuasi*' books. Even though I had not yet been to school, my brother relied on me for help with his homework.

Tracking the scent of my mother, I crisscrossed the streets of Karatina, but noone claimed to have seen her, not even in Three-In-One, or Veeginia's Hair Salon, or the Mkorino woman's sausage and chips shop. I wandered as far as the ridges of Mukurweini and Ithanga, and shading my eyes, scanned the Mountain-of-God and westwards to the Yatta Plateau squatting on the horizon.

I described her, layer upon layer like the topographical contours I'd later cover in school, even though forming the words caused me pain. It forced me to see her as another, separate and different from me. To basket-weaving market women, and bushy-haired men, and bent tobacco-chewing old people, shiny-buttoned policemen, vaselined schoolgirls, bow-tied waiters and loud *matatu* touts, I said, "My mother is tall. Her skin is the soft yellow of mashed cooking bananas, and her lips are tinged with pink. She has big breasts and hips and buttocks, but when she tightens her belt, her waist is narrow. Muscles bunch up in her calves like isolated potatoes, but her legs are slender. Unlike Cousin Wangui, my mother's voice trips over certain letters, but it is rare. Her hair is in the latest curly-kit fashion. She likes beads and bangles, and the itchy music of Congo. But the Western music makes her cry."

I discovered that, in a house full of women, motherless children often sleep hungry. Sometimes food brought with it diarrhoea. Once, broken glass in water cut my tongue. But when a snake appeared in the bed I shared with my brother, and Senior-mother cried about the invasion of Evil Spirits in her house, and brought the New Deliverance pastor to cleanse us, it dawned on me that I would have to halt the search for my mother.

Even then I sensed that beauty and truth are the privileges guaranteed to bite themselves in time. At eleven, wasn't I as enticing as an almost-ripe mango, firm to the touch yet yielding, and bursting with juiciness inside? Wasn't my skin Ambi-light and Johnson's powder soft? Didn't my breasts shout, "Hello, Hello" from across Mukurweini ridge to the facing ridge of

Ithanga? Wasn't my back straight and my legs strong from ploughing the land of my father? When I crossed the Sagana, didn't the frogs croak, "Kairitu, but you're beautiful, Kairitu, but you're beautiful!"

I was hoeing my father's fields one dusty afternoon, glad to be away from Senior-mother and her twin chorus, when my father came to work his *jembe*. He hammered it into me, then twisted and turned over my ground. He hurried away to hide in his room.

It took me a long while to stagger to mine, and on the way the twins glared at me like I was faking pain to get off from digging. Senior-mother smelled the air and disappeared into the kitchen. It was not yet dark when she knocked on my father's wooden door to deliver him his food. He ignored her.

"Jesus Christ!" She beat her head against the door. "My house is falling."

I lay on my bed, the rags from my mother's cut-off skirts soaking up my bleeding, and vomited. Nobody came to wipe my mouth.

It took me three days to decide that, if this is what had to happen, I would milk its truth to feed mine. On my mother's spot in the yard, I styled my hair and taught my eyes to flutter promises.

So my father ploughed a pliant daughter, gratefully and repeatedly slithering his sperm into my bitter receptor. In turn, he enrolled me in school with money earned from Senior-mother's, Hope's and Grace's maize and potato digging. And my father said, "The offspring of a leopard scratches like its mother."

On weekends I resumed the search for my mother. I came home with meat that everybody ate, and it dulled the volume of their complaining. I let the *matatu* drivers plough me – Muriuki with his stained teeth, English-speaking Nehemiah, whose wife now taught me in school, and even wiry old Gakuru. For two years, I let them plough me until Nehemiah finally confessed that he'd driven my mother one early morning.

Such a meticulous man was Nehemiah. Exactly three and a quarter miles between my home and the homestead of his teacher-wife and children, he'd wedged his *matatu* into the bushes at such an angle that no glint of it could be seen from the road. He'd collapsed the rear passenger seats, folded his clothes, and cushioned the floor beneath our naked bodies with a Raymond blanket.

Like pebbles cast in water unaware of the ripples or even the depth they'd sink, Nehemiah's English words landed.

That on their way to Nairobi, he'd stopped to fill his *matatu* at the Shell BP station near the River Chania in Thika. That she'd slipped away and when he'd caught up with her crossing the bridge near the Blue Post Hotel, she'd waved him away despite his pleas. That he'd sat in his car in the parking lot only to see her disappear with a cowboy-hatted man who drove a white Peugeot.

Though there was a measure of guilt in his voice, Nehemiah insisted that he'd only done what she wanted, and that if I continued to be good to him, he'd do the same for me.

How was I to swallow the words of a man who'd helped steal my mother? Gooseberries raised their heads on my naked flesh. I had to snatch breath in tiny sips. Later when I read about the slave trade, I recognised how ancient my anger, but at the time, I rustled in my clothes, and drew out my father's penknife.

Perhaps it was shame or shock or fear, or just too dark for him to see, but all Nehemiah did was tremble as I unfolded my body to slash his caratoid artery.

I was not even suspected for Nehemiah's murder.

When I passed my primary school certificate with top grades the same year as my brother, my father wasn't that pleased because secondary school for us meant a sharp increase in fees, and reduced the opportunities for his ploughing. From his coughing I also sensed he feared I'd disappear from him. But he sold an acre of land because having a bone to lick is better than having to gather up limbs in hunger.

In my third year of secondary school, I gave birth to my daughter. She was retarded, of course, being that she was my father's.

With her suspicions confirmed, Senior-mother beat her flustered wings to spread the gossip. Her disciples spread the Word and it multiplied.

When the elders and the location chief and his sub-chief and the shiny-button policeman came to mediate over the matter, I refused to talk.

I could deal with my father's renunciation of me as though the incestuous devils had only plagued me. I could deal with being thrown out of home with my blank-face daughter as though the sight of us reminded them of their own vulnerability. I could stomach the spitting and hissing at the market where I tried my hand at hawking, my daughter drooling on the *khanga* next to me. After all, retribution dates to the beginning of time. And weren't these the biblical weapons of condemnation by a mindful, church-going public eager for me to exit their domain?

If I sound bitter, it's only because this bend on my road had delivered another surprise. My daughter moved her toothless mouth to gurgle at the sky in crooked ways, and her tender limbs spasmed. But she so intensified the scent of my mother that I sometimes fainted with gratitude and yearning.

It was Uncle Erasmus who finally said, "What a waste of a good brain," and used his connections to find us a home. We moved into the mission of Our Veiled Sisters of Mercy. Why should I have been surprised that so many teenage fruits of incest, homelessness, and murder incubated in this home of red brick and hard-waxed floors, heavily decorated with sacramental votives, crosses and candles? After all, what girl walks freely wherever and whenever she wants?

Of course we wore pious faces for the nuns, and they in turn taught us skills. With my daughter beside me, I learnt to sew and bake and even took mechanic classes. Two years later, I departed with a KCSE certificate and a just-in-case paper in my hand that declared me a competent maid, mechanic or wife-in-waiting.

A flat, wide space existed between the dark, expressive islands of my daughter's eyes. Her face was broad and brown, her head as thickly haired as my mother.

Only I understood her, but not all the time. It was as though she kept losing words, and the more formed the thoughts, the more the words escaped. Despite my encouragement, she could barely string three together.

Trying to capture the depth and breadth of her thinking, my daughter's hands flapped like the wings of captured widow birds. I sensed how beautiful her wordless thoughts, how sophisticated. I frustrated her most when I was closest to understanding, and she broke things or hit me.

My daughter needed help to express herself and soothe her body, so I begged Uncle Erasmus for more help. He raised the funds through a family harambee to put me through a teachers' training college. Most of the money came from his daughter Wangui in America, but even my born-again father contributed.

A Luo lecturer from Maseno, rubbing his steel-wool hair on my breasts, claimed my smell intoxicated. He added that his passion was psychological, not just a physical feeling. When I laughed he frowned, and invited me to 'Come-we-Stay'. And since lightning didn't strike at the same place twice, he added, he'd accept my child, and expected me to bear him many children. He was a stout man who drank too much Pilsner Lager, but spoke with the assurance of one used to being heard. So I heard him.

I enrolled my daughter in St Clementine's Boarding because the headmistress explained that, while I should not expect miracles, my daughter was not an idiot just mentally challenged.

I'd already confessed the bitter portions of my background, but my Luo man began to sulk over my missing pregnancy as if I'd deliberately misled him. In fact, he'd often asked me to repeat details, and had once concluded that my history served as a tragic metaphor for Africa just before he turned me over to plough me.

I offered to leave him because of this sulking. He replied that it was too late as I'd clearly applied on him a powerful *mganga's* concoction that bound us.

But that was not the reason I followed him to the lecturer's dining room hiding a knife in my sleeve. I found him bowed over a bowl of tomato soup, white bread and a Pilsner Lager on the side, and slashed his neck.

My daughter's school had called to find out when we expected to send a payment. Using his commanding voice to convince them of his good intentions, my Luo man collected my daughter from school. In our two-bedroom house, he sat her on a dining-room chair and stared at her until she'd vomited on herself.

When I arrived she was gurgling at the ceiling. As I tried to gather her and wipe her mouth, my Luo man prodded my stomach. His words reminded me of my father, "It seems a dried-up tree cannot bear a green one."

I took my daughter back to school in a hired taxi, where I told the clear-spoken headmistress the version of the story that I thought most likely to secure the padlocks of the school-gate in future.

Then I returned to seek my Luo man because I feared what might happen. And I killed him because, despite the intimate things he knew that bound us, he terrified my daughter.

When she heard the news, the clearly spoken headmistress contacted the Legal Aid for Women (LAW). The LAW arranged for my legal defence. But on the wings of my brutalised history, they also wanted to raise awareness of the terrible plight of the girl child, and the issue of domestic violence.

"As a representative of over 300 000 teachers in the country," said a tired-looking lawyer in a striped suit, though I was yet to qualify in that profession, "your voice is bound to cause ripples, and furthermore, the publicity will help your defence."

"You are to be admired, after all," added her colleague who wore a maroon suit, "because instead of taking the easier route of abortion, you took on the burden of mothering your –" she'd coughed at this point to delicately swallow the word 'father's' "– baby."

But to the microphones and photographers, the interviewers and lookers-on, I appealed for news of my mother. I said, "My mother is tall. Her skin is the soft yellow of mashed cooking bananas, and her lips are tinged with pink. She has big breasts and hips and buttocks, but when she tightens her belt, her waist is narrow. Muscles bunch up in her calves like isolated potatoes, but her legs are slender. My mother's voice trips over certain letters, but it is rare. Her hair is in the latest curly kit fashion. She likes beads and bangles, and the itchy music of Congo. But the Western music makes her cry."

I wondered about the accuracy of my description – maybe she had changed – because when I said these words, people looked at me without answering. Their eyes searched me up and down, and then lingered on mine as though puzzled that I could not see the answer.

Perhaps I landed in Kamiti because of the confusion that followed this publicity. Every time I emerged from the back of the police Land Rover during the trial, people pointed, sniffed, hissed, or kissed the air at me. Even in court, Judge Kipketer kept banging his gavel to restrain the commotion.

Listeners called in on Citizen and Capital and Kameme FM to comment on my story. Some said I was desperate or unfortunate. Some said the publicity was a clever ploy to avoid the price for murder. Women said it was unjust that men got away with rape and defilement. Men said women should not equate rape with murder. Kikuyus said it proved nothing good resulted from consorting with an uncircumcised Luo man. Luos cried for my blood to avenge theirs. But the only comments that hurt my ears are those that said I had no mother.

In my years lived amongst the condemned in Kamiti prison, I've read every letter sent to me by the clearly spoken headmistress who said that the lawyers of LAW had raised the funds to keep my daughter in school.

Sometimes I ask myself, what if my mother had not run away, what if my father hadn't raped us, and what if my daughter could speak clearly. I even ask whatever happened to Mercy, Charity, Hope and Grace. But then I realise that this pondering is just as useless as the question my Luo man in college asked in his examination paper, 'How might Africa have developed if white people had never appeared on the scene?'

Or the questions they asked in those interviews arranged by the suited lawyers – "Why do you seek your mother? At what cost?" and, "If you find her, what will you do with her?"

When they bring my daughter to visit, the prison guards shake their heads at the tremors of her body and her drooling. They look away. But with every visit, my daughter so intensifies the scent of my mother that I sometimes faint with gratitude and yearning. That's when a foolish thought visits – I wonder if my mother is hiding in her. She giggles when I tickle her armpits and back and buttocks searching for my mother.

After I tickle her, she sits on the floor opposite me. Her hands flutter less and the islands in her eyes reflect deeper. She grasps my elbows, her body jerking only a little, searching to see if I understand her meaning. Gooseberries raise their heads on my naked flesh. I have to snatch breath in tiny sips because when I look inside her eyes, we're floating on the Sagana, she naked, me in a billowing petticoat, daring the current to deliver us past the facing ridges of Mukuruweini and Ithanga; beyond the old Mountain-of-God, and further west of the Yatta Plateau where the Sagana becomes the crocodile-infested Tana. In my fear I thrash, but she grips me hard as we return again and again to brave the crocodiles of the Tana.

Muthoni Garland lives in Nairobi. She won a BBC award for a short story in 2002 and was published in the first issue of *Kwani?*

Transition

Muthony wa Gatumo

SOMEONE IS YELLING and banging at the door.

"Kamau! Kamau!"

My dad? *Ai*? *Kwani*, what's happened? Who wants my dead dad?

The door opens and out comes a burly figure, dressed in a magnificent navy-blue uniform. A cap with embroidered golden wings sits above the fat round face.

"Kamau! The captain and the rest of the crew are all in the Crew Coach downstairs waiting for you!"

Ohh-o! Someone is addressing me by my surname! And it's the Flight Purser, boss of any Inflight Crew, who is doing all that yelling.

It's also 0500 hrs GMT, and exactly two hours before our flight back to Nairobi takes off.

In twenty minutes time, I should be all showered and dressed up and flashing a permanent 10 000 watt smile – at least – at a crew of passengers of very different degrees of sophistication and persuasions, on board flight KQ 120J.

Two hours ago, one of the people at the Front Desk at the Holiday Inn Heathrow or Intercontinental Hotel Zurich or Athens, and I can't even remember where else, tried to place a wake-up call to my room *lakini wapi*, nothing happened. So here I am now inside my very worst nightmare possible.

I awake with a start.

Hot sweat is streaming from my body and soaking the bed.

How I dread these nightmare-causing early morning flights! I think to myself.

My mind's eye zooms around the darkened room, sensing the multi-channeled giant screen telly on the gleaming mantelpiece, the mini-bar with miniature liquor bottles. Beer. Chocolate bars. Nuts... At the furthest end stands the electric kettle. Nescafe and Nestle hot chocolate, Chamomile and Fruit 'n Spice herbal teas. Instant soup. Sugar. Milk. Biscuits...

On one beige wall rests a perfect Van Gogh replica, next to a Joan Miro print of bold black strokes crisscrossing a splashed, sprinkled and scribbled rainbow.

But in the very next instalment of that very same second? My wide-open eyes catch a glimpse of the illuminated radio clock blinking the real time at me.

2.35am, 2.35am, the clock mocks.

5 years later in Nairobi, Kenya.

A Pentecostal choir of dogs howl at distance. Cats play bitch, cursing. A horny mosquito decides to seduce me...

Damn! Now I'll have to get up and kill that blood-sucking mini vamp, because malaria's just too dear a disease to have in these days of inflation and 'very bad economy'.

Aiee! I try to move and my spring bed squeaks and squeals like rats on heat, the paper-thin mattress dipping, curving and curling with every movement made. I land on the ground with a thud and blindly feel my way to the electric switch surrounded by the snores, vinegary human gas, plus French-accented sleep-talk of my sleeping roommate Aminata The Lovely.

"Ma! Njeeri! He was reech!"

This is how Aminata usually greets me each morning.

"A beautiful man! A white! Reech!"

Aminata then swans around our 12' by 12' room; dancing around the small iron table and two wooden chairs between identical camping beds that all stand on a crackling vinyl carpet. "We go to dis 'otel... Beautiful! Biiiiig! With a lot of *mzungu* man, yo!!"

Unlike me, Aminata never has nightmares about her past. She's always engaged in fantastic movie-like dreams that always end up with her riding off in a stretch limousine towards the setting sun, accompanied by a super-rich white dude. Reeech!

I kill mosquito Dead. Knock, knock. Who's there? Amos. Amos who? Amos Kito... Sorry Amos Kito, I say to the tiny red smear on the wall.

145

Other spots and similar smears decorate our room. Like greasy fingerprints from myriad past lodgers. Strands of reddish blonde synthetic hair flapping on peeling brown paint. Something black. Something purple. And something else yellowing green for which tissue paper was surely invented.

Then cockroach.

Bigger than ones that get blended together with centipedes, grade worms and beetles the size of Brazil, into some smoothie from hell, in that popular TV programme called *Fear Factor*, where the drinker of the horror soup eventually gets to win $100 000.

However, my attention is not one hundred percent on the goliath roach. It's totally focused on the table and Aminata's loaf of bread, plus the Blue Band margarine beside cutlery engraved MKGH.

Ancient faded papers posted on the four walls say 'Mama Koi Girls' Hostel's Rules and Regulations'. These rub shoulders with calendars from 1980, 1992 and 1976, plus J. Lo's famous butt in a recent publicity poster, Janet Jackson's two-widely-spaced-oranges-shaped 'dashboard', together with a mile of pictures featuring anonymous blue-eyed blond male persons, pulled out of old magazines – I imagine – courtesy of Mam'zelle Aminata.

There're also ripe bananas and a hard Jaffa orange inside the thin black plastic bag supposedly well hidden under Aminata's bed.

★★★

9.45am

"Your meeting is when?" Aminata is carefully studying her face in the mirror over our solo metal sink. Thin, perpetually perplexed eyebrows. Studded tip-tilted nose. Polished skin. She opens her mouth wide and checks out her tongue. Then teeth. And then adds more pink lipstick and a generous splash from Jean Paul Gaultier's woman-shaped perfume bottle.

"Ten-thirty," I reply.

"Emille. My brother. 'E bring 'is ka. We drop you." Aminata takes a mouthful of coffee plus a generous bite of a fresh, fat *mandazi* doughnut from the cafeteria down the corridor. Swiss Café it's called. And is ran by Mama Koi's rather matronly daughter Koi. I start to salivate.

Emille? Mmm… Last month it was Jean Claude, 'my cousin from Rwanda'. The other month Otey, 'my uncle from Ghana'. And there's even been one or two Chinese-looking chaps, who are recently discovered long-lost twice- or thrice-removed relatives, I suppose… Didn't man evolve in Africa, I can hear Aminata explaining, hands on hips in that threatening West African way?

★★★

11am. British Council Auditorium. It's Buzzing.

A well-fed, rather young red-haired man from the podium seizes the microphone.

"Foist a'd loik to welcome you all to this hare Writers' Creativitay Workshop," his lips pout and pluck like a goldfish. "As we have limited toim a'd loik us to foist introduce ourselves, one ata toim, beginning with that laidey ova there." He points at me. The others around him remain mum.

"Richford Clarke from BBC Wales will start us off. Ty will be soived at 12 sharp. Barbara there'll taike ova til lunch toim, at one thatey. Okay? Okay!"

Standing up on rubbery feet, I soak in the many eyes stinging at me.

"Eh... eh... Thank-you. Thank-you Mr Wilfordshire, Mr Clarke, Ms Barbara... and all of you ladies and gentlemen for inviting me here today." I feel the pairs of ears cocking and noses twitching in a natural quest of scenting me out. Who the hell is this one now, they seem to say. What the fuck could she have written surely, they obviously are asking. I ignore them all and waddle on.

"Thank-you very much for having me here today," I reply. "It's a great honour, privilege and honour to be involved in this eh... workshop, where I hope to learn all that I can learn and benefit as a writer. Thank-you. Thank-you very much..." Words, which have always been my childhood sweethearts, desert me at this juncture and my mind goes blank.

Finally. And after a long pregnant silence. Mr. Wilfordshire asks me the hardest question all, "What is your naime?"

"Eh... eh... actually my real name, eh what I mean to say is, my official name is Margaret Kamau, but I eh... usually choose to use Njeeri as my writing name, which is actually my home name really..."

In the fog of apprehension and intimidation that now surrounds me, I hardly hear the command "NEXT!" which prompts the smooth flowing tirade from the others; fellow workshoppers, dapper and draped in sophistication, well-cultivated execution, articulation and finesse that I only last experienced as long words read in the last book that I read I dunno when...

147

Hey. Am Symone Ghiroba and I work at…
Hi. Am Atieno Gitau from…
Wassup. Joey's ma name and I do graphics for…
Cheserem… Mary… Raju… Ashley…

★★★

"So…" She's completely bald and has an eyebrow ring and dark-brown lipstick that matches her dark-brown eyes. "You said *ati* you're called?"

I feel my own cornrows tighten around my head like a sisal baseball cap. Wanjera the expert hairstylist at Embu Town had made the *kamatana* lines extra fine and extra tight, "to last at least 2 months".

My sensible Sunday Best outfit of matching blouse plus pleated long yellow skirt, bought during the last market day before relocating to Nairobi, at Manyatta township which is only twenty minutes from Mt Kenya, now feels and maybe even looks like a colourful polyester tent billowing in the sun in a typical Saturday afternoon wedding reception party, in comparison to the sea of casual jeans and sweatshirts swimming around me.

And *ai*!? *Ati* a whole Asian-Muhindi Indian girl actually saying '*ati*' like a true Nairobian?

Kwani when did this transition take place?

Before I left the city of my birth after quitting the career of my fantasy in search for self and the initial song of my soul, my art, Kenyan Asian-Muhindi young women wore long dark hair and were ideally slim virgins-in-waiting, who strictly concentrated on learning the delicate art of being a very good wife and mother.

They might have been allowed to polish up their mathematical skills, perhaps for when they began their prescribed lifelong part-time job at their father-in-law's shop in Ngara or Parklands, only after they'd successfully produced sufficient offspring. Where they'd henceforth supervise the daily selling of clothing materials, plus at least a hundred different spices or cereals. With the ever-present help of Kalonzo or Wanyonyi; the ever-faithful African Shop Assistant, who'd been assisting shop since World War One… *Kwani* when had this new breed taken over?

I remember the Asian girl's question about my name. Which is a question that literally catches me off guard nowadays. Much more than the shock of enjoying a one-on-one attention focused on any part of my person, and especially my mind. Which might be – or not – a natural side effect from my recently ended exposure to the hive-like traditional African network of my parents' village, where everybody's role in life is precisely prescribed by virtue of their sex and age.

"Eh… am Margaret Kamau," I manage to mumble. "And actually Njeeri."

She's tall but curvy and takes a delicate sip from her long, thin brown cigarette. She then blows perfect rings towards the high ceiling of the auditorium. "Rita Shah," she smiles.

It takes me a while to digest that she's just introduced herself to me and not just called me a name. My right hand begins to twitch. We are now all having ty and sandwiches the size of matchboxes at the recess young Wilfordshire mentioned.

"Nyery? You said *ati* you're from?"

"Uhm… Upcountry, eh I went to shags for a long break and I only just got back to the city last month… hch hch… but I eh was born right here in Nairobi, actually…" I over-explain about my recently ended upcountry sojourn as usual.

"Oh. So you now work for?"

Again am caught off guard.

"Eh… nowhere… eh, I mean, am self-employed… a freelancer…"

"Oh. So. Whom have you been writing for then?" Meaning, according to the Nairobi culture at least, are you important enough? Are you worth knowing? Do you have important connections? Will you amount to anything? Plus the very equally important, should I waste my time on you?

"Ah… this and that here and there… heh heh." Meaning that for the longest time, I've only had one or two stints with wannabe tabloids who pay their writers peanut husks in year-long instalments. A column in a magazine that died after only two belches. A stint with a porn rag whose staff writers remain anonymous as a policy. Bla… Bla… Bla…

"Oh."

Rita's interest is almost dead now, so I very quickly jump in with, "The BBC! Eh… I write for the BBC…"

Of course I forget to mention that that was once upon a time when that snap I took of Gaka, my grandmother, picking coffee, was accepted for publication by one of the BBC's Worldservice magazines. For their regular SNAPS page where even Maasai headsmen and Gikuyu chicken farmers often have their stuff accepted. This bluff ensures that I henceforth belong to the 'is important enough, worth knowing, has connections, will amount to something and the time wasted on me will not be time wasted at all' social category...

"Huh?"

The brown eyes light up, interest resurrecting.

Rita sips her cigarette. I sip my tea and bite my matchbox sandwich, then Barry White's voice asks, "What about the BBC?"

Joey is slender. Has illegally smooth skin. Perfect white teeth. Musky. Expensive. Wassup.

"Eh... am fine, thank-you." I swallow my tea and finish off my sandwich. My tummy still growls in protest nonetheless, because thinly margarined loaf and a hard Jaffa orange stolen from Aminata's secret stash at 2.36am just doesn't cut it. Again I wonder what we'll have for lunch. And again my hand feels abnormally hot.

Rita and Joey lock lips.

"Njeeri works for the BBC," she smiles, almost wetting her ears.

Joey's dark eyes smoulder. Okay, they didn't. But dark eyes on handsome men are supposed to smoulder, right?

What really happened was totally different, totally mortifying. As Joey pulled a seat, my right hand shot up from me quicker that a blink.

Rita stopped smoking. Joey's mouth dropped open. And my renegade limb stood poised in mid-air, begging for a handshake. Handshakes are as African as black is, after all. A reflex action. A natural reaction.

However. The poor guy gulped. Rita gulped. And I gulped too after a while, as I tried in vain to pull down the aforementioned stray appendage. So Joey shook it, almost blushing. A limp, sweaty, shaking virgin handshake.

"Sorry," I mumbled, as I observed a thick rope of shiny sweat pop on Joey's fine forehead; long, wide and smooth just like my dead father's.

★★★

I remember that his handsome smooth dark face was always expressionless – my daddy's was. Especially when he slowly chewed each mouthful of the food that my mother – Maami – ordered me to serve him every night, "as practice for when you get married".

This was always and exactly one hour after daddy walked through the door. After he'd shed his favourite overcoat-for-all-seasons bought in England in 1966, when the Kenyan government gave him a six-month-long job-related scholarship to study there. After he'd taken a long shower where he whistled gentle Anglican Church friendly hymns that were nothing like the loud Pentecostal Church friendly, hearty spirituals that were generously garnished with loud blasts of 'God-inspired spiritual languages' that had a lot of *Habara rara hobeshare!!!* Languages still spoken by the angels to date. Languages that Maami was and still is very conversant with.

"What did you learn in school today?"

That always came after we had all toiled through Rwamba the maid's culinary offerings, of *ikwa* – a super-dry cassava mash – or *gwaci* – boiled sweet potatoes – or her particularly all-time-favourite maize meal *ugali*, which came with a salty meat, pea and carrot stew. Then we drank water 'to wash it all down', ate fruits 'to help digestion' and to also ensure that "you don't come out of the toilet with red eyes and the prominent throbbing facial veins of trying of push and push and push," according to Rwamba.

After the table was cleared, any misbehavior of the day was accurately recited by Rwamba to, "your daddy and then you will see!"

'You will see' normally amounted to two or three quick knitting-needle lashes in the butt or a week-long curfew after school, depending on the quality and the quantity of the crime committed.

As I carefully narrated about my school day to daddy, Maami and Rwamba would be in the kitchen busy banging pots and pans. "Njeeri, bring the dirty cups if you've finished the Milo, ehe?" Maami would soon shout, "Dirty dishes left in the sink at night only feed cockroaches..."

"Cockroaches are very bad! Cockroaches bring bad diseases! They are the world's dirtiest animals! Is that a cockroach?! Kill it quickly! Here. Hit it with this slipper!!"

My mother hated cockroaches. She always talked about cockroaches. During the weekly Maami-special thorough-scrubbing Sunday evening ritual, where I'd get scoured down head to toe with a big *muratina* loofah, Maami still talked about cockroaches.

"When the nuclear war comes, cockroaches will survive – do you know that?"

She'd read about it in her favourite KiSwahili language newspaper *Taita Leo*.

"Everything will die but all cockroaches will remain alive... imagine!"

By then, she'd be working on my neck, turning my head this way and that, sometimes clasping it between her knees to steady me as she worked on my back. Rwamba would be nearby, gleefully on stand by with yet another bucket of fresh warm Dettolled water, that Madam would soon use to rinse her only offspring with. Then after Maami and Rwamba averted their faces, I'd be instructed to wash myself 'down there.' After exactly two and a half minutes, my mother would snap, "*Bas!* Enough!" a signal for Rwamba to quickly scoop me in a large towel and vigorously frisk me dry.

★★★

"Will you have a drink?" His coffee-coloured skin is too smooth for a guy, I heard myself observing for the umpteenth time. Joey flagged down a bow-tied waiter and ordered drinks for us without consulting me. I didn't mind much though, since I figured that I owed him one for embarrassing him like that with that unpremeditated handshake in public. How could I have forgotten the protocol, in this new world of mmuah-mmuah European air-kisses and quick dry hugs, at most? At least the man was a gentleman and had obviously forgiven me for invading his sacred Personal Space, which is a new African word now commonly used in modern cities and towns around Mama Africa.

For the whole three-day duration of the workshop, Joey, Rita and I somehow found ourselves seated or standing together during the numerous intervals. And especially while debating with the special guest author Marcus Toma Amenyi, whose ideas and insights seemed to go northwards, whilst ours headed down south in principle.

We respected the astonishing thirty-year-old author, needless to say. Because he had written his first book – primary school mathematics set book – at 19. His first novel, titled *Beyond the beyond* made the New York Times' Top Ten Bestsellers list when he was 21, a feat that ushered in numerous international literary awards. And the one million shillings coveted Artist's Grant from Men's League – that outfit that is headed by some dreadlocked millionaire from Chad, for Marcus's 'exemplary display of original literary genius, especially and including his amazing command of the Show and Tell technique'.

But it was always Barbara from the podium who had the task of plying us apart after the string of heated arguments that followed every paragraph of Marcus's speech. As she yet again tried to explain that none of us was right or wrong, in the long run. Because literature – like art – could be seen as abstract.

"Words are the paints which writers use to paint their individual imaginations," the lady explained carefully. "Some of you will be drawn to reproduce reality as it is commonly perceived, coming up with portraits and pictures of objects already in existence. Some of you won't, and thus combine these perceptions and come up with a completely original version of reality…"

While others like ourselves – obviously – could be compared to Joan Miro's dark strokes on splashed and sprinkled light. Or even like a literary Picasso, where the eye of a story was allowed to roam and subsequently appear on the knee or chin. Yes indeed, nothing at all was wrong or right because eventually each part gets its place in the whole picture, for all is fair in art, as it is in love and war. That was our group's argument.

Richford Clarke from BBC Wales belonged to Marcus Toma Amenyi's school of thought. He talked of the importance of capital letters and full stops in their proper places. Insisted on correct diction and prior planning, outlines, paragraphs, bodies, startings and finishings…

Our co-ordinator, the rather young Mr Wilfordshire, had on the other hand only appeared on the first day.

On the very last day however, I witnessed each of the workshop's participants troop one by one to Wilfordshire's corner office on the second floor, enter tentatively, stay for about ten minutes and then exit with a rather perplexed look on their individual faces.

When my turn arrived, I was surprised to see lines upon lines of beautifully covered books entirely fill the four walls. The only places where books were absent were the floor and ceiling. He looked up from something that he'd been busy scribbling and gave me a toothy smile.

"Njeery! Come in! Close the door!"

His blue eyes seemed to look right through me.

"So. How did you like this workshop? Did it help you at all?" Somehow his initially heavy accent seemed to have disappeared.

With two sets of ty and lunch for three whole days, I'd already privately concluded that this workshop was very good for me indeed.

"Am glad that you got exposed to so much experience and professional insight, as you say Njeery," Wilfordshire pronounced, after listening to my standard reply.

I then noticed that on the mammoth cedar-wood desk, huge for one so petite, stood a medium-sized carton box, into which the man now dipped one hand. Maybe, I anxiously thought, Wilfordshire was now going to offer me some money? As some sort of artistic grant to help me implement all the important points that the Writers' Creativity Workshop had taught us? Some very good money? Please please God, please?

Earlier that morning, Mama Koi's daughter Koi, who was also the hostel's accountant, administrator and manager, had summoned me to her office next to Swiss Café.

"When will you pay all dha money? If you don't pay all dha money tomorrow, don't come back here today!"

Koi had savoured each verbal bite the way she did the cream cakes that she loved so much.

The reality was that I was now not only homeless, but also had no access to all my worldly belongings, which would soon be confiscated by Koi, who doubled up as her mother's auctioneer as well...

"Yo! Njeeri! I 'ave no money to lend you, yo!" Aminata had wailed dramatically when I explained my predicament the previous night. Emille, her brother, had gone back to I dunno where and so Aminata was once again hunting for a new male relative to adopt her...

And of course I understood her position in regard to my current dire situation...Just like I understood Maami's utter disgust after I left my 'very very well-paying' job years ago, in order to pursue the 'silly-silly' so-called job of 'writing-writing foolish-foolish things'.

Apart from a roof over my head and a hot meal on the table when the going got too tough, any other help from her was synonymous with that biblical camel still struggling to go through the eye of a needle.

After my father died, Maami soon became the permanent chairperson of Holy Hill Pentecostal Jesus Christ Is The Only Lord, Savior, King And God Amen Church Without Borders. Rwamba stayed on to help Sister-In-Christ Bethie with her increased workload. And I guess that should mean that they lived happily ever after...

I don't think that I've totally forgiven daddy for dying on me like that; going off to bed one night and not waking up the next morning, just like that... But that's another story.

So here I was now at Club Kidogo with Joey and company, 'catching pints'.

"*Si* you can tell-tell us a little-little how the BBC works? Maybe you can get jobs for us too? Even if it's freelancing, it's better than to be *zubaaring* idly over here in Africa waiting-waiting for peanuts at the end of the month..."

I don't know who among the present company had suggested that, but here I was now sipping at my fifth Guinness and coke and watching Rita sway interestingly on the circular dance floor right in the middle of the premises. With another girl. The place was quite packed with the hippest, yuppiest generation X, Y, and Z Nairobi crowd.

My mind still swirled with the last word spoken by Wilfordshire that afternoon, and especially his last action.

"Usually. At the end of the Creativity Workshops. Throughout which we keenly observe and access each participant. We give each one of you a little something that will help you further your writing career on a more focused and concentrated footing. Use this gift wisely," the man added.

The three bottles that he gave me are still in my small *kiondo* handbag.

'One to be taken three times a day before meals' is neatly typed on each labelled container, which houses a mixture of blue, yellow and green tablets.

I wonder if they are seeds. Maybe if I plant them on some fertile ground they will each take, bud and then sprout forth a big, mighty tree. One with internationally acclaimed fruits the size of Brazil that just might make it to the Top Ten New York Times' Bestsellers List.

Or maybe not. Who knows...

Rita comes back to the table and gives me a drunken hug.

"Hey! BBC babe! Why the long face... eh? You wanna another drink... eh?"

Her companion, the other tall girl, smiles at me through clenched teeth. Mariah — she is called — 'not Maria', but Mariah as in Carey.

'Because cabs are too expensive' we all end up at Joey's digs 'because it's the nearest and the largest'. 'Because his bed is big enough' we all pile on top of it, half undressed 'because it's too too hot tonight' and obviously because of all those pints we have thus far consumed.

I don't know why Joey ends up on top of me — finally — but I know why I tightly hold on to his penis as he grunts and moans and jabbers in Sanskrit; a long dead language...

Maybe it's because good Anglican girls need sex too — at least once in a while... Maybe it's because the condom we're using keeps rolling down and slipping off Joey and I am not drunk enough not to notice it, and to just blindly ride this welcome wave, until I soar high enough to forget that am homeless and jobless, and eventually reach up and touch God's very face...

What I also notice is that I bite my tongue each time the word 'daddy' threatens to spill from my mouth...

Days from now, I will again notice the loud echoes of throbbing spasms between my legs, as I walk around Nairobi City, pretending to window shop, visiting friends and a smattering of relatives for meals and forced conversations, as I wait for the evening and the next drinking spree planned by Joey and company 'after work'…

I also know that during the next few days, when Rita turns and places her gentle soothing hand on my bare breast and then tentatively tries to kiss me… I will kiss her back.

Muthony wa Gatumo was born and bred in Nairobi, Kenya. Her first attempt at playwriting, titled *Snores Like a Man*, won second prize in the BBC Worldservice African Performance annual playwriting competition in 1995. Some of her poems have appeared in anthologies by The International Library of Poetry, plus in *Kwani?* literary journal. Her articles and short stories have also been published elsewhere.

Dying in the Name of Love

Zazah Khuzwayo

FIVE YEARS OF DEMOCRACY in South Africa and people were already expecting, hoping and even demanding major changes or miracles from the government. Some were working hard to better themselves and bring about change in their society. While others were expecting to have big houses. Everything was supposed to be free. Education, medical care and even job offers while they sat at home and did nothing.

I was living in an apartment on the South Beach in Durban at the time with three other black women who came from disadvantaged backgrounds. We were trying to find greener pastures, now that we blacks were allowed to stay anywhere in town and move around as we wanted. I stood on the balcony overlooking the sea. I could see the ships at the anchorage. Some just look at those ships as ships but I look at them as full of seamen with dollars and pounds.

I moved inside into the lounge where everyone was staring at *The Bold and the Beautiful* one of the boring, stupid and predictable dramas that allows people to live in the dreamland of Romeo and Juliet and not think about what the future holds for them. They live for these junk soapies, and for the next show and they have no plans for their life. They dream of this knight in shining amour who will come and change their whole life and they even know what he looks like. He's got a six pack. He is a Brad Pitt look–alike, and is very good in bed. He has got lots of money to look after them and their kids.

They are all black but he must be white or if he happens to be black he must be from overseas and most of all he mustn't speak their language.

I said to them, "I am going to vote before it gets darker. Is anyone coming or have you voted already?"

"I don't care," Fikile replied. She had her nose and tongue pierced, and a tattoo on her back. She had a French sugar daddy that paid her bills and a young Croatian seaman who left a long time ago but she still wrote to him. She waited and hoped one day he would come back. She even had a sangoma who promised her that her *muti* will bring him back to her arms.

"Where did I put my ID book?" I said.

Fikile carried on, "Gosh, are you out of your mind? What has this black government done for us? I have no time to vote for all these crooks. There are no jobs, too much AIDS and the president is travelling all over like a Minister of Home Affairs."

I kept quiet at first but then I wasn't going to allow her to walk all over me without getting back at her. I replied saying: "Do you think the Government is going to leave his office and come here to offer you a job? And stop you from practising unsafe sex when all the billboards, magazines and TV programs are telling you every day to use free condoms. Keep this in your lazy mind, no one is going to employ you if you have no skills."

They got more defensive.

Thuli was another one. Her biggest dream was to marry an Italian guy or any young guy who was white and had lots of money. She was in her mid-thirties, but everybody envied her body. She had a brown belt in kickboxing and she was proud of it, as it was the only certificate she had.

"*Hayi bo!* You think you know everything because you have some rubbish Bantu education and stupid certificates. But you are sitting here with your casual job that makes you work like a donkey and gives you peanuts. While your boss is making millions from your sweat. I happen to get more money from guys than what you are making at your work, busy studying things that are not taking you anywhere."

Fikile followed with her words, "Ah because you running your old man's lousy secondhand bookshop and because he gives you lots of money you think you are better than us. Does he still get it to stand up for you?"

I ignored that question and responded, "Oh, wow, girlfriend, at least I have dreams and a direction for my life. I can recognise what government is doing because I educate myself with the little I get. But it's strange when you have money from your boyfriend you go and buy the most expensive clothing and try to look like Jennifer Lopez or any other supermodel you can never be. When things go wrong you will start blaming the government who never fulfilled its promise, the family that never gave you an education, your stepfather who abused you, God who doesn't like you, the Italian or American guy who left you with a baby and disappeared without a trace and most of all, the whites for oppressing our people. It will go on and on until it is too late. You start drinking and blame somebody who made alcohol. *Ekse ngiyavaya* I will pass by Costa's for a drink."

Costa's was a pub not far from the beach where the Germans, English, Afrikaners and the others would come to meet the black and coloured (mixed-race) women. They drank with them, some even developed relationships and all the latest gossips around town were found there. I enjoyed meeting people there. My flatmates thought Costa's was for low-class people.

As I was on my way out Thuli had to have the last word, "That's all you know – to study for stupid courses, drink with the hobos and go out with old white men."

That felt bad, but I was on my way to vote while they all vowed they would never vote. But I remembered Robert Kiyosaki saying in his book, 'Criticism blinds while analysis opens your eyes. Analysis allows winners to see that critics are blind. To find out what everyone else missed is a key to success.'

I made my way to the streets. All the posters of politicians were up. Black faces, white faces with promises. Mandela's face was smiling and I smiled back at him. You can't help but admire his face; it is like that of a newborn, innocent baby. I looked around at all the tall buildings that were well renovated. I felt the sea breeze on my face from the Indian Ocean that had delivered all the Indians into our city to come as labourers and they have filled our city. People were climbing in and out of these *doof-doof* noisy, flashy kombis which graced our beautiful city, not forgetting our Model Cs, kids who went to expensive multiracial schools to speak and dress like Americans. They all had dreadlocks and afros but their behaviour was from New York or some city I have never been to. When we were growing up our mothers taught us to perm and relax our hair in order to get a job and be welcomed in the western society. But we still respected our traditions and the elders.

Here in this city were the Zulu warriors who fought the English and Afrikaners until they decided to unite against them. What an accomplishment by the Zulus! Not only to unite a powerful Zulu nation but also to help their enemies to unite.

I looked across the street and the street child carrying a plastic container with glue stopped digging in the bin and started dancing to the sound of the music from the kombi that had stopped to pick up passengers.

"*Mayebabo*! I almost passed the voting station." I entered and produced my ID book to show that I had registered. They put a mark to show that I had voted. I knew already which party I wanted. I dropped the paper into the ballot box. And the voting process was much quicker than I thought it would be.

I went to Costa's for a beer and listened to the new gossip around town and played the jukebox. Everybody was hoping the ANC would win and one of the English guys who was a regular asked me, "Has Mandela found you a job yet? I heard you've been studying."

"*Baas*, they used to call you; I have no time to waste on people like you."

They giggle in a group and one fat German shouted, "Now that you have a boyfriend you have no time for us."

I left Costa's and went back to the flat. But I remembered what had happened before I left. I didn't know what my flatmates were feeling right now. Well it didn't matter what they were feeling; I had to find a way to talk to them if wanted to go out and have fun with them again.

I forgot we were still one family and that we shared so much besides being flatmates. I almost forgot the reason I left home was much the same as theirs. *Eish*, I hate my life; it is like a cycle of tragedies. First your mother marries the bastard who abuses you and denies you an education. You find love from your first boyfriend and then he forces you into sex and beats you up, leaves you with a baby and an infection as a bonus. Your family treats you like a whore for having a baby so young and later your mother dies because your father stressed her to death. You run away and find others like you who hate their past and their traditions that never protected them. They have lost faith in black men. But you are full of dreams. You think you are better than they are and you try to change them.

It was already dark. I went into a supermarket to buy a five-litre carton of white wine.

That's when a white hobo smelling of alcohol started pestering me for R5. I told him "Do I owe you R5? Just get out of my way."

While I was inside buying wine I felt guilty. He is not the one who started apartheid. He might have been the lazy one. I bought him a pie instead of giving him money. Life is changing. I never thought I would see a white man sleeping on the street when I grew up.

I entered the flat with the wine, made my way to the kitchen and grabbed four wine glasses. I shuffled across the dining room to the lounge.

The black naked body of Thuli greeted me. She was painting her nails, her make-up kit in front of her. Her eyes glowed when she saw the box of wine.

"Yeah, innocent little bitch, great thinking." Then she shouted, "Girls! Wine is here!"

Theresa and Fikile came out of their room as soon as they heard Thuli shouting.

The room became quiet and the sound of wine flowing into their glasses was heard.

Thuli started the conversation. She always acted like an auntie we never had. "*Wena*, Zinzie you can study, vote, pretend to be somebody you are not but the fact is you are *mahosha* and once a bitch always a bitch. You heard Snoopy and Dre's song that you can't make a housewife out of a whore."

Teresa started to giggle.

Fikile added to what Thuli was saying: "Yeah, when her sugar daddy is away she is with us on the dance floor shaking her ass for the seamen. And she not only shakes it. She dances on top of the table for the Greeks to shove their dollars next to her private parts."

And Teresa added, "Then she will lie and say it's her birthday and tell the story of her growing up poor and her parents who could never afford to make a party for her. In minutes the table will be filled with the champagne and all sorts of liquor she will order, then the bitch will take home the Captain or the one with lots of money even if the guy is one step away from the grave."

There was a happy, cheerful mood and everything that was said was turning into a joke: the wine was at work. And we were all getting ready to go the Seamen's Club.

Thuli followed, "And you are going to make a change and be like Mother Teresa. You! The biggest bitch in town." While we were drinking we were waiting for the driver to come at 11pm to take us to the Seamen's club.

"Okay," I screamed, "Now it's my time to defend myself."

"But seriously, Ma. Oh, firstly we all came to the city to make a living looking after our kids and send food to our families right?'

"Oh Mamfundisi is preaching again," and the laughter went on.

161

"Guys, it is time to go *wena*. Zinzi, do you ever give yourself a break? One of these days you will end up confused in a mental institution."

"I do get a break when my sugar daddy takes me on holidays. I just want you to have dreams."

"Ooh *wena* Zinzi the new bitch on the block, this is how we live and we love it. Let's go. The driver should be outside," Thuli said as she stood up.

The next morning I woke up with a terrible *babalaas* dragging my feet along the passage to the kitchen fridge to look for anything that would cure my hangover. Milk was in front of me. It always worked for me. I had to get ready to go and open the bookshop. When I got there, to my surprise a dark, good-looking young lady was sitting at my computer.

"Hi, and you are?" I asked disgustedly.

"Pinky."

She had an unfriendly tone and looked like she was about to tell me I was fired and she was taking over the shop.

"Who put you here?"

"Andries told me all about you. You always come late and he is losing money."

"Oh yeah, now I would like you to listen to me. The computer in front of you is mine and we are in the shop together as partners. I would like you to get out of here, make your way to his flat or relax on the beach if you have nothing to do."

Before she reached the door I shouted, "Oh, I see here you have sold some books and CDs. Can I have that money?" She quickly reached for her bag and handed me the money.

"Great, that felt good removing the bitch from her new throne." My mood changed quickly to bitterness and anger. The bastard could have fuckin' told me he was leaving me for a young bitch. I felt a bit old. Maybe this was his way of punishing me for sleeping around and refusing to live with him.

I grabbed the phone and called him at work. They told me he was in a meeting. I banged down the phone. Now I was boiling inside. The day was going to be long. I started sweating, couldn't even smile to the customers who came in. I wanted an explanation. Maybe this would give me enough time to plan my revenge on the bald, sweating old Afrikaner. "How can he betray me like this?"

I heard a knock at the door and there he was. He entered, carefully closed the door behind. The streams of sweat rolled down from his face to his neck as he opened his hairy arms to hold me. But I refused and then moved to the corner of my bed.

"So this is it. You went and found another woman and even sent her for a show to our bookshop. Are you not the one who told me to leave my German guy? You were going to make my dreams come true. Is this how you betray me, without a warning?"

"Zinzi, you can't blame me. I asked you so many times to come and live with me. I want to have a baby with you. I have enough money to look after you and your kid. I thought you could trust me by now. You are about to get your diploma, you have a driver's licence. I have taught you everything you needed to know about business. I sign a cheque for you every month. What more can I do to stop you from sleeping with the seamen and settle with me? I love Pinky and she has agreed to come and live with me and we will have a baby together. You are a strong woman; you will find your feet somewhere. I don't think you love me enough."

"Mmm, that is very rich, Andries. First of all I have principles, I might be a street girl but I am human and I have boundaries. You are separated from your wife you did not divorce, because your family would take away your inheritance if you divorced her and married a black woman. You really want us to have sex without a condom but I don't know your status. I am not prepared to take that risk and I don't want your wife and kids to come and kick me out of your flat when you die of a heart attack or anything else. Plus I am not ready to have another baby. But I didn't say I don't love you. I still need you."

"Zinzi, I have already made promises to her. I can't leave her now."

"Okay, since you have made up your mind about her, I have to ask you to do me a favor. The shop was my idea. We will close it and I will take the deposit. If we find a buyer, I will also keep the money and you will sign a cheque for me for R20 000 so I can move to Cape Town to start a new life."

"Are you insane or what? Why so much money and why Cape Town?"

"In CPT there are no bad friends or hookers I know. I will need accommodation and I need to leave some money for my baby girl. While I try find a job I will need money."

"I can't afford that money."

"Well if I call your racist family in Bloemfontein and your wife and tell them about your life you will lose a whole lot more than this, so please understand, as much as you love your new young girlfriend I love my life."

That felt really good. I got him where I wanted to. I had seen how a person got blackmailed on TV. Now it was my turn. Why was it not called 'whitemail'? That sounds decent.

"Andy, as of next month, I don't want to be here. For me to change my life I have to be far away from everybody including you. You can go now and think about it and I will see you at your office tomorrow."

"Please don't come to the University."

"I cannot come to your flat. There is a new madam. Please leave me alone now. Bye bye," as I pushed him out of the room and banged the door in his face.

I made sure my friends didn't hear our conversation. I didn't want anyone to know about my plans to leave town.

Andries decided to give in and do as I had told him to. I moved to Cape Town. Found work in a hotel as an assistant manager, and Mike the owner of the restaurant in the hotel liked me and we ended up sleeping together. I guess my friend Mbali was right. Once a bitch always a bitch. At least this time I was in love.

Work and studies seemed to occupy me; back at home I still had to make time for my child's homework. Mike and I were very happy as we decided to get engaged. I felt guilty as I did not know how to tell him I had been on the street. I was hoping if he ever found out he would accept it and forgive me.

Two-and-a-half years later I decided to visit Durban. I got to Durban and the town was busy with people preparing for December holidays. I was looking forward to going to Costa's bar to play the jukebox and catch all the latest gossip.

Rebecca Malope's Gospel song played on the jukebox and I met one of the old girls who happened to know everything that was taking place around town.

I ordered two beers and sat next her. "How is it, Choma?"

"We thought you went to Cape Town with your child and forgot us."

"No, I have been busy. But, hey, I went to Thuli's flat and was told they moved out. How are they?"

"Those high-class friends of yours who don't mix with the hobos like us because they think they are white. The Seamen's Club has no money anymore. All the ships have taken on cheap labourers, like Filipinos, Indians and Turkish."

"So what seems to be the problem?"

"The problem is they get paid less and they like white women better. You know they come from poor countries. A white woman is their dream come true."

"Okay, Choma, I understand but where are Thuli and the others?" I asked, calling the waiter for another round of beers. To get more information you always have to buy more beers here. I was looking forward to spending time with old friends.

"Thuli got married to an Italian guy who has disappeared for the past six months. Now she is selling clothes to look after his baby and she has moved back to the township. But now she doesn't look fit, she looks skinny."

"Another one, Fikile, paid a lot of money for that sangoma to bring back the Croatian guy. Recently he came back. They got married. I heard they were both on drugs and she was busy trying to have a baby for him when she got sick and died of AIDS. I guess he moved back to Croatia before she died because he wasn't around for a funeral."

She said, "Can you repeat that song by Rebecca?" I stood up and did so, even though it was strange to listen to Gospel music in a pick-up bar.

"What happened to Teresa?"

"Oh, Teresa. Her English boyfriend heard that she was dying of TB and she did not treat it. The father of her kids came and took the kids to England and left her to die. Ehh, Choma, nobody came for her body. The government had to take care of her."

I kept quiet as tears were filling my eyes and carried on drinking. A few years and all this had happened. I wished I had left a contact for them. I felt guilty, but then it was too late. I was never going to see them again. Were we really friends? Or just flatmates, who drank together, lived together and chased the seamen for money. Later other friends showed up and we carried on drinking, dancing until the morning. At least I didn't have to pick up any man for money.

Zazah Khuzwayo is the author of *Never been at home*, which is being published by David Phillip and she has also written for a few magazines. She is a freelance tour guide for KwaZulu-Natal, and was nominated for Checkers/Shoprite Woman of the year 2004.

City Centre Saga

Jackline Melisa Makena

TWO WALLS SANDWICH AN alley. A dim alley. Archaic to the last, the twelve-foot Asian shop wall on my right recites, among its layers of green mould, the sights it has seen. *Kamau was here 1952...* that's when white *Afandes* herded Kikuyu folk into reserves. *Vote for Kenneth Matiba...* the 1992 political warlord thought the wall was a worthy gallery for his black and white newsprint portrait. Soon afterwards, it began soaking with the blood of capitalist martyrs, prey of socialist muggers. 2002... *Uhuru na kazi*: the newest political slogan painted in red with a finger. This time the campaigners didn't care to brush it with wheat flour paste and stick up those forced-smile politician faces. Only the other wall across the clogged drainage trench got that privilege.

I call this wall Priscilla. Peacock-pride, pebble-studded, dust-powdered Priscilla. Quite the long-necked, long-legged African babe. She is the brainchild of some ambitious Nairobian, proprietor of the storied building next door. He has painted *Usikojoe hapa* signs on her but they still wet her feet with diluted urea.

It's ten o'clock. I can't sleep. A train of wind whistles down the alley. Like rice grains falling from the winnowing tray, a heavy downpour masquerades itself as a light shower. Dasani's teeth chatter in staccato beats. He moans and slowly pulls his old, sisal-sack blanket over his head. And slowly his bare, clammy feet stick out on the other side. The *thighiriri* – those menacing, tiny, black ants – inhabiting the blanket stir into a frenzied dance all over his body. Like a hungry child at its mother's breast, a Dasani water bottle, half full of dried gum, clings to his mouth. His coffee brown teeth clasping the bottle are sticky with plaque. I can literally see the vile stench oozing from his black gums. He turns over, lies on a pillow of chewing gum. He doesn't stir.

Tired of pretence, the heavens crack and let out a heavy deluge. The clogged drainage trench floods and mucky green sewage water bathes Dasani's jigger-infested feet. The *thighiriri* drown. The sisal-sack blanket gulps buckets of water and belches. Bad blanket breath, stale and dusty. He doesn't stir.

The garbage heap near his head pulsates with worms and rats. Protein, vitamins, carbohydrates! It's ripe at last! I had better get to it before the city council trucks arrive. Idiotic City Council... where should Dasani and I fill our tummies? What's wrong with Nairobi's garbage-heap restaurants?

Frustrated at Dasani's indifference, the downpour ceases. I quickly set my suction pad to work on the meal. Heavily fermented Delamere yoghurt for the starter. Sour, tomato-sauced French fries for the main course. Tender, pudding-like banana for dessert. A few drops of rain-diluted *Ribena* for wine. A water-soaked newspaper to dab the corners of my suction pad. *Voila!*

It's warm now... I'm sleepy. Crickets have begun strumming their hind legs. Drop after drop of rain trapped in Priscilla's gutter pounds the bottom of a Milo tin... ta, ta, ta. Steadily, the crickets rise from bass to tenor, tenor to alto, alto to soprano. A sharp scream suddenly drowns the cricket orchestra. The air is instantly still...

A muddy puddle in the pavement swallows a foot and spits it out again. Someone's coming... Someone's running towards our dim little alley. Dasani shoots up. His countenance is ice cold with panic. He crouches. His eyes run up and down the alley. I fly up and down the alley.

Moi Avenue is bald-head bare. A peek at Tom Mboya Street and I see a man. Running with stooped gait, he loosely carries a thin *panga* in his left hand on which his right hand rests. He is clenching his teeth tightly. A glittering pearl necklace is peering out of his shirt pocket.

More screams. The Meridian comes alive with bustle. I can already see tomorrow's headlines, 'Tourist at the Mercy Of Gangster'. Dasani doesn't care for headlines. With dread his eyes dart about the alley. He is afraid even to breath. Suddenly, he sees them... the carton boxes! He dives under them.

Into puddle, out of puddle, into puddle, out of puddle, the man draws nearer. Soon he arrives. He nervously scans the alley. All is clear. He staggers towards the sewage trench and crouches before it. He dips his hand in and shuts his eyes until ridges of flesh appear at their corners.

Soon he shakes the mucky water off and stares at the deep gash mingling with his veins from the wrist to the elbow. Fresh blood streams out of it like chocolate paste out of a squeezed eclair. I draw nearer, his blood draws me, but he frantically waves his hand over the wound.

He glances at the *panga* still in his hand. It is still bloody. "*Jinga…*" he curses as he flings it towards the carton boxes. They shift about as though writhing in pain. He turns sharply, totally mesmerised. For a moment he hesitates. Then like one struck by divine revelation, he inches towards the boxes. Instantly he raises the boy Dasani by the neck.

"*Unanicheki hee?*" he asks, accusing Dasani of spying on him.

Their eyes hold as the man's fingers tighten around the fragile neck. The boy gasps. From his constricted throat comes a grunt, a defiant grunt… "I cannot die." He pounds the man's face but those fingers only tighten.

"*Kuna damu, amepita hapa,*" shouts a patrol policeman pointing at the trail of blood on Tom Mboya Street.

Into puddle, out of puddle; a rush of feet. They are coming with their torches.

The man drops Dasani.

"*Ukiscream nitaku…*" says he to Dasani sliding his index finger across his throat.

Dasani swallows hard. He is too afraid to even move away from the torrent of blood bathing his chest from the man's hand. His eyes dart between the man standing over him and Moi Avenue. He wants to jump up and scuttle down the alley; but his legs are paralyzed by fear.

The thin man is wearing a pair of blue jeans. They are slit at both knees. The rolled-up sleeves of his shirt hide his tattered cuffs. The formerly white, stiff-collared Manhattan shirt is now brown and thin. It has intense yellow patches under the armpits. His chest, taut as a drum, is like a staircase to nowhere. The cut on his right cheek lengthens his fat lips. He looks like he is smiling.

He panics and skids down the alley with the pearl necklace still in his hand.

"*Nitakupata,*" he says promising to return and finish Dasani off.

He crosses Moi Avenue, goes past the bazaar and disappears onto Biashara Street.

Hot in pursuit, the policemen pick up the *panga* but hardly notice Dasani among the carton boxes. He lies there, breathing quietly, until the voices fade. Then, he kicks off the boxes and sits up. He rubs his neck gently, staring at the hand the *panga* grazed. I look up at him, enjoying the tiny trickle of blood. He frowns and slaps his other hand over the wound.

So much for charity. He leans against Priscilla searching for me among the mould layers on the other wall. He wants to squash me. Soon he shuts his eyes, perhaps returning to his slumber.

Suddenly, he opens his eyes wide, jumps to his feet and races down Tom Mboya Street. I linger behind. Should I pursue the selfish brute? After all, he is running to Soja's throne outside Odeon. Yes, Odeon the famous cinema hall. Latema Street is the domain of *matatu* drivers and touts by day "...*beba, beba, beba,* Westlands, Kangemi, *beba...*" as they urge passengers into their vehicles but at night, Soja, the king of *chokoraas* – street children – and his council of elders sit there. Each night they bore a new hole in the ozone with their rubber-tyre bonfire. And in African spirit, they sit around it sniffing gum.

Anyway, curiosity pulls me off the wall, and I flutter my wings in the wind towards Latema Street.

Eleven-thirty o'clock. I turn into Latema Street, my wings threatening to tear off my body. The spiracles in my abdomen are dilating too wide. My exoskeleton was definitely not made for these kind of flights.

Sitting on a corrugated-iron sheet wall of a new building site opposite Odeon, I watch. Glowing like a black pearl, a boy of about eleven years of age dances around the fire. He has smeared old black grease on his face, upper arms and chest. Except for the thick, mountainous mat of hair on the top of his head, he is shaved clean. Something of witchcraft, he chants the names of the kings of *chokoraas* and sneezes. Gum vapour has gone deep into his brain. The lesser *chokoraas* seated around the bonfire are equally stoned. They let out, in unison, a cry of jubilation after each name.

There is nothing childlike about Soja. This twenty-five-year-old has outgrown gum. The girls are in Koinage Street right now playing prostitute for his expensive marijuana tastes. The five elders of his council have lately acquired these tastes too. The only stick he allows them passes from one hand to another among them, at the foot of the staircase, each boy hoping it's not gone before he has had his second puff. Soja likes their desperation. His glassy eyes laugh for his mouth as he watches them. His white crown of lice has badly mutilated his hair. He thrusts his fingers into the scanty bush and gives his scalp a rough massage. Afterwards, he puts a stick of marijuana to his flaming red lips and quickly forgets his itchy troubles.

"*Maze* Soja," pleads Dasani.

I see him. There he lies on his stomach under Soja's foot. His back is quite the straight and stiff footstool for the *akala* sandal Soja is wearing. His Dasani bottle of gum lies next to him. A young *chokoraa* is crawling towards it with sparkling lust in his eyes. The king is puffing away. His mind is far away. Perhaps he is thinking of the police who daily harass him or the parking field he and the elders will raid tomorrow. Either way, he is oblivious to Dasani's pitiful pleading.

"*Maze* Soja, *nimecheki* Cruda *akitoka raid. Jo karibu anidedishe*," Dasani tells of the man who almost killed him.

Soja doesn't care.

"*Maze… jo siunifanyie maconnection*," Dasani implores for protection from the man Cruda.

Soja suddenly drops out of his cloud. He stares at the boy. Dasani courageously looks into the king's face. Soja raises his left eyebrow. Dasani still stares at him boldly. Angrily, Soja digs his *akala* into the boy's back. He spits at him.

"*Fala*," Soja yells, "*sinilikushow uingie* CLAN *ukadinda?*"

That's where Dasani went wrong; he refused to join the CLAN – *Chokoraas*' Lethal Association in Nairobi, as the government has lately baptized it. Had he been seated among the lesser *chokoraas* tonight, he wouldn't have encountered the long-lipped thug Cruda and even now, the clan would have formed a bronze wall around him. I have heard them talking. They say when Othis accidentally witnessed the murder of an Asian trader outside his shop on Biashara Street two years ago, Soja struck a deal with the murderers. A few girls as slaves and an oath of silence. That was all!

But Dasani cowered away from the initiation rites. I hear he won't dance naked among the garbage heaps along Nairobi River or let Soja circumcise him with the blade – a rusty communal razor from the early 1990s. Indeed the knife of their forefathers, a former generation of *chokoraa* who are now wanted gangsters in their thirties. You see Dasani went to school until Standard Five and he had a so-called Hygiene teacher – Odijo – until he was eleven. Perhaps that's where the problem really lies. I saw him dance when President Mwai Kibaki announced the free education policy two days ago.

"*Maze* Odijo…" Dasani tries to explain Standard Five Home Science to the king.

"*Fala…* Odijo, Odijo, Odijo," yells Soja.

By now, the fire wizard has ended his dramatic chants. The clan is dead silent, each boy sniffing his gum in bliss. The elders' single stick is gone. Their eyes are on the stick Soja is raising to his mouth. He takes a long puff then, watching them, he throws the remaining stick to the ground near his foot. Hungry wolves, they jump over each other. Othis pushes some boy's face into the dust almost snapping his neck as he crawls over his companions. He grabs the stick victoriously only to have Soja's *akala* on his back. The king wiggles his index finger and Othis has to give up his prize. But as he relights the stick, Soja pulls out a new stick from his shirt pocket and sets his grumbling elders at peace.

He raises his foot off Dasani, and carelessly waving his hand says, "*Ishia*." Dasani hesitates to go and lets his head fall into the dust. Raising his face again, he clasps his hands in supplication to this deity Soja.

"*Maze* Soja," he begs.

"Othis…" Soja calls for security.

Dasani rises as quickly as the hungry, red-eyed bulldog jumps to his feet. Grabbing his gum bottle from the young *chokoraa* who has been acquainting himself with it, he backs away from the bonfire. Some eyes are on him; others are on his gum. Suddenly, the fire wizard stands up and deliriously bounces around the fire. He halts and copying Soja's gesture shouts, "*Ishia… Fala*." Faithful as dogs, the lesser *chokoraas* take up the chant, "*Ishia, Fala, shia…Ishia, Fala, Ishia*."

Midnight. Dasani runs. I fly to Soja's head and settle on a bush of his hair. Generous king, he doesn't mind.

Her legs wide apart, she digs her teeth into it and brutally tears off a huge chunk. She chews it slowly, savouring every moment, until a bright-orange juice oozes out of the corner of her mouth. She sticks out her pale tongue and licks up the juice. Bite after bite into the mango, I try to help her with the juice but she blows me away. Her fingers are already tributaries to the rivers of mango juice streaming down her hands yet she won't let me have some. Market women!

A customer is coming. She throws the soggy mango seed into a garbage heap a few feet off and wipes her mouth with the *khanga* tied round her waist. I race for it but someone else picks it up: Dasani.

"What's he doing at City Market?" I wonder.

The tourist at the Meridian died. The newspapers screamed this headline today morning.

Dasani sucks the seed hurriedly and glances over his shoulder. Then he pushes it all into his mouth and walks away from the garbage heap. He lowers his eyes and only raises them periodically to inspect the faces of those he encounters. He doesn't notice me sitting on his upper lip. Contrary to his norm, he doesn't kick pebbles today.

Suddenly he stops. A woman standing in front of a cybercafé display window is staring at him angrily. She is wearing a luminous-yellow nylon overcoat. Her one hand on her hip and the other raised like a cobra about to strike, she walks towards him shouting. Certainly a City Council worker! He spits the mango seed on the pavement, sticks his gum bottle into his mouth and runs. Two seconds later, he goes round the corner and doesn't stop running until he is on Moi Avenue.

Avoiding the pavement, he walks alongside the cars parked on the street. Today, he doesn't look at the gold-coated watches in the Asian shops' display windows. Soon, he stares down last night's alley, which is across the street. His sisal sack is still there. He will need it tonight but he hesitates. Both sides of the street are thronged with Nairobians hurrying away to their individual undertakings. A car is coming down the street. He hides between two parked cars until it passes by. Then he crosses the street, enters the lonesome alley and grabs his sack. Without looking behind, he joins Tom Mboya Street.

Touts are busy herding passengers into their *matatus*. Soldered together like metal coffins, these vehicles cough black smoke as they crawl to their various destinations. "Twenty bob, twenty bob, *kila kitu* twenty bob," shouts one hawker, declaring her merchandise goes for twenty shillings. "*Mia, mia, mia*," cries another hawker as he raises into the air a bra worth a hundred shillings. Dasani rolls up his sack and painstakingly eludes the notice of fellow pedestrians.

Down Tom Mboya Street he goes, towards the Meridian. He is shaking even in this warm sun. His eyes pass over buildings nervously. A *matatu* almost knocks him down when a woman walking up the street brushes hard against him pushing him off the pavement.

"*Jinga*," shouts the *matatu* driver as he speeds off.

Dasani stares at the back of the woman. He then glances up and down the pavement. He sighs. Tucking his sack neatly under his armpit he walks on. He stares at the entrance to the Meridian through the corner of his eye. Business as usual: taxis in, taxis out.

"*Mwizi… chika huyo mwizi*," a female voice urges.

"Thief… stop that thief," takes up a manly voice in English.

A choir of pedestrians, each singing in his or her own tongue, quickly builds up.

Dasani looks up the street. The choir mistress is the same woman who almost killed him a few moments ago. She is pointing. She is pointing at him. Fellow pedestrians turn sharply looking for the thief. Those across the road stand and stare. Perhaps the thief will run into their hands. The supposed victim pushes through the thickening crowd of confused

Nairobians. She is still pointing at Dasani and shouting.

He panics. He drops his sack and slips between two women. He runs like a cat that has spotted a dog among the garbage heaps at City Market.

"*Mwizi, mwizi, mwizi,*" roars the crowd behind him.

I watch from the head of one of the men running after him. I cannot accompany this time. Yes, when they catch him, they will throw a rubber tyre over his neck, bathe him with paraffin and set him ablaze.

He seems to know this well as he bravely stretches his leg muscles. Ducking cars on Murang'a Road, he jumps into the Globe roundabout. He pushes his frail, hungry, weather-battered body towards Nairobi River. A stone missile assaults his head and he falls. Determined and bloody, he stands up and continues running. The crowd grows louder, "*Mwizi, mwizi, mwizi.*"

Dasani stumbles on and soon slides down the bank of the river, landing in the water with a splash. A man launches a huge stone – more like a boulder – after him. We wait. One minute. Five minutes. Fifteen minutes. He doesn't surface.

"*Kamedrown,*" a man in the crowd declares Dasani drowned.

Each man turns to his neighbour and congratulates him for having helped rid the city of yet another pickpocket. Thirty minutes later, almost everyone is gone. Yes, everyone except Dasani's supposed victim who is standing beside a man. The man who hauled the boulder. He is standing with his hands crossed over his chest. His leather shoe with a hole at the big toe heavily rests on Dasani's gum bottle. He is staring into the river intently. Soon, a smile spreads on his face. The cut across his right cheek makes his smile too long. I can no longer see him now; the man on whose head I'm sitting has walked round a corner. At least he doesn't mind flies.

Jackline Melisa Makena was born in April 1987 in Meru, Kenya. Daughter of a single mother, she began her writing career at age fifteen when she self published – with her mother's help – her first novel *The Mystery of the Twin Web*s (renamed *Twin Webs*) in 2003. She was the EVVY Award winner in the Young Writer's League (USA) essay contest in 2004. She has recently finished her secondary school education and is looking forward to starting university in September 2005.

While hoping to penetrate book markets all over the world with *Twin Webs* and its sequel, Africa remains her foremost concern, being both her homeland and a continent in desperate need of more stories told by its own children.

1955!

Tony Mochama

Dedicated to Capt. Jack Lemroy, whoever he is, who drew the painting 'L'Aviateur' that hangs in an airport in Belgium, for no discernible reason.

THE YEAR IS 2004. George W. Bush is still president of the You-Knighted S.A. Everything is not cool. In Brussels, at the airport, a sign kind-a floats on the wall. It says 'Belgium Comma a view from the sky', that is all. There is no view, although the sky's pretty all right. Also, light for 1am.

Instead of a view of this *Belgiese* floor-to-sky windows system, there is a row of buildings with yellow lights spilling out onto runway. The lights are like glares from malevolent cats' eyes, and the buildings stretch on into infinity. It is *not* a pretty sight.

Inside the airport lobby, a man on a motorcycle vacuum cleaner vacuously goes round and round a Greek pillar of Lenin in repose, his motorcycle vacuum cleaner's cleaning fall-feathers spread behind his machine like a peacock tail. It ain't a pretty sight, too.

The man is African. He goes round and round, and round, 'n round – 'n round and round and round – his thoughts mean nothing to the world, but are related to himself. He thinks of his wife, a waitress, and the way she doesn't respect him. In fact, he is sure, she is fucking the café owner in the place where she works, 8am-to-midnight. He recently found out, (from a friend of a friend, who knew a friend), that the job is pretty much a 12-hour shift. Two days on, then a day off, two days on, then a day off, and so on. 12-hour shift! That's eight-to-eight. So the question is, and he poses it: 'Where the fuck does his wife go from 8 to midnight?' You tell him this, because it is driving him crazy, which is why he drives his motorcycle vacuum cleaner in savage circles. Plus, she didn't tell him she had off-days! She, the slash – his wife – is Flemish.

An African woman is crashed out on an airport couch. Entry-visa shit, and all that shit. They'll probably report, then deport, her tomorrow. Tonight, she sleeps. At the airport, on the couch. He sees her in phases and fragments, as he drives round and round. First, he sees her face, lower lip hanging open in zzz land, like an open window during the parade after your soccer team has won a glorious cup. Kipling occurs. She's beautiful. Then he sees her feet (round and round), toes polished in purple, then her butt, then the top of her head, then the face again... Round and round he goes, taking her in, in circumferences.

There is music in the air.

It says: *This is where I came in, this is where you must go out*, and *I'm a loser, baby, so why don't you kill me?* and *Tcha-tcha, tcha-tcha, tcha, tcha-tcha, I'm Nelly, from Nellyville!*

All music to him these days is vile. Why? It is because his wife loves, no, fucking adores, music, and hearing music reminds him of *she,* and she reminds him of her dishonest work schedule. He loathes the way she comes in at 1am, all smiles and sated hugs, at an impossible distance from him. He stands there, pathetic, watching her remove her coat, and look at him (smugly he thinks) with her green eyes... and chat happily about how 'exhausted' she is, and what a 'horrible' day she's had at work, and so on. For someone so exhausted from horrid days, he thinks she's way too fucking happy. Her boss is 36, the son of the departed owner of a chain of restaurants called Mafia Menu. The man fucks his wife and runs restaurants he inherited for free. The father is Russian, and he's heavily invested in Brussels, in more than one way.

That's why our guy took the night-shift.

To dodge the 1am meetings.

At 1am, however, he cannot help obsessing.

She's coming home now! He dropped her off a block away to camouflage. She's smiling on the *Belgiese* streets, although it's autumn and she's Flemish! She has a way. She is expecting me. With no sheer dread. Am I so h-o-p-e-l-e-s-s other men have to...? and so on.

He took this job, he took the night shift – and now he needs to pee.

The African chick is still asleep. She, like a loyal sentry, has not stirred from her focal position in the couch. He needs to take a pee pretty badly. He needs to because Europe is so cold, and his wife is hot, and life, generally, is lukewarm.

175

"Being African must be hard," our man thinks, then strolls into '55 with a hard on.

1955 isn't hard to find. He just opens a door that he thinks leads into the lavatory and there he is!

At first, he thinks he is on the runway. It looks like the runway, anyway, with the thin strip of grey ribbon that is the tarmac running straight on into the horizon.

There is something very correct about this scenario, but like a cube inside a Rubik, the 'corrected-ness' of it all is inside a very wrong situation.

For example, a man somewhat unfortunately caught down on a, say, runway would be somewhat afraid. Perhaps very afraid. Such a man would be scared of being run down out of turn at the behest of a Boeing. Or being squashed by a Concorde (not knowing that Concorde had done its swan song). Or being mowed down by an Air-bus. Ground into Tar-mac-adam, like the thingies ingrained in Pistachio or the randomly painted cubes inside a Jean-Sartre Picasso paintin'.

Fear may be natural.

Our man, curiously and not out of courage, isn't at all fearful. To him, the air down here feels *dead,* like when one is surfing television channels and somehow reaches the remote outpost of television country… like channel 88 or 123 and all the action is 71 clicks away.

Life in this place feels remote.

Our man, however, still needs to pee.

It is an urgent and compelling act. There is something of the emergency around this need to pee. He could do it right there, by the dead grass, or right here, on the runway, but the cats' eyes call to him. Maybe there is a lavatory in there – for some reason, buildings tend to have them and maybe our man has a reservoir of good manners left over from childhood and is not the kind of guy who randomly urinates on walls and trees and other half-way places.

So he walks to the hanger, aware of his soft dead footfalls on the hollow ribbon of runway – tap tap, tap tap – vaguely wondering where everyone is.

There are some folk inside the first hangar he opens.

There are at least fifteen of them, and they are all strung up by the neck, they are all dangling from the noose, from the neck, from the neck upwards, their eyes are bulging out of their sockets, from their neck downwards, they are all footloose. They are all sticking their necks out, and they are *dead*. Our man decides, right then, to hell with the consequences and lets loose a nice burst of piss that soaks his pants good.

When he used to drink Carlsberg, Bud and other beer with his wife, he always went to the lavatory a lot. She said he had weak kidneys and would probably die from kidney disease or from a cyst, and now he guesses she was right – about the weak kidneys.

What he will die from, he thinks, is fright as he slowly backs away from the gruesome scene, hardly feeling the pee trickle and negotiate its way down to his knees. It takes massive will to force his badly trembling fingers to stop shaking enough to e-knoble the hanger door and push it open. Yup! Same show here. *This* film is running on two screens simultaneously. What the heck, the hangers stretch all the way to the horizon on Runway Street, and it is feasible this is the only show in town.

Our man walks and watches, with horrified fascination, at the way the curiously dead yellow light plays against the bloated, now wax black or rancid green, faces of the damned. Some are in the nude. Some are not. Most are men; there is an old African woman swinging from the ceiling in her own little corner of finale; most of the men are draped in rasta-hair, with features hardened from life forest, *changaa* but mostly death… these guys didn't die easy! They hang like barbecured chandeliers, dotting the scene like dark, dirty angels on the Devil's Christmas tree…

This time round, our man vomits, violently, and splotches of last night's fast food end up on his shirtfront.

He staggers out of there, head reeling with dead-fuck. Now he has pee in his pants and vomit on his shirt. He's never been more ready for a date than he is today.

He stumbles, no, careens, up the runway, moaning "O God no", "O God no" until it sounds like a song, but our man know he is only singing to himself. There are not gods here, he knows. Maybe, have never been. If God were here, he either left of his own volition, or was exiled to Siberia by some Whiter power.

It seems to dawn, the sky turning a funny purple-blue colour, and our man has gone so far up the runway he is beat with terror and tiredness; he thinks of his wife asleep at home, on his Yochi Pochi bed, curled up under the duvet he bought, sleeping the sweet sleep of the sexually sated, yet she hasn't fucked him for five and a half months. Then he thinks of this place, hangers swarming with victims of some recent mass hangings, for whatever purpose.

"Wazzup?" he screams at the sky, slack-jawed, "Wazzuuuuupp?"

He thinks of his wife, and her two-timing life; he thinks of this Mass

Gallows world he's in, wife, mass gallows, world, wife, mass gallows, world; he thinks, "she's a whore" and "this ain't Disneyland" and he screams "wazzuup" at an absent God, and kneels on the grass by the tarmac to weep.

When he looks up, he sees – through his fear-stained face. It is like watching life through a Cellophane paper, seeing an outdoors airport bar called The Dambusters and, yeah, sure – the dam has burst and the troubled waters of his life are threatening to draw him in, then drown him in a deluge of delirium.

Our man's tongue feels – prods actually – almost automatically, the sockets in his teeth. There are four gaps in his mouth, just as there are gaps in Time, and at least another dozen teeth in his mouth are defective – some with jagged, little given edges or yellow film creeping over them like furtive roaches on a futile mission; gift-wrappin' fro a ver' bad men givin' unpleasant present. You could get teeth like tha frem juzz sittin up in your little flat in Belgium, eating chocolates as you wait for your factored up, up-factored white wife to come home; eating chocolates to infect a little sweet into your bitter life. Or you could get teeth like that from three years hard living in the forest, hiding from Brits out to kill your ass because you are a 'rebel' – teeth like that from sustaining your scrawny boo-dy on a diet of wild berries, arrow roots and, when you're hungry enough from sucking pulp, with only the occasional field-turned-forest rat, for protein.

Yeah, you could get teeth like shit because you dare not use your homemade firearm (which you learnt to cook up in Burma during World War 2 as a gun carrier-corp) because noise is a Judas when you're a man-on-the-run. Besides, ammo is precious, ammo is for killing Brits, but mostly for killing your fellow Agikuyu who will not take the oath to expel the enemy from the homeland. *Mzungu Arudi Ulaya, Mwa-frika Apate Uhuru.*

Besides, to get that ammo you had to raid a *Mzungu* police post in Karen where they got six of your guys… so why waste ammo on animals because you are hunger, and your comrades died getting this ammo-shit? So you go hunger, because hunger is a smaller price to pay than death. That's why they call *it* the 'Ultimate Prize'.

Teeth, too, have their tale – even if it is a green-and-yellow movie.

All our man wants out of God's blue sky is a beer – and a little ska muzik to cheer him up. "Da-doo-dee, dalala, da-doo-dee–" and so on. His wife hates ska. He likes it because she *hates* it. It's not, though, a ska-man's world.

What's the point of hovering around (while your wife fucks up) or hoovering on the periphery of life (because the Brits want you dead) if you cannot obliterate the present through a cold *Kanywaji*? Or, for that matter, a hot vodka?

"Mau mau and de-definated coffee?" our man asks, in some confusion. "What the fuck are you talking about?"

The British woman-gal behind the counter looks (even more) shocked, then stormy.

Her thin lips become two pencils pressed in-between the hands of a schoolmaster about to give you the hiding of your life. She's got bluish-greenish eyes that would be pretty if they weren't about as cold as a Swiss banker's wife's bottom might be when the middle has dropped out of some ultra-cold European winter. Her eyes flash lightning. "Now, look here, you fucking *kaffir*, don't you dare brandish your bloody American vulgarities in my pub, otherwise I'll have Mike whip the bloody hell out of your black bottom. Do you understand?"

Our man wonders why his thoughts are beginning to hurricane, why a tsunami of rage is building up dangerously in his mind, yet even football world players of the year, striker Thierry Henry up-front in 2005, have no immunity about being described as dark excreta by Spanish National coaches, who have shit-for-brains and talk shit in soccer pitches that sends their fans into paroxysms of verbal diarrhoea…

Besides, the Brit (bitch) reminds him of his wife, with her red head, and blue-green eyes, and button-nose and freckles, and thin pencil mouth – but mostly, the contempt in her eyes that reduces him to a small segment on the periphery of the boundary-line between here-and-nothingness.

His thoughts no longer rotate in helpless cycles now, are no longer, are from ceiling fan. They are violent, directed thoughts – like the arrow an *Mkamba* hunter aims at fleeing prey – his thin frame like an exclamation mark in the landscape – or, those funnel-shaped miseries of African mosquitoes that look like a little boy's 'Happy Birthday' dunce-cap, but are really nothing more than malaria-in-a-cone on the open road where for two seconds you caught Elvis singing *Don't mess with my…* and you never get to know whether it is tutu or blue suede shoes. Because the car, or the tune, got away. It is called Doppler's effect, physicists say. It's called life, our man thinks.

"Don't call me shite…" he says, his voice low like an iceberg awaiting ships in the Black Sea.

"Shite, shite, shite, shite, shite, shite, shite, shite…" she screams; her voice fades off... like the way after you've passed by in a fast car, with an open top up some radio shop.

He's at a small bar in his local town in Kilgoris, having come home for the December holidays. He's the local hero — at least for the week in between December 24th and January 1st when he's literally throwing *wang'u* (liquor) at the local people because the year's paid off in shillings... and the drunker he gets, the bigger his garage in the capital city of Nairobi becomes.

Jukeboxes, not deejays, are still the mainstay in this shady dive in Kilgoris and our man strolls over to one, the only one, decorated with Chris-mas-tree lights that flicker colours.

He wants to play some real Western music to these X-mas drunkards, something like *Dance like an Egyptian* or *Ra-ra Rasputin, Lover of the Russian Queen, some really thought he was God* will show these country hicks a few tricks, a few tricks about sophisticated big city tastes.

Our man walks into The Dambusters' bar at what looks like 10.52am to him, going by the position of the sun, wondering if they take Euros here, because Euro is all he has going for him, here in 1955, not tarnishing Euro that hasn't happened yet, in 1955, just seeing the white girl behind the counter in odd 1955 clothes that he has seen in the TCM movies, when he cannot get shut eye coz he's thinking of his hot, white waitress wife servicing a Russian mobster who's already heavily invested in Brussels' Eateries and Belgian thighs — shutting out the sounds of Copenhagen shrieks by gobbling won gobos of choc-o-lata, o yeah.

And he plops down in front of the bar-counter, weary from dead-fuck, and orders a Tusker.

She's obviously British — with a dirty red head. She'd be pretty if not for the pinched, Brit mouth that gives her face a mean look like a semi-disgusted Doberman bitch or a comma, in the wrong place for a wrong sentence, if she did not look so comically shocked... and he smiles for the first time, drops her his 'famous wink', the same one he used to shellshock his wifey the first time they met, back in Kenya when he was somebody — the owner of a garage up at Upper Hill where they met after her hired tourist's car broke down before she discovered that the pleasure of fucking Russian gangsters far surpasses the pleasure of marrying African owners of Upper Hill garages who came home so wiped from call-gals' work they cannot the fuck keep it the fuck up.

"Can... may," he corrects himself, "I have a warm Tusker?"

The redhead in the 50's dress is staring at him with the same shocked look one would have if one ran into a Ukranian bear in the middle of morning traffic in Manhattan, so he glances over her shoulder out of discomfit, and there's a mail-cutting of the really young Elvis from some British newspaper on the wall... and there is no sign of a Tusker on the black-wood bar shelf. Just rows of Bells, and Johnny Walkers – with Guinness and Pilsner beers beneath, like the sentries of higher powers.

And 'sentry' makes him think, twice, of the African gal back at the airport barge who lay in visa-free state for many hours, because her beautiful face does not make sense to European immigration officials, and he asks, "Which country am I in?"

And the girl, white behind the counter, finally seems to find her tongue (which some Russian cat called Pieterovysky had taken away) and says, "Are you by any chance one of the Wilson Mechanics?" in that inquisitive tone of voice the Brits have to a tart.

"No," our man counters, still in his hoovering overall, "I am one of the *Mike and the Mechanics* crew – y'know?"

Relief, instead of laughter, washes over her face – like a welcome flashflood, quite in contrast to the deluge that engulfed him before he discovered the dam-busters, and the welcome thought of *kinywaji*.

"One of Mike's mechanics," she repeats, seemingly more to herself than to anyone else, including him, "Good. And yes, you must always look over your shoulders those days, what with this frightening Mau Mau business going on all over the bloody place. It's so *déclassé!*"

Our man.

The music fascist.

Discovers that juke-boxes too are dictators – and instead has to settle for Kenny Roger's *The Gambler* because that is what is there, and while the old beer goes on about how *you've got to know when to hold enfold 'em, walk and rum away*... our man goes about the business of 'tuning' or flirting. With Wanjiru. The local barmaid who may, or may not, sleep with him tonight in the cheap one-bed lodge-room above their heads, and who may or may not be HIV positive. But it does not matter, all things considered.

He has condom.

If she does not sleep with him, he shall still have condom and no disease, and if she sleeps with him, he shall not have the condom. If she is not HIV, he shall still have no condom and no disease, and if she is HIV, he shall have no condom and still no disease.

To paraphrase the English naturalist, Ray, Venereal Disease is the Tax paid for Random Pleasures, and whatever the meaning of life is, condoms are the Answers. Out of the Conundrum into the light.

In his Africa, *this* Africa, many things don't have any meaning and when things are meaningless, fuck them!

But don't fuck them for fuck's sake. Have accessories.

Have condoms. Have a slippery mind, and slippery years, and a good ear for music (unlike those two twits in loud plaid shirts – yellow and red – who have drunk too much *keroro* and are loudly demanding that the music be changed... and that brand of amusing idiocy can only be imported from Ukambani).

But mostly, have rage!

Everybody, who is somebody, knows that – from Phyllis Diller who said *never to go to bed mad, to stay up and fight*, to Emily Dickinson who advised that anger *soonest fed, soonest dead* to the Maya Angelou who knew a *rage is like fire and burns everything clean* to Ephesians that advises, *let not the sun go down upon your wrath*.

And who is our man to defy an American Comedian, prim English authoress, authoritative African-American black female writer *and* commentator; to God himself – who could be Ra-sputin – all at the same time? Writers, legends, feminists and gods all have authority. And authority is someone that you dare not defy – just like gravity.

So he fucks her harder against the counter, his hand holding her red hair and the right hand, the one with the knife... still pressed against her throat and he mutters, "So now I'm in real *shites*, right?" and it is in the same guttural 'scream and die' tune of Radio-Moscow dial he'd used earlier...

And the music in his head goes: *There was a mad man, in Russia long ago, and his beard was long, and his eyes were flaming gold!* but it's not 1917, it is 1955 – and Elvis Presley approves of what he is doing because he is still smiling at him from his vantage point on the wall, and has one thumb up. Elvis and Eminem – the only two good white musicians who ever lived, our man thinks – Elvis stole the thunder from Afro-rock in the fifties, and Eminem stole the lightning from black rap at millennium, and yet the bastards think the black people, in America and everywhere, be *the* thieves?

Or maybe it is 1987 in his favourite bar in Kilgoris Town and Wanjiru, the local barmaid (in the pre-proper-AIDS Era) is shyly asking – "So, man, how is the big, city, of Nea-ro-be?"

And he's saying – "It is hot shit, with discos like starlight. Maybe one day, baby, I'll take you there." If you promise to do me, he do not add – and she's smiling, all coy, like a six-year-old retard, saying. "Oke! A would re-a-rrr-y like that." "Yeah, you'd like it," our man says meaningfully, and maybe she does, but not in 1955 because this bitch is screaming like a shit slut determined to shatter the sound barrier, and he wonders if he should slit her throat – trachea 'n all – because, in the jungle, ammo is expensive, and noise is a Judas, and he doesn't like white bar-women who call him 'black shite'.

In fact, ever since he discovered his wife was not just a hard-working Brussels waitress, but also a Russian Mafia-banging tart, he does not especially tolerate the insults of arrogant white women, *not* in 1955, not anytime soon, and he wonders why they can't all be like the subservient barmaids of Kilgoris – *if* you overlook their thieving ways with wallets when you are catching your power-naps.

Those ones let you slap their big, or little, asses as they sashay by – and don't mind that, when you want to catch their attention, you yell: "*Wee, Malaya na matiti ku*bwa!" (Hey, you prostitute with big tits) or "*Hey, we Malaya na rasa ndogo!*" (Hey, whore with the flat bottoms), "Bring me a beer here!"

Crudity is the currency in local dives, be it Kilgoris or be it anywhere.

"Black *shite*" was the real dam-buster, in our man's case.

A man's life could be his suicide-bomb, not any different from the TNT-belts strapped around some Palestinian freedom-fighter or Iraqi insurgent's waist – and the powder could be having Time and Country taken away from you – by a whore of a wife who comes home, *ex nililiso*, exhausted at 1am, exhausted by dalliances with Russian gangsters who could shoot up a man, or an omelette, any given hour, on order. Or, time and country taken away from you, the powder could be from stumbling into a lavatory and out into 1952 – in a jungle called Ngong Forest where you hid for three years and ate tree-bark for breakfast and rat for dinner, for protein – because you are an insurgent in the fifties. And one day you got fed up of feeding on bark-rat, and fed up of hiding, and because a man must 'stay up and fight', you got out of Ngong Forest and trekked past elegant mansions in an area called Karen named after a Dane called Blixen who thought y'all Africans were children. Okay *enfant terrible,* you wandered into an airport of light aircraft called Wilson where you did not know was the plane of an aviator, a heroine, called Beryl Markham, who was the first woman to fly non-stop across the Atlantic and 'straight on till morning' – although the twilight of her life was sad-dish.

But you did not care. The fates of white women, spawn of Country Snatchers, didn't concern you. All you knew was the alarm was about to be raised by a collaborator, a black home-guard, in a mechanic's uniform – that lay in stark contrast to your rags that once were clothes. About, because you know, because of the rage, you slew – and later you found out he worked for a man called Mike Holmes who was perfectly capable of whipping your black bottom red... not blue, because blood ain't ice, and its colours are constant!

You found this info out of a pinched mouth of a British woman, because computers are foreigners like a reluctant IBM; a redhead who called you 'black shite' in our new Dead-Mechanic's Skin – and your TNT-belt just went off, with catastrophic consequences for the crowd of one.

"You should not only have looked over your shoulders," our man says with a final thrust, "you should have looked at the sign that said *Danger – Roadworks Ahead*".

Sometimes, the most dangerous 'shite' is that which is most obvious. Sometimes, not.

Over his shoulder, a shadow creeps up on him like a plague... it's right-hand arm side – Holmes is elongated with a wrench. There is a tremendous crack, like the lightning that sometimes tears African skies apart, a pregnant woman giving that last, triumphant push to birth. Afterwards, exhausted, she smiles, tired-like, as a little new miracle squeals into the world. It is a moment of breath-taking joy, but the baby – un'ware – still shrieks indignantly, even as new mom holds it up in loving hands, before cuddling it in the start of a lifetime of indescribable affection – that only the death of the one, or the other, will break.

The pain that splits our man's head is so bright that for a second, everything is illuminated, like walking through a dark African town or country scape on a stormy night – then the lightning comes and, for a second or two, everything is lit up in a sheen of terrifying yet glorious blue-fire light, so that life seems to have been frozen into a Kodak moment. Field fire you could send as a postcard. "God is taking photographs," children used to say when young, running and laughing from the African rain. Wish you were here – blue-fire light illuminating countryside so that, for a second, the fields are all lit up. Elvis in neon, corn-ears frozen in the blue-fire moment, green fields of static harvest lit up in a pearlish-white colour... or... it's in a town.

You are walking on a dark city street when it happens. Lighting happens. Blue-fire city occurs, the shadow of another pedestrian, like Batman in still – only he's a mugger. A cat caught in mid-jump, from one dustbin lid to the next. The feline motion frozen – frightened to mid-air stillness by *God-fire*! The sharp edges of blue-white building come askew, knives being sharpened by the Grinder-man, who sharpens knives in lives teeming with them. Everything cuts!

1955 shatters when it hits the ground. It is like that Michael Jackson video with the rain falling in slow-mo, or could be from a Crown Paints advertisement. Then the Kodak moment is gone.

Darkness descends – and our man's last thought is that he has suddenly gone blind – unlike Charles in that 'Ray' film where things, like tree-trunks, gradually became **A**-mbiguous, **B**-lurry, **C**-loudy, before **D**-arkness descends.

Death does not descend suddenly, like an African sunset. It takes its time, like dying light during a Saint Petersburg white night, when the vodka still tastes sweet 'n succinct on the lips – and everywhere.

The year is 2005.

George *Dubya* Bush junior is still president of the United States of America, and none the wiser for it!

Six am steals in through cheap curtains and into the seedy room at the La Belle Hotel. Euro-Dawn's fingers lightly comb red hair with pink fingertips, before Euro-Dawn's palm spreads across the corpse-like features of Chantal, asleep.

She comes awake violently, blue-green eyes shooting grey bewilderment across the room, before realisation turns bewilderment into red rage.

On television, the porn-channel is still on, advertising an upcoming 'Lord of the Rim' programme, or something ridiculous like that.

Timor is gone. Chantal is alone.

Timor, owner of Mafia Menu is gone, so Chantal is alone – but that's not the way this script is supposed to be working.

The plan was to sleep together in this seedy hotel called La Belle – that happened. The plan was for was for *them* to wake up together, Chantal and Timor, drive over to Chantal's place in central Brussels, wake up that no-good, can't-get-it-up, airport-hoover-cleaning husband of hers, and tell him, *marriage's up, you can pack up and go back to Africa, or you can stay here and do whatever the hell you please, me I'm packing and going.*

The plan was for Timor, then, to take off with her to his native city of Saint Petersburg and set her up with her own perfume line.

"We'll call it Chantal No. 1," he'd whispered in his low and slightly menacing voice, after one of their marathon lovemaking sessions. His *Rrrrs* roll deliciously.

That was the plan!

And in her mind's eye, Chantal could see her perfume-line taking over Russia, before rolling westwards like a *blitzkrieg*. She could see herself with two beautiful children – a girl and a boy – frolicking in Timor's *dacha* in the outskirts of Saint Petersburg… but she'd also have apartments in Paris, Budapest and one also here in Brussels.

Meanwhile, she dresses rapidly, blind panic making her hyperventilate violently, and she staggers out into Steenwegopaarschot Street – shady and red light, but still in the morning light, with little human or mechanical traffic.

The early morning sun dances against dilapidated buildings lightly, Sammy Davis in a good mood, but this rare beauty literally being played against grim lives is wasted on Chantal.

Panic still holds her in its iron grip, like a dictator's fist around a fragile cup of a tea. Further down the streets she comes across a small group of nine-, ten-year-old early birds. They could be Turkish – or they could be Moroccan – she doesn't care, they are all Arabs – and they giggle when she passes by.

Chantal throws – no, hurls – such a filthy look of ill will at them that they are stunned into silence. Even the scruffy dog that they are with instinctively shrinks into the little space available between Stunned Silence, and the Arabic graffiti scrawled into a Steenwegopaarschot wall.

When she gets to the Brussels North station, she gets into a near empty train and soon she is pounding on the door of her Brussels apartment that she told her husband they can afford because she gets lots of tips from Russian mobsters at the Mafia Menu restaurant, when the truth is that Timor has been paying rather generously for some of his *in*-investments in Brussels.

A woman who showed up at a rural African man's door at 6.36am in the morning, after an inexplicable night-out is as likely as not to end up in hospital… if not on page 5 of the Daily Standard as a 'casualty of a domestic dispute'. Obituary, with history and a story.

In Europe, anything goes, in the age of the femme *fatal feminist*, and in this case, it is our man who seems likely to go as pounding the front-door, panic giving way to rage, Chantal screams, "*Ouvre, sale negre*, or I'll have you deported so fast you won't know if your ass is in Cape Town or Cairo."

Still, he does not open, so she shouts even shriller until a neighbour –
a short, fat bespectacled fellow with a white face that looks like dough –
emerges.

They have been living here eleven months now, but have never
exchanged a word. Now they exchange words.

"*Als je nie ophoud met al dat lewaai zal ik de politie bellen*," which involves
something about making racket, immediate cessation and calling the
police.

Chantal's is an educated response. "Fuck you!" she screams, her face a
flaming Flemish red, an African tomato.

He stares at her through his thick bifocals, that make him look like
some anonymous railway ticket-man staring blindly at one, through a
booth in *Nowhere, Europe*.

"So now he's a 'dirty nigger'," the accountant says, a nasty, faceless
smirk spreading across his dough face. "What about you giving yourself to
Slavs in the back of big cars across the park, uh? You think I do not see
you when I'm on my midnight jogs uh? I'm keeping an eye on you, I'm
keeping my eye on you."

And with that tempting revelation, the accountant darts back like a bat
into the anonymity from whence he'd emerged.

After she has stopped shaking, Chantal remembers the spare key in her
handbag and let's herself into the apartment.

It is quarter to seven in the morning – and the apartment has been
swept clean. Everything is gone, except for the telephone in the hallway
that stands on a black mahogany table from Africa... and the clock on the
wall that says that it is indeed quarter to seven.

Chantal lets out an ear-splitting shriek of rage, then rushes to the
telephone to tell the Belgian police that her thief of an African husband has
stolen everything in her flat – down to her knickers. And hey, they better
be on the look-out and block all the pawnshops and hand-me-down
clothes stores in Brussels that have lately, thanks to the Arabs, sprung up.

There is a message on the answering machine

It can only be from one man – Timor it is. It is he who says: "*Gonvno*,
you listen to me very carefully. You are nothing to me anymore but whore.
Am finished with you.

"This is why our last fuck was at the *La Belle*, where whores like you
belong. You spoil everything when you become bore with your fantasies,
Chantal Number One, and so on." His voice, dark as bats, laughs – a low
hack that she used to think sexy as hell. Now, all is *hell*. "I'm not taking

187

you, anywhere. If you come to my restaurant or bother me, you will be involved in accident so bad your face will require re-construction… If you survive! My advice would be to stay with your husband. Good wives stay, and support, husband. *Dasvidanya.*"This is good-bye, in Russian.

Then there is a silence that stretches on into infinity, which is the end of the tape.

When the police come, having been told that the black man upstairs is busy killing his wife, Chantal is naked – and the glass is everywhere.

The windows are shattered on the floor, as is the wall-clock. The telephone will not make any more calls this year, or any other year after this. The clock doesn't work, and the phone does not work, and Chantal's mind doesn't work; the only thing that still works in this apartment, it seems, is the Brussels Police force.

They responded quickly to the imaginary homicide, and stopped Chantal bleeding further. She had stripped naked, and they linger a few extra seconds covering her up, in order to savour her nudity a little while longer.

The black mahogany table is on its side among the shredded glass. It did not escape her wrath. But it still is intact.

A man walks up St Petersburg's Nevsky Prospekt, the early-morning sun in his face. When he reaches the Beer Garden, he cuts sharply left – and out of the summer. A youthful Russian drunkard has his manhood out, and is peeing on the base of the statue of General Kutzov, the man who chased Napoleon out of Russia.

Nearby, two of his drunken mates stagger about, laughing uproariously, clutching half-empty bottles of Stolichnaya Vodka and encouraging him on.

A pigeon flying overhead swoops low, and shits on one of their heads.

"The ghost of Kutzov," the Russian man thinks, as he cuts across into St Isaac's Cathedral Square. An old *babushka*, in gumboots, is painfully wheeling a young blond man up the ramp – and to the church. The blond man is a soldier who lost his feelings, both physical and emotional, to an accurate Ingushetia sniper in Chechnya.

This paralysis has left him with a burning hate of everything – even God – only his grandmother, the woman who wheels him up the stairs, is spared from his loathing despair.

The other Russian, the Walker, hesitates a moment – wondering whether he should walk on, or help the old lady wheel her grandson up.

Walk on, he decides. This is Russia, because when the shit hits the Neva, the shit hits the Neva.

Old age and Chechen snipers are just part of Russian life. Nothing can stop 'em. Timor enters a new club he's just opened called Tropez on Sixth Kazanshkaya Street. It is still full, mostly of foolish Americans spending their money as if there is no tomorrow. And, he guesses for these people, tomorrow is always today.

If Timor were interested in authors, it would be an apt time to quote W. Somerset Maugham to the doorman of Klub Tropez perhaps? He could look the seven-foot Igor up in the eye and sigh, "The future will one day be the present, and seem as unimportant as today." But American authors aren't Timor's thing.

Russian strippers *are*, and he walks into Klub Tropez, pinching breasts and nipples liberally, like some farmer in an African stock market that deals in Zebus and Friesians.

And when his club manager, a psycho in a sharp blue suit, walks up to him at the bar and asks what happened to the 'Belgian whore' he was supposed to bring to run the Klub Tropez strippers, Timor smiles and says, "*Dermo*! The kunt has ambitions of becoming perfumieri, like Estee de Gautierrr. So I leave her bar-haind in Belgium."

The two men laugh heartily-hack-hack-hack and the beat goes on.

Our man.

His last day on earth could be spent calling Brussels at 1.55pm, operating lovingly, urgently, to his wife on the telephone – the way they do in Hollywood romantic comedies – telling her how much he loves her, and how if only she'd leave the Russian, he'll forgive her and everything will be right as the African rain.

The African rain from his childhood, not the snowflakes that coloured her days of innocence, in beautiful, blinding white light, in the little Dutch town of Mol.

She stared out of her small window in Mol, at the snow falling outside, with the same intensity our man stares outside of his little window at the prison yard outside.

They are building the gallows.

The year is 1956. He cannot call his wife in Europe because I.T. and T. does not exist. Nor does his wife. And if I.T. and T. exists, they certainly do *not* do long-distance calls.

He shares his cell with another man.

The fellow is sick and dreadlocked, and shivers violently in his thin blanket on the floor.

His chest is bare, the colonial authorities having reduced him to mere underwear. The lice are everywhere, but his eyes burn with defiance.

He coughs, spittle flies like MiGs.

Our man, against the window, thinks the man-on-the-floor has tuberculosis, but then again it is hard to worry about TB when your gallows is under construction.

"What's that noise outside?" The man-on-the-floor finally manages to croak.

"Carpenters," our man says resignedly, then hastens to add, "They are making beds!"

The-man-on-the-floor sees the lie in his eyes, and laughs a sardonic, doomed laugh, "Ha, ha, ha. No doubt to go with the hotel-standard blankets they've provided us with."

"Why are you in Kamiti?"

Our man, against the window once more, is in a crude, kangaroo courtroom, governed by English law, English justice. Lady Law is blind and British. He is charged by a prosecutor who saw "live action against the Mau Mau rebels in 1952" – but who does not add that he's responsible for at least three coloured children in the area around Timau, and none of the young, black women wanted to exercise their reproductive rights – who alleges that our man is a "Mau Mau insurgent".

The penalty is death. Lady Justice swings her scales (made in the UK), and agrees.

"I heard you were caught red-handed raping a white woman in a Nairobi West airport bar last year. That is why you are here." The-man-on-the-floor's eyes seem to dance between light amusement and deep disgust. Then a coughing spell engulfs him, and he adds, "No doubt, man, you done doing your part in the struggle for freedom."

The neck-ties are everywhere, and *they* select one for him, and knot it carefully around his neck.

For some reason, it reminds him of Chantal, of the early days in Brussels when things were still cool between them, the way she knotted his airport tie, her blue-green eyes laughing *with*, not at, him.

When it still did not seem ridiculous to wear a tie to work, only to cover it in mechanic's overalls and hoover a few square feet of Belgium clean.

When he still did the day shift.

They put a black bag over his head – where do they make black head sacks? In Cornwall, or Belfast perhaps? – more for them not to see grotesque death mask struggles, the shifting expressions, than for him not to see the dying of light.

He remembers Chantal, tying his tie in Belgium.

He remembers a childhood tongue-twister that went: "Kantai can't tie a tie? If Kantai can't tie a tie, why can't you tie a tie, like Kantai?" Perhaps because the kids who recited these poems were in bourgeois schools, and Kantai was, is still, a Maasai, perpetuated in poetry? *Ars longa, Vita brevis...* Chantal.

He recalls their honeymoon, somewhere in some bay overlooking the Indian Ocean, somewhere in Mombasa. The way, early one morning, they went out for a walk on a little path alongside a cliff – holding hands, the way people in love do, thinking of nothing as the humid Mombasa air embraced them in its light-headedness.

Out of the cliff side, hundreds of Northern Carmine Bee-eater birds suddenly exploded, colourful balls fired out of a Russian cannon, their long, central tail-feathers clubbing a sly signature through the sky, dipping momentarily towards the ocean as if to drown – before disappearing into the sky, into oblivion.

Our man tries to cling to this image, of him and Chantal watching the magic, open-mouthed, watching the morning magician of Mombasa pull flying hankies, or bunnies, out of the cliffside.

A sinister image of an airport hangar, of bulging eyes and uselessly dangling feet, threatens to sweep the coastal image – a dark cloud, drowning Rara the sun goddess.

Something falls out beneath him. Maybe gravity.

Then the sun is out again, and the Carmines, all turquoise-blue and crowned in green, are flying again.

Tony Mochama is a poet and journalist working in Nairobi whose work has been published by *Kwani?*

Letter to a Friend

Charles Mungoshi

IT'S A LONG TIME SINCE I last heard from you or about you, Fungiso. I can't remember whose turn it is to write. It doesn't matter. Not anymore. Not now. Really, it doesn't matter, Fungi. I just hope that you're still there, that you haven't started the long journey across the desert like so many of our age these days.

Or, maybe, you have forgotten about me? Maybe you are now happily married, with two little bright kids – a boy and a girl – and living with your handsome, loving husband somewhere in the northern – low-density – suburbs of the city? Remember our long – oh, so long – talks that would go on and on and on far into the night? You were always waiting for someone, or expecting a letter from someone: Leon, Zondo or Anxious. You always had more than two or three at the same time then. But never, you said, never at the same school as we were.

"Get someone to love you Sarai," you used to tell me. "A girl your age, beautiful as you are, without a sweetheart? You must be sick or something!" You just couldn't believe it was possible to live without a boyfriend, could you? It was just as unnatural as someone who didn't visit the lavatory after a heavy meal of *sadza* with *harurwa* and *masondya,* you said.

Did you finally get him, Fungi – the man of your dreams? I got mine, Fungi, or rather, he got me! Anyway, I also remember the many nights we would walk the four kilometres – sometimes in a heavy downpour and sometimes in bright 'lovers' moonlight' – as you called it – back home with you crying and cursing all the way: "Men!" – and you would spit so far it hit the opposite shoulder of the road – "Men! They are worse than dogs! Tell me Sarai: why do we waste our time giving them our love? They will leave the piece of bone offered to them on a silver platter to chase after a passing warthog!"

Tell me, Fungi: who did you finally 'catch'? Is it Zondo? Or Leon? I rather liked Mike – with his big teeth and wide mouth and eyes that cried, tightly shut, when he laughed that echoing laugh of his! Had I been given a longer time with him, instead of the last two hectic exam months of our last year at school, I would have – *ahiwe*! But then, you were such an eagle – *chapungu chaicho* – when it came to laying claim and holding on to what was yours! I'll never forget how you nearly tore Greta Shanga to pieces when you heard that Leon had been walking her along the narrow path into the hills! (Or was it showing her the path along which her people came into this land? You always had such a graphically filthy mouth on you, Fungi!)

This isn't why I am writing this letter at all. This isn't why I am sitting here in the half-darkness of the guttering candlelight as night falls over me in this grass-thatched pole-and-mud hut or shack at the farthest end of St Mary's Katanga Settlement on Manyame River, writing this long-overdue letter to you. The real reason why I am writing is – well – by the way, do you still tell dreams?

Because, Fungi. Because I finally got him. Or he finally got me. Does it matter now? I got him. He got me. Name? You won't believe it! Mike. But not your Mike. This one is a false alarm. In fact he is not Mike at all. He is one of those fakes who think if they keep their own names the world will stop going round for them. His real name is Mhike! An unshod heel. A slippery eel! He ran away from me, Fungi. He ran away long before I buried my nine-month old son, Luke. Before my mother, without my say-so, had taken custody of Rita, my daughter, who is only one-and-a-half-years old. He panicked. He peed in his *kwasa-kwasa* dancer's trousers and disappeared into the soot, like the proverbial long-tailed rat, when I told him what the doctor had said about Luke's illness. He knew that Luke was going to die and he left me to handle the darkness alone. Scum.

I had been living in the family home in Glen View Three then.

"You can go and do whatever you want to do with whoever you want to do it with wherever you want, but I am not letting you drag my granddaughter in the muck with you!"

That was my mother, throwing my clothes and things into the muddy yard. She had ripped Rita off my back where I had tightly secured her with an *mbereko*. And she had stood in the doorway, fuming: the wronged, righteous mother!

I hit her, Fungiso. I hit my own mother. In a blinding, blood-red rage

I hit her! She shouted at me for the benefit of the other children. My younger sisters and brothers, six of them, some old enough to have babies of their own, just gawked and gaped at me silently, accusingly, as I stormed out of that house, packed my scattered clothes into my old, battered school trunk and left that place without saying goodbye or looking back. I could tell that they were terrified of me. None of them could understand this thing that had happened to me.

Whenever any of us did something my mother didn't approve of, she would always drag in our father's character to conk us on the head with it. It was worse for me since I was the eldest child and looked exactly like my father. One day, my father walked out of the house in the morning and didn't come back in the evening. Nor any other evening of any day after that. We heard later that he was living with an old flame of his, a shebeen queen, a *kachasu* swiller like him, somewhere in the St Mary's Katanga Settlement. My father had been a *madhobhabhini*, a dustbin man – as we called them – employed by Harare City Council. He used to work the Glen Norah–Glen View rounds. He must have been an embarrassment to my mother. At least he was to us, especially when other children whose fathers had better jobs, pointed him out to us as he hung precariously from the tailgate of the municipal rubbish truck shouting orders to the driver: "Ho!" as they approached a dustbin, then he'd jump down agilely – almost like a monkey (I sometimes felt extremely embarrassed) – picked up the filthy bin as if it were nothing, heaved it onto a dirt-besmirched shoulder and ran with it to the truck where a colleague in the truck grabbed it off him, emptied the contents into the truck and threw the bin down to the ground where it fell with a loud, vengeful bang. "*Handei!*" Father, now mysteriously back on his tailgate perch, would shout at the driver to move on to their next destination – another dustbin.

Poor mother! The sight of her husband like this twice a week must have been one of the most unbearable crosses in her life. You see my mother must have had her dreams as a young girl. She comes from a not too bad family. And my father? He had played the trumpet in one of the most popular bands around town. Mother must have built the most dazzling dreams on father's reputed soaring notes. Now she can only remember those tunes. And she remembers other memories, too, memories, I am sure, she doesn't want to remember.

"You see that man in the Benz, sitting in the back?" she had said to me once when we were just wandering around town, pointing at a passing car. "He is a minister," Mother said. So what? I said to myself. And when she saw that I wasn't going to comment, she said, as if to herself: "He once asked me to marry him; he was not a minister then." Later on when I had almost forgotten who she was talking about, I heard her say, "You could have been his daughter."

Well, I am my father's daughter. My earliest memories of Father are of him coming home from the beer hall, singing, drunk as a drugged fish – *sehove yadya chitupatupa* – as mother used to say. She would then of course proceed to unload a lot of verbal filth on his head and Father's response? He would just laugh it off saying: "You can run your mouth till it's silted up and runs dry like the Save River." He would then tell us stories of his day at work. On his best days, which were always when our mother had been really nasty with him, he would put all of us to bed and tickle us to rib-aching laughter and sleep.

As far as I can remember, there hadn't been a single day father came home sober. Now he'd been gone for two years. And every Thursday and Sunday of every week of those two years, mother had gone to church. In a Mother's Union uniform. At home she prayed daily: "Please make him come home to his children. No children can be called children without their father's presence." Maybe just maybe she did love him – and still does love him – what do you think Fungi?

I certainly loved my father. And if he is still alive, he is now my only hope. Maybe my decision to go and live in St Mary's has been prompted by a vague desire to be near him, a dim hope that one day, maybe, I might run into him on the street or in a pub, somewhere (who knows what this thing might make me end up doing?).

Well, my family is not the reason why I am writing you this letter. It is not the reason why I am sitting here in the dark, swatting mosquitoes to death by the dozen.

Fungiso, I finally met him. He drove a BMW – Be My Wife. I thought he had thought it up himself and it seemed very clever to me. Scum. Somebody had thought it up long before he was born! He would drive to our home and spend hours talking to my mother, making her laugh. She was impressed. I don't blame her. She said: this is the man to marry, Sarai. And I said, yes, Mother, yes, yes! Well, he paid a little something. We couldn't locate my father and an uncle stood in as Father. Fungiso, the least said of this rat the better. He ran away. He panicked – *When I needed you most* – remember those songs we used to swoon to and cry over at Nyika Growth Point in Mudhara Vodo's shop? Too late now. He drove that BMW into my belly twice and I brought two children into the world...

Go on! I can almost hear you laughing. I can see you holding your sides, rolling on the ground as you used to do, mussing and messing up your hair – your beautiful hair. (And that joke schoolboys always had running among them about you and *zvibayamahure*! But they never could win because you didn't care, and how you would make them all look like snot-nosed babies still wetting their mothers' backs!)

I can hear you laughing, Fungi, even now shouting to your latest 'catch': *Listen to this nonsense, darling! Do you remember Sarai Chakafugwabodo? That thin, wispy waif of a girl who used to think that boys hide pangas and canon-shot in their shorts? The one who would pray for the ground to open up and swallow her each time she smelled a boy near her?* I can still hear your ringing laugh, Fungiso.

You knew how to hurt me with that laugh that brought so much sunshine into those days at Gwindingwi Secondary School. For that laugh I forgave, and still forgive, you the daily pranks you never tired of playing on me either in the classroom or the netball pitch. The netball pitch was always full of laughter and sunshine then. It seems so long ago now.

Tell me, Fungiso: are you well? Don't laugh. All of a sudden, those words: to be well, seem to recede farther and farther from me with each breath I take. Just to be well. Nothing else. *Can you feel it, Fungiso?*

I ask because – because – it is true, Fungi. It is true. It is so maddeningly, frustratingly, frighteningly true that I just can't bring myself to believe it. That – that – all of a sudden – *usingambozvifungira* – you are not well! Not just for one day. But forever, Fungi, forever and ever amen! *Do you hear what I am saying, Fungiso?*

Even now, as I sit here in this gathering darkness, I would have laughed into the face of anyone who came to me suggesting that such a thing can happen to real people. Each morning I wake up expecting to hear someone knocking on my door to tell me that there has been a mistake, that it's all a big monster of a dream, that that doctor has been diagnosed insane and has since been imprisoned for life, that I can any minute rise from my bed again and walk out a free woman in the laughter and sunshine of my youth. It's so true that I spend most of the day trying to laugh it off, trying to laugh it all away.

Yes, Fungiso. For the past four or so months that I have known about it, I haven't done anything else but laugh. I laugh so much you could boil an egg on my face – it's so hot! – and now the laughter scares me. It seems to belong to someone else. I have never heard this kind of laughter all my life! This is the kind of story that only happens to other people: to Connie,

Rudo or even Marwei. They were that kind of girl at school. But me? Sarai Chakafugwabodo? Tell me, Fungiso. Please, please do tell me. Could you ever imagine, even in your wildest dreams, such a thing happening to this thin, wispy waif of a girl who lived innocently with her grandmother maMupakwa, in Bikita, while her parents were in Harare? Why me, Fungiso? Why me of all the unhappy people in God's wide wide world – why? Couldn't he have given it to those who deserved it? If he had wanted any names he could have asked me – or you – and we would have given him a whole school register of names!

It's when the laughter comes that I ask this question: why me? I am still too young, Fungiso! The worst times are when I am walking down the street, or buying vegetables in the market. It is then that, as I laugh, talking to someone I know, exchanging jokes, it sneaks in on me stealthily, without any warning at all, and conks me on the head: I am laughing, and suddenly I see the dark, haunted look that comes into the eyes of those I am talking to, the black, bottomless, shut-coffin silence that freezes their lips to a wind-blasted dryness as recognition and fear rampage inside them, and the poor struggle they put up as they try to laugh it off, to contain the panic inside social and civil bounds.

It is then that I know, as I have never known anything in my life before, that, although they are not moving away from me physically, they are moving away from me in their minds. *They are shutting their doors on me. They are forgetting me even as I am looking into their smiling faces.*

Well, I won't panic, Fungiso. Maybe today – these things happen, you know – maybe today, I will bump into my father. He is bound to understand these things, he's had his own problems with drinking, he's just got to understand what's going on with me. What do you think, Fungiso? Or, if he doesn't, well, I have always loved his talks and jokes. Maybe I will be able to tell him to persuade Mother to let us both come home, since she is always praying for him to come back. Maybe she also misses me now and she will just let me come back home with Father and we will be together again. Even just for a day.

God! I am tired, I didn't know that even just a little talk could cost so much.

Charles Mungoshi, the well-known Zimbabwean author of *Waiting for the Rain*, was shortlisted for the Caine Prize in 2000 and highly commended by the judges in 2004.

From Toyitoyi to Oyi Oyi

Dumisani Sibiya

INSTEAD OF THE SOFT lips of his beloved wife that would normally kiss his lips as a form of greeting every time after a hard day's work, that early evening, as the front door flung open, Mr Ndimande was greeted by the open black lips of a gun. He had tried several times to put the key in the hole but the key did not open the lock. The key simply turned. It seemed rather too loose. When he held the door handle he realised the door was not locked. He wondered why his wife, MaNdlovu, had left the door unlocked when the drug-influenced thugs, like vultures, hover around the streets of the township looking for fresh and regular victims. The lips of the gun that pointed in his direction as soon as he entered the house answered all the questions he had been asking himself.

It was a three-bedroom house in Diepkloof, Soweto. Three beds, a kitchen, lounge, dining room and bathroom. He and his wife MaNdlovu had not yet been able to furnish it in the way they would have loved to. It was their only valuable asset: it reminded them of their love, the society's struggle and their role in it. His wife was basically everything he needed. Her strength and unflagging support was beyond measure. The love they had for each other was the treasure they cherished...

"Keep your big mouth shut! Be a good boy and remain safe from my anger." The gunman, wearing a balaclava, gave instructions as he drew closer and closer to him. Blood-red eyes peeped through the two holes of the balaclava. Mr Ndimande, the government official, had almost frozen with dread. A strong smell of marijuana filled the whole house, making him even more scared.

"But-but..."

"No buts! I told you to shut your big mouth!"

Ndimande saw his impending death; he had to behave himself if he wanted to see the beautiful sun again. He wondered for the very first time where his wife could be. Perhaps she was no more, he thought. This thought sent shivers down his spine. If she were dead, he too would be better dead. He would not be able to endure the pain of her death. He definitely had to find out about her even though that might annoy the invaders. He wished someone would come to his rescue. His thoughts were interrupted by another masked body, which appeared from his bedroom. It was a one-legged fellow. He hopped and came close to the two. He spoke to his colleague as though he did not see Ndimande.

"It's your turn, *broer.*"

"Ho grand, comrade," replied the first gunman undoing the button of his trousers. "*Ke tlo shapa* two rounds. But I think we should tie this bastard first and make sure he is harmless. We must take him to the bedroom so that he cheers us up when we enjoy ourselves. We need his full support when we do it," he said with a forced giggle that came from under the balaclava.

"Brothers, please do not do that to me," Ndimande pleaded with a feebly hoarse voice, shock boldly written on his face. "Let's talk guys. If you need money, I will give you." He could not bear the thought of these two men raping his wife in his own bedroom. That was the worst humiliation he could ever experience.

"We are not here to play, *uyaverstana?* You are boasting to us that you have all the money in the world! *Uyaphapha, ne?* Hold your horses, boy. You tell us where the money is!" intimidated the big voice of the one-legged fellow. Ndimande had God to thank that he only got a slap on the face, and not the deadly bullets of the gun that was still pointing in his direction. Cold drops of sweat, one after the other, trickled slowly from his back to his buttocks.

"An inch of movement will be enough to send you to heaven. *Siyezwana?* Stand right where you are, and lift your arms up! So be a good comrade, *broer.* The one you used to be during the days of toyitoyi. Where is the money?" said the one-legged gunman.

"The money is in that wardrobe. But countrymen, what have I done...?"

"Shut your mouth before I slay you bastard!" said the other guy with his trousers round his ankles and his eyes looking at the bedroom door. He went to the wardrobe and, after searching for a few minutes, got a few

R200 notes. He put the money in his wallet. Ndimande kept inside all the words he wanted to say. He wished he were near the headboard where his gun was kept. As if they read his thought, the two men grabbed him, as a vice-grip would, and tied his legs together with a rope before dragging him to the bedroom.

They entered the bedroom. The smell of sex and marijuana filled the room. His beloved wife was on the bed, whining helplessly like a dog left outside in the cold. They let him sit on the chair. He could not help but break down in tears when he saw his wife, especially when he recalled what they had been through together…

They met many years ago. It was love at first sight for both of them. They were seventeen and fifteen or so. It was during a sports tournament. In the football category their schools played in the final match of the tournament. He was not a soccer player, but came to cheer for his school team. It was during that moment of jubilee and joyful noise that he was attracted to her. She was not very beautiful but far from ugliness. She was a short, plump girl, with beautiful legs and well-combed black hair. Her teeth were as white as milk. She looked extremely calm and respectful. There was something about her eyes he could not explain. He had momentarily felt scared. But something inside him pushed him to approach her. He gathered the courage and told her how much he loved her. Although she loved him, three months of negotiation passed before she agreed. Three years later they got married, a small traditional wedding.

Just before their son was born – he later died of some strange illness – Ndimande was severely tortured, arrested and, later, forced into exile in Swaziland for participating in the June 1976 Soweto uprisings, a march of school pupils against the introduction of Afrikaans as a medium of instruction in schools. They communicated sporadically as husband and wife for almost seventeen years. Distance that kept them apart made them love each other even more. They always dreamt, longed, hoped and wished they would be together one day. When Mandela was released from the jaws of Robben Island, Ndimande and his wife's hopes of coming together rose even higher. After seventeen years of loneliness, they were together once again.

It was very hard for her to accept him after he was away for such a long time. She felt very strongly that he betrayed her love by going into exile. She would not take any of his elaborate explanations. "The struggle came first! Our love came second! My womanhood came third and last!" MaNdlovu had said bursting with anger.

Things took longer to get back to normal. His wife, unlike many wives who betrayed their exiled men, was still childless. When they had sex (three weeks later) for the first time after close to twenty years, he could feel she was like a virgin. They cried together and told each other how much love they had for each other.

Their love grew day after day. When they were together they would remember the good old days. They wanted all the sweet memories to live with them and never be buried in the past. They constantly said how much they loved each other. They had held each other so tightly as though they were glued, like saliva and tongue. A new dawn had come for them and it was marked by the country's first-ever democratic elections on 27 April 1994. He endlessly thanked his God and his ancestors for giving him such a wife...

Now MaNdlovu, the bone of his heart, was on the bed, with legs forcibly stretched apart. Her hands were fastened tightly on the headboard. Half of her face was covered with a cloth. There was a tennis ball-like thing in her mouth, to make sure she did not raise any alarm.

"You do not make noise, OK! If you make noise you will go to heaven," said the one-legged man while his colleague mounted Ndimande's beloved wife. "You know why you are here, Ndimande. So start clapping while the comrade is enjoying. You know we are comrades; we have to share. We all fought for freedom and we must enjoy the fruits. Like many people who fought for freedom, I also lost my leg during the struggle. Remember the 1976 Soweto uprisings, which led to your detention? That is where I lost my leg too."

"Does that give you license to rape my...?"

"Shit! Who do you think you are talking to? I am not here to play! Don't waste my time with bullshit talk! *Jou foken hond!*"

"Better kill me, man!"

"Who do you think you are talking to?" He moved a little closer to him, "We will do that, don't you worry! Your hour has not come yet."

Ndimande felt his body burning with anger. He wanted to say something but no words would come out. A stream of tears started to run down his face. Did that one-legged fellow think he was a coward? Did he not fight with commitment to set the people of the country free? Is he not still working faithfully to deliver the promises of the ruling government and fulfil the expectations of this people? It was only last week that an article about his good work was published in a weekly newspaper. Had he not created hundreds of jobs for the Gauteng province's unemployed youth? Was that how people of the province wanted to thank him? Flames of wrath raged from within him. He wished this man could come closer to him. One blow would be enough to send him dizzy. If Ndimande could only get his gun, these thugs would surely regret it and curse the days that ushered their presence on earth. He did not clap. He got a slap that threatened to tear the skin off his face. Then he started clapping his hands.

"Clap, clap, man! You also sing. Yes, you are getting there. Good boy. Clap a bit more." The sighs of the man on top of his wife made him restless. If his feet were free he would be able to take his gun. Making him feel the pain of helplessly watching the rape, and forcing him to cheer as if he appreciated what they were doing, made the cruelty of these men's deed even more vivid.

The man on the bed wailed without weeping, almost like the siren of an ambulance. It was only temporarily. He then sighed and gasped with relief as though something had really been troubling him, and he was now free from it. He jumped out of the bed. His body was wet from sweat. Sperm was still dripping from his penis as he walked about. As he walked toward Ndimande, the one-legged man undressed. He was amputated just above the knee. Within a split second his knife was up, ready to tear the flesh of Ndimande's wife. Ndimande was horrified at the size of the man's penis. It must be one of those Shangaan men. It is believed that once they take a woman no one will ever satisfy her again. He could not help thinking about the pain his wife was going through. He fell off the chair.

"No time to play monkey tricks. Clap! *Masepa! Ake re o clever wena, ne?* You think you are smart? Today is today. I want you to feel all the pain that we are going through!" said the other fellow to Ndimande, touching the balaclava as if to reassert his authority.

"But brother..."

"*Ek is nie jou broer nie, ne*! I told you to clap your hands," he said raising his hand as if to hit him with the rifle butt. Ndimande stared at him, his eyes glowing with anger mixed with hatred.

In a flash of lightning, the bed, wardrobes, dressing table, curtains, the carpet, and everything in the bedroom, soon transformed and melted into thoughts about his fate. He had to find a way to escape. If not, he would die. As old people say, although a cat may be small, it can deal a dog a few blows. He had to do something quickly…

"You have stopped clapping hands, bastard! *Uyabhluza, swayini?* Blues and booze!" The gunman looked at him and shook his head left and right before he spat. Ndimande clapped once or twice. All he could see was an encroaching death. There was no way he could get his gun. As they say, you never remember the good old days unless you are facing the bad new ones. He was going to die and leave behind his major youth development project, in which he was encouraging the youth to transcend the era of *oyi oyi* – that is vibe and drugs – and be more active like the youth of the '70s, what he calls the toyitoyi generation. He had created hundreds of jobs for the youth. It appeared to him everything was soon going to become a thing of the past. He would not let anyone take his life very easily. He tried in vain to loosen the rope that married his legs together, forever. It would not let him…

Ndimande jumped and opened his arms in an attempt to catch the gun-toting man. He could not catch him. The one-legged gunman hopped away like a frog. He cocked the gun, came closer, ready to blow Ndimande's skull into pieces. "Do not ask your death of me; it is too early for that. We need to talk first. But I warn you…" he pressed the trigger and shot Ndimande in one leg. Ndimande, in agony, became more and more certain that this man with one leg could be Sabelo, a fellow nicknamed Broom because of his extraordinarily long beard that looked like he was going to sweep the floor with it. They grew up together but neither became close friends nor enemies. When Ndimande was actively involved in the political struggle in the 1970s, Sabelo or, Broom, as he is called, was gradually graduating as a hardened criminal under the guise of political activism. It was discovered very late that during political rallies, he would use the opportunity to burgle houses while the owners were attending rallies.

When discovered he ran away. The struggle continued and Sabelo disappeared without trace. He was still not found when the police, who colluded with the apartheid government, tortured and arrested Ndimande and other political activists. Ndimande learnt only when he was in exile that Sabelo had been back to the township only to meet his fate at the hands of the police. He was shot during an armed robbery and was later amputated. So went the story of Sabelo's lost leg.

"*Jwale ke nako ya ho re* we reveal ourselves to you. First, Jack, untie the *foken* woman. I want to kill this bastard before her eyes before I kill her too," said one of the men, his eyes turning as red as blood. While the one-legged guy was busy untying MaNdlovu, Ndimande was whining in pain. The leg of his cream trousers had quickly turned red.

"My name is Nyokovane," he said and unmasked himself. Ndimande, whose eyes had turned red too, did not recognise Nyokovane. "You probably remember the poet who used to recite during rallies?" Silence. "That was me. I can see you are growing bigger and bigger because of the fruits of freedom which we all fought for." While he was talking, MaNdlovu was still lying as though she was dead. The one-legged collected a few bracelets from the dressing table drawer, and later, with his balaclava in his hand this time, came closer to Nyokovane and Ndimande. His beard wanted to sweep the floor.

"We all fought for freedom. We did not go to Robben Island or exile. We have never been to Lusaka but the fact is we did fight. When some activists were away, we made sure the country and its economy progressed. Most of all we lived in severe fear of being arrested. Now we are free. We all deserve a fair share. We need money and fancy cars. We are also dead tired of the government that is increasingly becoming one ethnic group. I like your use of the phrases 'Toyitoyi and *Oyi oyi*'. We fought together during the times of toyitoyi and now that it is *oyi oyi*, joy, financial freedom, peace and dance, you and several other comrades are pretending not to have known us before. Please note that this has nothing to do with you as a person. This is only but a beginning... I will give you a few minutes to say what you want just before you undertake a long journey to heaven or hell," Nyokovane sighed with relief. Meanwhile MaNdlovu had just woken from unconsciousness. Only Ndimande could see her because the two gunmen were facing him with guns in their hands. She seemed to be quietly looking for something lost.

"*Bantakwethu*, please, do not kill me..." Ndimande's speech was cut short by the thundering sound of several shots that made him dirty his pants. Both one-legged man and his accomplice fell on their faces.

Dumisani Sibiya was born on 29 April 1976 in Nquthu, northern KwaZulu-Natal, in South Africa. He holds a Master of Arts in Publishing Studies from the University of the Witwatersrand. His debut novel, *Kungasa Ngifile*, won the silver medal in the Sanlam Prize for Youth Literature. His collections of short stories due to be published are: *Imikhizo* and *Izinyembezi*.

The Snake

Veronique Tadjo

I REMEMBER YEARS AGO, the roads were not like this. So many potholes now. The road appears to have caved in on itself. Our car fights with mud, sand and stones. Plastic bags on either side of the way stick to the dusty bushes and hang from trees like strange fruits. Dirt. I remember a different place. I used to marvel at the sky, the light so magical with its heavenly blue that would make me dream. Today, I can only see grey clouds heavy with pollution, looming over us, menacingly. *Matatus* and lorries send fumes in the air, coughing sickness and discomfort. Is it me seeing all this or has the country changed so fast?

Then, at last, at the end of the broken road, nature welcomes us, still alive with extraordinary beauty. That is why we have travelled such a long way, why we have left the city and our ordinary life behind.

Lying in my bed, I can hear everything: the sound of insects flying around and the lonely call of a night bird, a prolonged, monotonous series of loud, sharp notes, '*tchew, tchew, tchew…*' with little variation. Muffled voices seep through my tent. Suddenly, somewhere in another tent, someone breaks into laughter. I hear drops falling on the canvas roof. I am aware of nature and its power. The crater hides away in darkness, its mouth open, swallowing the sky. The air is fresh. A cricket has settled on my pillow under the mosquito net. I flick it out and lose sight of it somewhere on the floor. Will it come back to bother me in my dreams?

I am far away from everything. It feels like a new beginning. I am alone and that is how it should be. Alone, but with you.

We have come here to write stories, those that inhabit our minds, those that had refused to come out, those we dared not tell. We have come to craft tales so we can feel whole again. Like a sculptor ready to carve a piece of wood, we look within ourselves for inspiration.

Each story must be told anew. There is no tale that has never been heard before. So we must use old and new words to craft our art, trust our instincts and keep our imagination alive. Our hearts stay young and our minds curious about everything. Trying to make magic with words. But if we don't really feel those words, we will fail to make a difference.

The story I am going to narrate was given to me by a man I met in a foreign land and who carried many tales in his travel bag. He would pick one out at random and give it to whoever wanted it. When I heard this story, which comes from Sicily, I held out my hand. He looked at me for a moment and said: "Do what you want with it. It is here for the taking. I collected it from someone else."

"Thank you," I replied gratefully while I quickly slipped the story into my pocket. From then on, I thought about it. It came up when I was sleeping. It came up when my eyes were open. It came up when I was looking at life, the way we are, the way we behave towards one another. Then I saw how relevant it was to us, too. How much it meant to me.

With the pink flamingoes on one side of Crater Lake and the Colobus monkeys perched high up in the trees on the other side, I took a deep breath and started writing. I made the story mine. I made it ours.

Now, if you don't like my story or if you have heard it before in the same way, you can eat me up or throw me out. But for the moment, listen:

There was an old woman who lived in the middle of the forest in a small hut that she had built with her own hands before her husband died. Years ago, they were cast out by the people from their village because her husband had fallen ill. A mysterious disease that scared everybody so much they thought the sick man would bring death to all of them if he and his family were allowed to stay. She ended up alone with her daughter, a very beautiful young girl with dark wide eyes and a marvellous smile.

The two women were at one with their surroundings, communicating with the animals of the forest, speaking their language and respecting their ways. They were also very familiar with the many spirits and ghosts who lived there and were careful not to infringe on their territory. They gave them small offerings and sang praise songs. In return, the spirits were generous. The land was fertile. Fruits were abundant and there were plenty of fish in the river. The wildlife was kind to them, never hurting them or stealing from them.

The only regular visitors were the cattle herdsmen who passed by on their way to greener pastures. They only came during the dry season but they would never forget to bring some warm and frothy milk for the two women. It was delicious and comforting. The daughter loved to watch the herd trampling the soil, raising dust into the air, their horns pointing at the sky.

The old woman taught the girl how to gather plants with a healing power. She taught her, among other things, how to recognise the fever tree whose bark can cure malaria, and the camphor leaves that chase away insects and make the skin fragrant. She also showed her how to collect acacia wood, which is hard and makes the best knobkerries, and *lileshwa* roots that can cure all kinds of sickness. The girl became such a skilled gatherer of plants and herbs that the old woman would prepare them and go to the market-town where she would sell them while her daughter stayed at home.

The young woman loved to sing while she was sorting out the herbs. Her voice was pure, strong and haunting. When the birds heard her, they would stop their chirping and quarrelling. In fact, all around her nature paused to listen.

One day, as the old woman had gone away to sell the herbs, her daughter was alone in the hut. The king's son was hunting in the forest. He had already killed an impala, which he had tied up on his horse leaving a trail of bright-red blood behind him. He had strayed from his path when he stumbled across the deserted compound. When he saw the hut, he got off his horse and knocked on the door. Silence. He knocked again, this time much louder. When the daughter came out, he asked for some water because he was very thirsty. She brought him a calabash of fresh water from the big earthen pot and waited for him to quench his thirst. Then she immediately went back inside, closing the door behind her.

But it was already too late. The king's son had seen how amazingly beautiful she was. He was struck by her graceful features. She had hardly said two words to him, but he was at once overcome by a powerful and dark desire to possess her.

He knocked on her door again. Silence. Raising his voice, he ordered that she open the door for him. He was used to getting what he wanted and was not prepared to accept a refusal.

"Open the door, beautiful girl. I just want to talk to you."

"I can't," she replied. "My mother is not here. Please, come back another day."

"Don't be afraid, come out. I am Prince Karati, son of Nabongo, king of all this land. I need to see you."

Silence.

"Listen. I am not playing, now. Come out immediately or I'll have to remove you from there by force!"

Still, the young woman did not open the door. Enraged, the king's son broke down the door and barged into the hut.

The daughter screamed and kicked, scratched and pushed but he was determined and she was completely on her own. As she struggled, desperately looking around for help, she saw a silvery snake that was sliding along the far corner of the hut.

"Since nobody is here to save me," she cried, "I call upon you, oh snake, to bear witness to my suffering."

The prince took no notice of what she said and continued to force himself on her.

"May you never marry in your entire life!" she screamed.

When the king's son had finished, he simply got up and left the hut without once looking back. Outside, he found his horse, jumped on it and rode at full speed towards the palace.

It was the end of the day. The birds were whistling in unison. A red-headed weaver was perched on the roof of the hut. Now that the heat had subsided, the small animals of the forest came out of the bush. Dik-diks and mongooses drew closer as if to look for the young woman who usually greeted them and gave them bits of food.

When the old woman returned, she immediately sensed that something was wrong. She questioned her daughter but the girl remained silent. She did not want to reveal her painful secret for fear it would hurt her mother. She couldn't hide her pain, though. She spent her days doing nothing and looking very sad. She did not sing anymore. She stopped gathering herbs and sat miserably on a rock staring with vacant eyes in the distance. She did not eat and became very thin.

After a while her mother stopped asking questions as she could see it perturbed her daughter. She would just hold her tight, stroking her hair and whispering kind words to her. She would also go into the forest to find rare herbs with which she would make concoctions for the daughter to drink.

The old woman made fewer trips to the market. She did not want to leave her daughter on her own as she refused to follow her. But she had to go because they were poor and they needed honey, salt and many other things.

One day, at the market, the old woman heard a rumor that the prince was soon going to marry a beautiful virgin. Her innocence was without doubt and she came from one of the finest families in the land. There was great joy and excitement. Everybody was looking forward to the wedding ceremony and to the feast that would surely follow. Ten white bulls had already been chosen for slaughter. The drummers were stretching more tightly the skin of their instruments.

But by the end of the day, when the old woman was ready to go back to the forest, she heard some worrying news. As soon as she got home, she said to her daughter: "Listen to this. The king's son wants to marry a beautiful virgin but he has a snake wrapped around his neck, and nobody can get rid of it. Whenever anyone tries to remove it, the reptile only tightens itself around his neck even more and nearly strangles him to death."

"He deserves to die," thought the daughter.

However, after a couple of days, she decided to go to the palace. When she arrived, the atmosphere was gloomy. The kingdom was virtually in a state of mourning. The guards took one look at her and refused to let her in. But she insisted on seeing the king and declared that she knew how to free his son from the deadly grip of the snake.

The king, who was now beside himself with worry for the prince's health, accepted to receive her. He was ready to try anything to save him. She was led to the young man. He was lying on a wooden bed with a snake wrapped around his neck. His eyes were bloodshot and bulging. He was trying to breathe but all that could be heard was a continuous whine. He was sweating heavily and his legs were jerking uncontrollably. It was obvious that he was slowly choking. The diviners and healers gathered around him and watched helplessly.

The girl asked them to step aside and came near to the prince's side.

"Look at me! Look closely!" she said. "Do you recognise me?"

"No," replied the king's son, but the snake tightened itself around his neck.

"Have you forgotten how you barged into my hut and forced me to submit to your will? Don't you recall how I called on the snake to bear witness to my suffering? Don't you recall I told you that you would never be able to marry?"

"No," repeated the son of the king, not daring to look up at the young woman. The snake tightened its grip, making him scream in agony.

"Yes, yes, yes! I remember everything."

The snake released its grip a little.

"And now you want to marry a beautiful virgin? What am I supposed to do? Did you think of me?"

"No," he said. "I did not think of you."

She looked at him intently. Anger was written all over her face as she tried to remain calm. Everybody was petrified. The king intervened: "If you can free my son, I shall give you anything you want: money, servants, jewellery. Just say what you want and it will be brought to you immediately."

It was as if the daughter had not heard what the king had just offered to do. She declared in a voice that betrayed her outrage: "From now on, prince, you will think of me every day for the rest of your life. Although you won't see it at times, the snake will remain close by, ready to strangle you if you forget me for one moment. You will not marry until you find enough love in your heart to erase the suffering you have inflicted on me. You will honour my name and all the men in this kingdom will respect womanhood as we have always respected manhood."

After this, the king's son broke down in tears. The snake released its grip and disappeared from everybody's sight. The daughter bent over the young man and put some herbs into his mouth. Then she turned round and left without once looking back.

And this is where the story that was given to me would normally end.

I guess we should be happy for justice has been done even though temporarily. But I have been left wondering: whatever happened to the daughter after she left the palace? It is commonly assumed that she went back to resume her former life in the forest and that her mother continued to care for her. With time the daughter found her joy again although she was never able to marry because she did not like men at all. She learnt more about the healing power of plants and her reputation grew well beyond the borders of the kingdom.

It is equally possible that soon after, the old woman died and her daughter was forced to leave the forest. She settled down in the market-town to start a new life, finding small jobs here and there to survive. She thought that her past was behind her. Yet, one day, she heard a faint knock on the door. When she opened it, she found the prince standing in front of her. He did not look the same at all. In fact, she almost failed to recognise him. But he held out his hand and asked her to marry him.

Or perhaps, she never saw the king's son again. She became so destitute she had to sell herself, having lost both her strength and her ambitions.

No, maybe something entirely different occurred. After she went back to the forest, she could have given birth to a small baby boy. What would she do then? Bring it to his father so he could take responsibility for him? She could also choose to abandon it in the woods to be devoured by hyaenas. But it did not fit her character. Chances are she would raise the boy in the forest passing her knowledge on to him over the years.

There could be, of course, a completely new story around the child. Would he grow up hating his father, wanting to take revenge on him until one day he would gather an army and destroy the kingdom? Or would he spend his life, seeking his affection, yearning for him, desperately wanting to be recognised, accepted, taken in?

The truth is, we don't know whether the Prince was capable of changing to become a true man at last or whether he continued with his brutal ways until the snake strangled him to death. Suicide or sheer mindlessness?

Which ending should I give this tale? What powers do I have?

★★★

Now, I am back at home doing my normal routine. Like every morning, I read the newspaper from cover to cover. After that, I go to my room, close the door and start writing.

But this time, I can't. I have to stop. One of the stories I have just read in the newspaper is so gruesome it haunts me. The rape of a baby. Suddenly, writing tales seems totally meaningless.

The air in the room has become stifling. I switch off my computer and go out to take a breath of fresh air. In the streets, I see people going about their business. I meet a woman sweeping the road, a homeless man carrying his belongings on his head. Cars pass by. I walk to the park and watch a family enjoying the sun. The parents are lying on the grass while their children throw a ball at each other. A huge tree casts a protective shadow over them.

And I ask myself, "Is it at this point that my tale really ends?"

Veronique Tadjo is a writer and painter from the Ivory Coast. Born in Paris, she grew up in Abidjan where she attended local schools and subsequently became a lecturer at the National University until 1993 when she took up writing full time. She has lived in several countries and is currently based in Johannesburg. Her latest book, *Reine Pokou*, is on the subject of Queen Pokou, founder of the Baoule Kingdom. She also writes for the young.

Retail Therapy

Chika Unigwe

WALKING ANAESTHETISES ME. I walk until my head no longer feels like it is stuffed with a balloon about to burst. From the restaurants around the central square, I can smell spices and vegetables in which mussels are coming open. This replaces the smell of sex in my nose.

But my thoughts do not clear. Pictures jump in my mind, frenzied, one on top of the other. It feels like I am looking at a screen with superimposed pictures. The ground beneath me swirls and starts to suck me in. The croissant and coffee I had this morning force their way back to my throat, threatening to spill out. I lean against a lamp pole and shut my eyes. I take deep breaths. One. Two. Three. Four. Five.

The madness clears and a memory that refuses to fade pushes itself forward.

★★★

It was a Saturday morning at the Brussels National Airport. I had just got off the plane from Nigeria. Swaying like a model, my dreams in the black leather bag slung across my left shoulder, I walked over to the immigration counter on my left: the one with the slower moving line of mainly black people clutching passports in one hand and dragging heavy hand luggage in the other.

"Name?" The immigration officer's tone was routine. Bored. Like a pupil reciting a poem at assembly.

"Mary Eze."

"Address?" He glanced at me as he flipped through to the page with the visa.

"Baarlestraat 101, Beerse."

The address was easy to remember.

He said something in Dutch. "I don't speak Flemish. Sorry." I smiled and tucked a stray braid behind my ear.

I hated Mary Eze for having braids in the passport picture. I loathe having my hair braided. The tugging always gives me a headache. I much prefer just having my hair permed and held in a ponytail.

"French? *Parlez vous Francais?* You speak French?" The voice was firm. Like a school teacher.

"No."

"How. Long. You. Live. Here?" His words came out slow and deliberate. His eyes never left my face.

"Six years," I muttered, suddenly realising that my palms were starting to get clammy.

He looked at me again. "Please. Stand. Here. At the side." He motioned for me to move away from the queue so he could attend to the next in line. My passport lay open on his desk. I thought of the Nigerian girl, Amina, suffocated in the plane by the *gendarmes*, the Belgian policemen escorting her back to Nigeria after her asylum request was turned down. A necklace of sweat formed around my neck and I wiped it off.

Kunle had assured me that white men could not tell the difference between one black woman and the other and that I was safe with the passport he had got me. "Sista, nobody go ask you any quession. Oyibo go just look de face, look you, pass you on. Welcome to Belgium!" He had laughed when I asked him how I could convince the authorities I was Mary Eze. Married to a Belgian. Been living in Belgium for so long without speaking the local language.

I transferred my bag to my right shoulder and unbuttoned the denim jacket I had on. I felt the urge to untie the laces of the Nike canvas shoes I was wearing. They suddenly seemed too tight.

I never wanted to come here. America was my first choice. "The *lend* of the *Buhraaave end* the *Fuhree*." That was what Ikem called it. He said in America, one became rich simply by wiping old people's butts. And one could abuse the president right to his face and go free. "Not like here, *men*," he said. "Call Obasanjo a coconut head to his face and you'll spend the rest of your days in Kirirkiri maximum prison, being fed nothing but water and stale bread. This country is shitty, *men*."

Ikem and I met one Friday night at Tastee's in Opebi. I was

concentrating on the chicken pie I had ordered when a man asked if he could share my table. I almost burst out laughing because Lagos men do not need anyone's permission to sit wherever they want to sit. I nodded a yes, intrigued by the man in a cream-coloured t-shirt and black cotton trousers. I stole a look at him before he sat and I thought that apart from the fact that his torso looked long in comparison to his legs – giving him the look of the etiolated shadow of a much taller man – he was not altogether bad looking. I saw that he had ordered *jollof* rice and I told him it was a good choice. "Really?" he smiled and that was when I noticed his dimples, my Achilles' heel as far as men were concerned. He said he lived in the States and had just come home on vacation and did I know a good club he could go to at the weekend? We talked about Lagos: its frequent power failures and its unbearable heat. We sat at the table long after we had both finished eating. And the next day, we went clubbing together at Cazmic, the new nightclub in Ikoyi.

We saw each other almost everyday and we pried into each other's lives. He told me of his home in Atlanta with its four bedrooms and a garden. He told me of his wide plasma TV, huger than any I had ever seen at Mega Plaza. "It covers the wall of my TV room, *men!*" His stories fed my dream of a better life away from the dust of Lagos. From the mosquitoes that bite with viciousness in the rainy season. From the smell of death and decay which pervaded my father's one room *face me I face you* apartment where I still lived, cheek by jaw with rats and cockroaches. Three years after graduation, I was still unable to get a job as my father did not know anyone who knew anyone who knew anyone influential enough to get me a job.

Ikem was going to be the answer to my prayer. A man I loved who would take me away from the rut my life was falling into. We were going to have three children: two boys with their father's dimples, deep enough to hold water and a girl who would be a mini me. We had their names planned. Even chosen the schools they would go to.

But then Chinyere happened. Chinyere with the very thick ankles and the splayed toes that made her look like an elephant with duck feet.

I had heard from a mutual friend that Ikem had asked her to marry him. When I confronted him in his house, my anger blowing a hurricane that cracked his favourite Nina Simone CD in two, he said it was nothing personal, but, "One had to be pragmatic, *men*. I don't even enjoy sleeping with Chinyere but she is a nurse. And nurses are hot in America, *men*."

I looked around the room and noticed the framed picture of the two of us mocking me. I picked it up and hurled it at his head. It missed and hit the blue wall behind him. It smashed and fell, face up on the cream rug I had helped choose. A star of cracked glass formed on our smiling lovey-dovey faces. I had wanted the glass to shatter, to pierce Ikem with its jagged edges.

"I will do three jobs. I will clean. I will scrub. I will wipe octogenarian butts. I will find something. I have a degree for heaven's sake!" I wailed.

"Baby," he said, his tone amused, "a BA in Linguistics won't guarantee you a well-paying job in the States, *men*. Baby, understand. Life in *Yankee* is hard, *men* and with a working nurse by your side, your life is made easier. You will always have a place in my heart. I will always love you." He laid a broad palm on my shoulder and I shook it off.

"You money-loving son-of-a-bitch!" I hurled at him. I cursed him and his children to come. They would have their mother's thick ankles and stagger on three feet. I cried until snot clogged my nose. "I will make it to America," I promised him, wiping the snot with the back of my hand, and I had every intention of making that come true.

Three weeks later, I was at Randle Avenue meeting Kunle, a man whose contacts a former classmate of mine, Ngozi, had given me. She said he was one of the few people in Lagos who could get me an American visa through the backstreets of Surulere.

Ngozi with a BSc degree in Microbiology worked for Kunle on a commission basis. For every customer she got him, she got 10 percent. "The pay is good, I can't complain," she sighed, when I asked her if she did not want to leave the country. "I searched for a job for an entire year. I thank God, I finally got this one. It pays my siblings' school fees and keeps me dressed. Those who want to leave, let them go. Me, I will stay on," she concluded. There was no way I could stay on in Nigeria. The place had no future for me. I would go to America, make loads of money and build a proper house for my parents. A house where they would not have to share a bathroom with five different families. And my mother would have her own kitchen to preside over rather than worry every day that one of the other women who used the communal kitchen had stolen some of her palm oil or pinched some salt. I did not care how hard I had to work to achieve that. "Me, I want to check out. I'm tired of this place," I told her. "*Ike aguwugo m.*"

"An American visa costs 500 000 Naira," Kunle said, picking his tooth with a splint off a chewing stick.

"I don't have half a million naira, Sir," I said. My voice came out

216

squeaky. Like a plastic toy. I was aware of the silence in the closed room, a silence broken only by the humming of the air conditioner behind the lanky man swivelling on a chair.

Five-hundred-thousand naira was beyond me. I could not lay my hands on such an amount even in my dreams.

He did a 360-degree turn on his chair and removed the stick from his mouth. He placed it on the table and clasped his palms together, as if he were saying a prayer. Resting his chin on the tip of his fingers, he declared in a voice that sounded like a dog barking, "America is not de only abroad, you know." Smiling and showing off a gold tooth that glittered like a promise, he continued, "Dere are other places, you know."

"Like where? London?" I asked.

"No. No. Not London. Dat road don close. De immigration people dere don wise up. Spain. Belgium. Italy. All dese ones I can get you for 200 000. Everybody wan go America. But you can make money in any abroad. Anywhere is better dan dis our godforsaken country." He picked up the splint again and began to pry something loose from a lower tooth.

I knew nothing about Spain. Italy had the mafia. And all the second-hand cars that congested Lagos roads came from Belgium. That gave it an edge over the rest. It made it seem somehow familiar and confirmed for me that it must be a rich country.

The officer who tapped me on the shoulder and said, "Follow me, Madam," had the build of the Michelin man in the TV advertisement: small head, a huge middle and very skinny legs. The rings around his stomach did not wobble as he walked, like I had expected them to. They seemed turgid, cast in iron.

He entered a small room with three tables, a desktop PC on each table and a fax machine. There were two other men in police uniforms seated at two tables. He took me to the third, right by the door and sat me down opposite him.

"So, what is your name?" he asked, his face plain. Like cardboard paper.

"Mary Eze."

He pulled out a drawer and brought out a magnifying glass.

"Real name?" he asked again, holding open the passport. He brought it close to his face and shutting his left eye, peered at a page through the magnifying glass.

"That's my real name," I answered, twisting the copper bangles on my left wrist.

He sighed and dropped both passport and magnifying glass on the table in front of him. He stretched out a podgy arm and reached across his table for a thermos flask and a mug. I watched him fill the mug with coffee and close his right hand around it. His hand looked like that of a well-fed baby, dimpled at the base. He took a sip, bringing his head down to drink so that it was as if he was bowing to a god.

"I ask you again. What's your name?"

"Mary Eze," I repeated, hardly opening my mouth for fear that if I did I would surely cry.

"I will have to check your luggage, madam," he said as he lifted himself from his chair. My black *Samsonite* suitcase was beside me. The other two policemen, one with hair the colour of the rising sun and the other with brown hair the shape of a mushroom, had their eyes on the suitcase.

Michelin man pulled on a glove, opened the suitcase and dug his gloved hand in. I knew he would find nothing incriminating there because Kunle had warned me against taking any documents that would reveal my real identity. Yet, the tightening around my ankles got worse. When he lifted a pair of red underwear and swung it over his head, the three of them laughed.

Fifteen minutes later, he had checked both my handbag and my suitcase. Emptying my compact powder case, an eyeliner with a broken tip and Revlon lipstick on the floor. He had unfurled crumpled sheets of paper with a list of some shopping I had to do the day before I left. *Uziza*. Spinach. Cowrie beads. *Akamu*. Dried fish. *Ogili*. He scanned the papers meticulously; a doctor performing surgery; but they revealed nothing to him.

"What is your telephone number?" His English was better than that of the immigration officer. It flowed without any hitch.

I swallowed. I did not know that. Kunle had not covered that for me.

"Madam, this is a stolen passport and we are going to charge you." His voice was cold steel. "We are going to take a fingerprint and then I shall advise you to tell me what your real name is and how you came across this passport." Someone came to the door and said something rapidly in Dutch and Mushroom hair walked out. Michelin man typed out a document and took my fingerprint. "We keep you here and wait until I hear from the Ministry of Foreign Affairs. Now, I go on pause." When he got to the door he stopped and said, "What you have done, madam, is very serious. Very serious." Then the door clicked behind him.

The officer with hair the colour of the rising sun got up from his chair and came and stood beside me. For the first time, I noticed that he was the tallest of the three. He had the blue plastic eyes of a doll.

"I am Carl," he said.

I did not respond.

"You are very beautiful. Beautiful. You are beauty queen in your country?" He rolled his 'Rs' when he spoke.

Silence. The room seemed to be closing in on me, its walls coming together to sandwich me between them.

He moved closer and squatted so that his lips were close to my ears. The air in the room was filled with the stench of garlic that came from his breath when he spoke.

"See, Günter, my colleague, yes?" He made every sentence sound like a question. "Günter he is *raacist*. He don't like black woman, no? But me, I don't mind. Me, not *raacist*. Yes?" I bit the inside of my cheek. It hurt. He grunted, his breath hot against my ear, "Twenty minutes is all I need. Twenty minutes and you can walk out of here," as he stood up and drew me up in one fluid movement, pushing me against the table. "If Günter come back, you are in trouble, no? Big trouble." He spread his hands out to show me the expanse of the trouble he thought I would be in. He continued, "Twenty minutes and you walk out. No?" He panted, his breath coming in short spurts like someone who had just run a marathon. He stood behind me, trousers down at his ankles. I imagined I had flown off and was perched on the ceiling watching this blue-eyed man and a woman who looked like me. I could feel the hardness of his manhood against my buttocks as he cupped his hands over my breasts and groaned as he came, "Aah, ooh, *mijn negertje*. Beautiful. Beautiful."

And afterwards, he tore up the paper with my fingerprint on it and said, "Go. Go before the rest come back. Me, I am not *raacist*. Black and white, we are the same, see? Like chocolate mousse and vanilla mousse. De-fe-re-nt, but same, no?" He gently pushed me out, his blue eyes blazing.

Even though I hurt between my legs and tears were scarificating my cheeks, I said thank you, because he could have had me put in prison or deported.

And because, already, my morality was beginning to discover new countries.

★★★

There is a light snow shower falling. It looks like someone is sprinkling salt from a huge salt shaker. Antwerp is at its prettiest when it is covered in snow. A pristine whiteness that hides the dog poo and cigarette stubs that litter especially the Schippersquartier where I live. A one-room house with a glass window overlooking the street. I am the centre of that universe. My house is not too far from De Grote Markt Square and the Cathedral and the souvenir shops and their horde of tourists, mainly Asians with digital cameras and multiple shopping bags, smiling and taking pictures of each other. Yet a tourist would have to wander to find the Schippersquartier, neatly tucked away, hidden from sight like dirty laundry.

I walk behind a Japanese couple holding hands and giggling. They are young, probably in their teens. They have the confident gait of people in love and this seduces me. My ankles are starting to hurt in my high-heeled boots. They feel like they are encircled by ivory anklets, *odu*, the sort Onitsha women wear when their husbands take new titles. Anklets heavy as guilt. My stomach rumbles like the goods train that ferried coal from Enugu to Kanfanchan. I follow them into a restaurant and sit at a table dressed up in white, right beside theirs. If I listen hard enough, I can hear their conversation. But they speak mostly in their language. I order *frietjes* and *stoofvlees* and while I eat, I listen to them *oohing* and *aahing* over their food as they reach the peak of their culinary orgasm. They look satiated. With life. With love. And the thought depresses me.

I leave the restaurant and walk over to the Meir. My feet have a soul of their own. They understand that I am running out of work clothes, and so they lead me to Hunkenmoller, the lingerie shop sandwiched between Zara and the Euro shop where everything from toilet rolls to t-shirts sell for one euro. I walk into the shop and I am flanked on all sides by underwear of different colours and inclinations. I pick up a red one, consider it for a minute and drop it. Red is cliché. I run my hands through an array of underwear. I let the fabric make love to my hands. Finally, I make my choice: pink, black and yellow g-strings with their matching bras. The g-strings are trimmed with lace, reminding me of wedding cakes decorated with icing. "Nice choice. *Mooi,*" the shop assistant smiles. She knows me.

Outside, it is still snowing. I walk out and I am swallowed by the anonymity of the city.

Dr Chika Unigwe, a Nigerian living in Turnhout, Belgium was a 2004 Caine Prize finalist. She is also a recipient of BBC and Commonwealth short story awards as well as the author of two EFL books published by Macmillan, London. Her debut novel, *De Feniks* is published by Meulenhoff (of Amsterdam) and Manteau of Antwerp.

A Day in the Life of Idi Amin Dada

Binyavanga Wainaina

1983. IT WAS THAT time of the day when the streets of Nakuru seemed to stand still. A Monday at 11: even the hot, dry breeze was lazy. It would glide languorously collecting odd bits of paper, have them tease the ground, threaten to take flight, tease the ground. Every so often there would be a gathering of force and a tiny tornado would whip the paper into the air, swirl dust around, dogs would lift their ears, tongues lolling, then burrow their faces between their forelegs as the wind collapsed, exhausted. Children were in school, long lines of spittle reaching their desks as they tried to keep awake.

Even Daniel Arap Moi, the Kenyan president, who usually woke up at 4am, was now taking his nap – trying to summon his favorite dream: that the entire nation of Gikuyus were standing in line at his gate to await execution, cash and title-deeds in hand to hand over at the gate.

Idi Amin Dada hunched over Mrs Gupta Shah like an insistent question mark, jabbing. She was chewing hard at a bit of blue, gold and red sari, trying to keep from screaming out loud; they had put on a movie on the video and set it loud to muffle the sounds: some Bombay song: *Chal Chal Chal Merihethi...* On the screen Idi could see a pouty maiden at the edge of a cliff, and a man with a giant quaff of hair and sideburns sang in a shrill voice. She leapt off the cliff, and he followed her in a few seconds... they lay draped elegantly at the bottom of the valley; their fingers touched and they died, then the nasal Hindi music escalated in intensity, went beyond drama, beyond melodrama, and achieved genuine Bombay Belodrama.

Idi Amin Dada jabbed deeper into Mrs Gupta, his plantain-sized fingers digging deeply into the folds of her stomach, which usually undulated serenely between two wisps of sari as she hummed her way through the day.

"You want my banana?"

"I vant your banana Idhiii? Give me your banana Idhi…"

"I give you my banana till you are fed up."

★★★

This was Idi's room; was also Idi's afternoon workplace. Had been for twenty years, since the early 1970s. This morning, every weekday morning, Idi would drop Mr Shah at the grain mill his family owned. At nine he would drop the petulant maharajah at school: The Shrival Manahaval Shah Academy For Successful Gentlemen Who Will Go To Oxford and Cambridge. *We start to train them at 5 years old! Book Now For Half-Price Discount on Swimming.*

The maharaja's mother would beg him to get into the car, "Oh my baby Pooti-poo, my Mickey-Mouse, my *Diwali gulam*, don't cry babe…"

Mr Shah remained silent; sometimes he tried to imagine this rosebud managing the grain mill and failed.

As soon as the car was at the gate, the maharajah would wriggle to the front passenger seat of the Mercedes.

"Idi — buy me goody-goody toffee gum or I tell Mammi-ji that you pinch me here."

This routine had ceased being a to-fro conversation. Idi would extract a wad of goody-goodies and the boy would stuff the toffee into his mouth and launch into muffled brags about Sapna's father's car or Rakesh's trip to Disneyland.

Idi was once in the army, and was used to handling such humiliations with a deadpan face and a slight flaring of his nostrils. He always dropped off the prince without argument before rushing back to fuck the prince's mother in the ironing room.

Piles of freshly ironed clothes sat on a boat-shaped basin next to the bed, clothes Idi had ironed last night. Vishal's (the bookshelf had been moved to this room since Prince Number 1 left for Oxford: the top row full of Louis L'Amour cowboy thrillers; the bottom row had a copy of *Heart of Darkness*, scribbled all over with A Level notes and next to it sat V.S. Naipaul's *A Bend in the River*. Idi Amin Dada was asking questions today: jabbing questions that sank deeply into Mrs Shah. She gave a low gnashing answer that blew soft cardamom-flavored wind into his ear – these were slow, long probing questions. He grunted in assent. Idi had a lot of questions. Every 11am he asked them.

He loved ironing. Every afternoon he would put on some Bollywood film, and turn the Shah family's washing into crisp battalions of soldiers. He loved shrugging shirts into broad, identical shoulders, arranging them in wardrobes, watching them stand at attention. They were his to command. A Natural Leader, his sergeant had called him. The room was once a stable, but was now a servant's quarters. At 6pm exactly, he would go to the shower, and smoke a joint and dream of shining brass buttons; dream of the embrace of a Luganda woman – sucking at his nerve endings like a fish; turning and twisting him around; smelling not of ginger and turmeric; but of musk and steamed bananas and Nilo beer.

The 1960s were full of landslides: as the British Administration screeched to a halt those that were waiting for a trajectory to come and grab hold of them were left stranded. In those days being dutiful mattered, *not* taking initiative – when they had decommissioned the special forces, afraid that they would remain to leak what had really happened in the forests and the African townships in the '50s; some had auctioned themselves to the new leaders – as bodyguards; as hired fists: these guys climbed up dizzyingly. Amin had waited for his loyalty to be rewarded; had hung about Nakuru – 10 miles from the barracks waiting for the call. In 1970, he was about to give up; was about to hitchhike to Uganda and sell illegal liquor in Arua like his mother had done, when he had found a frail Indian man being pulverized by a 10-year-old parking boy, outside the wholesale market, with market women cheering the boy. He had rescued the man. And he got a job. It wasn't bad: Mrs Shah was exactly the same as Sergeant Jones: insistent, fanatic about time, a goddess of routine.

Idi had joined the army as soon as age would allow it. It was his way out of a life that seemed aimless. His mother had sold liquor, and her body, to army officers. He loved his mother to distraction. At thirteen, he had beaten a thirty-year-old Acholi private who had come to their home to insult his mother.

At fifteen he was six foot four, and when Sergeant Jones had seen him walking in Arua, he had offered him a place in the army at once. Idi was terrified of whites; and he could sense that Jones feared and was fascinated with him. Jones would spend hours with Idi in the boxing ring, teaching him new skills. He loved to punch Idi softly; to wipe sweat off Idi's back; to test out Idi's muscles – always gruffly, always lingering. During a bout, his adrenalin pumping, sweat flying, Idi was like a machine: looking for every angle to kill; never angry. Clinical. He loved it, loved holding onto himself, loved the control of violence. One day he caught Jones's eye, saw the fear in it – fear – and Idi felt like God, standing there showing his power; the feeling was almost sexual.

Idi rose up the ranks in the army because he was the dream soldier. He had no father – had no problem being a boy to his superiors. He took his punishment with a wry mischievous grin, followed by a *Yessir Afande!* He loved to catch Mau Mau terrorists – it was all a marvellous game. Most of all he loved the gruff pride that Jones would flash when Idi had done something exceptional. He shrunk like a child at Jones's criticism. One day he drunk *chang'aa* and came to barracks with a prostitute (he loved older women). The sentry who challenged him was floored. Jones found him in the gym, thrusting away. He slapped Idi twice, and sent the woman away. Idi did not talk to anybody for days. Three days later, after winning the Gilgil Barracks Boxing corwn for a second time, Jones patted him on the back, and Idi grinned widely and said, "Now I am the bull, *Afande*."

★★★

Mr Shah liked to spend the morning working on his novel: *Conquerors of the British Empire.*

He was already 1 000 words into the novel, and was still finding it impossible to squeeze characters into the dense polemic. His theory was simple: that India, already with a foot in the door in Kenya, should take over the continent, and use this leverage to take over Britain.

It is the only way to make a National Profit from hundreds of years of British Rule: the more territory we control, the more we can dictate the cost of raw materials, the final profit will be manned by our guns. We must be Lords of the Commonwealth, and let the English carry us on their backs! Why build afresh when we can inherit what is already there?

His first-born son, Vishal, was disdainful about the book.

"Rubbish Dad. Pseudo-religious xenophobic polemic Dad. V.S. says the Indian Industrial revolution is petty and private. If Nakuru Shahs and Patels are fighting over 10 shillings, who will unite us? We are greedy Dad... V.S. says we are 'a society that is incapable of assessing itself, which asks no questions because ritual and myth have provided all the answers, that we are a society that has not learned 'rebellion'. Maybe Daddi-ji you need to read some real literature before writing this. The Russians?"

Vishal was brought up by Mrs Gupta to be the dream prince she had expected to marry all those hazy, plump years ago; to be *not* his father; not her father. Vishal treated them as if they were trinkets: colourful mantelpiece trinkets who chimed once in a while, but who were so divorced from any viable reality they could only be treated with contempt. It gave his father a twisted sense of pride to hear his son thus: what a man I am to produce a son so un-Dukawallah; a son for Oxford. But he was hurt. Now what would accompany his quiet mornings at the office?

When he was nine, Vishal had composed a song, which he liked to sing at birthday parties to scandalise everybody (except the Punjabi Kalasingas who liked his mettle). He sang it to the tune of a nursery school song about a Kookaburra.

Duka-wallah sit by de ole Neem tree
Merry Merry King of da Street is he
Run Dukawallah run
Dukawallah burn
Dukawallah hide your cash and flee

***

Between 2 and 4pm you can find Idi Amin at Nakuru Boxing Club. For years he has been the Nakuru Boxing Champion. He is getting older now, and some young bucks are challenging. Modesty Blaise Wekea is short. Very short. It is said he once lifted a harrow over his head while working as a casual in the wheat fields of Masailand. He is copper coloured to Idi's black. It is his speed – the unbelievable speed of those bowed legs with thighs the size of a grown man's waist. But there is something else. When he first exploded into the Nakuru boxing scene people saw a future world champion, "*Aii Alikuwa kama myama!*" The discipline of the army added to his natural ferocity to make him unbeatable.

He was not hungry anymore. He had finetuned his life to perfection over twenty years: there was no threat anymore.

He had no wife: many lovers, soft, yellow Gikuyu women desperately looking for a man with some skills – they complained that Gikuyu men were disdainful of frills – saw sex as a quick efficient drill; *wira ni wira* – work is work. Idi's giant physical size, his soft and gentle eyes and wicked smile, his reputation for controlled violence, attracted many women.

After his sparring session with a nervous young man with even larger limbs than his, a young man so scared of violence he could probably kill in

225

fear, Idi had a soda with an old friend, Godwin, the only fellow Kakwa in Nakuru. Pojulu was a tailor for an Indian family: the Khans. Idi speaks his language badly; he was better in Luo and Acholi – army languages. But when he was six or seven his mother had taken him to Yei town in Sudan – and he had fallen in love with the mango-lined avenues and the gentle character of his people. Children were generally a nuisance in the colonial Labour Lines of Arua; in his maternal grandfather's home, just off Maridi road, five miles from Yei was heaven. He was free to run and play as far as he wanted. Adults would swell to accommodate him – he would eat in the homes of strangers. His grandfather had told him the history of the Pojulu, his clan:

He tells me about the history of the Pojulu.

Death comes in many ways. For centuries, Pongi, the sickness of sleep, blighted the people of Bari, the children of Jubek, the submissive; son of King Mukunyet the wise.

Generations ago, Jubek was posted to a place that came to be known as Juba town. Godwin tells me Jubek does not deserve this privilege. He was a coward, he says. He was reluctant to fight the Dinka, and keep them out of their territory.

The Bari army was divided into six groups. Each bore a secret codename. The leaders of the group were determined by their abilities, or character. They would determine what action to take.

Eventually a group of frustrated soldiers took it upon themselves to defend Jubek from the North from the Dinka. Mundari was their codename. Mundari means 'a hostile force that acts without orders'.

Paparrara are the descendants of Jubek. This name was shortened to Pari. This became Bari, some time after the arrival of the first Turko-Egyptians in 1820. The letter 'P' does not occur in the Arab alphabet. Today, there are six groups of Bari peoples, named after the six groups of the Bari army: Kakwa, Pojulu, Kuku, Mundari, Nyangwara and Bari.

The people of Pisak are Pojulu, named after a great hero. Onyanyari was a leader of one of the six forces. A mild-mannered man. Polite. An astute politician. Because of this skill, he was sent to the Zande kingdown in the North-West to try to persuade them to let the Kakwa penetrate the area. His force was known as Pojulio, which means 'Come My Friend'. This group of Bari speakers is now called the Pojulu.

Godwin speaks to him about Sudan. About Inyanya 1 – the war. About old heroic days; about rumour and gossip coming from Yei town. Idi loved to hear the stories; would always ask Godwin to repeat stories he had memorised already. Idi has vowed to die in Yei. One day. They would eat and drink soda and *mandazi* and talk till the sun started to set and Idi made his way to his room to do the ironing.

★★★

The only person in the household who threatens Idi's job is Vishal. Since Vishal started to sprout whiskers he has been hostile to Idi. After reading Eldridge Cleaver, he took to calling Idi 'The Supermasculine Menial'. He once asked his parents if they did not think that a man as animal as Idi would not one day attack them?

"You need to read V.S. Naipaul. He understands the black man," Vishul said to his parents.

As crime has increased in Nakuru, Idi has become more indispensable. Two years ago he cornered three thugs, beat them all up, and was left with a knife-wound in his belly. The Shahs are fearful – scared of the seething Dark out there. The presence of a tame Giant Dark is a consolation. Sometimes Idi thinks that Mzee Shah knows what he does with his wife every afternoon. But maybe he does not mind so long as it is secret. Mzee Shah is a man of peace – and Mrs Gupta Shah has been less bullying, more mellow, mewing even sometimes, since she and Idi started fucking.

He had caught her wailing one day in the living room, after Vishal had gone to Oxford. He had tried to slide backwards slowly out of the room; but she had leaped at him and grabbed him and wept on his shoulder, leaving long snail-trails of snot on his khaki shirt. Her mood had changed abruptly, and she attacked him: teeth and nails; her body so incoherent she had come by rubbing herself on his knee.

He likes to see the fear/desire in her eyes; the surprise at his gentleness, when she expects the thrust of a lion, of a legend about Black Men, related among giggles and whispers while *samosas* are being cooked and Gujarati Aunties are talking raunchy. He likes to ask her questions: see her eyes answer, Yes. You are a man.

He does not mind being a HouseBoy.

He is happy.

Binyavanga Wainaina won the Caine Prize in 2002 and on his return home founded the Kenyan literary journal *Kwani?* which has already provided another Caine Prize winner (Yvonne Adhiambo Owuor in 2003) and a shortlisted candidate (Parselelo Kantai in 2004).

Rules

The Prize is awarded annually to a short story by an African writer published in English, whether in Africa or elsewhere. (Indicative length, between 3 000 and 15 000 words.)

'An African writer' is normally taken to mean someone who was born in Africa, or who is a national of an African country, or whose parents are African, and whose work has reflected African sensibilities.

There is a cash prize of $15 000 for the winning author and a travel award for each of the short-listed candidates (up to five in all).

For practical reasons, unpublished work and work in other languages is not eligible. Works translated into English from other languages are not excluded, provided they have been published in translation, and should such a work win, a proportion of the prize would be awarded to the translator.

The award is made in July each year, the deadline for submissions being 31 January. The short-list is selected from work published in the 5 years preceding the submissions deadline and not previously considered for a Caine Prize. Submissions should be made by publishers and will need to be accompanied by twelve original published copies of the work for consideration, sent to the address below. There is no application form.

Every effort is made to publicise the work of the short-listed authors through the broadcast as well as the printed media.

Winning and short-listed authors will be invited to participate in writers' workshops in Africa and elsewhere as resources permit.

The above rules were designed essentially to launch the Caine Prize and may be modified in the light of experience. Their objective is to establish the Caine Prize as a benchmark for excellence in African writing.

The Caine Prize,
The Menier Gallery,
Menier Chocolate Factory,
51 Southwark
Street, London SE1 1RU.
Telephone: +44 (0) 20 7378 6234.
Fax: +44 (0) 20 7378 6235.
Website: www.caineprize.com